TAKE THE

LONG WAY

HOME

Other Books by Rochelle Alers

ALONG THE SHORE

BREAKFAST IN BED

HAPPILY EVER AFTER

HEAVEN SENT

HIDDEN AGENDA

HIDEAWAY

HOME SWEET HOME

THE INHERITANCE

ROOM SERVICE

THE BEACH HOUSE

THE SEASIDE CAFÉ

VOWS

ROCHELLE ALERS

TAKE THE LONG WAY HOME

KENSINGTON PUBLISHING CORP.
www.kensingtonbooks.com

TAKE THE

LONG WAY

HOME

Prologue

It takes a long time to grow an old friend.
—John Leonard in *Friends and Friends of Friends*
by Bernard Pierre Wolff

Present day, New York City

Claudia Fortenza had just closed her eyes when the telephone on the bedside table rang. Reaching over, she picked up the receiver. "Hello."

"What's up, roomie?"

She was suddenly alert. "Yvonne?"

"Yes. I'm downstairs in the lobby. They wouldn't give me your room number."

"It's 1215. Come on up."

Claudia hung up and slipped off the bed. She had taken a car service from the Hudson River pier and checked into a Midtown hotel after disembarking from her transatlantic trip from Le Havre, France, to New York. She'd sent Yvonne Chapman-Jones an email of her itinerary, informing her best friend that she'd planned to spend two days in New York City, then fly down to Mississippi to visit her parents' graves, before going on to Raleigh, North Carolina. It was there she would stay with her daughter and grandchildren for the next two months.

Claudia had nearly lost count of the number of years since she had last stepped foot on US soil. Once she went through customs and presented her Italian passport, the impact that she was no longer an American citizen caused her heart to sink like a stone in her chest. At the time when she'd decided to give up her United States citizenship, Claudia had felt no remorse because she'd believed the country of her birth had continually betrayed her race.

Her people were denied rights given to them at birth by the Constitution, and many of the militants, radicals, and leaders championing equal and civil rights for all Americans had either been assassinated or imprisoned. And if it hadn't been for her daughter and grandchildren, Claudia knew she never would've come back. Her grandparents, parents, and aunt were dead, while her last surviving relative, at the age of 109, was living in Paris as an expatriate.

She heard three rapid knocks on the door followed by another two. Claudia smiled. Yvonne hadn't forgotten their signal. She opened the door and was rendered motionless once she realized her former college roommate hadn't come alone. She hardly recognized the man standing behind her. "Ashley?"

Within seconds, her past and present merged as she found herself enveloped in a tangle of arms, she attempting to escape the kisses on her face and hair. Seeing her friends filled her with an indescribable joy she hadn't felt in weeks. If anyone could be called her rock, it was Yvonne. Her college roommate was her witness when she'd married Robert. She'd also been by her side when she'd buried him. Yvonne had also sat with her the night before she boarded the plane that would take her from the country of her birth.

Although Claudia had extended invitations for Yvonne and her family to come to Italy for vacations, her friend always declined because of her fear of flying. Holding Yvonne at arm's length, she took in everything about her in one sweeping glance. She'd put on weight, but who didn't as they aged, and her hair was completely gray. A profusion of twists pulled into a bun and rimless bifocals made her look professorial. Her deep brown skin was clear and virtually wrinkle-free, giving credence to the adage that *good black don't crack*.

"You look beautiful, my friend. Y'all come in and sit down." She directed them into the sitting area of the bedroom suite. The *y'all* had slipped out unconsciously. Despite speaking fluent French and Italian, Claudia still spoke English with a cadence that identified her as someone from the American South.

"You're the beautiful one," Yvonne countered as she sat on a club chair. "Isn't she, Ashley?"

Her gaze shifted to Ashley Booth. He was one of four men in her life who'd been responsible for her maturing from an innocent girl into a worldly woman. If she and Yvonne hadn't changed much, Ashley had. At the age of eighty-seven he was four years their senior yet looked much older. He was a mere shadow of his former self. It wasn't only the drastic weight loss, but it was as if his once vibrant personality had faded. She still could remember the exact moment she had been introduced to the tall, sophisticated investment banker. Most people who met Ashley for the first time found themselves drawn in by his charismatic persona.

"Yes, she is. It's as if time has stood still for you," he said to Claudia.

Claudia smiled at her former lover. "Hush up, Ashley Booth. You're still a silver-tongued devil," she said teasingly.

Ashley Booth hadn't realized his knees were shaky until he had to grope for the arms of the chair to assist him as he folded his body down to the cushioned seat. When Yvonne had called to let him know Claudia was returning to the States, he'd thought she was playing a joke on him, yet she'd managed to reassure him their friend was coming back, but she wouldn't be staying long. He'd asked Yvonne if he could accompany her for the reunion, while extracting a promise from Yvonne not to tell Claudia he was coming along.

The only thing that had changed about Claudia was the color of her hair. There was still a trace of gold in her fashionably styled short, curly, silver hair. Their eyes met and held as a hint of a smile tilted the corners of her mouth, a mouth he'd kissed many times when they had shared their lives together.

It'd been more than fifty years and he still thought of himself as a king of fools for not asking Claudia to marry him. And it wasn't as if she hadn't given him an out when she told him if he loved her, she wouldn't leave the States to accept an overseas position with a Rome-based bank.

Claudia had remarried; it was then Ashley realized he'd lost her forever. And if he had it to do all over again, he would have gotten down on his knees to tell her that he loved her, and that he wanted them to spend the rest of their lives together.

"I hope y'all haven't eaten, because I ordered room service."

Claudia's drawling cadence broke into Ashley's musings. "I don't eat much nowadays. I have a sensitive stomach," he admitted. "It probably comes from dousing my food with hot sauce back in the day."

Yvonne gave Ashley a level look. "What's the expression? A hard head makes for a soft behind. In your case it's an ulcer. I used to warn—"

"What can't you eat, Ashley?" Claudia asked him, interrupting Yvonne.

"I stay away from fatty fried foods and anything with acidity."

"What are you eating now?" Yvonne asked him.

"Foods high in fiber."

Claudia stood up. "I probably ordered everything on the lunch menu, so you can select whatever you want to eat."

Ashley stared at the tips of his shoes. He hadn't noticed the scuff marks when he'd put them on earlier that morning. There had been a time when he never left the house unless his shoes were shiny enough for him to almost see his reflection. But that was then, and this was now.

So many things had happened in the world and in his life since the day she'd left the States for Europe. Ashley Thaddeus Booth saw other women after Claudia, slept with them, but refused to commit to a relationship that would lead to marriage. He wined and dined women, while earning the reputation as a love-and-leave-them confirmed bachelor, willing to show a woman a good time while enjoying whatever they were willing to offer him.

However, it had been different with Claudia. She'd been special, a standout among all the women he'd known, but somehow, he wouldn't permit himself to love her because he feared it would make him not only weak but vulnerable. He'd witnessed firsthand how his father had ignored his wife's infidelity, which made him a weak man in Ashley's judgment.

There came a knock on the door, and he stood up when Claudia walked over to answer it. A young man pushed a cart into the dining area and set the table with bottles of water and wine, plates, glasses, serving pieces, and covered dishes. Reaching into the pocket of his slacks, Ashley removed a monogrammed money clip and slipped the man a bill.

"Thank you, sir. Just call room service when you're finished, and someone will come and clean up everything."

"You didn't have to do that," Claudia said, once the man left. "I was planning to leave the gratuity on the check."

Ashley waved his hand in a dismissive gesture. "I don't get to tip folks much anymore because I rarely eat out, so please indulge me, Claudia."

Smiling, she nodded. "Okay."

*   *   *

It was like old times for Claudia when she, Yvonne, and Ashley got together to eat, drink, listen to music, or discuss current events. She'd noticed Ashley opted to drink bottled water while she and Yvonne drank wine. He'd eaten a green salad, a small portion of skinless chicken breast, and steamed carrots.

"Where are you living now, Ashley?" she asked him.

"I'm renting an apartment in a Harlem brownstone."

"What happened to your place on Riverside Drive?" Claudia had spent countless nights in the spacious high-rise apartment overlooking the Hudson River. Although she and Ashley hadn't officially lived together, she'd stayed at his place more than she did at her studio apartment.

"Once the building went co-op, I bought the unit. After a few years, the board kept raising the maintenance fees and that's when I decided to sell it."

"We used to have some good times at your place whenever you and Claudia threw a party," Yvonne said to Ashley.

Claudia nodded in agreement. She and Ashley had become a much sought-after couple among their social circle of elite Black peers.

"My party days are behind me," Ashley said, smiling. "I'm lucky if I can stay awake long enough to see the late news."

"Do you still go out to Sag Harbor?" Claudia asked. Ashley's parents owned a beachfront home on Long Island, and as their only child she expected he would inherit the property.

He shook his head. "No. My father sold it after my mother passed away a year after you left the States. He claimed he couldn't live there without her. A few years later he was diagnosed with dementia, and I had him move in with me. I hired someone to look after him when I couldn't be around, and after a while his doctor recommended he go into an assisted living facility. Although he was given the best medical care he quickly deteriorated, and within six months he was gone."

"I'm so sorry, Ashley," Claudia said. "I really liked your folks." The Booths were who she'd thought of as Black aristocracy.

Ashley lowered his eyes. "They liked you, too." He paused again, as if deep in thought. "Yvonne told me you lost your husband a couple of months ago."

Leaning back in her chair, Claudia exhaled an inaudible sigh. "Yes. Giancarlo died in his sleep." It was the second time she'd buried a husband and thankfully Giancarlo's death was peaceful, while she still believed the Ku Klux Klan were responsible for Robert Moore's so-called accidental death.

Yvonne's cell phone pinged a ringtone and she pushed back her chair. "Excuse me. I must take this call."

Ashley half rose, but stopped when Claudia rested a hand on his arm. "Don't get up, Ashley."

He smiled and a network of tiny lines fanned out around his eyes. "Old habits die hard. Speaking of husbands, Claudia. You know I should've asked you to marry me."

A slight lifting of an eyebrow was her only reaction to his pronouncement. "Really? And if you'd asked, I would've turned you down because you didn't love me."

"But I did, Claudia."

She gave him a lingering stare. "When was that, Ashley? It couldn't have been when we were sleeping together because you never uttered the word. Not even when we had sex."

A beat passed. "You're right," he admitted under his breath. "It was after you left, I realized that I did love you. And I've never stopped loving you. I suppose that's the reason why I never married."

"You never married because you wanted to pick and choose who you dated or slept with," Claudia said in a quiet tone. "You liked being called the Black Prince of Wall Street and having women at your beck and call."

Ashley sighed. "Maybe. But it wasn't that way with you, Claudia. I gave up all those women once I met you."

"And should I assume you reverted back to the old Ashley once I left?"

Ashley pressed a fist to his mouth as he closed his eyes. "Not really. I did see women but not as much or often." He opened his eyes. "I'd changed. You'd changed me."

"Are you involved with a woman now?"

"No. And it has been a while since I've entertained one. But things would be different if we were married."

Claudia curbed the urge to laugh in Ashley's face. He'd waited more than a half century to ask her to marry him when he could've done it before she'd moved across an ocean to fall in love and marry a man who would make her his wife and the mother of their children.

"I'm sorry, Ashley. Two husbands in my lifetime are enough. I don't need a third."

"How about a friend, Claudia?"

"I could always use a friend." She paused. "Do you have a valid passport?"

Ashley nodded. "I renewed it a couple of years ago, even though I hadn't planned to go anywhere."

"I'm going to give you my daughter's cell phone number in North Carolina. I'll be staying with her family until the end of August. Then I'm sailing back to Europe. If you want to come with me, then call me before Labor Day so I can secure passage for you. If not, then this will be the last time we will see each other."

"To visit or to stay?"

"That's up to you, Ashley. The invitation is open-ended."

"What if I choose to stay?"

"As I said. The choice is yours. And if you choose to stay, then you can live in the guesthouse on my property. And if you don't call, then I'll return alone."

Ashley ran a hand over the back of his neck. "Well, do I have time to make a decision?" he asked, before reaching into the breast pocket of his jacket and handing her his cell phone.

"That you do," Claudia countered, as she programmed Daria's number into his Contacts and returned the phone to him.

She wanted to tell Ashley that she still had feelings for him, but not those that would translate as romantic. There had been a time when she did love him—enough to become his wife if he'd asked. But that was the past.

"What did I miss?" Yvonne asked when she rejoined them at the table.

"Not much," Claudia admitted.

She chatted with her friends for another half hour before Yvonne said she wanted to drop Ashley off and drive back to Mount Vernon before getting stuck in rush-hour traffic. Claudia hugged and kissed Yvonne, and then Ashley before they left, wondering if it would be the last time the three of them would be together.

Claudia wondered if Ashley would take her up on her offer to return to Italy with her, or if he would decide this encounter would be their last. Either way, she planned to spend the rest of her life as an Italian citizen in the Eternal City.

Claudia took deep breaths to relieve the constriction in her chest, the closer the driver came to the town limits of Freedom, Mississippi. She had planned for a car service to pick her up at the Gulfport-Biloxi Airport and drive her to Freedom, then on to Raleigh. The trip from Mississippi to North Carolina was estimated to take more than twelve hours, and she'd called her daughter to expect her arrival sometime later that night.

When she'd left what now seemed a lifetime ago, she'd vowed never to return. However, before Claudia made the decision to move to New York, she'd offered to take Sarah Patterson with her, but her mother had refused with the excuse that she never would've been able to survive the frigid winters and therefore decided to move back to Biloxi. Sarah wouldn't say it, but her eyes spoke volumes. She did not want to believe her only child was deserting her.

They passed through downtown Biloxi, and Claudia stared at the Black-owned bank where she'd secured a position after graduating college. She'd applied to several other banks in the city but was told they didn't have any positions that would match her qualifications. She had politely thanked the men for taking the time to interview her when she'd wanted to tell them they were bald-faced lying bigots because she had as much or even more education than most of them. She finally garnered an interview at one of two colored banks and was hired on the spot.

Even when the US Supreme Court ruled segregation to be unconstitutional and the WHITES ONLY and COLORED ONLY signs had begun to come down, Claudia struggled to forget what she'd experienced when living in Mississippi.

Fifty-eight years.

That's how long it had taken Claudia to find her way back home. But then she had to ask herself, where was home? Was it Freedom, Mississippi, New York City, or Rome, Italy? She'd spent more time away from Freedom than she had lived there, yet there was something about the all-Black town that had called out to her, that made her want to embrace it while inhaling the recognizable scents that had been so much a part of her innocent youth.

She closed her eyes and took a deep breath. It smelled the same but with subtle differences. Back then it had been an odor of curling wax in her mama's beauty parlor and the lingering fragrance of Old Spice wafting through the connecting door to her daddy's barber shop.

And she'd always associated mouthwatering aromas with her grandmother. Earline Patterson had gained the distinction of being one of the best cooks in all of Freedom. The chicken she'd fried in a cast-iron skillet with lard *and* butter was without equal among her peers. Her biscuits, cornbread, smothered cabbage, and pound cakes also received unanimous raves from anyone fortunate enough to sit at her table or able to sample a portion at church socials.

They were all gone: Mama, Daddy, and Grandma, her aunt, uncle, and her two husbands. Some were buried in the cemetery here in Freedom and another in a foreign land. Bending slightly, she placed a single white rose on the graves of her parents, grandmother, husband, and other long-deceased relatives.

She'd lingered longer than she had intended, because the late-spring suffocating heat made breathing difficult. She left the cemetery, walking to the car where a driver held open the rear door. "I'd like to stop downtown before we leave for North Carolina."

The tall man nodded. "Yes, ma'am."

Claudia slid onto the rear leather seat and closed her eyes. She didn't know why, but suddenly she felt old. She was eighty-three, yet there were times when she felt as if she'd lived two lifetimes in one. A sad smile lifted the corners of her mouth when she thought about the four men who'd impacted her life. First there was Denny Clark, then Robert Moore, then Ashley Booth, and finally Giancarlo Fortenza.

She opened her eyes, her mouth softening in a tender smile when she thought about her first husband. Robert had taught her how to love herself, and in return she loved him selfishly. Claudia's smile slowly slipped away as a wave of sadness swept over her. The love she shared with Robert was short-lived, and when she sought to withdraw emotionally from every man, Ashley Booth came into her life with the velocity of a twister sweeping up everything in its unleashed power. Ashley had introduced her to New York City's elegant Black society. Her involvement with Ashley gave Claudia the confidence she needed when she was reunited with Giancarlo, who initiated her into a world most women dream of but would never experience.

Claudia still could not understand the strange hold Denny had on her, and she knew this visit to Freedom wasn't only to visit the graves of her loved ones but also to symbolically bid Denny goodbye forever.

The Town Car maneuvered smoothly over the paved road leading to downtown Freedom. Claudia peered through the side window, staring at stores that no longer resembled those from her childhood. Her mother and father's beauty parlor and barbershop now housed a chain drugstore. The candy store was gone, replaced by a Baskin-Robbins. Freedom had come into the twenty-first century boasting a fast-food restaurant, car wash, pizza parlor, florist, and a variety store advertising everything from small household appliances, beauty products, candy, and discount cards and candles.

"Please let me out here," she directed the driver as he pulled over, parking along the street facing the town square. Claudia waited for the man to get out and open the rear door for her. She placed her hand in his, allowing him to assist her to stand.

Bittersweet memories assailed Claudia when she exited the car to walk along the main street, stopping to peer into windows of several stores. The heat was proving to be unbearable, and when she turned to go back to where the car was parked, she collided with someone. She mumbled an apology before she glanced up to see somebody from her past. Suddenly she felt a chill as if she'd been doused with a bucket of ice when she recognized the man with the cold blue eyes— eyes that would haunt her to her grave.

She managed to step around him and headed back to the car. The driver got out at her approach and opened the rear door. Claudia collapsed on the rear seat, her heart pounding painfully in her chest. And when she looked out the side window she saw the man, standing motionless, staring back at her. Despite the years, she'd recognized him, and he seemed to recognize her. Reaching for a bottle of water, Claudia removed the cap and took a swallow.

"Are you cool enough back there, ma'am?" the driver asked.

She forced a smile. "Yes, thank you."

"I'm planning to stop in Mobile, where you can stretch your legs and get something to eat before we continue."

"That's fine." Claudia would've agreed to anything if they did not make another stop in Mississippi.

Once the car began moving, she chided herself for wanting to come back to a place where she'd endured fear and unhappiness, but knew she had to because she needed closure. Claudia did not want to admit to herself that her life was like a book—with a prologue, and then filled with many chapters until it concluded with an epilogue.

It didn't begin in 1940—the year of her birth—but in late spring, 1952, when she'd met Denny Clark for the first time.

PART ONE

1950s

DENNY CLARK

Chapter 1

Extending your hand is extending yourself.
—Rod McKuen, *Book of Days*

Claudia Mavis Patterson made an auspicious entrance into the world in the small, all-Negro town of Freedom, Mississippi, in the spring of 1940, surprising her parents because her mother had had no indication she was even pregnant.

As an only child she'd grown up pampered by her business-owner parents. Earl operated Freedom's only barber shop, as his father had before him, while Sarah was the owner of one of two beauty parlors in the town of 1,837 residents.

Claudia was troubled by an indiscernible restlessness not found in many children, and by the time she'd turned eight she had become aware of it for the first time. She loved Freedom, but she wanted to be elsewhere whenever she opened a book. Books had become her lifeline to the outside world. Her aunt Mavis, her mother's older sister, gave her books as gifts rather than toys or dolls.

Mavis Bailey, who taught grades one through eight in Biloxi, told her niece that books enabled her to glimpse into a world beyond the boundaries of Mississippi. Claudia read about people who lived in China, England, Germany, and Italy. She'd overheard some of the older residents talk about bad White people, but her parents usually hushed them up or sent her away so she wouldn't listen to their private conversations.

She was curious about some of the White people she occasionally saw whenever her family left the environs of her hometown, seeing repeatedly the WHITES ONLY and COLORED ONLY signs, signs that were unnecessary in Freedom. Resigning herself that Freedom was her home, giving her all she could wish for as a child, with its own school, movie theater, business district, and a hospital with a permanent staff of two doctors and three nurses, she felt protected. However, everything that was safe and idyllic came to a startling end in the spring of 1952 for twelve-year-old Claudia.

It happened as she walked home from school with her best friend, as she did every day. She always looked forward to her walks with Janice Mason, because Janice knew things most girls their age were not exposed to until after they were married.

"Why must you fib about things?" she asked Janice.

"I'm not fibbing, Claudia. I swear I saw—"

"Don't swear, Janice," she interrupted. "You know God will strike you dead if you swear."

Janice stopped, resting one hand at her waist. She stared at the long-legged girl whose body had yet to begin to show the feminine curves of a young woman on the threshold of puberty. It was apparent Claudia Patterson was going to be a beautiful woman. Her thick, curly brown hair was styled in two braids that were pinned across the crown of her head. Her face was slender, with exceptionally high cheekbones, her nose short and straight and her mouth wide and handsomely generous. Her complexion reminded Janice of a baked peach. It was as if the sun had kissed her cheeks, turning them a velvety red-gold brown.

"I did see them doing it," she continued in a soft whisper.

Claudia's large, light brown eyes widened. "Doing what?"

"You know."

"I don't know, Janice."

Janice moved closer to Claudia as a battered pickup truck came down the dusty road toward them. The driver slowed and executed a U-turn. His passenger stuck his head out the window. Grinning and displaying a mouth filled with tobacco-stained teeth, the man's light blue eyes squinted at the two girls. He pursed his lips and a stream of brown spittle landed only inches from the toes of their black patent-leather Mary Janes.

He doffed an imaginary hat. "Afternoon, *ladies*. Wanna ride?"

Both girls shook their heads, too frightened to speak. They knew not to speak to strangers, especially White ones. And these two were what colored folk called *cracker trash*.

"Leave 'em 'lone, Bobby," the driver ordered, squinting at Claudia and Janice. "They ain't nothin' but babies."

The man the driver had called Bobby licked his thin, stained lips. "Not the blacker one. Look at them tits on her."

Janice pulled her books closer to her chest to conceal the swell of growing breasts that had become her greatest source of pride. Her body had begun developing at nine, and now at twelve was full and lush with a feminine ripeness some women twice her age would never claim.

"I said leave 'em 'lone," the driver repeated.

Bobby winked at Janice. "I likes them black and ripe. And you sure is a beauty. I'm going . . ."

Whatever he said was lost in the noisy sound of the truck's engine as it sped down the road, raising a cloud of lingering dust. The books in Janice's arms fell to the unpaved road. The tears filling her eyes spilled over and streamed down her silken ebony cheeks. The sound of the books hitting the ground pulled Claudia out of her shocked stupor.

Lowering her own books, secured by a leather belt, to the

road beside her best friend's, she pulled Janice against her body, holding her tightly. The two girls comforted each other once they realized how close they had come to harm.

"The Lord is punishing me," Janice cried against Claudia's shoulder. "He's punishing me for sneaking out at night and peeking through the window when Mister Bill and Miss Hester were in bed together doin' it."

Pulling back, Claudia stared at her friend. "You were spying on them?" Janice nodded. "That's a sin!" she said accusingly.

"I know." Janice pulled a lace-trimmed handkerchief from the pocket of her dress, wiping her runny nose. "I ain't gonna do it no more. I swear, Claudia."

"Don't swear, Janice!" she screamed, temporarily forgetting her fright.

"I know. But I'm so scared." She gave Claudia a questioning glance. "Wasn't you scared of those men?"

She wanted to lie but didn't. "Yeah. I was plenty scared, too."

"You going to tell your daddy?"

Biting down hard on her lower lip, Claudia shook her head. "No. I don't want trouble. Daddy would go hunting for those two rednecks and he would wind up dead. And you know we're not supposed to take the long way home."

"You're right," Janice agreed. "We don't say anything. Cross your heart and hope to die."

"Cross my heart and hope to die," Claudia repeated, making an X over her left breast.

Picking up their books, the two girls quickened their pace and turned off at a clearing and took a shortcut to the residential section. They hadn't gone more than a hundred yards when both heard a weak, wavering cry for help. It sounded like the mewling of a kitten, but then a kitten couldn't talk.

Janice's slanting dark eyes widened as she stopped and turned slowly. "What's that?"

"I don't know," Claudia replied.

The burning rays of the hot spring sun did not reach the ground through the overgrowth of towering pine trees as the girls listened, trying to discern where the noise had come from.

There was another moaning sound. Janice shook her head, taking a step backwards. "I'm going, Claudia."

"Don't . . ." Her words died on her lips as she stood and watched Janice run away. "Fraidy cat," she whispered.

What she did not want to admit to herself was that she also was afraid. But her curious nature always got the better of her. She'd asked her mother why, so many times that Sarah would say, *Hush, baby. Just accept it.* But what she did not want to do was accept it. She had to have an answer. That's why she'd suggested taking the longer road home from school instead of the more direct route. She wanted to see as many places as she could beyond Freedom's boundaries.

She heard the sound again and followed it to a dilapidated building leaning at a right angle in a clearing nearly obliterated by an overgrowth of trees and shrubs, and moved closer. A small shriek of fear escaped her parted lips as she stared at the body of a White boy curled into a fetal position on a pile of dirt. She gasped, then clapped a hand over her mouth when she saw hunks of flesh hanging off his back. It was apparent that someone had whipped him and then had left him to die.

He raised his head from the dirt at the sound of her voice. Opening his eyes, he stared up at her, his tortured gaze filled with a suffering she'd never seen. Not even in an injured animal. Her dog had broken away from his restraint several months before and wandered into a trap set for a raccoon, breaking his front legs. The pain in her pet's eyes was not as intense as the one she saw in the boy's eyes with his bared back festering with open wounds. An army of insects had invaded the blood pooling around him.

Her first reaction was to run. Why, she thought, was she suddenly coming face-to-face with White people within a span of minutes when in all her twelve years of living she had never exchanged a word with them?

"Help me," he groaned, closing his eyes at the same time his head fell back to the ground.

"I . . . I can't," she stammered.

"Please. Oh, God—let me die."

Even though he'd closed his eyes, Claudia still saw them. They were the same blue eyes as the man in the pickup truck. Staring at the fallen body, she realized the boy posed no threat to her. He lay bleeding, unable to move. Although he appeared taller than she was, she doubted whether he weighed more than she did. She could see every rib in his emaciated body. But who, she wondered, had whipped him, and dumped his body near a colored town? And she was mature enough to know that any White person found beaten in a town filled with Negroes was trouble for her people.

"I'll be back," she promised. Turning away from him, Claudia took the same route as Janice, running in the direction of her grandmother's house.

Slowing her steps as she approached the large white house with the wraparound porch, she spied Earline Patterson sitting on her rocker, sewing, and listening to her favorite series on the radio, which sat on a table inside the house close to the screened door.

"You're late," Earline stated, not looking up from piecing squares of fabric together for her latest quilting project.

"I'm sorry, Grandma." She climbed the half dozen steps while trying to slow down her runaway pulse. "I stopped for a minute."

"It was more than a minute." Earline stared at her over the top of her glasses. A slow smile creased her unlined dark face. "No harm done as long as you are all right."

Dropping her books to the porch floor, Claudia leaned over and kissed her grandmother's cheek. "Afternoon, Grandma."

"Afternoon, grandbaby." Earline waved her away. "Go in and change outta those clothes. You hot and sweaty. What you do? Run home?"

She bobbed her head. "Yes, Grandma."

"Who was chasing you?"

"No one, ma'am. But I found someone who needs help."

Earline dropped her sewing to her lap and gently removed her glasses. Snow-white hair blended attractively with her mahogany-brown complexion. At sixty-two Earline Patterson was still a fine figure of a woman. She was tall, five-nine, and full-figured. Her skin was still smooth and youthful looking. There were only a few laugh lines around her dark eyes.

Claudia recalled her grandmother talking about her first and only love, Joe Patterson, who'd passed on in 1939, and Earline continued to cherish his memory by not marrying again or taking up with the men who'd occasionally come calling on the attractive widow. Her grandmother bore Joe two sons, Joe Junior and Earl. Joe Junior lost his life to a Japanese bullet in a jungle in the South Pacific during the Second World War, and there was a time when Earline said she would never get over losing her son four years after burying her husband.

"Who, child?"

"A White boy in the woods."

Vertical lines creased Earline's forehead. "A white what and where?"

"A White boy in the woods," Claudia repeated. "Someone whupped him bad and left him in the woods. He's going to die if we don't help him, Grandma."

"Did he say who whupped him?"

Claudia shook her head. "No. He just asked me to help him."

Earline blew out a breath. "I've lived long enough to know if that White boy did die near Freedom, colored folks would be blamed and lynched even if they didn't do it. Who else knows about him?"

Nobody, Grandma. Janice was with me, but she didn't see him."

"Where is she now?"

"She ran home."

"I hope that girl knows to keep her mouth shut."

"She will," Claudia said confidently. She knew Janice's mother and father would beat her senseless if they knew she hadn't come directly home. They claimed she was "too fast" for her age, and both kept a close eye and tight rein on her.

"Go change outta your clothes while I get my medicine sack."

Claudia picked up her books, and then ran inside the house, letting the door slam noisily against its frame. She raced up the staircase to the second-floor bedroom that she occupied whenever she stayed over at her grandmother's house.

Unbuttoning her shirtwaist dress, she kicked off her patent-leather shoes at the same time. Within minutes she'd changed into a sleeveless white blouse and cotton pants. A pair of white tennis shoes had replaced her Mary Janes.

Her grandmother was seated behind the wheel of the old Packard, waiting for her when she pushed open the screened door, this time holding it before it made the annoying bang against the frame.

"It's not far into the woods, Grandma," she said, slipping onto the seat beside Earline.

The woods were close to the house, but Earline had no intention of walking in the heat. Things were going on in the world that did not directly affect Freedom, but something told her Freedom was about to change. She prayed the change would not begin with the White boy in the woods.

Turning on the engine, and shifting into gear, she slowly let out the clutch and the shiny black car rolled forward.

A strained silence filled the inside of the car as Earline and Claudia stared straight ahead, each lost in their private thoughts. Earline wanted to reprimand her granddaughter for walking through the woods. If she hadn't, she would not have come upon the White boy. But then she could not chastise her for wanting to help another human being, even though she doubted whether the favor would be returned if the boy had found a Negro begging for help.

She had lived long enough to have witnessed the evil of racial prejudice that her people had endured and continued to suffer throughout the South, first under slavery and now Jim Crow. Fortunately, Freedom's cloistered all-Black environment had spared it from the reports of an occasional lynching.

"Was I wrong, Grandma?" Claudia's voice broke the strained silence.

"Wrong about what, child?"

"Wanting to help that White boy?"

A smile softened Earline's tightly compressed lips. "No, baby. You are not wrong. God loves all of us, white or colored, good and bad. We will let Him do the separatin' and judgin' when the time comes for Him to set this evil world straight. Right now, we must do what we can to keep the Devil from gatherin' as many souls as he can before the Lord Jesus stops him."

Claudia nodded, pleased with herself. She had done the right thing to want to help the White boy. "Over there, Grandma," she said, pointing and directing Earline to the clearing where the boy lay.

Slowing and stopping the car, Earline put it in neutral and applied the brake. "Stay here," she ordered, reaching for the burlap sack resting on the seat between them.

"But, Grandma. I saw him already." There was a hint of

panic in her voice. Earline gave her a warning look that spoke volumes. It was a *don't cross me, girl* look that older folks gave whenever children sought to challenge their authority.

"I'll wait here." Everything about her was resignation as she fumed inwardly. It was she who had found the boy. It was she who had gone for help. And it was she who knew where he lay hidden near the abandoned shack.

A shiver of fear caused the hair to rise on the back of her neck when she saw her grandmother reach under her seat and withdraw a large handgun. She had seen the gun enough to know it had belonged to her Grandpa Joe. She never met her grandfather because he'd died the year before she was born, but she had heard stories about his courageous exploits when he was in the Great War and had received a bright shiny medal for his heroism. Her grandmother had a faded photograph of Grandpa Joe standing proudly at attention, the medal pinned on the shirt of his uniform while Joe wore a proud, tight-lipped smirking grin.

She had overheard her grandmother say to some of the other grown folks that she kept the gun because it was trained to shoot White folks with deadly aim. All she had to do was squeeze the trigger and the bullets found their mark. Now she wondered whether a bullet would end the life of the boy in the woods the way some people shot an injured horse or dog whose life could not be saved. She prayed he would not die, and she prayed he would not be put to death to end his suffering like her dog whose legs were crushed in a neighbor's trap.

She sat in the car, praying and waiting for what seemed hours when it had been only fifteen minutes. Staring at the towering trees draped in Spanish moss, Claudia failed to see the beauty of the surrounding landscape. The woods were dark and cooler, while the trees and underbrush concealed one from prying eyes and wagging tongues. She knew some of the older kids spent time together in the woods after dark, doing things they did not want their parents to know about—things she'd heard whispered about but did not yet fully understand.

Her eyes grew wide when she saw her grandmother coming toward the car, carrying the boy in her arms as if he weighed no more than a tiny infant. Her burlap sack, hanging from her wrist, swayed and bumped against her thigh.

"Open the back door," Earline ordered. A sheen of moisture beaded her forehead as she carefully made her way to the parked automobile. Claudia jumped from her seat, raced around the driver's side of the car, and opened the rear door. "Spread that quilt out on the seat. I don't need him stinkin' up my car."

Claudia noticed the odor coming from the bruised body for the first time. It was the sickening smell of drying blood and body secretions mingling with infected flesh. Working quickly, she unfolded the handmade quilt and laid it over the rear seats. She swallowed back a rush of nausea, struggling to keep from losing the contents of her stomach because of the overwhelming stench.

Earline laid the boy on his belly, wrinkling her nose. Dirt and grime lined the back of his neck and matted hair. It was apparent he did not bathe regularly. Dirt had darkened his skin and he could have been taken for colored if one did not see his eyes. But then there were Negros in Freedom who had inherited their light-colored eyes from White ancestors who had been unable to resist a Black woman's body.

Slamming the door with a solid thud, Earline reclaimed her seat behind the wheel, replaced the gun under the front seat, and handed Claudia her medicine sack. Her mouth was set in a hard, tight line. What she intended to do went against everything she had been taught about White and Black people. She would take a White boy into her home to save his life. And if she hadn't been a God-fearing Christian woman, she would have left his dirty, scrawny butt in the woods to die.

Giving her only grandchild a quick glance, she shook her head. Claudia was a good girl, but she was too soft and trusting. She'd brought home more stray dogs and cats than any child in Freedom. Now she had her taking home a near-dead White boy.

Earline planned to save his life, and then send him back to wherever he came from. And if he died—she refused to think of what she would do if he did.

Chapter 2

A little kindness from person to person is better
than a vast love for all humankind.
—Richard Dehmel

Claudia placed a hand over her nose. "Why does he smell
so foul, Grandma?"

"Cause he's po' White trash," Earline said, as she, too,
scrunched up her nose at the odor coming from the boy on
the seats behind them.

"How can you tell White trash, Grandma?"

Earline frowned as she drove slowly along the narrow trail
leading out of the wooded area. "They don't take a bath
every day. And some are so po' that they don't eat right. The
kids must drop out of school if their folks are sharecroppers
and they have to help work the fields."

"The Wilkins family is like that. And they are colored like
us. So, does that make them Black trash?"

Earline shook her head. "No, grandbaby, they ain't Black
trash. They just lowlife, no-account colored folk. That is why
your mama and daddy preach to you to get an education.
With book learnin' you don't have to be beholden to no man
or no woman. You can hold your head up and be proud that
you somebody."

"I'm already somebody, Grandma."

"You are. But when you become a full-grown woman, you have to be somebody special. You must make your mark in this world."

Claudia nodded, and she wanted to remove her hand from her nose, but with the sour, sickening odor, that wasn't possible. She knew she would never be trash or no-account because no one in her family was lowlife. Her granddaddy Joe had had his own business even though he hadn't had more than six years of schooling. Her grandmother managed to finish the eighth grade before she had to drop out to take care of her younger brothers and sister when their mama died giving birth to her twelfth child.

It was her mother's people, the Baileys, who were educated. They came from Biloxi. Sarah Bailey completed high school but refused to go to college after she met and fell in love with Earl Patterson. Defying her parents, she married Earl and moved to Freedom. Earl worked in his father's barbershop and owned it outright after his father died. He'd used the money from Joe Patterson's life insurance to expand the business to include a beauty parlor for his wife.

Sarah Bailey Patterson was one of three girls born to the Baileys. The two remaining daughters attended and completed college, both becoming teachers. They were fiercely independent women who rejected the advances from men who sought to *tame* the uppity Bailey sisters. The attractive, intelligent women had many suitors, but never accepted any of the marriage proposals presented to them.

Claudia wanted to be like her aunts. She wanted to go to college; she wanted to be able to debate on any subject, and she wanted to set up a home like theirs and invite her close friends for elegant suppers or afternoon tea.

But then she also wanted to be like her mother, too. She wanted to have a business, make her own money, and marry a man like her father who loved his wife and wasn't ashamed to admit it openly to all his friends.

"I'm going to drive around to the rear of the house," Earline said, breaking into Claudia's thoughts. "I want you to open the back door so I can carry him without someone seein' me."

"Yes, ma'am."

Earline maneuvered the Packard until it was less than six feet from the rear door. She shut off the engine, and opened the back door. Using the quilt, she pulled the edge of it until the limp body hung half-in and half-out of the car.

Claudia stared at her grandmother as she lifted the injured boy. "Is he heavy, Grandma?"

"Not too much. It's just that I don't want to hurt him mo' than he already is."

Claudia figured he couldn't weigh that much, the way his ribs showed through his flesh. Her grandmother was right about his kind not getting enough to eat. Even though colored families in Freedom were poor, few went hungry. They raised chickens and hogs and cooked big pots of peas, beans, rice, and stews along with biscuits and cornbread. Many of them had gardens with collard greens, cabbage, tomatoes, green peppers, and cucumbers.

She followed Earline down a flight of stairs to a root cellar. The space was dark and cool even during the hottest weather. It was on these occasions Claudia and her parents came to Earline's to set up cots to sleep in the cellar. The last time was the prior summer. All the South was ravaged by a severe, unrelenting heatwave. Crops withered and died, and the loss of livestock and human lives shattered records.

Earline laid the unconscious boy on his side on a narrow cot in a corner. There was enough light coming from a high, narrow overhead window for Claudia to see the deep lacerations crisscrossing his bony, narrow back. Her grandmother retrieved a kerosene lamp from one of the many shelves lining the cellar walls, turned up the wick, struck a match, and lit it. She bit down on her lip to keep the strangled cry from escaping. Whoever whipped the boy sought to kill him.

Earline glanced at Claudia over her shoulder. "Get me a couple of towels, a bar of lye soap, and two sheets. I'm going to take off his clothes and then clean him up."

She waited for her granddaughter to race up the cellar steps, allowing her to undress the boy without Claudia seeing him naked. He hadn't worn a shirt or shoes, and only having to remove his grime-caked blue jeans made her task an easier one. His penis was cradled in wisps of light-colored hair. He was developing into a man while the rest of his body had yet to catch up. His hands and feet were large, indicating he could grow up to be a tall, large man if properly nourished. She concealed the lower part of his body with the quilt.

Earline had filled a small metal washtub with water from an outdoor pump by the time Claudia returned with what she'd asked her to bring. "Go upstairs and do your homework while I wash him up."

"It's Friday, Grandma. I don't have homework."

"I made some lemonade. Get a glass and have a few gingerbread cookies with it."

Claudia didn't move. "I'm not hungry or thirsty, Grandma."

"Get outta here, girl, and let me get to work." Earline gave her an angry scowl. "This boy don't have no clothes on under this quilt."

Needing no further prompting, Claudia turned and fled up the cellar steps. She did not want to be like Janice Mason, spying on naked people. As she made her way to the kitchen, Claudia was unable to forget the dirt-streaked boy whose face resembled those of angels she'd seen in a book. It was hard to tell the exact color of his hair, but it didn't appear to be too dark. His lashes were long and lay on high cheekbones like feathered silk. But it was his nose and mouth that had reminded her of the angel. His nose was straight and narrow, and his mouth was pink and too beautifully sculpted for a boy. Claudia decided it would look a lot better on a girl.

Standing in the middle of the kitchen, Claudia stared at the new stove and refrigerator. She loved her grandmother's house—especially the kitchen. And she loved coming to the house after school rather than going to her own house, which was closer to Freedom's business district. She'd told her parents that she didn't like being home alone once classes were dismissed for the day, and she had gotten them to agree to let her go to her grandmother's and to sleep over on Friday and Saturday nights. These two days were the busiest for the barber shop and beauty parlor when folks made appointments for haircuts, press and curls, marcel, and finger waves. All the primping and preening was for Friday and Saturday parties or dances, or for Sunday church service. Claudia rarely visited the barber shop or beauty parlor. Her mother washed her hair at home and pulled a barely warm comb through the strands to straighten her curls. The few times she had ventured into her parents' businesses she was astounded by the spirited energy of men debating everything from the world's situation to baseball, music, religion, and Joe McCarthy's Red Scare. The women were different. They were more subdued, talking quietly and shaking their heads when someone disclosed some well-kept secret. What surprised Claudia was that her parents rarely contributed to the discussions. They listened and sometimes grunted in agreement or wagged their heads vigorously in disbelief.

Earl and Sarah Patterson claimed barber shops and beauty parlors were places where lives and reputations could be ruined by misleading information coming out of the wrong mouth. They could ill afford to lose a customer by having someone accuse them of *I heard that you said I said*—

Janice Mason insisted the Pattersons were rich, even though Claudia denied it. She had explained to her friend that her family did not have money problems that some other Freedom citizens experienced because her parents were good businesspeople. All she knew was that her parents were friendly and treated their customers fairly, and each paid their employees a decent wage. What Claudia had not understood was the abject poverty affecting many colored families in

Mississippi. Many worked as sharecroppers, owning little or no land of their own. Land they'd toiled on when their ancestors were enslaved. They were the first to experience the ravages of tough times if crops failed or if the national economy fell into a recession.

What she did not tell Janice was that the woman who assisted her mother at the beauty parlor, or the young man at her father's barber shop, were not permitted to handle any money. Customers knew to pay Earl or Sarah directly. The money was stored in cigar boxes, was counted after closing and secured in a secret place in the Patterson home before it was deposited in a Biloxi bank on Monday mornings. A percentage of the proceeds were always deposited in an account in the same bank in Earline Patterson's name, thereby enabling the older woman to live in comfort with the additional income.

Earline never revealed to anyone how much her husband had left her. It was a known fact that Joe Patterson had *sat* Earline down. She never worked, and he paid someone to help Earline to clean her large house. She claimed she did not trust another woman to cook for her husband; she was too superstitious to allow someone to slip something into Joe's food and work a *root on him*.

At the beginning of every December, Earline withdrew ten percent of her savings and bought herself a little something for Christmas. Last year it had been the refrigerator and stove. The year before it was a washing machine. Her grandmother hadn't decided what she wanted for this coming Christmas.

Claudia wandered restlessly around the kitchen, her tennis shoes making squeaky sounds on the waxed linoleum floor. What was her grandmother doing to the White boy? Did she expect him to live? Or would he die? Who had beat him? Why did someone dump him in Freedom? Had he been beaten by White or colored?

She walked over to the refrigerator and took out a bottle

of lemonade. Claudia shook the bottle to stir up the sugar that had settled on the bottom, removed the cap, and filled a glass with the pale yellow liquid. She replaced the cap and set the bottle on the top shelf in the refrigerator, and then took a large gingerbread cookie from the crock on the countertop where Earline stored flour, sugar, grits, and cornmeal in matching containers. Alternating taking sips of lemonade and biting off flavorful pieces of the cookie, she sat at the round oak table and waited.

The sound of Earline's footsteps on the cellar stairs brought her to her feet. "Is he going to be all right, Grandma?"

Earline entered the kitchen, nodding and smiling. "He will. If he don't come down with a fever if those cuts become infected."

"What did you do for him?"

"I put a cinquefoil poultice on his back after I tried cleaning him up. It should not be long before the bleeding stops."

Claudia watched as her grandmother washed her hands in the kitchen sink with the sliver of lye soap, and scrubbed her nails with a small, hard brush. "How long do we have to keep him here?"

Earline rinsed her hands and forearms under the running water, then repeated washing and scrubbing them again. "Until he can make his way outta here on his own two legs."

"How long will that be?"

"Can't tell."

Claudia sat down and finished her cookie. The feeling of restlessness was back. This time stronger than ever. She couldn't sit still. "Do you want me to help you with supper?"

"I could use some help."

"What you fixin' tonight, Grandma?"

"I thought some smothered porkchops would be nice."

"With rice, cabbage, and cornbread?"

"Yes, baby, with rice, cabbage, and cornbread."

Claudia stood and went over to Earline, curving her arms around her waist, while inhaling the familiar scent of Evening in Paris on her generous bosom. Her grandmother was going to cook her favorite foods.

"Thank you."

Earline flashed a tender smile and then kissed Claudia's forehead. "You are welcome."

Because she knew Claudia would be her only grandchild, she doted on her. A week after she had buried her eldest son, she scheduled an appointment with a lawyer in Biloxi to draw up a will. She hadn't planned on joining her husband and son in Heaven for a while, but she had wanted to make certain her grandchild would be financially taken care of. It wasn't that Earl and Sarah could not provide for their child, because they could. What Earline wanted was for certain items that had been in her family for generations to be passed down through blood kin. And it wasn't that she didn't like her daughter-in-law, but Sarah wasn't blood.

Claudia had asked how long the boy in the cellar would stay with them, and Earline wanted him gone, and as soon as possible. She knew it wasn't Christian-like to turn him out where he surely would die, but then she didn't want him under her roof either. Other than the pot-bellied sheriff who came around asking about some no-account colored making trouble, she never had any White person on her property. And even when the sheriff came, she always made him stand out on the porch because she wasn't about to let him come in through her front door. Not when she had to go around to the back door at a White person's house.

"What do you need for me to do?" Claudia asked.

"Start by washing your hands. Then you can get the pots I need to cook the cabbage and rice."

The kitchen was filled with the sounds of running water and clanging pots. Within twenty minutes the aroma of diced sautéed onions and bacon ends filled the space. Earline worked quickly, washing and rolling cabbage leaves into cylinders, and then cutting them into long, thin shreds. She had filled a large wooden bowl with the shredded cabbage before she handed it to Claudia to add to the large pot of simmering onions and bacon.

"Put them in slowly, stirrin' them until they get limp before you add another handful. Meanwhile, I'm going downstairs to check on that boy."

It wasn't long before Earline returned to the kitchen, her forehead furrowed. "He's runnin' a fever. Infection must have set in."

Claudia stopped stirring the pot. "What you gonna do, Grandma?"

"Make up some wild sarsaparilla tea. Before long he'll be sweatin' out all those poisons."

Hesitating before she dropped another handful of cabbage into the large pot, Claudia glanced at Earline. "Can I give him the tea?"

"No! I want you to stay away from him. Do you hear me?" Silence followed her question. "Claudia?"

"Yes, ma'am. I hear you."

Earline stared at Claudia, seeing tears in her eyes. "I didn't mean to holler at you, baby, but you have to stop pesterin' when I tells you something. That boy don't have no clothes on, and you don't need to see him like that."

Claudia smiled through her tears. "I don't mean to pester you, Grandma. It's just that if I don't ask, then I won't know whether I can do something. That's all."

"You right about that, baby. If we can get some pants to fit that boy, then you can help me take care of him."

"Don't you have old pants that belonged to Uncle Joe Junior?"

Earline thought about the large trunks in the attic with memories from her past. She had held on to items that were milestones: her sons' first baby shoes; report cards from school; locks of hair from their first haircuts, and their first pair of long pants. She was certain there would be something in the trunks that would fit the boy.

But what she did not want to do was defame her dead son's memory by offering his possessions to a southern White boy. However, he was helpless after being beaten close to death, but she did not fool herself into believing that if he recovered, he would be any different than some of the hateful people of his race. She knew little snakes grew into big snakes, and of all the animals God created, snakes were the most cunning and deadly.

Earline had heard stories about how people found snakes helpless and frozen whenever frost swept across the state, picking them up and putting them to their bosom to warm them. Then without warning they'd bite the person, causing severe injury or death. She didn't know how she knew it, but the boy in her root cellar was a young, helpless snake.

"After we eat you can help me find somethin' in the attic for him to put on," she reluctantly conceded.

Claudia effected a slow smile as she angled her head and glanced up from under her lashes. Earline had noticed the gesture enough to know that her granddaughter would never lack for male attention or company. Although she looked like Sarah, she had inherited Earl's charm. Both were a winning combination.

Earline filled a small enamel pot with water and set it on the stove to boil. She searched a tall, narrow closet for several glass jars containing roots and herbs and located the one she needed. As she rubbed the leaves between her palms the shredded particles floated into the boiling water, filling the kitchen with the distinctive aroma of sarsaparilla. She had learned her healing skills from her grandmother, and it was her intention to pass them along to her own granddaughter, because she'd found Claudia to be a quick learner.

Claudia alternated stirring the cabbage and a pot of boiling rice while her grandmother retreated to the root cellar to give the boy the sarsaparilla tea. Warm, homey smells mingled in the kitchen, smells she treasured. She loved cooking and relished the sense of peace and protection a home offered.

Whenever she was at home with her parents or grandmother, she forgot about the talk of another war or atomic bombs. She had turned five the year the United States dropped two bombs on Japan to end the war, and the photographs of the deaths and destruction gave her nightmares for years. Then there was talk about another war—a Cold War.

She did not understand the difference between a cold war, or one fought with guns, tanks, and bombs, but the talk of any war frightened her. Her grandfather had fought in one war and her only uncle died in another, and whenever her teachers lectured about the Communists in Korea and the possibility that war could erupt at any time, Claudia wanted to run away and hide. She was too young to think about dying or watching bombs blow people apart. And each night before she went to sleep, she prayed for peace.

Earline rejoined her in the kitchen. She showed her how to fry the pork chops and put aside the pan dripping to make a savory gravy. The yellow cornmeal mixture with eggs, melted butter, canned milk, and a tablespoon of sugar filled a pan and was put into the oven to bake until golden brown. Claudia refused to eat cornbread unless it was her grandmother's. Not even her mother could make it sweet and buttery enough for her.

Afternoon shadows lengthened with the setting sun as dusk descended on Freedom, while Earline and Claudia sat at the kitchen table eating and listening to the news on one of the three radios in the house. Earline didn't read much, yet always felt the need to keep up on what was going on in the world. The rumors of war and Senator Joseph McCarthy's charge that the Department of State had been infiltrated by Communists earlier that year unsettled everyone in the country, but she wasn't bothered. She had no more sons to send off to war and Earl, at thirty, was too old to be drafted to fight.

As she sat listening to the announcer's voice, Earline decided it was time she purchased a television set, because she wanted to see the images of the actors on some of the programs she listened to on the radio. "I'm fixin' to buy myself a television for Christmas," she said quietly.

With wide eyes, Claudia sat up straight. "Really, Grandma? You are really going to buy one?"

Earline nodded. "I want to see all those colored boys who play for the Brooklyn Dodgers instead of listening to them on the radio or seeing pictures of them in the magazines. Good ole Jackie Robinson, Roy Campanella and Don Newcombe."

Vertical lines appeared between Claudia's eyes. "I didn't know you liked baseball that much."

"Didn't before them colored boys started playing on those White teams. All before, they had to play in the Negro leagues. Your Uncle Joe Junior, God bless the dead, tried out for the Homestead Grays, but didn't make the team. He fell asleep under a fan and came down with a stiff neck and shoulder. He couldn't throw or move his head. Plumb broke his heart."

"When do you listen to the games, Grandma?"

Earline chewed and swallowed a piece of cornbread. "Different times. Sometime in the day and sometime at night." She paused. "Let's finish up here, so we can go up to the attic to see if we can find some clothes for that boy."

Chapter 3

Kindness is never wasted. If it has no effect on the recipient, at least it benefits the bestower.
—S. H. Simmons

The naked bulb Earline had switched on gently swayed from the ceiling rafters, throwing light and dark shadows over boxes and trunks stacked neatly around the yawning space. "I have everything marked," she said to Claudia. "Look for something with Joe Junior's name on it."

"Here's one." It hadn't taken Claudia long to locate a trunk with a yellowing tag with her late uncle's name.

Earline pulled over a wooden crate, sat down heavily, and sprang the lock. Sighing, she closed her eyes and compressed her lips. Opening the trunk reopened the wound that had taken years to heal. *People ain't supposed to bury their children.* But she had. The United States government sent his body back with several medals pinned to his chest. She was told he had died a hero. Being a hero didn't mean spit when Joe Junior couldn't travel the state of Mississippi like a free man. He had gone and given up his life for a country where he was still in bondage.

"Do you want me to look for some pants, Grandma?"

She opened her eyes and nodded as she watched Claudia gently remove folded shirts, socks, and several jackets. Seeing the clothes made her wonder about the mother of the boy in her cellar. Was she upset her child was missing? Did she believe she was never going to see him again?

"Take out some undiewears if you find some. If they be too big, he can always pin them up."

"Won't he need a bath before he puts on clean clothes?" Claudia asked.

Earline snorted. "He'd catch a death of cold if he took a bath like regular folks. I cleaned him up some, so that will have to do."

"Will he need socks, Grandma?"

"Not now."

"These clothes smell musty. Do you want to air them out first?"

"They smell a heap better than that child did before I washed him up."

As they retraced their steps, the telephone rang loudly in Earline's bedroom. Claudia raced to answer it before it stopped.

"Patterson residence . . . Yes, Mama . . . No, Mama." She extended the receiver to Earline. "Mama wants to talk to you."

"I don't know what she wants," Earline mumbled under her breath. "She just ought to save her money and her telephone units. She knows you already staying over." She took the receiver. "Yes, Sarah."

"Is Claudia minding you?"

"You know the child's not giving me any trouble."

"Maybe I should come over for a spell."

"There's no need to trouble yourself by comin' here. I'll bring her home tomorrow for supper."

"There's no need for you to get your back up. She is my child!"

"Watch your mouth, Miss Sarah. I know she's your child, but she is also my grandchild." Earline saw Claudia frowning. She knew the child didn't like it when she argued with her mother. And when it happened, she would not see her grandchild for at least a week. Then Earl had to step in to make peace between his wife and mother.

"I need her help with puttin' in a garden," she continued, hoping to pacify her daughter-in-law. "We gonna get up 'fore day in the morning 'fore the sun gets too hot." Earline flashed Claudia a facetious grin.

"If that the case, then can you bring her over on Sunday?"

"Yes, Sarah. I will bring her with me to Sunday school and you can pick her up before church starts. And tell *my son* that I'm fine, thank you. Good night." Shaking her head, she replaced the receiver on its cradle. "I don't know why, but your momma always makes me wanna holla."

Claudia gave her an expectant look. "Does it mean I can stay over until Sunday?"

Earline smiled. "Yes. We'll meet your folks in church on Sunday."

Claudia clasped her hands in a prayerful gesture. "Thanks, Grandma."

"Let me go put some clothes on that boy, then we can plan what we want to do tomorrow."

"I thought you told Mama that we are going to put in a garden tomorrow."

Earline made a sucking sound with her tongue and teeth. "I ain't studyin' Sarah. One of these days she's gonna work my last nerve and I'm not goin' to bite my tongue when I tell her just how I feel. She act like I'm goin' to take you from her."

It was common knowledge that Sarah Patterson was possessive of her only child. Three subsequent pregnancies had ended with miscarriages, and doctors had warned Sarah not to try for another baby. Several months after Claudia turned ten Sarah found herself pregnant again, and when she began bleeding and it wouldn't stop, twenty-seven-year-old Sarah was admitted to the hospital for a procedure to prevent further conception.

"How would you like to bake some pies using the fruit we put up last winter?"

Claudia clapped a hand over her mouth at the same time she spun around. "I want cherry and apple."

There were times when Claudia appeared much more childlike to Earline than most girls her age. She had noticed the subtle changes in her granddaughter's body that indicated she soon would become a woman and have a baby of her own.

"You want cherry and apple, but I want peach cobbler." Earline gathered up the clothes they'd taken out of the trunk and made her way to the staircase. "I want you to stay in the kitchen until I call you."

Claudia waited in the kitchen while her grandmother went down to the root cellar with Joe Junior's clothes. She stood by the door, listening for the sound of voices, then bounded down the stairs when Earline called her name.

The light from the kerosene lamp and several candles lit up the dark space. Her grandmother had planned to wire the cellar for electricity but hadn't gotten around to it. Earline picked up a broom and began sweeping up a layer of silt that had settled over the floor when Claudia walked over to the cot and stared down into the face of the boy lying on his side facing her. His pale blue eyes never wavered as he boldly returned her stare; the jeans her grandmother had given him were several sizes too big for him.

"What's your name?" Claudia asked.

His lids fluttered wildly before he closed his eyes. "Denny Clark." His first name came out strong and deep, the last cracking and ending in a high pitch associated with boys going through puberty.

"Where are you from?"

"Madison."

Claudia bit her lip. Denny Clark lived in a town less than three miles from Freedom. "Where's your mama?"

He opened his eyes and glared up at her. Claudia took a step back when she saw hardness settle into his delicate features. "She's dead."

She didn't know why, but Claudia felt a wave of pity wash over her. It was no wonder he was so dirty. He didn't have a mama to take care of him. "Who beat you?"

"None of your damn business!"

"Watch your mouth, boy," Earline warned from across the room. "That girl is responsible for saving your skinny, smelly behind. Show her some respect."

Denny shifted on the cot, turning over, and allowing Claudia a close-up view of his scarred back. The poultice Earline had placed on his wounds had stopped the bleeding, leaving the open wounds to drain a greenish-yellowish substance onto the sheet under his body. The cloying fetid stench nearly overpowered her.

Clamping a hand over her mouth, she turned and headed for the stairs, praying she wouldn't be sick from the smells that followed her. She took a glass from the kitchen cupboard and filled it with water. She drank the water and miraculously her stomach stopped churning.

"He's hateful and evil," she whispered as she recalled the cold eyes staring up at her. In that moment, Claudia knew it had been a mistake to have stopped and helped him. She should have run away like Janice and left him to die.

Anyone filled with that much hate did not deserve to live.

It was another two days before Claudia saw Denny Clark again. She'd refused to go down to the cellar on Saturday, and it was early Sunday morning before she prepared to leave for church services that she crept down to where he lay on the cot.

He was awake, lying on his side and staring out into space.

"Where did you go?" he demanded as soon as she came into his line of vision.

Claudia sat down on a folding chair close to him as tiny pleats from her delicate shirtwaist dress flowed over the sides. "Didn't your mama ever teach you any manners? When you meet a person, you're supposed to say good morning or good evening."

"I told you before that my mama's dead, and I don't have to say nothin' to a nigga."

Recoiling as if he had slapped her, and before she could stop herself, Claudia leaned over and struck him across the face. The gesture stunned him as much as it had her as she froze in shock and rage, then jumped up.

"Don't you dare call me a nigger, you lowlife trash. It's a wonder anybody would want to be around your kind. You smell like something rotten crawled up in you and died." Turning on her heels, her skirt billowing around her legs, she fled the cellar.

Denny watched her retreating until he couldn't see her anymore. The shock of her hitting him faded as the stinging in his cheek subsided. He hadn't meant to call her a nigga, but the word just slipped out. He had grown up hearing it whenever White people talked about Black people. It came to him as easily as saying *yes, sir* and *yes, ma'am*.

Hot, angry tears filled his eyes and overflowed, soaking the sheet and mattress. He wanted to see her again, smell her sweetness, and now she was gone.

"Damn you!" he cursed between clenched teeth, pounding his fist into the mattress.

He was angry with himself for chasing the beautiful colored girl away; angry with his mother for dying; angry with his stepmother, who was young enough to be his older sister, and angry with his father for trying to kill him when he found his second wife in bed with his son.

Denny had tried to avoid his stepmother, but she wouldn't leave him alone. He'd stay away from the house, didn't go to school, and hung out in the woods, but whenever he returned home, she was there pushing her body against his and touching his private parts.

He'd shamed himself whenever his body responded to her groping hands as she did things to him to release the pleasure that had made his cock hard. He knew he was sinning with his father's wife, but after the first time he released his seed inside her he couldn't stay away. Just being inside her hot, wet body allowed him to forget that everything they were doing was wrong.

It all stopped when his father came home early one day and found them together. He'd pulled him out of the bed and pounded him with his large fists until Denny lost consciousness. Bobby Lee Clark doused him with a bucket of water to revive him, and then picked up a whip. Denny remembered counting to eight before he passed out again. And when he woke a second time it was to see the face of the most beautiful colored girl he had ever seen, standing over him. He'd believed he'd dreamt her until he saw her again. What he had remembered so vividly about her was her smell. It was sweet and hypnotic—like a newly opened flower.

None of the girls he knew smelled like her. Most of them in Madison smelled like fried foods or lye soap. The exception had been his mother. She'd died in childbirth when he was seven. His recollections of his mother were that she took a bath every day with the perfumed soaps her mother mailed her from Jackson, and that she'd told him he was special. More special than her other children because he was her firstborn.

Memories of his mother merged with the image of the girl who had slapped him, and he cried until spent. Then he fell asleep.

Denny hadn't realized that he had been counting the days when he would see her again, but when she came down the cellar steps he was sitting up on the cot. Her grandmother had come earlier that day to wash him and give him another set of clean clothes. She also gave him a toothbrush and toothpaste so he could clean his teeth. He did thank her because he knew she had saved his life. The older woman had sat some distance away, watching as he shoveled spoonsful of chicken soup into his mouth, while reminding him he didn't have to eat so fast and if he wanted more, he just had to ask for it.

Denny had had little or no interaction with Black people and wondered if all of them were like the ones in whose house he was staying. The girl's grandmother had washed him, tended his wounds, gave him clothes to wear, even if they were too big, and had fed him. He hadn't realized how hungry he'd been when eating the soup with rice, chicken, and other vegetables. She had also changed the cot with clean linen that smelled faintly of Ivory soap.

"Good afternoon, Denny."

He cleared his throat several times. "Good afternoon. I'm sorry, but I don't know your name."

"It's Claudia. Claudia Patterson." A hint of a smile tilted the corners of her mouth. "You must be feeling better."

He nodded. "Yes, I am. Thanks to your grandmother."

"Grandma is the best." She came closer. "Do you have a grandmother?"

Denny shook his head. "No. They are both dead."

"What about your father?"

Denny's expression and appearance changed, like a snake shedding his skin. "He's not dead, but I want to kill him."

Claudia froze. Nothing moved. Not even her eyes. "Why do you want to kill him?"

"Because he was the one that whooped me."

"What could you have done so wrong that he would whip you?" Claudia asked.

"Because he found me in bed with my stepmother. The first time he brought her home telling everyone that she was his new young wife she started in on me. She's nineteen and because I was thirteen, she said she didn't want to have nothing to do with an old man, and because she and his son were teenagers they belonged together. Every time she darkened the door, she would touch my private parts. I tried staying away and even stopped taking a bath, but that didn't matter to her. After a while I gave in and fucked the horny bitch! I'm sorry," he said quickly when he saw the look of horror on Claudia's face. But it was too late to apologize. She was running up the stairs and closing the door before he could get up off the cot.

Denny cursed to himself because he knew he had frightened Claudia. He'd admitted that he'd sinned by sleeping with his father's wife, and after a couple of times he had come to enjoy it. And judging from her reaction, she also enjoyed sleeping with him. He had grown up fast, because at thirteen he was doing things with a woman that grown men bragged about. His stepmother was a bitch—a bitch that was always in heat. Days before his father found them together, she'd mentioned that her monthly was late, and Denny didn't know, if a baby was growing in her belly, whether it was his or his father's. He prayed it was the latter.

He lay down on his side and closed his eyes. Although his back was healing, he still couldn't lie on it because he hadn't healed completely. And as soon as he was able, he would leave and never come back. But then something didn't want him to leave, because Claudia had everything he yearned for: a stable home, a doting grandmother, and loving, protective parents. That wouldn't be a problem to ask to stay if he was Black; but he wasn't. He was White, poor, and uneducated, and now he swore an oath that when he grew up, he would be somebody. Someone folks would look up to and fear at the same time. What he had to figure out was how to make that happen.

Chapter 4

The most important thing a father can do for his children is to love their mother.
                    —Theodore Hesburgh

Claudia sat on a rocking chair several feet from her grandmother. An open book lay on her lap. She had attempted to concentrate on her homework and failed miserably. Even a week later, thinking about Denny Clark had continued to disturb her. She'd told herself that he was only a trashy White boy. That he got what he'd deserved for fornicating with his stepmother. Yet there was something about him that was so sad. At thirteen he should not have had to go through what he did with his stepmother.

"Those words ain't goin' jump off that page and into your head, Claudia Mavis Patterson."

Her grandmother's voice shattered her reverie. "I know, Grandma."

"What's the matter, baby?"

Putting the book aside, Claudia pushed to her feet. "He bothers me." She met her grandmother's eyes, knowing that she knew who she was referring to.

"You shouldn't be paying no White boy no mind."

"I know, but he's so sad."

Taking off her glasses and placing her quilting in the large wicker basket next to her rocking chair, Earline wagged her head. "He's not as sad as he's evil. I see death in that boy's eyes."

Claudia wondered, how could she tell her grandmother that Denny threatened to kill his father? That he had sinned by sleeping with his father's wife? "I guess I would be evil if someone beat the skin off my back."

Earline grunted. "It's not as if millions of our people did not feel the bite of the whip, child. And even though it's 1952 it's still goin' on."

"Not in Freedom, Grandma."

"No, baby, not in Freedom. But it happens in Mississippi and throughout the South. Now, finish your homework before your folks come to pick you up."

"Can I stay for supper?"

"Not tonight. Remember, Friday and Saturdays are ours."

Claudia forced a smile. "Yes, Grandma."

The two nights she ate with her grandmother were always more interesting than the ones she spent with her parents. Most times they came home tired from spending hours on their feet. Her mother prepared whatever was quick and convenient, and just as quickly cleaned up the kitchen.

Sarah usually came to Claudia's bedroom where they discussed what she'd learned in school that day, then she retreated to her own bedroom. Her father passed the time tallying his receipts, reading the newspaper, and listening to a few of his favorite radio programs before he turned in for the night.

Tonight, Claudia sat at her father's feet listening to the radio with him. She waited for a recorded commercial announcement before speaking. "Grandma says she's going to buy a television for Christmas."

Earl Patterson raised silky black eyes as he stared down at his daughter's upturned face. "She did, did she?"

"Yes, Daddy."

He smiled, displaying his straight white teeth. Everyone said Earl Patterson was his mother's son. He had inherited her smooth, mahogany complexion, expressive dark eyes, and her balanced features. His broad forehead was high, eyes set far enough apart to give him an expression of pleasant surprise. His nose was broad and wide enough to offset his full lips under a clipped mustache.

He wore his black hair close to his scalp, the style neat and fashionable. His obvious attractiveness was enhanced whenever he wore a suit. He favored double-breasted jackets that flattered his broad shoulders and trim physique. Rumor had it that Sarah Bailey had taken one look at Earl when he'd gone to Biloxi to conduct business with his family's attorney and decided on the spot that she'd wanted to spend the rest of her life with him.

"Are you telling me that you want to move in with your grandmother once she buys a television?"

"No, Daddy," Claudia said, with a giggle. "I want us to buy one, too."

"I've thought about it."

Springing up from the floor, Claudia settled herself on the arm of her father's chair. "Please, Daddy. Buy it."

"Buy what?" Sarah asked as she walked into the living room. She had changed her clothes for a nightgown and bathrobe, and had braided her long, wavy hair into a single plait.

"Claudia says Mama is thinking about buying a television for Christmas."

"I like the sound of that."

"You do?" Earl and Claudia said at the same time.

Sarah sat on the chair facing her husband. "Yes, I do. Even though we're not home much, I still would like to sit down and put my feet up and watch a few of the popular shows."

The light from a nearby table lamp illuminated the ivory undertones in Sarah's smooth face. Sarah's mother had been fair enough to pass for white to escape the evils of Jim Crow with her flawless magnolia complexion, dark gray eyes, and silky auburn hair, but had elected to embrace her blackness when she married Kenneth Bailey, who was as dark as his wife was light skinned. Sarah never mentioned her White grandfather who had made her grandmother his common-law wife under the guise that she was his housekeeper. She hadn't said so, but everyone knew she was ashamed of her White blood.

"Grandma says she wants to watch the baseball games."

"I suspect your grandmother wants to watch more than the baseball games," Earl teased, as he ran his forefinger down Claudia's nose. "I think I'll surprise her with a television before Christmas. Next Monday we'll go to Biloxi and order two. I'll get one for us and one for your grandmother. Now, don't you say anything to her, Button."

Claudia smiled at her father's nickname for her. "I won't, Daddy." She curved her arms around his neck and kissed his cheek. "Good night, Daddy." She went to Sarah and repeated the gesture. "Good night, Mama."

Sarah returned her kiss. "Good night, precious."

Earl and Sarah watched their only child walk out of the room. "I'm proud of her, Sarah." He was the first to break the silence.

His wife smiled and nodded. "You should be. She's a good girl."

Earl rested his head against the crocheted doily on the chair's back. "She's growing up so fast."

Pulling her lip between her teeth, Sarah stared at her hands folded in her lap. Earl was right. Claudia was growing much too fast for her. In another five to six years, she would be gone. She hoped Claudia would go away to college instead of marrying as she had done. Her head popped up and she stared at her husband. If she had it to do all over again, she still would've married Earl Patterson rather than attend college. She loved him just that much.

She'd graduated high school at sixteen, and she and Earl

were married a month later. By the time she was seventeen she was a mother. What had shocked Sarah was that she hadn't experienced any of the signs indicating she was pregnant. Her monthlies hadn't stopped, nor had she gained any weight. She'd conceived another three times, but the pregnancies never advanced beyond four months. She finally took her doctor's advice and underwent a hysterectomy. The last and final pregnancy had her close to death after she'd hemorrhaged, losing one third of her body's blood supply.

However, Sarah found solace in her work at the beauty parlor. Having to put on a brave face for her customers saved her from recurring bouts of depression. It had taken a year to recover physically, and twice that much emotionally.

Moving from her chair, she sat on Earl's lap. Pressing her mouth to his ear, Sarah placed soft, nibbling kisses around the outer edge. "Are you ready for bed, Daddy?"

Earl smiled, meeting her clear, hazel eyes. "Now I am." He stood, cradling her in his arms. "Turn off the lamp."

"How will you find your way in the dark?"

"I'll find it," Earl whispered, seconds before his mouth covered hers. He walked over to the table and Sarah leaned over and pulled the chain attached to the lamp, plunging the room into darkness.

"Careful, Daddy," she crooned, breathing heavily against his ear.

Earl made his way toward the staircase leading to the bedrooms on the second story. Placing his foot on the first stair, he managed to make it to the top and into their bedroom without falling or dropping his wife, and kicked the door closed.

Sarah's hands were as busy as her mouth. She kissed Earl while unbuttoning his shirt and pushing it off his shoulders, at the same time he placed her on the bed, his body following hers down. Sounds of heavy breathing reverberated in the darkened bedroom as articles of clothing were shed and discarded on the bed and floor.

She opened her mouth, arms, and legs to her husband, groaning in pleasure as his erection pushed into her vagina. It had been a long time, almost two weeks since they'd last made love. It was as if they hadn't had time for each other. The desperate coupling was over—much too soon for Sarah, as they lay side by side, spent, breathing heavily. She'd missed the passionate lovemaking that was the glue that held their marriage together.

"What do you say we close three days a week instead of two?" Earl asked once his heart rate returned to normal. "That way we can spend more time with Claudia."

Sarah turned, rubbing her distended nipples along her husband's muscled shoulder. Both businesses were closed on Sundays and Mondays. Closing on Tuesday would give them more time together as a family.

"I say yes."

Claudia lay on her bed in the room next to her parents'. The sound of her mother's keening had frightened her, but then she realized Sarah wasn't in pain after she heard laughter. Her father's deep chuckle followed, eliciting a smile from Claudia. It was apparent they were enjoying whatever they were doing.

The queasiness and heaviness in the lower part of her abdomen increased until she nearly doubled over in pain. Pressing her face into the pillow, she took deep breaths until the cramping eased. She waited, but thankfully the pain didn't return. She closed her eyes and waited for sleep to come.

Claudia woke feeling sicker than she ever had in her life. She felt hot, then cold, and her stomach heaved as if it wanted to purge everything she had put into it over the past couple of days. Dragging herself from the bed, she made it to the bathroom in time to throw up. Waiting until she was certain there was nothing left to expel, she walked on wobbly legs to the sink and rinsed her mouth at the same time her mother walked into the bathroom.

"What's the matter with you?"

Claudia rested her forehead on the cool porcelain sink, willing the tears not to fall. "I don't know, Mama. My stomach hurts, my head hurts, and my back is aching." She didn't see Sarah's eyes move downward, stopping when she saw the dark red stains on her pajamas.

Sarah blinked back tears and as she moved closer to Claudia and cradled her. "I know why you're feeling the way you do," she said in a quiet tone.

"Why, Mama?"

"You just got your period."

Claudia pulled away from her mother and glanced down at her pajama pants. "I don't want it," she cried.

"You don't have much of a choice, my child."

"But I feel so sick."

"It will pass." Sarah handed Claudia a cool cloth for her face. Pushing her daughter's hair off her face, she kissed her forehead. "You're a young woman now, Claudia. You must start behaving like one."

"I don't know how to be a woman, Mama."

"Yes, you do. You'll begin by washing yourself. Remember what I told you about keeping clean. I'll bring you what you need to protect your clothing."

"I don't feel like going to school."

"And you don't have to. You can spend the day in bed if you want."

Her mother's face wavered before her teary gaze. "Thanks, Mama."

Claudia waited for Sarah to leave the bathroom before she brushed her teeth, took off her pajamas and stepped into the tub. She pulled the shower curtain around the tub, slipped a plastic cap over her hair, and turned on the water.

Her mother had told her about menstruation and where babies came from, once she turned ten. What her mother told her was quite different from what her friends whispered among themselves. Some said you could have a baby from letting a boy kiss you, while others claimed all you had to do is let a boy rub up against you and a baby would start growing inside you. She hadn't believed them because what they'd said didn't sounded realistic. Her mother's explanation was much more believable.

Janice Mason had gotten her period, along with a pair of large breasts, last year. Janice also confessed to letting a high school boy kiss her. She said it made her feel good—especially between her legs. Right now, the only thing Claudia felt between her legs was pain.

She finished washing her body, patted it dry, and stepped out of the tub. Sarah had left a nightgown, panties, and a box of Kotex with a sanitary napkin belt on the small table in a corner. It took several attempts before she secured the pad in the belt for a comfortable fit. She slipped into the panties and then pulled the nightgown over her head. The sight of her mother and father standing next to each other in her bedroom wouldn't allow Claudia to take another step. Her father held out his arms and she rushed into his embrace.

"Congratulations, Button. Now I have two women in the house instead of one."

"I don't want to be a woman," Claudia said against his chest.

Earl chuckled and tightened his hold on her body. "You don't have a choice," he stated, repeating her mother's statement. "What do you say we go out tonight and celebrate you becoming a woman?"

Claudia sniffled. "I probably won't feel much like it."

"I doubt that. Your mama is going to stay home with you today. I'm certain after she takes loving care of you, you'll feel up to eating out."

Easing out of her father's embrace, she stared numbly at her mother. It wasn't often when Sarah Patterson did not go into her shop. "You're staying home with me, Mama?"

Sarah smiled. "Of course."

Claudia's gaze shifted from her mother to her father. "I suppose I'll be better by tonight if Mama's going to take care of me."

Earl nodded. "I suppose also." He kissed Claudia's forehead before leaning over to place a tender kiss on Sarah's mouth. "I'll eat breakfast at Velma's."

Sarah caught Earl's hand, lacing their fingers together. "I'll walk you to the door, Daddy," she crooned, at the same time a blush crept over her cheeks.

Claudia crawled back into bed and pulled the lightweight blanket up to her chin. In the span of a few days her life had changed completely. She'd had close contact with a White boy for the first time in her life, and she had become a woman.

A cramp seized her back, radiating around to her abdomen and she wanted it gone; gone along with Denny Clark.

Three generations of Pattersons sat at the large table in the restaurant everyone in Freedom called Velma's. Claudia sat next to her father, facing her mother and grandmother. She had recovered enough to join her family in celebrating her new womanhood.

"You look beautiful, baby," Earline crooned, smiling.

Claudia lowered her chin and smiled up from under her lashes. "Thanks, Grandma." Her mother had pinned her hair up in a sleek twist, with an abundance of curls falling over her forehead. The hairdo made her feel very grown-up.

Earl laid aside his menu and cleared his throat. "I'm sitting with the three most beautiful women in the whole state of Mississippi." The three women stared at one another and laughed. "What's the matter with y'all? It's true."

Sarah motioned to the waitress who stood several feet away from their table. "Earl, it's time to order," she said quietly.

He nodded to the waitress, and she moved closer. "What will you have this evening, Mr. Patterson?"

The Pattersons decided to order different dishes, thereby enabling all to sample from each plate. Claudia felt heat in her face when glasses of chilled lemonade were raised to toast her new status. Tears filled her eyes when Sarah lowered her head and cried softly. Earl exchanged seats with his mother, pulling his wife into his arms. Giving her grandmother a sidelong glance, she saw Earline dabbing the corners of her eyes with a handkerchief.

"If this is a celebration, then why is everyone crying?" she asked, fighting back a rush of tears.

"It's a rite of passage, Button," Earl explained.

"It feels more like a funeral than a rite of passage," Claudia countered.

Earl nodded. "You're right about that." He caught the waitress's attention and beckoned with a slight wave of his hand. "Please bring a bottle of your best champagne."

"Champagne?" Sarah questioned, placing a slender hand on her husband's suit jacket.

"Only the best for my daughter."

Earline sat up straight, while grunting softly under her breath. "I'll drink to that," she whispered, winking at Claudia.

Glasses were filled with the chilled bubbling wine and the toast was repeated. Claudia took a sip of the minuscule portion in her glass, frowning at the strange taste and the bubbles lingering on her tongue.

"Do you like it?" Sarah asked.

Claudia shook her head, pushing the glass away from her place setting. "It's too bitter."

"It's very dry," Earl explained. "Champagne is an acquired taste."

Scrunching up her nose, Claudia stared at the pale liquid. "I don't think I want to acquire a taste for it." She reached for her glass of lemonade, watching the adults become more animated as they each drank several glasses of champagne.

She thought about the photographs her mother had received from her sister who'd recently moved to France. Virginia Bailey was having the time of her life. She wore slacks, drank champagne, smoked cigars and cigarettes all while in the company of bohemian writers, artists, and jazz musicians. Her life seemed free and exciting, because she'd written that she did not have to confront racism like she had in the South. She had found a position as a tutor, teaching English to the children of wealthy Parisians, and had joined a group of expatriates who lived by their own set of rules. Claudia envied her aunt because she wanted to travel and meet exciting people who were confident enough to live their lives by their leave.

The celebration ended with slices of pie and portions of cobbler. Earl left a generous tip for the waitress, then escorted everyone to his car. He dropped his mother off first, kissing her before he drove the short distance to his own home. Claudia and Sarah waited for him to come around the car to open their doors and help them alight. He extended both arms, and they each looped an arm through his as he escorted them up the porch to the front door. He unlocked it, stepped in, and glanced around before standing aside for them to enter. It was a ritual Sarah and Claudia had replayed over and over through the years.

Rising on tiptoes, Claudia kissed her dad's cheek. "Thanks, Daddy. You've made today special for me." Turning to her mother, she hugged and kissed her. "You, too, Mama. Thank you."

Claudia climbed the staircase and went into her bedroom. She kicked off her shoes and unhooked her nylons from the garters attached to the belt around her waist and pulled the taffeta dress over her head. Her mother had given her a pair of her nylons to wear with the dress. It was the first time she'd gone out in public without socks. Wearing nylons did make her feel less like a girl and more like a woman.

She felt better than she had earlier that morning, but the bulky pad between her thighs was constant reminder of the show of blood that came from the most private part of her body. Putting on a nightgown, she retreated to the bathroom, where she washed herself and changed the pad. Then she unpinned her hair and covered it with an unflattering cotton nightcap. She returned to her bedroom, closed the door, walked over to the bed, and turned back the crocheted coverlet. A small object fell on the floor.

Bending over, she picked up a small gold box. She opened the box and her eyes widened in surprise. A gold locket, shaped like a heart, suspended on a chain, lay on a square of black velvet.

She held the locket under the light of a lamp. There was an engraved inscription on the back: *April 19, 1952 —Love Mama and Daddy.*

There were no jewelry stores in Freedom, so she knew her father had driven to Biloxi to buy it for her. She fumbled with the catch before she was able to secure the chain around her neck. The gold heart rested between her breasts over the nightgown. She whispered a promise never to take it off.

Her left hand rested over her gift as she padded barefoot out of her bedroom to her parents'. Their door was slightly ajar, and she could hear them talking softly. She raised her hand to knock on the door, but something stopped her as they came into her line of vision. Her father, cradling her mother in his arms, lowered her to their bed. The sight that rendered her motionless wasn't their passionate embrace as much as it was their naked bodies. The sight of Sarah's pale limbs entwined with Earl's darker ones was imprinted on her brain as he settled himself between her legs.

Forcing her gaze away, she turned and raced back to her room. Everything her mother told her about how babies were made came rushing back. Sarah had told her that she couldn't have any more children, yet she still offered her body to her husband.

Why?

She would ask her mother why the first chance she got to talk to her whenever they were alone.

Climbing into bed, she slipped between the cool sheets. Her day had begun miserably and had ended wonderfully. The gold heart was a testament to that.

Chapter 5

To know the value of generosity, it is necessary to
have suffered from the cold indifference of others.
—Eugene Cloutier

Janice Mason waited for Claudia as she did every day
school was in session. She spied her the moment she walked
through the front doors. "Where were you yesterday?" she
asked, falling in step beside her.

"I wasn't feeling well," Claudia explained.

Janice's sharp eyes spied the gold heart resting over a light
pink blouse. "Where did you get that?" she questioned,
pointing at her chest.

"My parents gave it to me."

"Was it for your birthday?"

"No."

Claudia and Janice skirted a group of boys and girls
milling near the faculty parking lot, waving and nodding to
students they'd known all of their lives.

"What was it for?" Janice questioned.

"It was to celebrate my becoming a woman."

Janice frowned. "Quit lying, Claudia. You're still a girl."

"I'm no more a girl that you are. I got my period yesterday."

Janice gave Claudia a long, penetrating look before realization filled her brilliant dark eyes. "You got it! I can't believe you finally got it. I thought you were going to be the last one in our grade to get it."

Claudia stopped and stared at her friend. Janice Mason was what people called an ebony beauty. Her complexion was only slightly lighter than her thick raven-black hair. Janice had learned at any early age that her large, slanting dark eyes and heart-shaped full lips were her best features and used them to her advantage whenever she smiled, displaying dimples in both cheeks. They were until her body began developing. Boys, and some men, stared at Janice in stunned appreciation. Their reactions reinforced Janice's awareness of her sensual beauty instead of making the twelve-year-old uncomfortable. Everyone but the two White men they'd met along the road the day Claudia found Denny.

"What made you think I'd be the last one?" she asked Janice.

"Everyone says you have no tits," Janice blurted out.

Embarrassment added color to Claudia's face. "How can you be a party to petty gossip, Janice Mason?"

"I wasn't gossiping, Claudia. I overheard Barbara Parker and Carol Edwards talking about you on the milk line."

"It's breasts, not tits. And they are wrong because I do have breasts," Claudia said defensively. "I'd rather have what I have than look like a cow that needs to be milked."

There were several girls at the school who still weren't old enough to attain the high school level, yet were as physically developed as their mothers or older sisters. These were the girls the high school boys followed and met in the woods after school.

None of the boys had ever approached Claudia, and this did not bother her. Her mother had told her to be patient, because she would have plenty of time for boys once she completed her education. Sarah said all she had to do was look at her aunts Mavis and Virginia. They were beautiful, success-ful, educated women who'd had lots of suitors.

"I told them it didn't matter whether you had tits—I mean breasts—because you're still pretty enough to have any boy in Freedom," Janice said, smiling.

Claudia's eyelids fluttered. "You said that to them?"

"Of course. You're my best friend."

Claudia hugged Janice with her free arm. "Thanks for tak-ing up for me."

Janice returned the hug. "Anytime. I must go. My mother had a fit yesterday because I was a half hour late getting home."

"Where did you go?"

"I was talking to Butch."

"Butch Washington?" Janice nodded as they began walk-ing. "I thought your daddy told you not to talk to him. You know what he did to poor Priscilla Owens."

"Butch said he never touched Priscilla."

"And you believe him?"

"I believe him when he says if she got swole up, then it wasn't by him."

Claudia shook her head, deciding to drop the topic of Butch as she and Janice turned onto the road leading to the business district. Butch Washington was sixteen and one of the best-looking boys in Freedom. His looks, brains, and the fact that his father and uncles owned a small cotton mill had all the young girls vying for his attention. But Butch didn't like girls who chased him. He preferred the ones who wor-shipped him from afar. Priscilla had been one of those girls. There was gossip that he and Priscilla were seen in the woods together, and three months later her parents packed her things, put her on a bus going up to Jackson to stay with her grandmother. Janice would not get away so easily, because Claudia was certain Mr. Mason would shoot Butch, his father, and his uncles, then wait for the sheriff, if Butch got his daughter in the family way.

"Slow down, Janice," she urged. "It's too hot to rush."

Janice slowed her pace. "What are you going to do for your science project?"

"I'm going to take botany. My grandmother can help me. She knows more about plants than anyone I know."

"I think I'm going for astronomy. I love sitting out at night and staring up at the stars."

They had a month left before school ended, and both looked forward to passing all their courses. Janice was an excellent student despite her flirtatious behavior, and Claudia was a good student. Her mother said if she studied a little more, she could be at the top of her class. Janice turned off on the road that led to her house, while Claudia continued down the main street. She walked past the beauty parlor and barber shop, waving to her father, but not stopping. The wooden venetian blinds covering the beauty parlor plateglass window concealed women having their hair straightened, dyed, or curled.

She smiled and acknowledged people she encountered on the street. Freedom was small, yet it was still thriving. It had lost citizens during the two world wars, while some had left to find work in northern factories. Only a few returned. Claudia felt safe in Freedom, safer than she did when she went to Biloxi with her parents. However, she knew she did not want to spend the rest of her life in her hometown. She made her way along a side street, taking a shortcut down the alley that opened out onto the road to her grandmother's house.

She reached her grandmother's house and found her sitting on the porch sewing and listening to the radio. A secret smile curved her mouth. She still hadn't told her grandmother that her son was going to buy her a television. Claudia's cotton blouse was drenched with sweat by the time she climbed the porch steps.

Earline looked at her over the top of her glasses. "You look plumb tuckered out."

"I am, Grandma. The sidewalks are hot enough to fry a piece of fatback in minutes." Leaning over, she kissed Earline. "Good afternoon."

Earline placed a hand on her granddaughter's moist cheek. "Afternoon, baby. Go inside and change into something cooler."

Claudia nodded and opened the screened door. She held it until it closed with a soft click. She wanted to take off all her clothes and lie across her bed wearing nothing more than a slip, because she didn't have the nerve to sleep naked.

She headed up the stairs to her bedroom. Gathering a sleeveless blouse and a pair of pedal pushers from a drawer in the highboy, Claudia walked into the bathroom and closed the door. It took twenty minutes for her to groom herself and change her clothes, emerging from the room enveloped in a cloud of honeysuckle-scented dusting powder. Her bare feet were silent on the stairs, and she retraced her steps and went into the kitchen for a cold drink.

The need to quench her thirst was forgotten when she noticed the open door leading down to the root cellar. A slight frown furrowed her smooth forehead. Had her grandmother neglected to close the door, or had Denny come up and opened it?

She made her way down the stairs to the cool, shadowy cellar. Waiting for her eyes to adjust to the darkness, Claudia noticed the door leading to the side of the house was slightly ajar. The position of the afternoon sun slanted a swath of light on the bare cement floor, and through the window over the empty cot where Denny had spent most of his time recuperating from his father's savage whipping. She glanced around the cellar and realized Denny was gone. She'd wanted him gone, but now that he was, she felt a sense of loss. Why? She didn't know.

Claudia walked over to close the door, and then she saw him. He had his back to her as he stood under a tree. It wasn't until he shifted that she realized he was relieving himself. She moved quickly to close the door, but not quickly enough. Denny had turned around. He stood motionless, staring at her. She now knew the color of his hair. It was an attractive combination of light brown and gold. It was long and wavy, falling over his forehead and the tops of his ears. Along with the deep gashes of flesh torn from his back, the bright sunlight revealed purpling bruises along his left jaw and under both eyes.

Denny stared at Claudia staring back at him. "I had to piss." He held up his pants with one hand and made his way toward her, taking small, wobbly steps.

"Why didn't you use the chamber pot my grandmother left for you?" Claudia asked as he approached her.

"I needed to get up and walk around."

He examined her delicate profile when she averted her head, his heart pumping wildly in his chest. Seeing Claudia in the full sunlight was like being kicked in the gut. Her skin wasn't as dark as he originally thought, but the shade of coffee with a lot of cream. Her eyes were also lighter than he had imagined—a clear light brown with large gold centers. He closed his eyes for several seconds and sucked in a breath. No matter the time of day she smelled the same—like the scent of a newly opened flower.

He swayed slightly, and Claudia reached out to steady him, but pulled back before she touched him. "You should go back inside and lie down."

Denny opened his eyes, unable to believe he'd found a colored girl who stirred emotions within him he didn't know existed. There were a few White girls in Madison who had caught his eye, but none of them disturbed him like Claudia Patterson.

He wasn't a virgin—his stepmother had seen to that, yet what he was beginning to feel for Claudia had nothing to do with sex. If she offered herself to him, he would take her, but something told him she never would. He knew she had been raised to be a lady, not a whore.

"Can I get something to drink? *Please.*"

"What would you like?"

"Anything cold."

"I'll be right back. You must keep the door closed to keep out the heat."

His eyes were fixed on her slender figure as she went up the staircase. There was something about Claudia that reminded him of a young colt. She was all legs. Minutes later she returned and handed him a glass of water and he jumped slightly when their fingers touched.

Claudia felt the static electricity at the same time. She'd drunk a glass of water before returning to the cellar to give Denny his. She waited for Denny to drain his glass, then held out her hand. He handed it to her, then eased his body slowly down to the cot.

"Don't go," he said quietly as she turned to leave.

Claudia felt his gaze on her back. "Why?"

"Because I don't want to be alone. Because I need someone to talk to."

She shook her head. "I can't stay. I must do my homework."

"Do it down here."

Claudia shook her head again. "No. There isn't enough light."

"There are candles and the kerosene lamp."

Claudia grew more uncomfortable with every minute she remained in the cellar with Denny, and headed for the staircase. A warning voice whispered in her head to leave him to the darkness. He was mean and wicked. He swore, threatened to kill his father, and had lain with his father's wife.

"Read to me, Claudia," he pleaded softly. "Please."

She stopped, turned around, and tried to make out his shadowed features. "Can't you read?"

Lowering his head, he stared at his bare feet. "Not too well."

She moved closer. "How much schooling do you have?"

"I completed half of the seventh grade."

"I'm in the seventh grade now. I only have another four weeks before I'm finished."

"Let me study with you."

Denny hated school, but he wasn't about to tell Claudia that. He would do or say anything not to have her leave him in the cellar alone.

"Let me ask my grandmother if it's okay."

He nodded, watching as Claudia walked away, the scent of flowers lingering long after she'd disappeared. Denny managed to swing his legs up on the cot and lie down carefully so as not to put any pressure on his back. Resting his cheek on folded arms, he closed his eyes and waited for Claudia's return. If she didn't come back today, then he knew she would return at another time. Waiting to see her made his convalescence tolerable. He was healing quickly, he ate well, and he was tended to better than he had been before his mother had died.

Denny closed his eyes, his breathing deepening until he fell into a quiet sleep for the first time since he realized he lay under the roof of a Black family. Dreams flitted in and out of his peaceful slumber. The nightmare of his father whipping him while Marilee laughed hysterically was replaced with the image of Claudia Patterson's delicate beauty, with her cradling him to his soft, scented body. He opened his eyes and sat up when she returned to the cellar, her arms filled with books.

"We will begin studying together tomorrow." She left the

books on a table, and then turned and walked back up the staircase.

Denny smiled. Studying together meant he would get to see her for more than a few minutes.

Denny sat next to Claudia on a burlap bag near the open door. He'd sat close enough to her that whenever he leaned to his right his shoulder brushed her bare arm under the sleeveless blouse. He hadn't heard a word she was saying as she read from the textbook on her lap.

He'd made certain not to drink the tea her grandmother gave him earlier that morning because he suspected it contained something that made him sleep more than he normally would. He'd found himself succumbing to as many as four naps during a twenty-four-hour day.

"Do you know where Madagascar is?"

"Somewhere in India," he answered, saying the first thing that came to his mind.

Claudia stared at him, smiling. "You're close. It's an island off Southeast Africa in the Indian Ocean."

Denny laughed. "I'm not as dumb as I thought."

A frown replaced Claudia's smile. "Don't ever say you're dumb."

He ran a hand through his hair, pushing it off his forehead. "My teachers said I was dumb. They said it enough for me to believe it."

"My mother said that I was never to let someone define who I am."

"But you know who you are. You're colored."

She frowned at the same time her fingers gripped the book. "I wasn't talking about race. It's like someone saying you're trash and that you will always be trash."

"Once trash, always trash. Like once a nigga, always a nigga."

Claudia jumped up and stood over him. "I told you before not to call me that."

Realizing he had said the wrong thing, Denny pushed to his feet. "I ain't calling you a nigga. I—"

"Don't say it!" she shouted.

"Okay. I'm sorry. I won't say it again." He saw that Claudia was shaking.

"We've studied enough today." She leaned over and picked up the stack of books.

Denny panicked. His right hand curved around her upper arm. "Please don't go." His eyelids fluttered as she stared at his fingers on her arm.

"Don't touch me," she said, the warning barely above a whisper.

He loosened his grip, but didn't release her arm, and leaned closer. "I won't hurt you. I would never hurt you."

Claudia met his eyes. Her gaze took in the soft, golden down on his cheeks and chin, the lump in his throat moving up and down as he swallowed, and the fading bruises on his neck and chest revealed by the unbuttoned shirt. She wasn't afraid that he would hurt her. She just didn't feel comfortable whenever he touched her. Men and boys, she knew, did not touch a girl or woman unless they were invited to do so.

"You smell wonderful." Denny's voice was soft, hushed. "You remind me of the way my mother used to smell." He tightened his hold on her arm and eased her down to sit beside him again. Then his hand fell away.

Claudia saw sadness in his eyes. "Do you remember much about her?"

"A little. My father has photographs of her when she was younger, but I don't remember her looking like anything in the pictures."

"She changed?"

Denny nodded. "She looked so young in the pictures. I only remember her looking old and tired. I heard some people say that she came from a good family in Jackson, and when she took up with my daddy her family disowned her.

They turned her out with the clothes on her back, so my daddy married her and moved her to Madison. Her mama used to sneak and send her those perfumed soaps she loved so much. After a while even those stopped, and Mama grew old and sad. Daddy said she didn't want to live and willed herself to die."

"Oh, Denny. That's so sad."

"I don't need no pity!"

Claudia's temper flared. "Do you always have to lash out at people who haven't done you wrong?"

"I have to get them before they get me."

"What have I done to you, Denny? My grandmother is taking care of you like you were her own—"

"Not you or your grandmother," he interrupted. "Y'all is different. I appreciate what you do for me."

"You sure have a funny way of showing your appreciation."

"I have no money to pay you back."

"It's not about money. It's about manners," she said.

"I know nothing about manners," Denny grumbled under his breath. "Having manners didn't stop my daddy from beatin' the shit outta me." Claudia reached over and gathered her books. "Where are you goin'?"

"Away from you and your nasty mouth. You cuss too much."

Denny stared up at her from his seated position. "That's because I don't have an uppity mama to teach me fancy words."

"My mother's not uppity," Claudia said in defense of Sarah Patterson.

"Like hell she ain't. You wouldn't act the way you do if she weren't."

"You have no right to talk about my mother."

Denny grunted. "You want to hit me again?" He rose slowly to his feet and looked down at her. "Is that what you want to do *Miss* Claudia Patterson? You want to hit me?" he repeated.

Claudia's breath burned in her throat as she struggled to control her temper. She knew Denny was goading her to fight with him. She had never hit anyone in her life before she hit him, and now that was exactly what she wanted to do. She couldn't hit him again no matter how angry he made her, because she didn't want to be like his father.

"No," she said, quietly. "I don't want to hit you. You've suffered enough." Turning away from him, she walked into the cellar, leaving him staring at the space where she had been.

You've suffered enough. Her words echoed in Denny's head. He had suffered and continued to suffer because he wanted Claudia. He wanted to take off his clothes and lie next to her. He wanted to see if the rest of her body had the same smooth, velvet softness as her face. She didn't like him touching her, but there was nothing he liked better than feeling her skin under his hand.

He hadn't been given the choice of being a boy for long. He had bridged the gap of childhood to manhood as soon as he'd entered puberty. Guilt and feeling dirty attacked him relentlessly whenever he got into bed with his stepmother, along with the compulsion to wash himself every chance he got. The need to wash proved pointless when Marilee followed him into the bathroom. There was no lock on the bathroom door, and he hadn't wanted to put one on it and alert his father as to what was going on between his son and his wife.

Bobby Lee Clark had done him a favor by beating him and dumping his body. He had gotten away from Marilee. But now he had to figure out what he wanted to do with his life. He was thirteen with no skills, no family, and no education.

Denny knew he was a hard worker. He would hire himself

out to anyone who needed an extra hand. He needed money to exist, so he couldn't be particular who he worked for or what he did.

He planned to stay at Claudia's grandmother's house until he was strong enough to strike out on his own. Although the Pattersons were decent people, they still weren't his kind. And he hoped he would find a way to repay them for their kindness.

Chapter 6

We all live under the same sky, but we don't all have the same horizon.
　　　　　　　—Konrad Adenauer

Two and a half weeks after Earline carried Denny Clark into her root cellar, she knew it was time for him to leave. Scabs covered his back, his bruises had faded, he'd gained weight, and she could no longer count his ribs.

Earline had filled a duffel bag with a couple of pairs of pants, three shirts, a half dozen socks, underwear, and an extra pair of boots. She had rationalized that Joe Junior didn't need clothes in Heaven. Another bag was filled with containers of food and an envelope containing two ten-dollar bills.

She left everything near the cellar door and walked away from Denny without saying anything, while doubting whether she and the White boy had exchanged more than fifty words since she'd brought him home. She did what every God-fearing Christian should have done for someone in need. Earline had offered him shelter and given him comfort and food. Now she wanted him on his way, because she suspected things were going on between Denny and her granddaughter that weren't proper or acceptable for a White boy and colored girl in segregated Mississippi. They had become friends.

Earline had no intention of telling Claudia that she sent Denny away; she would find out once she came over after school.

Claudia arrived at her grandmother's house, knowing she would not see Earline on the porch. Her father had purchased the television, and when it was delivered to Earline's house she was so surprised that she had to lie down to compose herself. Earline now sat in her parlor watching her favorite shows instead of listening to the radio.

"Good afternoon, Grandma."

Earline smiled over her shoulder. "Good afternoon, baby. How was school?"

"Good. I got an A-plus on my science project. I identified more plants than anyone else in the class. The teacher gave me extra credit for listing their medicinal purposes."

"Good for you. I told you that you are a smart one."

"Yes, you did, Grandma. I'm going to change my clothes, then I'll be back to watch television with you."

"No television until you finish your homework."

"Grandma," she moaned. "I only have a week left for school."

"You can learn a lot more things in a week. Homework first, young lady."

Claudia let out a heavy sigh, she went up to her room to change her clothes, then gathered her books to head for the root cellar. She usually did her homework with Denny, and she was surprised at how much he had learned and retained. He had even talked about returning to school in the fall.

She walked into the cellar and stopped. The diffused light coming in through the narrow window showed her what she did not want to accept. The cot was missing, along with Denny.

Racing over to the door, she opened it, blinking against the bright sunlight. Claudia looked around the backyard, her eyes filling with tears. He was gone. Her friend had left without telling her goodbye.

She turned to go back into the cellar, and something caught her eye. Then, she saw him. He stood under a tree, his arms crossed over a short-sleeve white shirt. Her gaze grew wide, and she realized he was fully dressed. It was the first time she had seen his chest covered. And there was something about him that made him so very dangerously attractive. Thick golden-brown waves covered one eye before he reached up and pushed them back. Bending slightly, she set the books on the grass and walked over to him.

Denny unfolded his arms, his intense stare taking in everything about Claudia as she moved toward him with the grace of a young deer. The sun glinted off the gold heart, suspended from the delicate chain, resting between a pair of small breasts. Her body had begun to fill out with soft, rounded curves. She stopped within a foot of him.

"You're leaving." Her question was a statement.

He nodded. "It's time I left."

"You were going to leave without telling me? Without saying goodbye?"

"I thought about it but changed my mind."

Claudia blinked slowly. "Why?"

Denny heard the breathless quality of her voice. Even her voice had changed from a high-pitched tinkling sound to a lower contralto register. Claudia Patterson had appeared to have grown up right in front of him and he hadn't been aware of it.

"Because you mean too much to me to desert you without a proper farewell."

Lowering her chin, she smiled. "You sound very proper, Mr. Denny Clark."

"You taught me."

"No, Denny. You're very smart. It's just that you must come to believe it."

He looked at the ground. "Being smart is not enough. For me to make it I must be the best."

Claudia smiled. "You told me I'm going to read about you in the newspaper. I hope it will be a happy story."

"I want to make history. I want my name to go down in history books like some of the men you told me about."

"You'll make it, Denny, if you continue to study."

He studied her delicate face, committing it to memory. "What do you want to do, Claudia?"

"I want to travel."

"Where?"

"Anywhere. As long as it's not in Mississippi."

An expression of panic crossed Denny's features. He never thought she would want to leave Freedom. Her parents were successful businesspeople. She was their only child and they loved her. How could she leave something so perfect?

"You . . . you can't leave," he stuttered.

"Oh, yes I can," Claudia retorted.

"You can't."

"Says who?"

Denny stared at her. "Says me." Claudia returned his stare for a full minute before she turned and headed back to the house. He followed her, capturing her arm and spinning her around to face him. "You can't leave *me*. Not when I feel what I feel for you."

Claudia wasn't given a chance to come back at him when she found her chest molded to his. She felt the heat of his body burn her breasts through her cotton blouse. His head came down, and she averted her face at the last possible moment so his kiss landed on the side of her neck. "Let me go!"

"Claudia," he groaned, burying his face in her hair.

The other times when he'd touched her and she demanded

he let her go, she wasn't frightened. Now she was. Before, he had only placed his hand on her arm, but this was the first time he'd contacted her body.

Her rising panic spun out of control with the press of his hardened flesh against her middle. Everything seemed to occur in slow motion for Claudia. She was struggling to get away from Denny, his mouth searching for hers, and the tops of trees, the sun, and the sky merged as she felt his suffocating heat.

"Don't you dare kiss me, White trash!" Without warning, he released her, and she fell backward, the grass cushioning her fall. Denny stood over her, hands balled into tight fists. Rage had distorted his features and paled his eyes, and at that instant Claudia feared for her life. She saw death in his eyes. However, she refused to give Denny the advantage of him standing over her as she pushed to her feet, not taking her gaze off his face. Running a hand over her hair, she tilted her chin in a gesture of defiance.

"Get off my grandmother's property and stay off." Her voice was low and quiet, as if she had asked him for the time of day. Not waiting to see if he would comply, she turned and went to where she'd left her books. She picked them up, walked through the door leading into the cellar, and closed it.

Willing the tears not to fall, she leaned against the door until she was back in control. It was over. He was gone.

Fool. How could she have been such a fool? She had treated him as if they were equals, as if their race hadn't mattered. She was everything Denny Clark wasn't, yet he believed himself better because he was White. She'd just learned a hard lesson at an early age.

She couldn't trust White people.

A violent trembling shook Denny like a leaf in a windstorm, and he waited for it to pass. He'd thought Claudia was different from others. She hadn't treated him like the trash everyone in Madison had called him.

A slow, evil smile thinned his lips. *Nigga bitch!* He wanted to shout out the two words to make Claudia as angry as she'd made him. He wanted her spitting mad. And he wanted her to hit him, so he would be justified in hitting her back. What he really wanted was to smash her beautiful face where no man would ever look at her or want her the way he did.

Denny walked three miles to the interstate. He'd thought about going back to Madison, but changed his mind. His rage had not subsided with the long walk in the oppressive humidity. Waves of heat shimmered before his eyes along with the face of Claudia Patterson calling him White trash.

He had fallen in love with her, while she hated him. He wanted to hate her and couldn't. More than anything else he'd wanted to hold her close, feel her warmth, inhale her sweetness. He wanted to take her hair down and bury his face in it.

And he wanted to fuse his flesh with hers, making them one. Going to bed with her would not be sinful. It would not be dirty. He knew he couldn't marry her, but he would devote his life to taking care of her.

A lone car came down the road and Denny put his hand out, thumb up. The driver slowed, stopped, and he opened the back door and deposited his bundles on the rear seat. "Thanks," he said, smiling at the White man chewing a wad of tobacco, as he slipped onto the passenger seat.

"Where you goin', boy?"

"Biloxi."

"You in luck. I'm headin' there myself."

Denny stared through the windshield of the late-model Ford. "Nice car."

"Thanks, boy. You from around here?"

Denny took a quick glance at the man who was close to his father's age—late thirties or early forties. He was smartly dressed in a pair of khaki slacks and a white cotton shirt. "Yes, sir. I'm from Madison." He'd decided not to lie. He wasn't wanted by the law.

"How old are you, boy?"

"Fifteen," he lied. He was tall for his age even if his body hadn't filled out.

"You in school?"

"No, sir."

"Then you must be looking for work."

"Yes, sir, I am."

"How would you like to work for me?"

Denny felt a rush of excitement eddy through him. How lucky could he be? "Yes, sir. Doin' what, sir?"

"A few odd jobs here and there. Can you drive, boy?"

"Yes, sir. I learnt to drive a tractor when I was ten." This time Denny was truthful.

"Got a license?"

"No, sir."

"I'll see about gettin' you one. I live in Hackersville. That's not too far from Madison. I live next to that town the niggers call Freedom. I travel to Biloxi at least two times a week on business, and I hate driving." Turning the wheel sharply to the right, he maneuvered off to road. "Come on around and drive."

Denny opened the door and walked around the car at the same time he and his new boss switched seats. He sat down, closed the door, shifted into gear, and gently pressed down on the gas pedal. The car glided over the smooth surface of the road like a duck swimming across water.

"The days I don't go to Biloxi you can use the car for your own personal business. The only thing I expect from you is that you always keep it clean. I can offer you a salary of twenty-five dollars a week, but considering you get your room and board free should make up for it."

Denny's eyes widened in disbelief. Twenty-five dollars a week! He would be rich in no time, especially since he didn't have to pay for rent or buy food. *Who's White trash now!* he wanted to shout at Claudia. He would show her.

"I accept your offer, Mr. . . ."

"Carson. Shelton Carson."

Denny's hands tightened on the leather-wrapped steering wheel, his knuckles showing with the increased pressure. His mother must be smiling down on him from above. He had just accepted a job to work for the highest-ranking member of the Mississippi Ku Klux Klan.

"What's yo name, boy?"

"Denny Clark."

Shelton Carson nodded slowly. "You's little young to be drinkin' but I think we can lift a glass of excellent bourbon to a long employment."

Denny sat up straight. "Yes, sir!"

Claudia toyed with the food on her plate. She'd turned a thinly sliced portion of ham over and over while staring out into space.

Sarah's questioning gaze met Earl's across the table. She lifted both shoulders at the same time, indicating with a barely perceptible nod of her head in the direction of their daughter. Earl put down his fork, stared at Claudia, and then shook his head.

"Are you feeling all right, Claudia?" Her daughter's head popped up.

"I'm okay, Mama."

"If you're okay, then why are you playing with your food?"

Sighing audibly, Claudia set her fork next to her plate. "I guess I'm not hungry."

"You guess?" Sarah questioned.

Claudia met her mother's eyes. "I'm not hungry."

Lines furrowed Sarah's smooth forehead. "Empty your plate and go to your room."

"Yes, ma'am."

Claudia stood up and emptied her plate. She knew Sarah

hated to see her rearranging portions of food on her plate. That and constant whining disturbed Sarah Patterson more than anything else.

Her footsteps were heavy as she made her way up the staircase to her bedroom. She sat on the window seat and stared out the window. A bright red-orange glow lit up the sky with the setting of the sun. Insects buzzed lazily in the Southern heat. Some of them flittered against the screens covering the windows as they tried penetrating the tightly woven mesh. Claudia listened to the cacophony of sounds; she fixed her gaze on the massive tree in the backyard covered with Spanish moss.

She closed her eyes, reliving the scene at her grandmother's house earlier that afternoon. What she could not forget was how she and Denny parted. She'd wanted to forget the press of his body against hers and the power in his hands when he'd held her captive. She also couldn't forget his smell. It was different from the sickening sour odor coming from him the day she and her grandmother first brought him home. He smelled of lye soap, but it was eclipsed by the natural scent of his clean flesh. It was warm and sensually musky, like her father's after he'd showered and splashed on bay rum. It was then Claudia realized that Denny Clark wasn't a boy but a man. The hardness between his legs pushing against her belly as they struggled silently said he was a man.

What had frightened her more than his touching her was her own body's reaction to his. After her initial shock and fear she'd felt the heaviness in her breasts and the throbbing in the secret place between her thighs. It was a warm, moist, exciting pulsing that had left her shaking with a desire for something she knew was wrong.

Claudia gasped and bit her lower lip. It had happened again! She recoiled as the heaviness in the lower part of her belly was followed by a soft pulsing.

"Claudia?"

She opened her eyes and scrambled off the window seat. Heat suffused her face, bringing with it a light sheen of moisture. Sarah stood in the doorway to the bedroom, her hands at her waist.

"Yes, Mama?"

Sarah walked into the room. "Do you want to talk about it?" she asked.

Claudia was certain her mother could hear her heart pounding uncontrollably although they stood more than six feet apart. "Talk about what?"

A hint of a smile softened Sarah's mouth. "Whatever it is that's bothering you. Remember, I once was twelve, too."

How could she tell her mother of the changes going on in her body? That those changes felt good? But then she and her mother never kept anything from each other—except that Denny Clark had lived in Earline Patterson's root cellar for more than two weeks and she had promised her grandmother that no one would know they had harbored him until he was well enough to leave Freedom.

She chewed her lip as she tried to form the words. "I . . . I don't know how to say it," she began hesitantly.

Sarah came closer and grasped Claudia's hands. "Come, let's sit down on the window seat." And once they were seated together, she smiled, saying, "Take your time, precious."

Claudia stared at her mother, marveling at her startling beauty. Naturally waving dark auburn hair framed her face like a halo. Sarah always wore her long hair in a French twist whenever she ventured outside of the house but left it down at home. There were times she threatened to cut it but didn't because Earl said he liked long hair. Tonight, she had not effected her usual single braid but had pulled it back and secured it at the nape of her neck with a delicate silver clasp. The hair ornament had been a gift from Earl for their tenth wedding anniversary.

"I don't know how to begin," Claudia said in a hushed tone.

"Begin at the beginning," Sarah urged quietly. "I won't say a word until you're finished."

Claudia nodded, then let out a breath. She looked down at her fingers entwined with her mother's. "You told me how babies are made." Sarah's fingers tightened on hers and she paused. "What I don't understand is why do a man and his wife do *it* if they can't have any more babies."

The seconds ticked as Sarah stared at Claudia with an expression of complete surprise freezing her features. "Go on, Claudia."

"What I need to know is what happens when a man wants to do *it*—"

"It's called sexual intercourse," Sarah said, interrupting Claudia. "You must learn to call things by their proper names."

She nodded again. This time the heat spread from her face to the length of her entire body. Now she was sorry she had brought up the subject. She should've just waited for the feelings to go away.

"Why would a man want to have sexual intercourse with a woman who is not his wife?"

Sarah frowned. "What happened, Claudia? Why are you asking me these questions?"

She met her mother's direct stare, deciding to tell the truth. "I feel—I'm feeling funny. Strange feelings I never had before. Down there," she whispered.

Sarah extricated her hands and pulled Claudia close to her body. "You would because you're physically a woman now. You'll have urges, desires. Sometime those urges make you think you're going to lose your mind if you don't do something about them."

"What do I do, Mama?"

"Wait for them to go away."

"But what if they don't go away?"

"They will, precious."

Easing back, Claudia stared at Sarah. "Do you have urges?"

"Yes, Claudia. I have a lot of urges. But it's different with me because I have your father. He takes care of them."

"With sexual intercourse?"

Soft pink color flooded Sarah's complexion. "Yes."

"But you told me a man and his wife only have sexual intercourse if they want to make a baby."

"There are times when they don't want to make a baby and they still make love to each other."

"Why, Mama?"

"Because it's God's unique way of bringing a husband and his wife together. When they share their bodies, they also share their love for each other."

"Does this mean I have to be married before I share my body with a man?"

"Yes, it does."

Claudia smiled. "And when I marry, I want to marry a man like Daddy."

Sarah laughed and hugged her. "If you find a man like your father then you will be a very lucky young woman."

"Thanks for talking to me, Mama."

"I want you to always come to me if something's troubling you."

"I will, Mama."

Sarah touched the tiny round gold earring in Claudia's ear. "You didn't eat your dinner, so how would you like a slice of sweet potato pie with a glass of milk?"

"No, thanks. I'm not hungry."

"If that's the case, why don't you get ready for bed."

"Okay, Mama."

"Good night, my precious."

"Good night, Mama."

Sarah kissed her on both cheeks, then stood up and walked out of the room, closing the door softly behind her, while Claudia sat on the window seat watching the stars light up the darkening nighttime sky. She listened to the frogs competing with crickets, while thinking of Denny Clark and wondering where he would sleep on this warm spring night.

A quarter of an hour later, she stood up and prepared herself for bed. She lay in the dark listening for the sounds coming from her parents' bedroom across the hall. She smiled and turned her face into the pillow under her head. Now she understood why her mother gave her body to her father. She had urges and he took care of them.

Claudia hoped that she would meet a man, marry him, and he would take particularly loving care of her urges.

Chapter 7

Temper, if ungoverned, governs the whole man.
—Anthony Ashley-Cooper, 7th Earl of
Shaftesbury

Claudia walked out of the Freedom School with a throng of noisy students and into the brilliant afternoon sunlight. Her gaze scanned the crowd for Janice Mason. They had only four days before the end of classes, and she wanted to talk to her best friend about their plans for the month of June. She never saw Janice during the month of July and the first two weeks of August because the Masons always sent Janice and her three brothers to Alabama to help their paternal grandfather work his farm.

"Don't pay for you to be looking for Janice because she done walked home with Butch Washington."

Claudia nodded to the girl who was in her History and Government class. "Thanks."

How could she? she fumed inwardly. How could Janice be so stupid. Did she want to wind up like Priscilla Owens—having a baby with no husband? Claudia skirted a small group of graduating seniors talking excitedly while clutching boxes containing their caps and gowns to their chests. Graduation exercises were scheduled for Sunday afternoon and the entire town was expected to turn out for the event. After diplomas where distributed everyone gathered in the field behind the school for an afternoon celebration. The number of graduating students always depended on the economy—whether it was the national economy or the state of Mississippi's. If times were good, then most young people were exempt from leaving school to find work to supplement their family's meager income.

Claudia knew she would finish high school and then go on to earn a degree, because her parents and grandmother had put aside money for her college education. She nodded and waved to anyone who acknowledged her as she walked away from the school and headed for the woods. If Janice had left the school with Butch, then she was certain they'd stop in the woods.

Quickening her pace, she walked as fast as the heat would allow her without collapsing. Seeing the tall pine trees growing closely together reminded Claudia of the last time she'd come through the woods. It was the day she'd found Denny Clark close to death. The urges she'd experienced after he'd pressed his body against hers vanished after a couple of days. Her mother was right.

She left the woods and had just made her way along an unpaved road when a dilapidated pickup truck whizzed by with a loud clatter, leaving a cloud of dust settling all over her. She knew her grandmother would have a fit if she saw her covered with a layer of dirt and grime.

The soft purring sound of a car's engine came up behind her and she slowed her pace, then glanced over her shoulder. The sun gleamed down on a black car rolling slowly beside her. It was hard to see the driver's face with sunlight glinting off the shiny chrome bumpers. Her heart pounded in her chest like the heavy beats of a bass drum. Out of the corner of her eye she saw the pale face of a White man. Seeing a White man would not have frightened her so much if she hadn't been alone; and she was alone without another soul in sight.

The car stopped and she heard the sound of a door closing. If she made it to the woods, then perhaps she could get away before the man caught her.

"Claudia!"

She blinked slowly. No White man knew her name—except Denny. She turned slowly and saw Denny Clark as he approached her. It had only been a week since she last saw him, and he'd changed. He appeared taller and heavier. He was dressed in a pair of khakis and a short-sleeved white shirt. He also wore a pair of new tan work boots. She watched him come closer, not realizing she had been holding her breath. How could he have changed so quickly? He hardly resembled the same boy from three weeks ago.

A bright smile softened his cold blue eyes. "Hi."

A tentative smile touched Claudia's lips. "Hi." They stared at each other, waiting for the other to initiate conversation.

"I just came around to see how you're doing," Denny said, breaking the pregnant silence.

"I'm fine."

Denny's gaze lingered on her face. "You look nice."

Claudia nodded. "So do you."

He glanced down at his pants. "I got me a job."

"Doing what?" she asked.

"Driving."

Claudia narrowed her eyes. "You're not old enough to be driving a car."

"Don't matter. I'm driving anyway."

"Who do you work for?"

"A man in Hackersville. He took me in and offered me a job. It pays really well, too."

"Which means you're not going back to school."

"Don't need to. I'm making plenty of money. I have my own room and don't have to pay for no food, and I get my laundry done free, too. I make as much money as any man around here."

"You still need school. How are you going to amount to something without school?"

"I will."

The two words were said so softly that Claudia could barely hear them. She stared up at Denny staring at her, shivering despite the sultry heat. There was something in his gaze that frightened her and suddenly she didn't know why she had stopped to talk to him. She should've known better. Especially after their last meeting.

"I must get home. My grandmother will be looking for me." She hardly recognized her own voice. There was no mistaking the quiver of fear.

Denny reached out to touch her arm and pulled back at the last possible moment. "Don't go—not yet."

"Sorry," she mumbled. Turning, she raced through the woods, forgetting that she was supposed to look for Janice and Butch. Damp wisps clung to her neck and forehead by the time she left the cooler, dark forested area behind.

Claudia made it to her grandmother's, yelled out a greeting to Earline, then raced upstairs to her bedroom to change. She closed the door to the bathroom and washed her face. She managed to brush most of the dust out of her hair. For the first time in her life, she wished she knew enough vulgar words to cuss at both Janice and Denny. If she hadn't gone to look for Janice, she wouldn't have run into him.

It wasn't that he did not act like a gentleman, because he had. He was nice to her, and he looked nice, but seeing him again conjured up feelings she wanted to forget. She made a promise never to walk home through the woods again—not for any reason.

Denny hadn't moved. Claudia had disappeared and if he'd had the power, he would have willed her to come back and talk to him. He also knew she didn't stay because she was afraid of him. But then she had a right to be. He had practically forced himself on her in her grandmother's backyard. His life had changed, and yet he couldn't change his feelings for her. He now slept on a bed wide enough for two people to turn over without touching the other. Always before, he'd occupied a small, narrow cot. His bedroom was spacious, with two large windows with curtains instead of the tiny bare one he'd stared up at for thirteen years.

The live-in cook in Mr. Carson's house was a colored woman who fixed all his favorite foods: grits smothered with soft scrambled eggs and lots of butter, fluffy biscuits, thick slices of fried slab bacon, fried chicken, and greens cooked with generous pieces of smoked pig knuckles. He had eaten nonstop for the first two days before realizing he would always have access to food. It wasn't that he hadn't eaten at Claudia's grandmother's house, because he had. He ate whatever he was given, while he didn't have the nerve to ask for a second helping.

Although Mr. Carson was married, Mrs. Carson was hardly ever around. His boss didn't have to work. He lived off the money left him by his father, who'd owned most of the properties in and around Hackersville. His income also came from sharecroppers who worked his land. He'd bragged about niggers being so dumb that they didn't know when they were being cheated right in front of their faces.

Denny had tasted his boss's premium bourbon and didn't like it because it was too strong and it'd burned his throat and chest. He'd emptied the crystal goblet, refusing more. What Shelton Carson hadn't known was that Denny Clark had been raised by an alcoholic father who when drunk was as mean as a rabid dog. And not wanting to be anything like his father, he had taken an oath never to drink liquor.

He thought sixteen-year-old Alice Scott, the White girl who had come to clean the Carson house, pretty. She had long, silky black hair, pale skin, and startling dark green eyes framed by thick black lashes. Her tiny nose had a spray of freckles across the bridge and her mouth was as red as the ripest strawberry. He'd found himself staring at her and wondering why he did not experience the same feelings he'd had whenever he was with Claudia. Alice was nice to look at once you recovered from her delicate beauty, but it was Claudia he wanted.

The image of Claudia in the full sunlight was branded into his memory. He could close his eyes and still see the gold in her light-brown skin. It matched the gold in her clear brown eyes. He'd wanted to stay away from her but couldn't. He'd waited two days to see her, after he'd driven Mr. Carson to Biloxi on business, where his boss was scheduled to meet with several elected officials who'd secretly supported their brethren in opposition to the 1950 United States Supreme Court's ruling in *Sweatt v. Painter.*

The court had ruled that equality of education entailed more than comparability of facilities, implying that "separate" was unequal. Racial quotas were recently abolished by the US Army, and Mr. Carson and the elected officials feared their children would eventually be forced to go to school with colored children. That was all right for people up North, but not for the South or for Mississippi.

Denny agreed with them. What was wrong with niggas anyway? Why couldn't they be satisfied with separate but equal? That was the way it was and always would be.

Claudia felt the thick, smothering tension the moment she walked through the door of the school building the following afternoon. A crowd of students milled on the front steps, spilling over to the grassy area shaded by massive oak trees. Most times everyone left the school property as soon as the dismissal bell rang; but today was different.

What shocked Claudia more than seeing students standing around was the hushed silence. The intense heat and the haze, which had not burned off with the rising sun, along with the dust that seemed to settle on everything because of the lack of rain, paled when she saw a White boy leaning against one of the trees lining the path to the entrance. She stopped on the last step, going completely still at the same time her heart pounded painfully in her chest. Denny Clark had come to her school! He wore a pair of dark slacks and a pale blue shirt. The shirt was the exact match for the cold blue eyes concealed behind a pair of sunglasses.

Dozens of pairs of eyes were trained on the tall, thin White boy walking confidently toward the entrance to the school. They parted as he neared them like a sweeping blaze burning a swath over a narrow ribbon of earth. Everyone moved— except Claudia. The pounding in her chest spread to her head, and she was certain she was going to faint away right on the steps. Waves of shimmering heat and shame and embarrassment were overshadowed by icy-cold fingers of fear. He had come to her—to her school, and the secret she and her grandmother had hidden for weeks was now open for all of Freedom to know.

Squinting behind his newly purchased shades, Denny measured her reaction. It was obvious she was shocked to see him. He wasn't scheduled to drive to Biloxi until later that evening, but a powerful, invisible force had prompted him to see Claudia again. The school year would be over in two days, and he wanted to talk to her about meeting him over the summer.

He stopped in front of Claudia, his shrouded gaze sweeping over her startled features. A slight smile curled his upper lip. He'd wanted to surprise her, and she was. He'd studied her facial expression enough to know whether she was angry, pleased, or reflective. There had been times when they'd sat together while going over her schoolwork and a faraway look would cross her face, where she would shut him and everything around her out. Those were the times he resented her. Resented her because she'd shut *him* out. He had wanted to be a part of her dreams and her life. He was only thirteen, and he had fallen in love. He was in love with the girl who had saved his life.

Claudia Patterson had become one of the angels his mother whispered to him about whenever she'd tucked him into bed. In that instant a rush of emotions swept over him. He missed his mother. He missed her delicate touch, her soft voice, and he missed her smell. A sweet smell so like Claudia's.

"Afternoon, Claudia," he said softly. He smiled at the soft gasps slicing the thick air. Denny wanted to shout at the others standing around watching him and Claudia: *Yeah, I know her. What you gonna do about it?*

"What are you doing here?" Claudia asked as her eyelids fluttered wildly. Her voice was barely above a whisper.

Denny pushed his hands into the pockets of his slacks. "I came to see you."

She glared at him, the shock on her face replaced by anger. "You had no right to come here." This time her voice quivered with rage.

Denny's temper also flared. "I can go anywhere I want."

"Not here," she retorted. "Not in Freedom."

He snorted at the same time he shook his head, tossing back a lock of wavy hair off his forehead. "Freedom—shit. You niggas ain't free." Claudia took a step toward him, but he was quicker. Denny caught the hand that had slapped him once before when he'd called her a nigga. His fingers tightened on her wrist, not permitting her movement or escape. Several of the older high school boys moved closer. "Stay back!" Denny warned. "This doesn't concern you."

"It concerns all of us when you touch one of *ours*," came a deep, booming voice in the crowd of students that had gathered to watch Denny and Claudia. "Let her be."

Denny hesitated, then released Claudia's arm. He was angry, angry with himself. He should've never come to her at the school. It would've been better if he had gone to her grandmother's house and waited for her to show up there.

He turned to face the small crowd closing in on him. He was scared, more scared than he had ever been in his life. It was the first time he'd faced a mob of Black people. "You niggas touch me and y'all be swinging from trees before sunrise," he said with false bravado. He was certain they could hear panic in his voice.

His softly spoken warning stopped all movement, and Denny saw what he hadn't expected to see: fear. They feared him. The threat of a lynching had stopped them in their tracks. He hadn't had much contact with Black people, but he'd grown up hearing his parents and other Whites talk about them. They said they were lazy and dumb, and if it weren't for White people they would starve to death.

"Is there a problem here?"

Denny shifted and met the gaze of a woman dressed in a light blue seersucker suit with a crisp, white cotton blouse. Confidence and strength showed in the face of the dark-skinned, middle-aged woman with deep-set brown eyes.

He shrugged his shoulders. "Ain't no problem."

"If that's the case, then please leave the school property." Her gaze swept over the students standing around in small groups. "Classes are dismissed. Everybody go home." All followed the principal's command except Denny and Claudia.

"Claudia?"

"Yes, Mrs. Walker."

"Come inside with me."

Nodding, Claudia mumbled, "Yes, ma'am."

Denny watched Claudia walk away and he panicked. He didn't want her to leave him now that he had set aside his pride and come to her.

"Claudia!" he shouted to her back.

Mrs. Walker turned and glared at him. "Get off *my* school property before I call the sheriff and have you arrested for trespassing."

Fear and the threat he would never see Claudia again made

Denny reckless. "You niggas are the ones trespassing. Why don't you go back to Africa?"

Mrs. Walker took a step toward Denny, and he pulled back his shoulders when seeing rage in her eyes. "It is apparent that you're not in school, because if you were then you would know that *your kind* are the trespassers in this country. There was another race of people here when Europe opened its prisons and poorhouses and sent their *trash* across the Atlantic Ocean. And I doubt very much if there is any royal European blood in your veins, young man."

Denny's hands curled into tight fists. "You nigga bitch. Both of you nigga bitches!"

Patricia Walker narrowed her eyes. "Get away from my school before I go inside and get something that will make you sorry you ever drew breath."

Tears welled up in Denny's eyes behind the lenses of his dark glasses, and for the first time he was glad he had spent money on them, because no one could see him cry. He'd wanted to save every penny he'd earned, but knew he had to buy clothes and several small items that he'd always coveted. And the sunglasses were something he'd always wanted. Every man he'd ever admired owned a pair.

Backpedaling, he pointed at Claudia. "I'm gonna get you. You're gonna pay and pay good."

Tears Claudia tried to hold back spilled over and coursed down her cheeks. Her principal knew she'd had personal contact with a White boy; all the students who had witnessed the incident knew, and it was only a matter of time before her parents would also know.

Mrs. Walker stared at Claudia, then placed a comforting arm around her shoulders. "Come inside and sit a while. You will want to fix your face."

Claudia shook her head. "I can't. I must get home."

"Don't worry. I'll drive you home."

Nodding, she returned to the school building with Mrs.

Walker and walked into the large office with the gold letters of MRS. PATRICIA WALKER, PRINCIPAL painted on the glass. She searched a pocket of her skirt, pulled out a handkerchief, and dabbed her eyes and moist cheeks.

"Please sit down, Claudia," Mrs. Walker said softly. The girl complied. The older woman stared at Claudia Patterson's delicate features. The girl had never been sent to her office during the eleven years she had been the principal at the Freedom School. And that meant Claudia was a good student. "You know I'm going to have to tell your parents about this," she continued.

"Yes, ma'am."

Mrs. Walker picked up a fountain pen lying beside a stack of blank paper. There was only the sound of the point as it raced across the paper, leaving a swirling flow of wet letters. She blotted the hastily written note, folded it, then slipped it into an envelope. Two pairs of brown eyes, one dark and the other clear and flecked with pinpoints of gold, met and held. She sealed and handed the envelope to Claudia. "I want you to give this to your father." She watched as Claudia slipped the envelope between the pages of her language arts book. "Now if you're ready, I'll drive you home."

Claudia wanted to tell the principal she wasn't ready; she didn't know if she would ever be ready for what she was certain to become a highly embarrassing situation for her parents. "I'm supposed to go to my grandmother's house."

Mrs. Walker nodded. "Then I'll take you to your grandmother's."

Once they left the school, the trip was quick and accomplished in complete silence. Claudia mumbled a thanks, pushed open the car door, and walked up the porch to Earline Patterson's large white house. Earline stood on the porch; hands folded on her ample hips. The expression on her face said it all—she knew. How could she have known so quickly?

Earline waved to the principal, then turned her attention to her granddaughter. "Afternoon, Miss Patterson."

Another wave of fresh tears threatened to fall. Whenever her grandmother was angry with her, she called her Miss Patterson. "Afternoon, Grandma."

"Right now, I'm Mrs. Patterson to *you*."

Claudia would've preferred her grandmother hitting her to shutting her out. Her chin quivered uncontrollably. "I'm sorry, Gran—Mrs. Patterson."

"Go to your room," Earline ordered, pointing at the door. "I just got a call from your mother and she and your father will be over within the hour."

"Yes, ma'am."

She said every prayer she knew as she raced up the staircase to her bedroom. Claudia knew what she'd done was serious if her parents shut down their businesses before the scheduled time for closing.

Throwing her books on the rocking chair, she stripped off her skirt and shoes and changed quickly into a pair of blue jeans and tennis shoes. Then she sat on the wooden chest at the foot of the bed and waited.

Chapter 8

Misfortunes one can endure—they come from
outside, they are accidents. But to suffer for one's
own faults—ah, there is the sting of life.
              —Oscar Wilde

Sarah Patterson's face was flushed with high color as she
pushed open the car door. This was one time she did not
wait for Earl to come around and open the door for her. She
had gotten a call at the beauty parlor within minutes of her
daughter's best friend telling her what had happened at the
school. It had taken all her self-control to finish curling, then
combing out her customer's hair before she walked to the
barbershop to tell her husband. Earl hadn't said anything. He
didn't have to. The throbbing muscle skipping along his lean
jaw and the steely look in his eyes revealed his rage. They
were fortunate that it was a weekday and business had been
slow, and they decided to close instead of waiting for walk-in
customers.

"Where is she?" Sarah asked as soon as her mother-in-law
opened the door.

"She's upstairs. Don't be so hard on the girl, Sarah."

Any hint of gold fled Sarah's eyes, leaving them a deep
green. "How many times must I remind you that Claudia's

my child, not yours. And I'll thank you not to interfere when I must chastise her."

"And how many times do I have to tell you to mind your mouth, missy. Your mama did a piss-poor job of raising you if you didn't learn to respec' your elders."

The natural color drained from Sarah's face, leaving it a sallow yellow shade. She took a step toward Earline, her eyes as wide as saucers. "How dare you speak of my—"

"That's enough!" The two words echoed along with the crack of the screened door slapping against its frame. Earl Patterson stood in the middle of the parlor, his features contorted with rage. "There's enough going on right now, and I will not have my wife and my mother fighting with each other."

Earline snorted loudly. "There wouldn't be no fight if your wife learned some manners."

Earl's dark eyes swung from his wife to his mother, then back to his wife. "Apologize to Mama, Sarah." His voice was deceptively calm.

Sarah's mouth dropped and she stared at her husband as if he were a stranger. "I will not."

His frown deepened. "I'm sorry, Mama, if Sarah disrespected you."

Sarah rounded on him. "How can you take her side, Earl? I'm your wife."

"What you said was uncalled for," he countered.

"But the Bible says that when a man leaves his father and mother and is united with his wife, they become one," Sarah argued softly.

Earl's mouth tightened under his clipped moustache. "I don't intend to talk about it. The only thing I want to talk about is why my daughter has taken up with a White boy," he said before he headed for the staircase.

"It's not the child's fault," Earline said.

Earl's foot paused on the first stair. "Whose fault is it?"

"Mostly mine," Earline admitted.

Earl walked back to his mother. Placing a hand under her elbow, he led her over to the sofa. "Sit down, Mama, and tell us what this is all about."

Sarah moved as if in a trance as she sat on a cushion at the opposite end of the sofa while Earl sat between her and his mother. Both listened as Earline related the events that led to her taking Denny Clark into her home and hiding him until he'd recovered enough to leave on his own. She hadn't wanted him to die in Freedom, where Black folks would be accused of beating him to death.

Earl rested his elbows on his knees and buried his face in his large hands. "I understand you tending to his wounds, but I still can't believe you put my child in that kind of danger."

"There was no danger," Earline countered. "He never came up in the house. And if he had I would've shot him."

Earl dropped his hands. "But you allowed them to be together. Anything could've happened. What if he had touched her. What if—"

"He didn't touch her!" Earline shouted, cutting him off.

"How do you know that, Mama?"

Sarah didn't hear her husband's and his mother's angry exchange. The conversation she'd had with Claudia, about sexual urges she'd confessed to having, flooded her mind. Had the boy touched her daughter, and had she liked it?

"Oh no, oh no," she whispered over and over as tears flowed down her face.

Earl's head swung around. "What's the matter, Sarah?" He cradled her as she wept against his chest.

"I . . . I think he . . . he touched her," she said, hiccupping through a fresh wave of tears.

Tightening his grip on his wife's shoulders, Earl held Sarah away from him. "What the hell are you talking about?"

It was Sarah's turn to confess what had occurred the night she'd sent Claudia to her room without eating dinner. Earl and Earline were shocked by Sarah's revelation, both mumbling prayers that the boy called Denny Clark hadn't defiled their daughter and granddaughter.

Earl released Sarah and stood up. "I'm going upstairs to talk to her."

Earline caught his arm. "This is woman's work. Let your wife handle it."

Sarah stared at her mother-in-law, nodding, their former hostility temporarily forgotten. "You're mother's right, Earl. I think it's best if I talk to her."

"You'd better handle it, Sarah, or I will." He walked out of the parlor, flung open the door, and stomped out to the porch to wait.

Sarah touched the corners of her eyes with her fingertips. "I'm sorry about what I said to you, Miss Earline."

Earline's expression did not soften as she waved a dismissive hand. "Go up to the child and find out what you can."

Claudia's eyes grew wide when she saw her mother enter the room. She didn't know why, but she had expected her father. Rising slowly from the bed, she stood ramrod straight, holding out the envelope Mrs. Walker had given her. Biting down on her lip to keep it from trembling, she stared at her mother's face. Her eyes were swollen, and bright red splotches dotted her cheeks. It was obvious that she had been crying. Her own eyes filled with tears, and as she put a hand over her mouth, the envelope floated to the floor. Her knees trembled seconds before she, too, collapsed on the floor and curled into a fetal position.

"I'm sorry, Mama. I'm so sorry," she whimpered over and over.

Sarah went to her knees, gathering her daughter in her arms and rocking as she'd done when Claudia was an infant. "It's okay, baby. Have your cry. Then we will talk."

Claudia cried until an attack of dry heaves rendered her unable to speak coherently. Sarah left her and called down to

Earl. He bounded up the staircase, lifted Claudia off the floor, and carried her into the bedroom he'd occupied during his own childhood. He placed her on the bed, and then lay beside her. Sarah felt as if she had been shut out until he raised his hand and beckoned her closer. She took his hand and allowed him to pull her down beside him. They lay together on the mattress, father, mother, and daughter, each seeking comfort from the other.

"Did he touch you?" Sarah asked Claudia quietly after a long silence.

Her slight intake of breath echoed loudly in the quietness of the space. "Touch me how, Mama?"

"Did he touch your body? Your private parts?"

"No."

"If he was angry with you, then why did he come to the school to see you?" Sarah asked as she continued with her questioning.

Claudia sniffled. "I don't know."

Sarah stroked Claudia's hair at the same time she kissed her forehead. "You don't have to worry about him bothering you again. Your Daddy and I will see to that."

She and Earl lay with Claudia, waiting for her breathing to change. It deepened as she relaxed enough to fall asleep. They slipped from the bed, left the room, closing the door behind them. She returned to the other room to retrieve the envelope. Earl's name was written across the front. Sarah walked into the hallway and handed him the envelope.

Pressing her body against his, she wound her arms around his waist. "What are we going to do, Daddy?"

Resting his chin on the top of Sarah's head, Earl exhaled a heavy sigh. "I don't know. He didn't touch her. We must be grateful for that."

Easing back, Sarah stared up at him. "I wonder if she's going to be like her great-grandmother."

"In what way?"

"If she's going to prefer White men to Black."

"Dammit, Sarah, don't start on that again."

"Don't use that tone with me, Earl Patterson," Sarah said angrily. "My grandmother allowed a White man to make her his whore. He had his own wife and children, and he *had* my grandmother. Do you know how many babies she lost before she finally had my mother? Five, Earl. She wanted his baby so badly that she risked her life each time she conceived. The sixth time was the charm because she finally carried my mother to term. She delivered her, then bled to death. She gave birth to a little girl whose complexion was so fair that everyone thought she was White. My grandmother sacrificed her life only because she'd wanted a White man's baby."

"And you think because Claudia has an encounter with one White boy that she's going to become his whore?"

"I'm not saying that, Earl."

"Then what are you saying, Sarah?"

"Nothing. You wouldn't understand."

"The one thing I do understand is that as much as White people profess they hate Black people, yet their men can't stay away from our women."

Sarah wanted to tell her husband that it was more than that, that there was no way he could understand what she had gone through when other colored folks made snide remarks about her White blood. She was too light to be Black and not light enough to be White. And what she'd wanted was to spare her daughter any unnecessary pain and had subtly warned her to stay with her own kind. But it was obvious Claudia hadn't listened. Sarah had believed living in an all-black town was the answer, but it wasn't because Denny Clark's presence had shattered its cloistered security.

An expression of unyielding determination settled into Sarah's features. She would protect her daughter—at any cost. "What's in the envelope?" she asked Earl.

He slid a finger under the flap and withdrew the single sheet of paper. "Mrs. Walker says that Claudia's association with a White boy put the entire school population in danger. She says there were threats about lynching. She wants to meet with us tomorrow morning before classes begin. She also says that Claudia should be present."

Sarah closed her eyes and slowly shook her head. "It's worse than we thought."

"What I want is for it to be over, Sarah!"

"It will be, Daddy," she said, placing a comforting hand on his arm. "We'll get through this together."

Earl nodded. "I hope you're right, sweetie. I sure do hope you're right," he repeated.

Claudia slept fitfully, disturbing images attacking her relentlessly. She opened her mouth to scream but no sound came out. She tried hitting the gaping mouth screaming *nigga* over and over, but her arm wouldn't move. Each time the word attacked her it shook the very foundation on which she stood. The sound was that of an explosion. The explosion, smoke, and the flames that followed scorched her exposed flesh, burned her eyes, and made it impossible for her to breathe. The realization swept over her that she was going to die. The gaping mouth spewing the hateful word announced her sentence: *death by hanging*.

She was lifted upward at the same time thick strands of coiled knotted hemp were looped around her neck. It tightened, cutting off her breath. Turning her head slowly to the right she saw the lifeless body of the boy who had challenged Denny to let her go, swaying gently from another rope. Darkness descended on her as she heard another man calling her name. Panting and gasping for breath, she struggled to escape.

"No, no, no!" she shouted over and over.

"Button!"

The man calling her name was her father. "Daddy, please don't let them get me. Help me, Daddy!"

"Wake up, Claudia."

Earl gave his daughter a rough shake, her head flopping limply. She was having a nightmare, but what truly unnerved him was the sound of terror in her screams. Tears streamed down her face and her arms flailed wildly. He pulled her off the bed and shook her again. Her body went limp, collapsing against his chest.

"Claudia," he said in her ear. "It's all right, baby. Daddy's not going to let anyone hurt his baby girl."

Claudia opened her eyes and threw her arms around her father's neck. "I had a dream where I was being hung."

"That wasn't a dream but a nightmare. You've been through a lot, so you would dream about it."

"Daddy?"

"What is it?"

"Denny did try to kiss me."

"What did you do?"

"I called him White trash, and he was so mad that he pushed me down."

Earl chuckled, tightening his hold on her slender body. "Good for you."

"I'd never let a White boy kiss me, Daddy."

"I know that."

Earline and Sarah stood outside the bedroom holding hands. They had heard Claudia's screams at the same time as Earl, but he had made it up the staircase before them. Earline gently squeezed her daughter-in-law's fingers, praying the child would not be so traumatized that she would have recurring nightmares about Denny Clark. Earline cursed the day Claudia had walked through the woods and found the boy and cursed her own decision to help save his life. She knew there was something evil about him the moment she saw his eyes. They were the eyes of someone without a soul; someone who was a messenger of death. Earl glanced over Claudia's head, nodding and smiling. She had relaxed enough to go back to sleep.

"What has he done to her?" Sarah whispered, as she pulled her hand out of Earline's.

"I don't know," Earline replied, shaking her head. "What I hope is that he hasn't broken her spirit."

"She's only twelve, Miss Earline. This could scar her for life. I've tried so hard to protect her from White people, but . . ."

"Don't beat up on yourself, Sarah," Earline said, cutting her off. "You are the best mother the child could have," she continued with a rare compliment. "If anybody's gonna be blamed, then it's me. I never should have had that little devil under my roof."

"You did what you felt you had to do, Miss Earline. Like you said before, if he had died in Freedom then no one would be safe from those hood-wearing, bloodthirsty murderers."

"What are you and Earl gonna do to protect her?"

Sarah inhaled a breath, then let it out in a long sigh. "I'm thinking of sending her to live with my sister in Biloxi. We'll drive down every weekend to see her. She can finish school there before she decides where she wants to go to college."

Earline felt her heart lurch. The pounding in her chest and the rising lump in her throat made normal breathing difficult. She always looked forward to summer and spending that time with her granddaughter. Even though she'd loved her sons, she had never openly expressed that she'd also wanted a daughter. A daughter she would teach to cook, sew, and pass along her healing recipes to. Without her being aware of it, Claudia had become that daughter.

Taking a deep breath, Earline stared at Sarah's stoic expression. "Has Earl agreed?"

"He doesn't have a choice, Miss Earline. None of us do, because if that boy comes back to see her, you know there's going to be trouble. Earl will shoot him. You'll lose another son; I'll lose my husband and Claudia will grow up without a father."

Earline nodded as a feeling of sadness gripped her. It was

akin to grieving, a grieving she hadn't felt since she buried her beloved Joe and Joe Junior. This would be the one time she would not interfere with Sarah and Earl's decision. They knew what was best for their child.

"Do what you have to do to protect the child," she whispered.

Turning on her heel, she walked several feet to her own bedroom. She stood in the doorway staring at the furnishings that silently told her family's history. The large bed covered with a faded quilt stitched by her own mother was where she had given Joe Patterson her supple young body for the first time. It was also the bed where she had given birth to both her sons. And it would be the bed where she would likely draw her last breath.

She wasn't an old woman—at least she didn't think she was, but Earline knew it was time she put her affairs in order. She would call the man who handled her insurance and financial investments to let him know she was ready to update her will. It was necessary because if Denny Clark showed up again looking for Claudia, she wouldn't have to worry about Earl shooting him because she would do it first. She would take his life as surely as she had saved it.

Chapter 9

Your worst humiliation is only someone else's momentary entertainment.
                    —Karen Crockett

Claudia walked between her parents as they made their way to the entrance of the school. The steady hum of conversations among the students waiting for the bell to signal the beginning of classes faded away until all that was left was a profound silence. She felt better when her parents moved closer, each taking her hand in a gesture of protection. A slight smile parted her lips. Claudia didn't care what anyone thought because she had her mother and father to take care of her.

She'd slept fitfully throughout the night, Denny's hateful threat attacking her relentlessly. She woke several times in tears, and when she finally left the bed to prepare herself for school she'd noticed her eyes were quite swollen. Sarah had placed cold teabags over her eyes to offset some of the swelling, but enough remained to let any and everyone know that she had been crying.

What she'd wanted to do was turn the clock back twenty-four hours and erase the day from her existence. And if she could turn back the pages on the calendar to the day she saw

Denny Clark for the first time, lying close to death, she would have. She should have been like Janice and run home. But she hadn't, and now she had shamed her family because everyone knew she'd had contact with a White boy. But on the other hand, her parents knowing of Denny's existence had somehow brought her family closer together.

Claudia stared straight ahead, but out of the corner of her eye she saw Janice. Their eyes met. An angry scowl distorted Janice's beautiful dark face seconds before she jerked her head away in a gesture of rejection and disgust, leaning closer and whispering something to Butch Washington. He nodded as a smirk flitted over his handsomely brooding features.

She did not want to believe it. Her best friend had turned against her. Janice, who had come to her defense whenever other girls talked about her not having breasts, wanted nothing to do with her. Pinpoints of tears pricked the backs of her eyelids, but she refused to cry. Not in front of the entire school population. Not when she'd spent most of yesterday afternoon and most of the night crying. Tilting her chin in, which she hoped was the haughty gesture she'd seen her mother effect, she walked through the door her father held open for her and Sarah and into the school building.

Earl knocked on the door bearing Mrs. Walker's name. Within seconds it opened, and a short, balding man stood in the doorway, his dark eyes behind a pair of rimless glasses taking in everything about Earl's tall, erect carriage in a single glance.

"Please come in, Mr. Patterson." He waited until Sarah and Claudia stepped into the office, then extended his hand to Earl. "Cyril Brown. I'm the president of the Colored Board of Education for this county. Mrs. Walker asked that I be present for this meeting."

Earl removed his straw hat, and took the proffered hand, grasping it firmly. "My pleasure, Mr. Brown. I'd like to introduce my wife, Sarah, and my daughter, Claudia."

Cyril Brown nodded in acknowledgment. "My pleasure, Mrs. Patterson, Claudia."

Patricia Walker rose from her chair behind the massive desk in the large office. Her impassive expression did not reveal what she felt or was thinking. "Good morning, Mr. and Mrs. Patterson. Please be seated."

Earl seated Sarah and Claudia, then took the straight-back chair between them. He'd noticed that Mrs. Walker had deliberately ignored Claudia, as a shiver of annoyance swept over him. The fact that a member of the board of education was present meant that this meeting was profoundly serious. Crossing one leg over the opposite knee, he placed his hat on his lap and stared intently at the two educators.

"I'm sorry to take you away from businesses this morning," Mrs. Walker began, "but what occurred on school property yesterday was so serious a matter that it cannot be ignored."

"I agree," Earl said in a quiet voice. His gaze met Sarah's as she turned slightly to look at him.

"You do?" Mrs. Walker asked.

"Yes, Mrs. Walker," Sarah confirmed. Her wavy hair was pinned up in a fashionable chignon and covered with a small pale peach cloche with a matching veil. The color was the exact match for her slim voile dress with a lacy crocheted collar. The delicate pearls in her pierced ears matched the single strand draped around her long, slender neck.

"We were not aware of our daughter's association with the young White boy; however, we have taken steps to make certain he will never bother her again."

"I'm relieved to hear this, Mrs. Patterson," Mrs. Walker said, forcing what passed for a smile. "But that still doesn't change the fact that my students were threatened, and my property is at risk."

Earl leaned forward. "Threatened how?"

"There was talk of a lynching," Mr. Brown said, while glaring directly at Claudia and not allowing Mrs. Walker to explain. "There are enough colored folks still being lynched in Mississippi through no fault of their own, without adding the citizens of Freedom to the list."

"Who is supposed to do the lynching?" Earl countered. "A thirteen-year-old boy?"

"I'm certain that boy has a father and other relatives who would like to ride into Freedom and hang a few Negros just for sport."

"It was his father who tried to kill him," Claudia said, speaking for the first time. "It was my grandmother who saved his life."

"You will not speak unless you're spoken to, young lady," Cyril warned. "I've consulted with the other board members, and we've all agreed that Claudia is to be suspended for the rest of the school term and the first two months of the upcoming school year."

Earl started to get up, but Sarah held on to his arm, stopping him. "Firstly," Earl said, "you will not talk to my daughter like you just did or I will knock you on your ass. And secondly, I pay taxes for her to attend this school, so if you're not ready for a lawsuit, then I suggest you reverse your decision to suspend her. There are only two days left for this school term—today and tomorrow. I will bring Claudia to school and pick her up after classes. And you better hope and pray that none of you mess with her, because there will be hell to pay for them and their folks." Earl pushed to his feet and put on his hat. "This meeting is over and I'm going to wait until the bell rings, then I'm going escort my daughter to her class."

Claudia couldn't believe Mr. Brown wanted to suspend her for the rest of the school term and two months of the upcoming school year. It wasn't fair. It hadn't been her fault that Denny had come to the school. He and Mrs. Walker acted as if she had invited him.

She was also shocked because she had never seen or known her father to threaten someone. But it felt wonderful to know that he was willing to defend her. She'd overheard Earl Patterson say on occasion that he would willingly give up his life to defend and protect his wife, his daughter, and his mother, and she had seen that firsthand when he'd scolded Mr. Brown for chastising her.

"Let's go," Earl said, at the same time the bell rang, signaling the beginning of classes for the day.

Claudia, flanked by her parents, led the way down the hallway to her classroom. "I'm here," she said, meeting her father's eyes.

"We'll wait until the late bell rings before you go inside."

"That's okay, Daddy. I'm going to be all right." She hadn't lied. Just knowing he'd told Mrs. Walker and Mr. Brown that no one was to *mess* with her gave her the confidence she needed to finish the school term.

Earl nodded. "I know you will."

Claudia smiled at Janice coming toward her, who looked away rather than meet her eyes. "Hi, Janice." She knew she'd lost Janice as a friend, but that no longer mattered. If she had been a true friend, then she would've stood by her and not acted like she wanted nothing to do with her.

"Didn't you hear Claudia speaking to you?" Earl asked.

Janice stopped and stared at the floor. "Yes, Mr. Patterson." Her head popped up. "Hi, Claudia."

"I know you and Claudia are friends," Earl said, "and I'd like you to put the word out that I don't want anyone in this school to mess with her, because I'm not going to go after them, because they're kids, but I will definitely talk to their folks about their children's behavior." He paused. "Do I make myself clear, Janice?"

"Yes, Mr. Patterson."

Although Claudia knew she was the reason why Denny had come to the school to seek her out, there was nothing she could have done to stop him. As a White boy in segregated Mississippi, he could come and go anywhere he wanted, while as a Black girl she was limited. There were WHITES

Only and Colored Only signs all over the South. However, there were no signs in Freedom—an all-black town founded by free slaves following the end of the Civil War.

Claudia hugged her father and mother, then entered the classroom to take her assigned seat. She opened her looseleaf notebook and pretended interest in a composition she had written for a book report. Two days. In another two days it would be over, and then she would be able to walk out of the Freedom School and not look back.

Once her parents decided to send her to Biloxi to live with her aunt Mavis, Claudia initially felt as if they wanted to hide her away to absolve themselves of the shame she had brought on the family. But now she was glad they had, because if she'd remained in Freedom there was no doubt she would become a pariah—an outcast in her own town.

Four days later Claudia sat in Mavis Bailey's parlor, listening to her schoolteacher aunt talk about the plans she had made for them. All the Bailey sisters resembled one another, but it was Mavis who most physically resembled their mother, with her dark red hair and gray eyes.

"Have you thought about what you want for your future, Claudia?"

Folding her hands in her lap, Claudia laced her fingers together. "I want to travel like you and Aunt Virgie do."

Mavis smiled. "Now I know why Sarah named you Claudia Mavis Patterson, because she had to know you would be more like me than herself. My baby sister doesn't like or is afraid of change, while Virgie and I are willing to take risks."

"Mama said Aunt Virgie loves living in Paris."

"That's because it is an exciting city."

"How many times have you been there, Aunt Mavis?"

Mavis ran her fingers through her boyish bobbed hairstyle. "Just once."

"Would you ever think of living there?"

"No. I like living in Biloxi and traveling to different countries every couple of years. Last year I spent the summer in Cuba, where I knew enough Spanish to communicate with the locals."

Claudia felt a rush of excitement eddy through her. She wanted her life to mirror her aunts', traveling to different countries and speaking other languages. "Do you also speak French?"

Mavis nodded. "Yes."

"Did you take it in high school?"

"No, I took Latin in high school and loved it."

"What about college, Aunt Mavis?"

"I also knew I wanted to be a teacher, so I majored in education, but my minor was Romance languages. I can speak and understand Spanish, French, and Italian. However, I'm not as fluent in Portuguese."

"Don't people in Brazil speak Portuguese?"

"Yes."

Claudia knew her life and future had changed the moment she walked into the small, neat, two-bedroom house belonging to Mavis Bailey. This upcoming schoolyear, thirty-five-year-old Mavis was to be appointed as an assistant principal in a private school for colored girls whose professional parents wanted the best education for their daughters, for them to be accepted into historically black colleges and universities.

"I told Mama and Daddy that I want to go to college."

"And you will, Claudia. Your father and mother are paying for you to attend a private school, and that means you'll have an advantage over those at the Freedom School. The class sizes are ridiculously small. Most classes have no more than six students to one teacher. And if you're having a problem with a subject, they are always willing to give you extra help. Sarah showed me your report card and your grades indicate you shouldn't have a problem getting into college."

Claudia knew it was going to take a while to adjust to being away from her parents and grandmother—that seeing them once a week for Sunday dinner wouldn't be enough. She would make new friends at her new school but doubted if she would ever feel as close to them as she had with Janice.

"Have you decided what you want to study in college?"

"I keep thinking about becoming a business owner like my father and mother, and that means I have to take business courses."

"As a business major you can decide whether you want to become an accountant, go into banking, or work for a large corporation. Meanwhile I'm willing to tutor you in different languages. You'll have six years before you graduate high school, and during that time I'll teach you to speak French, Spanish, and Italian."

Claudia's features became more animated. "How long do you think it will take me learn enough to be . . ."

"Fluent enough to speak the language?" Mavis asked when Claudia's words trailed off.

"Yes. Fluent."

"Two years for each is more than enough time. After a while, whenever we're together we will converse exclusively in either Italian, French, or Spanish. The quickest way to learn a language is to speak it."

"When are you going away again?"

Mavis's lids lowered over large gray eyes. "Not until you finish high school. I'll make certain you will get a passport before we leave for France. The trip will be my graduation gift to you."

Claudia stared wordlessly at her aunt, her heart pounding a runaway rhythm in her chest. Her life had changed at the exact moment when she saw the body of a beaten White boy in the woods in Freedom, and it changed again when she told her grandmother about him. The events following Earline Patterson hiding the boy in her root cellar had become frames of film for Claudia, culminating with her being exiled from her hometown. She would now spend the next six years not sleeping under the roof of her parents or grandmother, but under that of her aunt whose name she claimed as her middle one.

Her encounter with Denny Clark had shattered her innocence and had taught her a valuable lesson about trust. She'd helped save his life and he in turn had threatened her people. She had trusted Janice but she, too, had turned her back on Claudia when she needed her support. Her grandmother had preached to Claudia that she was a descendant of survivors, and it was only now that she felt like one.

With her aunt's assistance, she would finish high school, go on to college, and become a businessperson like her parents.

PART TWO

1960s
ROBERT MOORE

Chapter 10

Strangers are friends that you have yet to meet.
—Roberta Lieberman

Claudia had read countless books about France, but once the ship docked in Le Havre, she'd come to the realization that she was no longer in the United States. She and her aunt had sat in what was no longer identified as the Colored waiting room in the bus station, since the Supreme Court had ruled in 1956 that segregation on public transportation was unconstitutional, before boarding a bus with stops in Mobile, Alabama; Atlanta, Georgia; North Carolina; and finally Washington, D.C., where they'd gotten aboard a train to take them to New York. It wasn't until they were settled in their cabin on the ship that would take them across the Atlantic Ocean that she was able to completely relax after seeing the malevolent stares of some White people in the States whenever they'd shared the same space. She still did not understand their hatred of Black people who only wanted to live and let live.

It had taken more than twelve hundred miles of traveling from Mississippi to New York for Claudia to shake off the invisible shackles of Jim Crow that had continued to restrict her people from experiencing what it truly meant to be free.

She thought of Emma Lazarus's sonnet inscribed on the Statute of Liberty: *Give me your tired, your poor, your huddled masses yearning to breathe free . . .* The poet may have been referring to the new wave of European immigrants coming to the United States at the turn of the twentieth century, but had she forgotten about the poor, shackled, huddled masses of Africans who had been kidnapped from their homeland, chained together in the bottom of ships, and as cargo represented free labor, while as slaves they were fed, clothed, and reproduced at no additional expense to those who'd owned them?

Black people had built the country, made Whites wealthy beyond anything they could've imagined, yet they still were regarded as worthless and inhuman, while beatings and lynchings were still evident in Mississippi and throughout the South, as were race riots in northern states like Ohio, Nebraska, Illinois, and Indiana. However, Claudia hadn't recently celebrated her eighteenth birthday to believe all Black people in northern states were as free or considered equal to their White counterparts, but at least the racism wasn't as overt as it was in the South. She'd hoped that for the next six weeks she would be able to temporarily forget about the race relations in the United States and immerse herself in another language and culture.

The six years she'd spent living in Biloxi with her aunt Mavis had given her the insight to imagine what lay beyond the environs of Mississippi. As a teacher Mavis had demanded nothing short of excellence from her and she'd answered the call. Her foreign language courses began with two years of conversational Spanish, followed by another two years of Italian, and finally two years of French. Mavis would begin a conversation in Italian, and then without warning lapse into French, to which Claudia would have to respond in that language. There were occasions when Mavis wouldn't permit her to watch her favorite television program because she'd taken too long to reply. These were the times when she'd go into her bedroom and cry herself to sleep, while wishing she was back in Freedom with her parents and grandmother.

However, Earl, Sarah, and Earline had kept their promise to come and share Sunday dinner with her and Mavis every week, regardless of the weather, for six straight years.

"Are you feeling better?"

Mavis's voice broke into Claudia's musings. "Yes, ma'am."

She'd become seasick within hours of the ship pulling away from the dock and it had continued for most of the transatlantic crossing. There had been one storm at sea, and she had been forced to remain in the cabin for the duration. She'd heard there were medications to offset motion or seasickness, and Claudia was determined to find some before the return trip.

After going through customs, she waited with Mavis as a driver loaded their luggage into the trunk of his sedan. Virginia—or Virgie, as she preferred to be called—had planned for them to be picked up at Le Havre and driven to Paris.

All Claudia craved was a warm bath and a firm bed. The change in time zones had played havoc with her body's circadian rhythm. Paris was six hours ahead of Mississippi and despite it being early afternoon, her body reminded her it was time to wind down to ready herself to relax for the rest of the day.

The driver opened the rear door and Mavis got in, followed by Claudia. "If you don't mind, I'm going to try and get some sleep before we get to Paris," she told her aunt.

Not much about her aunt's appearance had changed during the six years Claudia had lived with her. The slight differences were one or two tiny lines around her eyes and several strands of gray in her dark red hair. She hadn't gained more than a few pounds, and at forty-one, with her tall and slender figure, she still was able to turn the heads of most men regardless of their race. Although her aunt hadn't married, Claudia knew she did entertain men who had come to call on her. She could not say for certain if Mavis and the men had had sexual relations, and if they had then they'd been very discreet.

Claudia hadn't been exposed to boys because she'd attended an all-girl school, but that didn't prevent her from overhearing her classmates talk about allowing boys to kiss them and feel them up. She was friendly with most of the girls at the school, but managed to keep her distance from becoming what she deemed as a *good friend*. Janice Mason had taught her: *once burned, twice shy* when it came to forming close relationships.

Six years were also responsible for a lot of changes for Claudia. Not only did she look different but her outlook on life was quite different than it had been since she'd been exiled from Freedom. She'd grown four inches and had reached the height of five-eight. Her body had also filled out, and although still quite slim, if she'd been wearing slacks no one would ever mistake her for a boy.

Mavis had encouraged her to pack light because she intended to buy her a set of new clothes befitting an incoming college freshman. Claudia had applied to several black colleges and decided to attend Hampton Institute in Hampton, Virginia. Her initial choice had been Cheyney University in Philadelphia because it was the oldest of all of the black colleges, but decided on Hampton because in Virginia her parents wouldn't have to drive as far to visit with her. Both Sarah and Earline had wiped away tears at her high school graduation, while her father couldn't stop grinning like the Cheshire cat. All were proud that she'd graduated near the top of her class.

"I think I'm going to join you," Mavis said as she kicked off her shoes. Leaning forward, she tapped the driver on the shoulder. "Can you please wake us when we get to our destination?" she asked in French.

"*Bien sûr, madame.*"

*   *   *

Claudia opened her mouth; no words came out once they arrived at Virginia Bailey's home. She was of the belief that her aunt Virgie lived in a Parisian flat or pied-à-terre, not a *hôtel particulier*. She'd studied as much as she could about France before her visit and was able to identify a château, a country manor house, and a *hôtel particulier*—a private residence or mansion in the city—in a single glance. And it was apparent Virgie had been paid quite well to teach English to the children of wealthy Parisians to live in such a grand house.

A middle-aged woman opened the door as their driver told her Madame Bailey's guests had arrived. She opened the door wider, speaking rapid French. The driver brought in their luggage and set it in the entryway. Claudia smiled, seeing her expatriate aunt for the first time in eight years.

Virginia Bailey, the eldest of the three Bailey sisters, appeared as if she hadn't aged one day since Claudia last saw her. It was if time had stood still for the forty-four-year-old schoolteacher. Her large gray-green eyes shimmered in a palomino-gold complexion glowing with good health. Her wavy brown hair with streaks of copper was styled in a chignon on the nape of her long, slender neck. A white silk man-tailored shirt, slim black linen slacks, and black leather ballet-style shoes completed her stylishly chic outfit.

Tears filled Virgie's eyes as she held out her arms. "I can't believe you're here."

Claudia hugged her aunt, the scent of an expensive perfume wafting to her nostrils. She kissed her silken, scented cheek. "Thank you so much for inviting me."

Virgie kissed Claudia on both cheeks. "I can't believe you've grown up so quickly. The last time I saw you, you were an itty-bitty thing." She held her at arm's length. "Look at you now. All grown up and ready to go to college. Your parents must be so proud of you."

"I hope they are," Claudia said in French. "And I thank you and Aunt Mavis for your graduation gift of this trip."

Virgie's eyebrows lifted slightly. "I see my sister has taught you well. She told me she was tutoring you in different languages and there's no doubt you've been a good student."

Mavis hugged her older sister. "Claudia is very bright, but there are times when she's just content to do just what is required to pass her courses."

Virgie stared at Claudia. "Your last name is Patterson, but remember you are also a Bailey woman, and as one you must distinguish yourself whether it is in education, business, or medicine. We are descendants of survivors, and you must make certain never to make them weep because you did something that shamed them."

Claudia lowered her eyes. She wanted to tell Virgie that she did when she'd befriended a White boy who had brought shame on her family and potential danger to the Black people living in Freedom. That she had been exiled from all she'd known for twelve years to live down that shame.

"I hope you're not thinking about what happened to you before you had to leave Freedom," Virgie said perceptively.

"I was," Claudia admitted.

"That's behind you, child," Mavis said, her voice rising slightly. "We all do things we sometimes later regret, but you can't fault yourself for saving that ungrateful boy's life. You're luckier than a lot of young women your age, Claudia. You have parents who want only the best for you. They've sacrificed not having their only child with them because they wanted to spare you the hostility you would've faced if you'd stayed in Freedom. They paid for you to attend a private school, and now college. They love you, and your aunties also love you, and for that you must be grateful."

Claudia felt properly chastised. "I am grateful, Aunties."

Virgie smiled at her housekeeper. "Ingrid, would you please show my niece her room."

The woman smiled and nodded. "*Oui, madame.*"

"Do I have the same bedroom I had when I was here before?" Mavis asked her sister once Claudia followed the housekeeper up the staircase to the second floor.

"Of course. I know how much you loved sleeping there, so I made certain not to assign it to any of my guests because I knew you were coming."

Mavis looped her arm through Virgie's as they made their way to an area of the residence Virginia had set up as a salon where she entertained artists, musicians, and avant-garde intellectuals several times a month.

She sat on a settee, watching as Virgie filled two crystal glasses with red wine, and then handed her one. "How are things between you and Jacques?"

Virgie took a matching silk-covered chair. "Things are the same." She took a sip of wine. "His wife is still living with her female lover, while their daughter has come here to live with me now that she's attending Sorbonne Université."

"Do you two get along?"

"Initially not at first," Virgie admitted. "I told her I wasn't here to replace her mother, but that if she was going to live under my roof then she had to abide by my rules. Jacques has spoiled her, so she has gotten away with a lot of things that could prove detrimental to her physical and emotional well-being."

Mavis slumped lower on the settee. "I don't want her to be a bad influence on Claudia, because our niece has been sheltered from things most girls her age are now experiencing."

"Don't worry, sister. I will talk to Noelle about what I expect of her during Claudia's visit."

"Sarah has trusted me with her child, and I don't want some wild girl to corrupt her morally."

"Like us?" Virgie said, grinning.

Throwing back her head, Mavis laughed uncontrollably. "We corrupted ourselves, Virgie. I had no idea that you had given James Wilcox your virginity months before I gave Philip Lawson mine."

A rush of color suffused Virgie's face. "When I came home that night, I swore Mama knew what I had been doing."

"I think she did, because she asked me if you and James had been spending time together. And of course I lied and said no."

Virgie took another sip of wine. "You know he'd wanted to marry me because he was my first."

"No!"

"Yes! He almost cried when I told him that I had no intention of being his wife just because we had slept together. That I was planning to go away to college, and I did not want to become some man's property."

"So, that's why he put out the rumor that the Bailey girls were uppity bitches."

Virgie sucked her teeth. "Uppity bitches or not, we were able to live our lives by our leave. I never begrudged Sarah for marrying Earl, but she went from Mama's house to her husband's without knowing what she could experience as an independent woman. That's why I told her she had to let Claudia go to college, because there was a whole world waiting for her outside of Mississippi."

Staring at the deep-red wine in her glass, Mavis thought how differently her life would've been if she had married and become a mother. She doubted whether she would've been able to travel much. And she wouldn't have been able to pick and choose with whom to have affairs. It was the same with Virgie. She'd met a man who'd gifted her one of the finest private homes in Paris in exchange for her companionship.

Mavis did not miss having a husband or children, because she viewed her niece and her students as her children. And it appeared as if Virgie had become a surrogate mother for her lover's daughter, while continuing to tutor the children of Parisians willing to pay tuition for their English lessons.

She set the glass on a side table. "I'm going to give Claudia a few days to get used to a different time zone before I take her shopping for clothes. We can't have her walking into Hampton looking like a ragamuffin."

Virgie laughed. "You are so damned bourgeoise Mavis. You always need to have the latest fashions and hairstyles."

Mavis also laughed. "Bite your tongue, Madame Virginia Bailey. I've seen photos of you wearing the latest French haute couture."

Running a hand over her hair, Virgie patted the twist on her nape. "I have a certain image to uphold. I'll go with you when you take Claudia shopping. I'm invited to a wedding a couple of weeks from now, and that's when I want to introduce her to some of my friends."

"Are you saying it will be like her coming-out?"

Virgie nodded slowly. "That's exactly what I'm saying. It's never too early to introduce her to Parisian society."

Claudia didn't know what to make of her roommate. Firstly, she had never shared a bedroom with another person. And secondly, she could never have predicted it would be someone like twenty-year-old Noelle Lesperance. As the daughter, and only child, of a financier and a dancer, Noelle was the epitome of a bohemian. Tall, rail-thin with raven-black hair and eyes, she'd played up her pale complexion with lots of dark eyeshadow, mascara, and ruby-red lipstick.

They really did not get to see much of each other during the day when Noelle rose early to socialize with her friends. She usually returned home at nightfall reeking of wine and cigarettes. She'd admitted that her father did not like her smoking, so she did it only when he or Virgie weren't around.

The spacious bedroom Claudia shared with Noelle was furnished with two canopy beds decorated in what she'd come to recognize as "toiles de Jouy" prints in blue and white solids, stripes, and checks. The bathroom was just as luxurious with a freestanding marble soaking tub and a heated floor set in twenty-four-inch squares of stone. She'd felt as if she had stepped back in time when touring the eighteenth-century private residence filled with priceless antiques collected by generations of Lesperances.

Noelle lay on her bed, watching Claudia hang up dresses, skirts, blouses, and slacks in an ornately carved armoire. Boxes of shoes were stacked on the floor next to a closet. "Have you decided what you're going to wear to the wedding tomorrow?"

Claudia glanced over her shoulder at her roommate. "Not yet."

"I think you should wear the floor-length black gown with the halter neckline."

"I was thinking the same, but I'm not certain whether I want to show that much skin."

Noelle scrambled off her bed. "Are you kidding? The dress looks wonderful on you. Everyone will think you're a Coco Chanel model."

Not quite. Claudia did not want to remind Noelle that Madame Chanel only used White models when hosting her fashion shows. Her aunts had taken her shopping to some of the finest boutiques in Paris where they'd spent hours selecting everything from underwear to formal dresses for her new wardrobe. She'd thought many of the garments were much too fancy to wear to class, and when she'd mentioned this to Mavis and Virgie, they'd replied that not only did she need to dress for success but also to impress. How was she going to attract a boy from a good family if she didn't dress the part. Aunt Mavis had given her a set of Samsonite luggage as a graduation gift, and her parents a brand-new typewriter for her to type her papers.

Claudia was looking forward to attending the wedding once Virgie announced it would be a Catholic nuptial mass, followed by a reception in the groom's seventeenth-century family château for 250 guests, which had been touted as the wedding of the season.

"Have you decided what you are going to wear?" she

asked Noelle. Earlier that morning Noelle had gone to a beauty salon where she'd had her straight hair permed and the result was a riot of loose curls framing her tiny, round face.

"Definitely not slacks or my father would have a heart attack. He complains that every time he sees me I'm wearing pants, and says if I turn out to be a lesbian like my mother, he will disown me."

"But he knows you like men."

"So did my mother before she married my father. I had just turned fourteen when I overheard them arguing because my mother was spending so much time with a woman in her dance troupe. Then, one day she packed her bags and left. A few years later he met your aunt and they've been together ever since."

Claudia walked to a chaise and sat down. "Do you like my aunt?"

Noelle lowered her eyes. "At first, I resented her because I kept thinking she was going to replace my mother, who I really love even if I don't approve of her lifestyle. But once I realized Virgie only wanted the best for me, I changed my attitude."

"Do you like my aunt?" Claudia repeated.

Noelle's head popped up. "I've grown to love her as if she were my aunt. I know she doesn't like it when I spend so much time away from home."

"What do you do when you're not here?"

"If I don't have classes, I meet my friends at various coffee-houses where we smoke, drink wine, and listen to poetry readings. Then, there are the jazz clubs that are popping up all over the city."

"Jazz is popular in the States, too, but a lot of young kids are listening to rock and roll. Even though everyone's talking about Elvis Presley, it was Chuck Berry who invented rock and roll."

"A lot of kids in the UK listen to rock and roll," Noelle

said. She moved over and sat at the foot of the chaise. "Would you mind if I asked you a personal question?"

Claudia gave Noelle a long, penetrating stare. "How personal?"

"Have you ever slept with a boy?"

Silence filled the bedroom as Claudia met Noelle's eyes. "No. Why?"

Noelle smiled. "I thought so."

"Why would you say that?"

"I've noticed men and boys staring at you and you seem to ignore them."

"That's because I'm not interested in any of them. Remember, I'm only going to be here for four more weeks. And that's not enough time for me to think about having a boyfriend."

"So, you do like men?"

Pinpoints of heat dotted Claudia's cheeks. "Of course, I like them. I'm only eighteen, and my focus right now is graduating college, not getting married or starting a family."

"I don't know if I'm ever going to marry, because I want to be able to come and go without answering to a husband. But marriage can only happen if I find a man willing to not place restrictions on me."

Claudia smiled. "Now you sound like my aunts when they say they don't want to be a man's property."

"And that's what we become once we're married. Even though French women have been given the right to vote, we are still fighting for equal political status afforded men."

Claudia didn't want to dredge up the discussion about rights—political or civil, because she would begin crying and not be able to stop. The photos in *Jet* magazine of the beaten and distorted face of Emmett Till lying in an open coffin had given her nightmares for months. The fourteen-year-old boy who had come from Chicago to visit relatives near Money, Mississippi, had been accused of whistling at a White woman, which led to his kidnapping and brutal murder by White men who had dumped his body in the Tallahatchie River.

Newspapers covered the murder trial in which an all-White jury found the two White men not guilty of murder after deliberating for a couple of hours. White Mississippians were angry because the northern press's interest in the case had spread throughout the country and had sparked outrage among Black communities nationwide.

"You're fighting for political equality, while as a Black woman living in America my fight is for equal rights under the law."

Noelle shook her head. "I don't want to talk about racism in America because I get upset."

"You get upset while I have to live it every day, Noelle."

"Have you thought about leaving the States and moving here like your aunt?"

"No. That's not a solution to the problem. To stand for justice, a person has to get involved. When Rosa Parks got arrested for refusing to give up her seat to a White man, the people of Montgomery decided to boycott all the buses."

"How long did the boycott last?"

"Thirteen months. People either walked to work or were picked up and driven by those with cars to get where they had to go. Black-owned taxi companies agreed to transport Blacks for the same fare they would pay on the bus—ten cents. Initially the Women's Political Council, an organization that began in the 1940s after dozens of Black people had been arrested on buses, had planned for a one-day boycott. But then the people voted unanimously to continue the boycott because they were sick and tired of the injustices that had been endured by thousands throughout the years. The result was the Supreme Court ruling that segregation on public transportation was illegal."

Noelle's eyes sparkled with excitement. "Oh, I would've loved to have seen that."

Claudia smiled. "The images were powerful and the economic impact of the boycott devastating for the city of Montgomery." She paused for several seconds. "Are you saying you would've been sympathetic to the boycott?"

"I'm going to tell you something, but you must swear that you won't repeat it to anyone. Not even your aunts."

"Is what you want to tell me going to make me upset?"

"I don't think it would because your aunt is my father's lover—or should I say mistress."

A beat passed. "You're seeing a Black man?"

"Yes. He's from Africa and is now a student at the Sorbonne," Noelle whispered.

"Is that who you sneak out at night to be with?"

"Yes." Two round red splotches appeared on Noelle's pale cheeks. "He's sharing a flat with another student who's there all the time, so we never have any privacy. We just lie in bed together talking about everything. He claims he wants to marry me and take me back to Benin with him, but I'm not certain whether I want to live in Africa."

"Is he willing to live in France?"

"He can't because he's a prince and is expected to return home after he finishes his studies to take his place among his people."

"But you would be a princess, Noelle," Claudia whispered. "You would be the wife of African royalty." She didn't want to believe that her new friend was dating an actual prince.

"I know, Claudia. But do you think his people would accept me?"

"They wouldn't have a choice. You'd be his wife."

"You're right, but I'm—"

"You're what?" Claudia asked when Noelle suddenly stopped talking.

"I'm still not certain whether I want to be any man's wife. Even if he's a prince."

"Do you love him, Noelle?"

She hesitated, then said, "I think I do."

"Then marry him and allow his family to become your family and vice versa. Not all men think of women as their property but as their partners. Just look at your father and my aunt. He allows her to live her life the way she chooses to. He may have given her this house as a gift, but it is her house and not his. She doesn't need his permission to invite people to come and stay, and I suppose if they were married it would be the same."

"Papa is different, Claudia. Even though *ma grand-mère* warned him not to marry my mother because she's a dancer, he decided to follow his heart because he was so in love with her. But in the end look how it turned out."

"It couldn't have been that bad, because they had you, Noelle."

A hint of a smile lifted the corners of Noelle's mouth. "You're right." Her smile vanished quickly. "I'll think about what you said about my prince."

"Now, I think it's time we get some sleep, so we'll look rested when we attend the wedding tomorrow."

Leaning forward, Noelle hugged Claudia. "I've always wanted a sister, and now I've found one."

Claudia returned the hug. "Thank you."

Chapter 11

He who says that he likes, hears what he does not like.

—Leonard Louis Levinson

"Don't turn around, Claudia, but there's a man who has been staring at you for a while."

Claudia took a sip of champagne, the cool liquid sliding smoothly down her throat. The first and only time she'd drunk champagne was the night her parents had taken her out to dinner to celebrate her becoming a woman and she hadn't liked the taste. But that changed the night her aunt set a glass at her place setting and everyone sitting around the table toasted her acceptance into college. She'd taken one sip and had become quite fond of the bubbly wine.

"Who is he?" she asked, not turning around.

She'd decided to wear the black halter dress covered with minute black beading that shimmered whenever it caught the light. The body-hugging garment with a generous front split showed off three inches of matching satin-covered pumps and her legs in sheer black nylons. A stylist had set her hair on large rollers and sat her under a dryer for what seemed hours. And when looking at her image in a mirror Claudia did not recognize herself. Luxurious waves floated around her face and shoulders and the resemblance between her and Sarah was remarkable, before the talented woman created a French-twisted ponytail. Her only jewelry was a pair of dangling onyx earrings.

"His name is Giancarlo Fortenza. He's very tall, very handsome, and extremely wealthy."

"He's Italian?"

"Yes," Noelle whispered.

"What is he doing here?" Claudia whispered back. She wanted to tell Noelle that her only interest in the man staring at her would be to practice her Italian.

"He's a friend of the groom. Don't move! He's coming this way."

Claudia took another sip of champagne at the same time she detected the subtle scent of a man's cologne that was a tantalizing combination of citrus and amber. She stared over her shoulder at a man whose face could've been the model for Michelangelo's *David*. When she did turn around, Claudia couldn't pull her gaze away from his thick, wavy blond hair and large, dark green eyes under sweeping light brown eyebrows.

"*Mademoiselle Lesperance. Pourriez-vous me presenter à votre amie?*"

Claudia bit back a smile. He spoke French with an Italian accent.

Noelle rested a hand on Claudia's bare shoulder. "Giancarlo, I'd like you to meet Claudia Patterson. Claudia, Giancarlo Fortenza."

Claudia extended her free hand, smiling. "*È un piacere conoscerti, Signore Fortenza.*"

Giancarlo's eyebrows lifted slightly as he took her hand, cradling it gently in his larger one. "You speak Italian?" he asked in English.

"Not enough," she said in the same language. He smiled; the expression so sensual that it took Claudia's breath away. He'd angled his head and stared at her under lowered lids.

She'd had scant interaction with the opposite sex once she'd enrolled in the all-girls school in Biloxi and she knew instinctually the man holding her hand was older and more worldly than the ones she would encounter in college.

"And I don't speak enough English. We can help each other," he continued, this time in Italian. "I can tutor you in my language and you can help me with my English."

Claudia felt Giancarlo's nearness disturbing and exciting at the same time. She was flattered by his interest in her, but also frightened because reminders of what she had experienced with Denny Clark were never far from her mind. And while Giancarlo was everything Denny wasn't, he was still a White man—albeit a foreign White man, and she wasn't mature or worldly enough to know the difference.

"I don't know, Signore Fortenza."

"Would it make you feel more comfortable if I asked your aunt?"

Now she was shocked. "You know my aunt?"

Giancarlo released her hand. "Yes. Virgie has invited me to her home on several occasions."

Suddenly Claudia wondered if he'd asked her aunt about her before his introduction, and if Virgie had approved of him approaching her niece. *What harm could there be?* she thought, if Virginia Bailey gave her consent that they could spend time together.

"Perhaps you can call on my aunt and let her know when a time is conducive for both of us to meet."

Giancarlo smiled, exhibiting a mouth filled with even white teeth. "*Merci, mademoiselle.* Will you save me a dance?"

Claudia inclined her head, watching as he walked. Putting the flute to her lips, she drained the glass.

"That went well," Noelle whispered in her ear.

She met the smiling black eyes. "You think?" Noelle was resplendent in all black: sheath dress with a peplum jacket, heels, and a small cloche with a veil.

"Of course, I'm not kidding. The man belongs to one of

the richest families in Italy. Their wealth comes from designing and building sports cars for those with enough money and willing to spend thousands of dollars on a superfast car like a Ferrari."

"I'm not interested in Giancarlo or his wealth. I just need to practice my Italian."

"I've known him to be quite charming."

"If he's that charming, why aren't you interested in him?"

"He's not my type, Claudia."

"And Giancarlo isn't my type."

"You don't like White men?"

"It's not that I don't like them. I just prefer men of my own race." Claudia wanted to tell Noelle that White men in certain regions of the United States were not only racist but evil. That they hung and burned Black people for sport. That they had no qualms when in 1921 they burned down Greenwood, a black neighborhood of Tulsa, Oklahoma, that had become known as the Tulsa Race Massacre.

She had no intention of getting into a debate with Noelle about the injustices which Black people have endured since the advent of slavery in America, despite laws written into the Constitution giving them rights equal to Whites. She'd found the conversations depressing *and* exhausting.

The wedding reception began with cocktails and delicious hors d'oeuvres in the château's courtyard and was then followed by a sit-down dinner in the grand ballroom comparable to the banquets presided over by centuries-old French aristocracy. Hundreds of waitstaff worked efficiently to serve and remove each course as if it had been choreographed in advance. Claudia couldn't identify many of the items on her plate, but salade Lyonnaise, potatoes dauphinoise and salmon en papillote had become favorites.

She'd been seated opposite Giancarlo, and she wondered if the place cards had been assigned in advance or if he had used his influence with the groom to seat him opposite her.

She acknowledged him with a barely perceptible nod before focusing her attention on the young man seated on her right who'd introduced himself to her as a cousin of the groom. He'd admitted that her aunt had tutored the groom and many in his family in English.

When Giancarlo saw the beautiful American girl enter the château courtyard he'd felt as if someone had grabbed his chest and squeezed his heart until it was impossible for him to breathe. There was something so refreshing about her natural beauty that he could not take his eyes off her. She didn't walk but glided over the cobblestones as she gestured gracefully with her hands when talking to Virginia Bailey. He'd sent up a prayer of thanks because he'd been a guest of Virgie's the last two times he'd taken holiday in Paris. She was known for opening her home on Sunday afternoons for those in the arts. The first time he'd come with his then-friend and now the groom, Jean D'Arcy, who'd introduced Madame Bailey as his English instructor.

Giancarlo had found the gatherings intellectually spirited, as those in attendance debated religion, politics, music, art, and how quickly the world was growing smaller because of many scientific advances. Virgie was a gracious and generous hostess and he'd looked forward to attending her salon with and without Jean.

When he'd asked Virgie if he could dance with her niece, she'd hesitated and then gave her consent. But she had also warned him that she was different from the other women he'd been seen with in Paris, and if she suspected he planned to take advantage of her innocence, then she would make certain he would never see her again.

Although her threat irked him, Giancarlo did not want to believe he would do something to Claudia that would bring shame on her. There were enough women in his life to amuse himself with that he didn't need to seduce a virgin. Despite being enamored of her, Giancarlo realized at thirty not only was he too old, but much too jaded for Claudia. She would help him improve his limited English while he would do the same with her Italian.

The wedding couple had planned for a band to play after the dinner concluded and Claudia found herself in Giancarlo's arms when the sextet played the popular international hit, "Volare," sung by Domenico Modugno. She'd never danced with a man before and felt as if she were floating on air when she followed his strong lead as he spun her around and around on the marble floor.

"You know this song?" Giancarlo asked, his mouth pressed to her ear.

"Everyone in the States knows this song," she said, smiling.

"Are you saying they all speak Italian?"

Claudia laughed softly. "No. But they are familiar with the lyrics even if they don't understand the words."

"Your Italian is incredibly good. Who taught you?"

"My aunt Mavis. She speaks French, Italian, and Spanish."

"And you?"

"I speak all three, but Spanish is my weakest. If I hadn't come to France this summer, I would've visited Cuba or even Puerto Rico."

"I'm glad you didn't, because I never would've been given the opportunity to meet someone like you."

"Why me, Giancarlo, when you could have any woman you want in Paris?" Claudia felt his fingers tighten on her waist, and she wondered if she'd gone too far in judging him.

"Come with me so we can talk without others eavesdropping on our conversation."

Claudia panicked. Where was he taking her? And why? Suddenly she cursed her inexperience when it came to interacting with a man, and she also cursed Mavis for shielding her from what young women her age should've been exposed to. She had never attended a school dance or a party with boys in attendance. She'd never even had a date.

"Where are we going?" she said to Giancarlo, as he led her across the crowded ballroom.

"Out to the courtyard."

She was able to breathe easier now that she knew they wouldn't be completely alone. "What do you want to talk about?"

Increasing his hold on her hand, Giancarlo led her down a long hallway and through a door to the courtyard. There were a number of people standing around in small groups, and others seated at tables topped with lanterns with lighted candles. He stopped in a dimly lit corner where they were afforded complete privacy.

"Us, Claudia."

She tried making out his expression in the waning daylight. "What about us?"

"Do you actually believe I would treat you like other women I know?"

She blinked slowly. "I don't know. You tell me, Giancarlo."

"No, I wouldn't. You're no more than a child—"

"I'm eighteen, and definitely not a child!" she said, interrupting him.

He exhaled an audible sigh. "Okay, I'll admit you're not a child, but you're not experienced in the ways of the world, *bella*, and because you're not I would never take advantage of you."

Claudia wanted to ignore his calling her *beautiful* in Italian, but the truth was she did feel beautiful with him. Everything about Giancarlo Fortenza made her aware of him as a man. She'd discovered he was the first man who made her heart beat a little too fast whenever he stared at her. And he also was the first man to hold her against his body, where she'd become aware of the acute differences between them. It was nothing like when Denny had grabbed her and attempted to kiss her. When Giancarlo cradled her in his arms, she'd felt safe—protected, yet something wouldn't permit her to let down her guard to feel completely comfortable with him.

"Thank you for letting me know that."

He laughed softly. "There's no need to thank me, Claudia. What I want is for you to trust me. Can you do that?"

She nodded. "Yes."

Dipping his head, he kissed her cheek. "Good. Now, let's go back and join the others before your aunts send out a firing squad."

Their meeting in the château courtyard had become the foundation for Claudia's relationship with Giancarlo. He arrived at Virgie's midmorning, and they would spend the day touring the city and stopping to linger at cafés. She'd grown fond of eating freshly baked baguettes with a variety of cheeses and drinking endless cups of French roast coffee made from freshly ground beans and on occasion espresso, which she'd discovered offset fatigue, while Giancarlo favored sparkling water and red wine. They alternated days speaking entirely in Italian and then in English. Then, every once in a while, they would lapse into French—the language Claudia felt most comfortable speaking.

Two weeks before she was scheduled to depart, Giancarlo said he wanted to take her to dinner at Le Relais Plaza, located in the Hôtel Plaza Athénée, where he'd always stayed when on holiday in Paris. When he'd hinted that designers Yves Saint Laurent and Christian Dior frequented the restaurant and would also send their models to eat there to show off their latest fashion designs, Claudia quickly agreed because she'd become obsessed with French fashion.

When she woke the next day, the housekeeper informed Claudia that her aunts were on their way to Bordeaux to buy wine to restock Virgie's celebrated collection of Sauternes, which were fantastic sipping wines and accompaniments to cheese, foie gras, tropical fruit, and caramel-based desserts.

She scribbled a note to Virgie and Mavis, informing them she was having dinner with Giancarlo if they returned home before she did.

Noelle helped her select an outfit that was appropriate for dining in one of Paris's finest restaurants. It was an off-the-shoulder, black-and-white silk dress, with a wide skirt ending several inches below her knees. There had been rumors in the world of fashion that designers were talking about raising the hemlines of women's skirts and dresses, but for now it was only a rumor.

Claudia still hadn't decided to cut her hair, like so many women were doing, although whenever she visited a salon, she had the stylist cut an inch off the ends until she worked up enough courage to wear a pixie cut. She'd just put the finishing touches on her makeup when Ingrid knocked lightly on the bedroom door to let her know Giancarlo had arrived and wanted her to have something. She handed Claudia a colorful shopping bag.

"*Merci, Ingrid. S'il vous plaît, faites-lui savoir que je viens.*"

"You're telling Ingrid to let him know you're coming when you haven't done your hair," Noelle said. She slipped off her bed. "What's in the bag?"

Claudia gave Noelle the bag. "Open it for me."

"*Merde, merde, merde!*" Noelle repeated over and over.

"What are you shitting about?"

"Come and see."

Claudia took the black velvet case from Noelle unable to stifle a gasp when she saw a pair of pearl earrings suspended from a cluster of diamonds and a strand of perfectly matched pearls with a diamond-encrusted clasp. "Oh, sweet heaven," she whispered.

Noelle removed the earrings. "Pull your hair back so I can put these in your ears."

"No!"

"Yes, Claudia. Grow the hell up! The man gives you a gift

and you don't want to accept it. What happened to being gracious?"

"But why, Noelle, would he buy me something so expensive?"

"Because he can, Claudia. I told you before the man is wealthy, so what he paid for these pearls will not make him a pauper. You said before that he's been a perfect gentleman, so he's not expecting you to open your legs for him because he's given you a gift. That is something he can get from a lot of other women."

Claudia knew Noelle was right. Not at any time had Giancarlo intimated that he wanted or expected more from her than friendship. Pushing back her hair, she let Noelle put the earrings in her pierced lobes. "Please hand me the brush so I can put my hair up." She styled her hair in a twist, and when she turned her head the light from the lamp on the dressing table fired the diamonds in her ears.

Noelle crossed her arms under her breasts. "Now you look like a femme fatale."

Claudia shook her head. "Not really." Even with her limited experience, she knew it wasn't in her personality to become involved with a man for money. Giancarlo's wealth wasn't why she'd continued to see him, because in another two weeks he would become someone she'd met while on holiday in Paris.

Giancarlo stared across the table, unable to believe Claudia had improved on perfection. He'd thought her flawless at Jean D'Arcy's wedding, but tonight was different, and it wasn't because she was wearing his gift. Everything about her silently screamed unabashed sexiness, from her bared silken shoulders to her full lips outlined in red lipstick that made him feel like a voyeur whenever their eyes met. And it wasn't for the first time that he wished he weren't thirty and she eighteen. If she had been older, and more experienced, their relationship would have been different. There were occasions when Claudia appeared much older whenever she talked about world events and what she wanted for her future, while he had to constantly remind himself of Virgie's warning about her innocence—which he'd translated into her still being a virgin. She'd demurely lowered her eyes when thanking him for the pearls, the gesture both charming and sensual.

"Are you certain you don't want another glass of champagne?"

Claudia smiled. "Very certain. I limit myself to two glasses, because I don't want to feel light-headed."

Giancarlo stared at the design on the handle of the knife beside his plate. If Claudia had been any other woman, he would've invited her up to his hotel suite and made love to her. Never had he forgotten that she wasn't any woman, but the niece of someone of whom he'd become quite fond.

"Do you want me to take you back home now?" They'd spent more than two hours at the restaurant.

Claudia gave him a dreamy smile. "No. I'd like to stay out a little longer. My aunts drove down to Bordeaux, and I left them a note telling them I was going out to dinner with you."

"Bordeaux is a long drive from here. When did they leave?"

"Ingrid said they left around eight this morning."

Giancarlo quickly calculated how long it would take them to drive there and back to Paris. The trip was estimated to take half a day. "If you're not ready to go home, then would you like to visit a jazz club?"

"Yes!"

Giancarlo hid a smile. These were the times when he found Claudia's childlike enthusiasm utterly delightful. He signaled for their waiter, signed the check, then rounded the table to assist her to stand. Curving an arm around her waist, he escorted her to where he'd parked his car. The sports car was the latest prototype a team of engineers had designed for Fortenza Motors, the company founded by his grandfather and uncles. He'd driven the car from Rome to Paris, and it had passed the test when he'd accelerated on straight roads and decelerated around winding curves without it shimmying or stalling out. His father hadn't determined a selling price, but Giancarlo was certain once it was advertised orders would begin to come in.

As she strolled along the path overlooking the Seine, arm in arm with Giancarlo, Claudia realized she'd fallen in love with the City of Lights. She'd shared dinner with him at one of the finest restaurants in Paris, renowned for well executed French classic dishes and excellent service, and had noticed Giancarlo was treated with deference not afforded some of the other diners, because he was a guest in the hotel.

He'd driven past a seedier section of the city populated by several underground clubs—some with questionable reputations, and she'd had her first glimpse of prostitutes enticing men to come and have a good time, and those addicted to drugs either stumbling or sleeping in alleys—to a brightly lit neighborhood with flashing neon lights and a string of outdoor cafés. Giancarlo had parked along a side street and minutes later a man came out from one of the buildings to drive the car into a carriage house where it couldn't be stolen or vandalized.

It was her first time visiting a jazz club and Claudia found herself caught up in the music as a few musicians played set after set, only stopping when someone new joined in. The place was dark and smoky, but the assembly didn't mind as they bobbed heads, tapped feet, and shouted in abandon when a riff went on for several minutes.

It was after midnight when they left the club, and for the first time in hours she was able to breathe air not filled with the smell of cigars, cigarettes, and what Giancarlo told her was marijuana. Heroin and opium were illegal in France, but that didn't stop people from abusing them.

Giancarlo dropped his arm and placed it around Claudia's waist. "Should I assume that you've enjoyed yourself tonight?"

Smiling, she rested her head on his shoulder. "You assume correctly. This is the most fun I've had since coming here."

Turning his head slightly, he pressed a kiss on her hair. "Are you ready to do it again tomorrow night?"

"Yes. What have you planned for us?"

"What about a dinner party on a yacht?"

"I don't know, Giancarlo."

He gave her a sidelong glance. "Why not?"

"I get seasick."

Giancarlo wanted to tell Claudia he was looking forward to spending time with her in a more intimate setting than a restaurant, but watching her reaction at the jazz club was a reminder that not only was she young but she had been sheltered, when she'd shyly admitted that he was the first man she'd ever danced with.

"How would you like to go to the Folies Bergère?"

Claudia looked up at him. "Isn't that where Josephine Baker performed her famous, or should I say infamous, banana dance?"

Illumination from a streetlamp bathed her delicate features, and Giancarlo couldn't pull his gaze away from her expression reminiscent of children on Christmas Day seeing wrapped presents under the Christmas tree. There were times when he found Claudia so childlike, but it wasn't the same when he attempted to imagine what she would look like lying naked in his bed. Whenever those images flooded his mind he got an erection, and rather than masturbate he'd lie on his belly and wait for it to go down as he fantasized making love to her.

"Sì, bella."

Rising on tiptoes, Claudia pressed a kiss under his ear. "What time should I be ready?"

Giancarlo turned his head until their mouths were mere

inches apart. "Seven," he whispered before lowering his head and brushing his mouth over hers. Her lips parted and he deepened the kiss, then quickly ended it once he realized what he was doing. "I'm sorry," he apologized in English.

Claudia smiled. "I'm not, Giancarlo. It felt nice."

He wanted to tell Claudia that it had felt nice to her, but it was agony for him. He didn't want to kiss just her mouth but her entire body from her hair to the soles of her feet. Giancarlo felt the flesh between his thighs swelling and he knew he had to get Claudia home before he did something that would prove disastrous for them both.

"It's time I take you home."

No words were exchanged during the ride to Virgie's house. The front door opened when Giancarlo got out to help Claudia from the sports car. And from the expression on Virginia Bailey's face, he knew she wasn't pleased to see him.

Virgie forced a plastic smile. "You look nice, Claudia."

Claudia nodded. "Thank you, Auntie."

"It's time you go upstairs and get ready for bed. Giancarlo, I'd like to talk to you."

He watched Claudia walk away, then pulled back his shoulders when he saw Virgie's mask of stone. "I didn't touch her."

"It doesn't matter if you did or you didn't, Giancarlo. When I gave you permission to take my niece out, it didn't mean you could keep her out all night."

"I took her to dinner, and then to a jazz club."

"I don't give a damn if you took her to midnight mass. I shouldn't have had to spell out that I didn't want you to take her to places that you take other women whenever you're here on holiday."

"What exactly are you saying, Virgie?"

"I'm saying you are no longer welcome in my home, and this is the last time you will see my niece."

Giancarlo nodded. *"Bonne nuit et au revoir."* Not waiting for a reply from Virgie, he turned on his heel and walked back to his car. He'd wanted to tell the woman that her need to protect her niece was stifling the young woman's emotional growth. There would come a time when Claudia would meet a man and she would have to make her own decision whether she wanted more than friendship.

Claudia found an envelope with her name written on it next to her plate when she came down for breakfast. She'd overslept—again. That was something she hadn't done in the States. The night before, she had taken a warm bath before getting into bed, yet she hadn't been able to fall asleep. Her mind was a maelstrom of images of what she'd shared with Giancarlo. She'd put his exquisite gift in the velvet case and stored it in a drawer in the armoire for safekeeping after vacillating about whether to show her aunts what Giancarlo had given her or keep it from them, because she suspected they would want her to return it. And that was something she didn't want to do.

Instinct told Claudia that her aunts really didn't approve of her going out with Giancarlo, but he hadn't done anything untoward to besmirch her reputation as their virgin niece. Claudia still could not understand why they'd sought to keep her chaste while both had had lovers. Only Sarah had married and was faithful to her husband.

What the Bailey women failed to understand is that Claudia wasn't completely ignorant when it came to sex. She hadn't slept with a man, but she did know what to do to prevent an unplanned pregnancy. There were several books in Mavis's extensive library on human sexuality and Claudia had read all of them from cover to cover. Articles in medical journals documented trials for an oral contraceptive pill being tested on more than eight hundred women in Puerto Rico, while condoms for men and diaphragms for women were also available to prevent pregnancy.

She wasn't ready to engage in sexual relations, but she did want to be ready and prepared if and whenever it occurred.

And she did have urges. They came and went without warning, and more strongly on days before the onset of her menstrual cycle. Her breasts were fuller and sensitive to the touch, and the throbbing sensation between her legs was so pleasurable that she had to bite her lip to keep from moaning aloud.

"*Merci*, Margit," she said, smiling when Virgie's cook filled a fragile hand-painted cup with steaming black coffee.

"Will mademoiselle like an omelet this morning?"

"Yes, please." She picked up the envelope and removed the notecard:

> *I'm sorry I can't meet you tonight because I must return to Italy on business. I will never forget your beauty, wonderful laugh, or our engaging conversations. Wishing you much success in college*
> *Fondly,*
> *Giancarlo Pasquale Fortenza.*

Claudia didn't know why but she felt like crying. She had two more weeks in France and her friend was gone. She reread the note, then replaced it in the envelope.

"Are you all right?" Virgie asked, as she entered the dining room.

Claudia nodded as she forced a smile. "Yes."

"Someone delivered that for you earlier this morning."

She tucked the envelope under the neatly folded linen napkin. "It's a note from Giancarlo. He says he must return to Italy for business."

Virgie sat down opposite Claudia. "I'm surprised he stayed this long. He usually comes for a couple of weeks before going back."

Claudia met her aunt's gray eyes. "I'm going to miss him."

"And I'm certain he's going to miss you, too." Picking up

her napkin, Virgie spread it over her lap. "Are you ready for your next big adventure as a college student?"

"Yes." And she was. Claudia was looking forward to freshman orientation and discovering with whom she would be sharing a dorm. Sleeping in the same bedroom with Noelle would make it easier to share the same space with another woman.

Chapter 12

A friend is someone who makes me feel totally acceptable.

—Ene Riisna

Claudia felt overwhelmed when she saw the number of incoming Black girls and boys with their families as they unloaded cars and trucks with suitcases and boxes before making their way to the buildings where they would spend ten months of their lives as Hampton Institute students.

She'd received her acceptance letter with a map of the buildings that made up the campus. She had also written down the courses she wanted to take during her first semester, hoping she wouldn't be closed out of any of them and be forced to substitute something she didn't want.

Her parents had come to Biloxi to drive her to Virginia, while her grandmother had remained behind in Freedom because she hadn't been feeling well. Mavis had tucked an envelope into the pocket of her jeans, whispering that it was a little something extra in the event of an emergency. Her aunt had given her two hundred dollars. Claudia couldn't imagine what that emergency could be because her father had set up a bank account in her name at a Virginia bank for whenever she needed spending money. She knew her parents had continued to put aside money from their businesses for her education, and Claudia had promised herself that she would work hard to make them proud of her.

She found her dorm room and walked in to find a slender girl wearing glasses staring back at her. She set down the Pullman and the case with her typewriter and smiled. "I'm Claudia Patterson by way of Biloxi, Mississippi. The roster says we're going to be roomies."

"I'm Yvonne Chapman from Harlem, New York City."

Claudia's eyebrows lifted. "Are you certain you're ready for White this and Colored that down here?"

"Now you sound like my father. He said the same thing to my brother, who is currently enrolled at Howard."

"Did I hear someone mention my name?" asked a deep voice behind Claudia.

She turned to find a tall man with the same nut-brown complexion as Yvonne. His dark eyes sparkled like polished onyx. Muscles in his biceps bulged under a short-sleeve white shirt as he cradled a steamer trunk to his chest.

"Claudia, I'd like you to meet my brother, Dennis Chapman."

Dennis carried the trunk across the room and set it down next to one of the beds, then extended his hand. "It's a pleasure to meet you, Claudia."

She took his hand, smiling. "I'm Claudia Patterson and the pleasure is all mine, Dennis."

"I take it you're from down here."

"Mississippi."

Dennis whistled softly under his breath. "There's always a lot of shit going on in Mississippi," he said under his breath.

"My brother is studying to be a civil rights lawyer. He claims he wants to be another Thurgood Marshall."

"He couldn't have selected another better role model," Claudia said.

Dennis winked at her. "I like the way you think, Claudia."

"Which side of the room do you want?" Yvonne asked.

"It doesn't matter. You got here first, so you can pick whatever you want."

Yvonne pointed to the Pullman. "Is that all you're bringing?"

Claudia shook her head. "No. My parents are bringing the rest of my stuff." The words were barely off her lips when Earl and Sarah walked in, carrying garment bags and large satchels.

She introduced Yvonne and Dennis to her parents, refusing their assistance in helping her get settled. She had two days before the scheduled freshman orientation, and she planned to take that time to become acquainted with her roommate and the layout of the campus. Claudia noticed tears in her mother's eyes as she kissed her, while her father gathered her close and whispered that he loved her. They were there, then they were gone, and she struggled not to break down because she was truly alone for the first time in her life. She was eighteen, physically a woman but emotionally still a child. Four years. That's how long it would take for Claudia to mature into the woman she wanted to become before earning a degree and taking her place in the world.

It had taken Claudia and Yvonne a couple of hours to put away their clothes and rearrange the furniture in the room to turn it into a comfortable living space with family photographs and favorite items from their childhood.

"You're going to be one of the best-dressed girls on campus, Claudia," Yvonne said as she stared at the skirts, slacks, blouses, dresses, and shoes that had been purchased in Parisian boutiques.

"They are gifts from my aunts when we spent several weeks in France," she explained.

Yvonne stared with wide eyes behind the lenses of her glasses. "You've been abroad?"

"Yes. It was a graduation gift. I was in France for six weeks."

"What are they going to give you once you graduate college?" Yvonne asked, smiling. "An around-the-world cruise?"

Claudia laughed. "No. If I want to travel after that, then it will be on my own."

"Did you fly to Europe?"

"No. We took an ocean liner. I was sick as a dog going, but somehow, I wasn't bothered with seasickness on the return trip."

Yvonne shook her head. "I'm afraid of heights, so you'll never see me on an airplane. Cars, buses, and trains will be my only mode of transportation. How was it living there for six weeks?"

"Incredible. I must confess that it took a few days to get used to that, as a Black woman, I could go anywhere I wanted without being denied access to shops and restaurants because of my race."

"Did you have a problem with the language?"

"No, because I speak French, Italian, and Spanish."

"You're kidding?"

"No, I am not, Yvonne." Claudia glanced at her watch. "Let's go and get some dinner and when we come back, I'll tell you all about my European adventure."

If Noelle had called Claudia the sister she never had, then it was the same for Claudia and Yvonne. They had bonded so quickly that they'd become inseparable when they weren't sharing the same courses. The weeks passed quickly and in-between going to class, studying for exams, and typing papers, she spent her Sunday evenings writing letters to her parents, grandmother, and her aunts.

Writing had become a source of therapy for Claudia, where she was able put on paper what she couldn't say in person. She wrote letters in French to Virgie, and alternated writing in Italian, French, and Spanish to Mavis. Her Aunt Mavis would return her letters with corrections marked with a red pencil. She'd smiled when she received a letter with only one or two corrections along with a letter grade. The ability to read and write in the language was as important as the ability to speak it.

One weekend in late October, Yvonne invited her to accompany her to Washington, D.C., for a Halloween party that was to be held near the campus of Howard University. Claudia agreed, because she was looking forward to spending time in the nation's capital and meeting students from another Black college. Especially one as prestigious as Howard.

"Are we going to check into a hotel?"

Yvonne's hand stilled from straightening her shoulder-length coarse black hair. "Listen to you, Miss Southern Belle. No, we're going to stay in an off-campus house that my brother and his friends are renting. Dennis says he'll give us his bedroom and he'll bunk on the sofa."

Claudia couldn't ignore the wave of heat suffusing her face. Every once in a while, Yvonne would chide her about being spoiled, when it was the furthest from the truth. Her parents weren't rich, in fact by normal income standards for the country they would fall into the poverty-level category. They owned and operated businesses that provided a service, and that meant they would have to depend on customers willing to avail themselves of their services.

"You're letting that comb get too hot, Yvonne. You need to let it cool a little bit before pulling it through your hair."

"My arm gets tired when I must go over my hair more than once. And what do you know about straightening hair?"

Claudia unfolded her legs and walked over to where Yvonne had plugged in a small electric stove and picked up the comb. "My mother owns a beauty parlor. And I've seen her straighten and curl enough hair to be able to do yours."

"Really?"

"Yes really, Yvonne. Just sit still and let me take care of your hair."

Claudia parted and braided her roommate's hair in sections as she applied a small portion of hair pomade to her scalp. She heated the comb, placed it in on a damp cloth to cool, then pulled it through Yvonne's hair. A half hour later Yvonne's hair lay on her shoulders in strands that resembled a wig.

Yvonne combed her fingers through the shiny black strands. "You sure didn't lie about knowing how to do hair. Once the word gets out that you can do hair, girls will be lining up outside the door for you to do theirs."

"Oh no, Yvonne. If you say a mumbling word to anyone about me doing your hair, this will be the first and last time I'll do yours."

Yvonne pantomimed zipping her lips. "My lips are sealed."

Claudia couldn't afford to take time out of her busy schedule to do the hair of other students. However, if her financial status had been different, it would've been a consideration. Her parents had paid the tuition for her freshman year, and her grandmother had set aside funds for her sophomore year, and her aunts Mavis and Virgie had pledged to cover the junior and senior years.

Both of Yvonne's parents were college graduates. Her father taught math and science in a specialized Bronx, New York high school, and her mother was a social worker who was employed by a New York City agency advocating for single women and their children. Yvonne had enrolled in Hampton as a science major with a goal to become a dentist.

"Do we have to wear costumes for the Halloween party?"

Yvonne shook her head. "Costumes are optional."

"Will this be your first party at Howard?"

"I came down last year for Homecoming and it was nonstop partying. Dennis panicked when I told him I was thinking of applying to Howard."

"Why would he panic?" Claudia asked.

"You don't have any brothers, so you wouldn't know they don't want their sisters to see them do things they shouldn't be doing."

"Does your brother have a girlfriend?"

"Yes. He's been going out with a girl who will graduate Spelman next year. Dennis has been talking about giving her a ring for Christmas, and the last time I spoke to Gwendolyn she claimed she's ready to become a lawyer's wife. What I had to remind her was that Dennis must finish up his senior year before enrolling in Howard Law. And that adds up to another four years."

"It's not going to be easy for him to support a wife if he's still student."

"I agree, Claudia. Wendy, as she likes to be called, is used to getting whatever she wants. Her parents have indulged her, and when I told her that she should wait until Dennis graduates law school before they marry, she claimed she doesn't want to wait that long. And that her parents are willing to financially support them until Dennis graduates and passes the bar."

Claudia whistled softly under her breath. "Indulged or not. It looks as if your future sister-in-law is afraid of losing her man."

"I tried to tell Dennis that she's too clingy, but he likes all the attention. Personally, I would find it smothering to have a man in my face all day, every day."

Claudia recalled what she had shared with Giancarlo when they did see each other every day over several weeks, and never during that time had she felt smothered or overwhelmed by his presence. And if she were honest, she would admit that she missed him; missed his occasional bungling of English words or colloquialisms and his patience when he corrected her Italian. Claudia wore the pearls Giancarlo had given her the morning she and her aunt boarded the ship to return to the States. Mavis smiled and nodded, silently signaling her approval. The earrings and necklace were currently in a safe deposit box at a bank where Mavis kept her other valuables. Mavis had also added Claudia's name to the account.

"Do you have a boyfriend waiting for you back in Mississippi?" Yvonne asked Claudia.

"No, because I've never had a boyfriend."

Yvonne gave her an incredulous stare. "You're shitting me, aren't you?"

"No, I'm not. I told you I'd transferred from a school in Freedom to an all-girls high school in Biloxi."

"Are you interested in meeting someone?"

Claudia wasn't opposed to going out with someone, but only if it did not interfere with her studies. "Who are you talking about?"

"His name is Robert Moore and he's one of my brother's roommates, and he is also a pre-law student."

She smiled. "I wouldn't mind meeting him as long as he's nice."

"He's more than nice, Claudia. He's shy, and I think he is a good guy who will not take advantage of a woman."

"He sounds wonderful. But can you answer one question for me."

"What?"

"Why haven't you gone after him?"

Yvonne laughed. "I can't because he's my first cousin."

A smile spread across Claudia's features. "That answers my question." Suddenly buoyed with the anticipation of going to Washington, D.C., and meeting Yvonne's cousin, her first thought was about what she would wear. Most of the girls at Hampton wore shirtwaist dresses to class, or straight skirts with sweater twinsets and loafers, and favored pants during the weekends.

She and Yvonne rarely left campus, and if they did it was to take a taxi to the Black neighborhoods in Hampton, where they could eat and sit anywhere they wanted. Claudia knew it hadn't been easy for Yvonne to become accustomed to segregation when she saw the WHITES ONLY and COLORED ONLY signs. She'd curse under her breath while damning all the racists to hell.

Claudia knew it would take time for the veil of segregation to fall, and that would only be achieved through the courts. Black colleges with law schools were graduating brilliant young lawyers who had taken up the cause for civil and equal rights for all citizens. She hoped Robert Moore would become one of many champions for freedom.

Chapter 13

True love begins when nothing is looked for in return.
—Antoine de Saint-Exupéry, *The Wisdom of the Sands*

I'm going to marry this girl. The thought popped into Robert Moore's head the day after he'd been introduced to his cousin's roommate, because Claudia Patterson possessed many of the qualities he'd been looking for in a woman since enrolling at Howard University. She was beautiful, poised, intelligent, confident, and she wasn't a party girl. He'd discovered that many female students who'd left home for the first time to experience total freedom tended to overdo it when their weekends began on Fridays and didn't end until Monday morning.

Robert gave Claudia a sidelong glance as he reached for her right hand and threaded their fingers together. Earlier that morning he'd invited her to walk with him through historic neighborhoods in the nation's capital, designed by architect Pierre Charles L'Enfant, and she'd accepted his offer.

"Something tells me you're not having a good time."

Claudia turned to look at him. "Why would you say that?"

"You looked lost at the party and right now you appear as if you'd rather be somewhere else. You hardly danced with anyone last night, and you spent more time outside the frat house than inside."

Claudia stopped walking, facing him. "It was my first house party and I found it too loud, too smoky, and I was sick of men who'd had too much to drink and tried to feel me up. But I do want to thank you for rescuing me when that boy began grinding on me."

"It was either rescue you or he would've faced the consequences for disrespecting you."

"I'm glad you did because I don't like violence."

"It wouldn't have come to that, Claudia. All I had to do was to tell a couple of the brothers what he'd been doing to you, and they would've escorted him outside with a warning to stay out and never come back. There are always some who act a fool because they've had too much to drink, but we draw the line when it comes to assaulting or disrespecting our women. There's no way I'd want you to go back to Hampton and spread the word that Howard brothers are dogs."

Claudia smiled, bringing Robert's gaze to linger on her parted lips. The night before, she'd worn a light cover of makeup, but this morning with her bare face and her hair styled in a ponytail she appeared so much younger than eighteen. "There are always a few bad apples in every bunch."

"Is yours-truly included in the bad bunch?"

"No, Robert. You are one of the good ones."

He brought her hand to his mouth and kissed the back of it. "Thank you."

Claudia wanted to tell Robert there was no need to thank her. She'd felt something she could not identify when Yvonne had introduced her to her cousin. There was nothing in his appearance that indicated he, Yvonne, and Dennis were first cousins. The only thing they shared were their complexions; however, Robert's features were more refined, and he'd lacked

Dennis's height and musculature. Yvonne had mentioned he was shy, and Claudia had caught glimpses of that whenever he failed to meet her eyes.

"What made you decide to attend Howard?" she asked.

"It was the only Black college in the South that I applied to."

"You were so certain you were going to be accepted at Howard that you didn't apply to any other college?" He nodded. "And if you hadn't been accepted?"

He lifted his shoulders under a navy-blue sweater. "I would have attended a college in New York City and after graduating then I would've applied to Howard Law."

"Did your decision to attend Howard have anything to do with Dennis becoming a student here?"

Robert stared at the tips of a pair of black and white high-top sneakers as they began walking again. "No. Dennis and I were enrolled at the same time because I'd graduated high school a year early. I'll be twenty by the time I start law school."

"That's young, Robert." She paused, smiling. "You're the first genius I've ever met."

"I'm hardly a genius, Claudia. When you have a mother who is a schoolteacher, you know you can't slack off."

"I know exactly what you're talking about. My aunts are schoolteachers, and one would get on me about not working up to my potential."

"Are you?" Robert asked.

"Yes. I've made the decision not to pledge a sorority because I fear it would interfere with my studies."

"I feel the same about pledging a fraternity, even though I'm friends with a lot of the frat brothers. Yvonne told me you speak several languages."

"What else did she tell you about me?"

Robert tucked her hand into the bend of his elbow. "Only that you're from Mississippi, speak several languages, and that you're a business major."

"I'll tell you all about myself over breakfast. My treat. It's not Sunday morning unless we have fish and grits."

"I'll agree to breakfast, but I can't let you pay for me."

Shy and proud. Claudia hid a smile. She didn't mind Robert's reticence because she'd found herself turned off by some of the Hampton male students who had come on too strong, who'd believed they were the answer to all her hopes and dreams. And whenever she'd rejected their advances the word had gotten out around campus that Claudia Patterson was a stuck-up bitch. She didn't mind being stuck-up, because she wanted the option of choosing who she wanted to date, not because some man was putting pressure on her to be seen with him.

"There's a little hole-in-the-wall about three blocks from here that has earned the reputation of making the best fish and grits and chicken fried steak in the district."

"Come on, Robert. What are we waiting for? Let's go," Claudia urged, pulling him to walk faster. She wanted to eat before her stomach began making noises.

Unfortunately, she and Yvonne were leaving Washington, D.C., later that afternoon to return to Hampton, and she wasn't certain if or when she would ever see Robert again.

"Do you plan to come to Hampton to see Yvonne?"

"No. But I will come if you'll allow me to see you."

Claudia bit back a smile. "I would like that, Robert."

"So would I. Do you think you'll find time to write to me?"

"I'll make time for you." And she would. Claudia would add him to the list of those with whom she wrote several times each month. Three weeks ago, she'd written Noelle, yet had not heard back from her. She wondered if her friend had continued to see her African prince, agreed to become his wife, and had moved with him to Benin.

She knew Robert coming to Virginia to see her would signal a change in her social life. It was much too soon to determine whether they would become more than friends, but she did hope he would come to like her as much as she was beginning to like him.

His shyness aside, Claudia was drawn to his quiet, calming personality that hadn't put her on edge like some of her male classmates. She wasn't certain she'd been viewed as fresh meat because she was a freshman or if they'd suspected she was a virgin. Noelle had finally admitted that her African lover hadn't been her first. That she'd slept with an older man the year she had turned sixteen because she was tired of being a virgin. Noelle had also admitted she was disappointed because it was nothing like what she'd read about in books or overheard other women talking about how much they'd enjoyed sex. There were no fireworks or toes curling for Noelle until she slept with Adjovi. Just one encounter with him had changed everything for the young Frenchwoman.

Unlike Noelle, Claudia didn't view her virginity as a burden—something she needed to get rid of. For her it had become a prize. A prize she would give once and hopefully to someone deserving.

Robert opened the door to a small restaurant he'd called a hole-in-the-wall. Tables were positioned close together to maximize capacity. It was minutes after eight o'clock in the morning, and most of the tables were taken. Claudia smothered a moan when the distinctive aroma of bacon and eggs wafted to her nostrils. If she had been given the choice of eating one meal a day, then it would be breakfast. Grits, eggs, bacon, ham, biscuits—and fried fish on Sunday mornings—were her favorites.

Robert rested a hand at the small of her back. "I see a table over in the back. I hope you mind don't sitting near the kitchen."

Claudia shook her head. "I don't mind at all."

They wended their way through tables with just enough space to walk sideways until they reached the last remaining table with two chairs. Robert seated her, then himself. She knew if her grandmother had witnessed his action, she would tell Claudia to keep that boy because it was obvious he'd been raised with good home training.

She picked up the plastic-covered menu, read it quickly, then handed it to Robert. "I see they offer shrimp and fried whiting with grits." Robert smiled and met her eyes, and Claudia wanted to tell him that was something he should do more often, because she'd found him to be a little too serious.

"I've had the shrimp and grits and it is phenomenal," he admitted.

Resting her elbow on the table, Claudia cradled her chin on her cupped hand. "What would a city boy like you know about grits?"

Robert's smile grew wider, making him appear quite boyish. "You think only Southerners eat grits?"

"Well, most of us do."

"I grew up eating grits. My grandmother used to make them every Sunday along with bacon or ham and eggs."

"Was your grandmother born down here?" Claudia asked.

"Yes. She left South Carolina for New York City during the Great Migration where she got a job in a factory making women's dresses. She married my grandfather, who was a building superintendent for several tenements a block from Central Park. They didn't have to pay rent for their apartment, and after buying food they were able to save most of what they'd earned. My grandmother lost two sons before she had two daughters: my mother and Yvonne's mother. Mom is very smart and skipped a couple of grades and she'd just turned sixteen when she enrolled in the City University of New York. The college is tuition-free, and she only had to pay a nominal amount for student fees but had to buy her own books. She would never admit it, but I know she was competing with her older sister, who was studying to be a social worker."

There was a pause in their conversation when a waitress

came to the table to take their orders. Claudia requested the shrimp, grits, biscuits, and coffee, while Robert chose ham and eggs, toast, and coffee.

"What about your father?" Claudia asked. Within seconds of the query coming off her lips, she regretted it when she saw Robert's crestfallen expression. "You don't have to talk about him if you don't want."

"He's dead and I'd rather not talk about him."

And because she assumed it wasn't a happy topic for him, she smiled and said, "Consider it moot."

His expression brightened. "Now, you sound like a lawyer."

She frowned, shaking her head. "I have no interest in the law except those that afford us equal rights under the law."

"Things are changing, Claudia, albeit slowly, because of new laws and organizations.

After the Montgomery bus boycott, local leaders established the Montgomery Improvement Association and elected Martin Luther King Jr. as the president for the organization. I'm predicting that it will be students who will be in the forefront of what will become the civil rights movement."

"Why should it take new laws when the Thirteenth, Fourteenth, and Fifteenth Amendments to the Constitution give us the right to be free citizens and with the right to vote?"

"Because this country was founded on laws, and it will take overturning some of those laws to right the wrongs, Claudia. For example, *Brown v. Board of Education of Topeka* in 1954 did not overturn 1896 *Plessy v. Ferguson*, because *Plessy v. Ferguson* wasn't about segregation; it was about separate but equal. And *Brown v. Board of Education* dealt with segregation in education. However, the latter did set in motion the overturning of separate but equal.

"Segregation in education isn't just in the South," he continued. "There are de facto segregation policies in many northern cities which affect wide disparities in educational resources between Black and White communities."

"But some of those schools are integrated, Robert," Claudia argued, her tone quiet.

"Yes, but then again it depends on the neighborhood. The residents of Harlem, New York, are predominately Black, so their children go to schools with other Black children."

"Did you go to an all-Black school?"

"No. I lived in a neighborhood with diverse races and nationalities."

"Do you think if you'd lived in an all-Black neighborhood, you would've gotten an inferior education?"

It took a while for Robert to answer Claudia's question as he thought about the what-ifs. What if he had attended an all-Black school where the books were outdated, and the resources unequal to their White counterparts? There were teachers who'd earned degrees from historically Black colleges that were not deemed accredited by the US Department of Education and were forced to repeat the courses in accredited colleges to be hired as teachers.

"I don't know. Maybe it wouldn't have made a difference, because my mother is a teacher, and that could've given me an advantage over other kids."

"You just answered my question," Claudia said accusingly. "If your mother hadn't graduated from an accredited college and been hired as a teacher, there is no doubt you wouldn't have skipped several grades to graduate early."

Robert rested his elbow on the table and gave Claudia a direct stare. "Are you certain you don't want to become a lawyer?"

"Very certain, Robert. Even today, women getting into law and medical schools is like attempting to climb Mount Everest. Even when women do graduate law school, they are initially denied admittance to the bar. We may have been given the right to vote in 1920 but we still don't have equal rights when compared to men." Claudia recalled Noelle complaining about Frenchwomen not having political equity with Frenchmen. "And what's worse is Blacks being deprived of their right to vote here in the South, where we're required to pay a poll tax, count the number of jellybeans in a jar, or recite the preamble to the Constitution. How many White people can recite the preamble to the Constitution, Robert? Probably none."

"Don't worry. That's going to change, Claudia."

"When, Robert?" she asked, her voice becoming more strident. "How long do we have to wait to become full citizens in this country? Immigrants who came here less than fifty or sixty years ago and are granted citizenship have more rights than we do."

"Change is coming, but we must use the courts to fight Jim Crow and dismantle segregation. There were civil rights lawyers before Thurgood Marshall, like Charles Hamilton Houston, who was the first general counsel of the NAACP. He worked to overturn the *Plessy v. Ferguson* case of 1896. And through his leadership Howard University received accreditation through the Association of American Law Schools. Howard Law is known as 'Black Ivy League' because of Charles Houston.

"Then there's Dr. Pauli Murray, who'd been arrested and imprisoned in 1940 for refusing to sit at the back of the bus in Richmond, Virginia. The following year she enrolled in Howard with the intent to become a civil rights lawyer."

"Did she?"

"Yes, but not at Howard, because she was thought too radical for her time. She'd changed her first name from Pauline to Pauli and had pursued gender-affirming medical treatment but was denied hormone therapy."

Leaning over the table, Claudia whispered, "She wanted to become man?"

"It appears that way. She was brilliant but was confronted by mockery at Howard about her discussions, and because of this she coined the term 'Jane Crow' to explain the various forms of sexist derision she'd encountered from the Black male students. She did graduate at the top of her class, earning the Rosenwald Fellowship that opened the door for Howard graduates to attend Harvard University, but Harvard Law rejected her based on gender."

"See what I'm talking about, Robert? Even at Black colleges, Black women were not valued."

"She did eventually attend the University of California's Boalt Hall School of Law where she would receive a Master of Laws degree. By this time, she was an up-and-coming civil rights attorney, but she was suppressed by McCarthyism, labeled a Communist, and lost her position with the US State Department."

Claudia closed her eyes for several seconds. "I remember coming home from school to find my grandmother listening to the McCarthy hearings on the radio."

Robert also remembered hearing and reading about Senator Joseph McCarthy's campaign to rid the country of alleged Communists and the socialist influence on American institutions. He also recalled his grandmother campaigning for Vito Marcantonio, who represented the American Labor Party and who was a socialist and avid supporter of immigrants, labor unions, and Black civil rights. When he'd asked his grandmother if she was a Communist, she'd angrily told him to stay out of grown folks' business, and he assumed that she didn't want him to go around telling people that his grandmother was a Commie.

"Joe McCarthy and his henchman Roy Cohn ruined a lot of lives. Cohn is also known for his involvement in the trial of Julius and Ethel Rosenberg, who were charged with espionage and executed as Soviet spies."

"Do you think they were wrongfully charged?" Claudia asked.

Robert nodded. "I do. They'd become scapegoats for the so-called Red Scare."

"Do you plan to practice law with your cousin?" Claudia

asked, once the waitress set cups of steaming black coffee on the table, along with sugar and a pitcher of milk.

"No. Dennis wants to join the NAACP, while I prefer working for a community organization like the Southern Christian Leadership Conference, which was founded in Atlanta, Georgia, last year. It is an offshoot of the Montgomery Improvement Association that successfully staged the boycott of Montgomery, Alabama's segregated bus system. Martin Luther King Jr., Ralph Abernathy, Bayard Rustin, Fred Shuttlesworth and others wanted a regional organization that will coordinate civil rights protest movements across the South."

Claudia bit her lip at the same time her eyes shimmered with excitement. "What types of activities are they planning?"

"Boycotts, marches, and other forms of nonviolent protests. A lot of Black communities are opposed to their methods because they believe segregation should be challenged in the courts and not in the streets."

"What do you think, Robert?"

"I believe in both. Mahatma Gandhi used nonviolent civil disobedience to effect social and political change in India and there's no reason why it couldn't be effective here. But we also must use the legal system to overturn laws based on segregation." Robert paused as the waitress set their orders on the table before walking away, then asked Claudia, "Which do you support?"

She lowered her eyes and peered up at him through her lashes. "I prefer boycotts and other forms of nonviolence. The Montgomery bus boycott ended because the city had lost so much money that they were forced to allow Black people to sit wherever they wanted. And it is always about money and amassing wealth. That's what drove the slave trade and is still evident today when our people are forced to pay for services where we are denied equal treatment under the law."

Robert's smile was dazzling. "I was hoping you would say that." Claudia had grown up under Jim Crow and when she talked about equal rights—for Blacks and women—he heard the passion in her voice, which meant she was willing to fight for whatever she wanted. He nodded. "Let's eat before our food gets cold, then you can tell me all about Claudia Patterson."

Chapter 14

I love you, not only for what you are, but for
what I am when I am with you.
—Roy Croft

Claudia felt comfortable telling Robert everything—
intimate details she had withheld from others, and that
included family members. She'd revealed her childhood dreams
about traveling and what she'd discovered when leaving the
States to experience another culture in France. She had also
told him about Denny Clark, and although she and her grandmother had saved his life, he'd turned on her because she'd
rejected him.

"He turned on you, Claudia, because he'd become obsessed with you."

"Obsessed or not, he was responsible for my being exiled
from my home, my family, and everything I'd known for the
first twelve years of my life."

Robert peered at Claudia over the rim of his coffee cup.
"Can you answer one question for me?"

"What is that?"

"Do you hate White people?"

His question gave Claudia pause when she recalled those

she'd met in Paris. "No. Not all White people are bad, just like not all Black folks are bad."

"Does that include the Italian man you met in Paris?"

Claudia chided herself for mentioning Giancarlo Fortenza. And why did Robert make it sound as if she'd had an affair with him? "Giancarlo is a friend of my aunt's, and he helped me perfect my Italian, while I did the same with his English."

Robert's black eyebrows slanted in a frown. "So, there was nothing romantic going on between the two of you?"

"Of course not, Robert. And there wouldn't have been because he is much too old for me." Claudia narrowed her eyes. "Why does it sound as if you're jealous, Robert?"

He sat up straight, his expression suddenly impassive. "You're wrong, Claudia. Why should I be jealous of someone I've never met?"

"Just checking."

"Just checking for what?" he asked.

A secret smile tilted the corners of her mouth as she contemplated telling the man sitting across the small table from her something that would probably shock him. "Whether you would become a jealous boyfriend." When Claudia saw his expression, it confirmed her thoughts. "I'm sorry if I shocked you."

Robert quickly recovered, smiling. "I'm not shocked, Claudia," he lied smoothly. "Even though we just met, I feel as if I've known you for years, because you're so easy to talk to."

"It's the same with me," Claudia confirmed.

"Are you saying I won't have to go through a gauntlet of Hampton brothers when I come to visit you?"

"Why would I ask you to come see me if I was involved with someone, Robert?"

He nodded. "You're right."

Robert wanted to tell Claudia that he'd met so many women who said one thing and did another that he hadn't known where he'd stood with them. It was why he'd refused to become emotionally involved with any of them. Getting a girl pregnant before graduating had become Robert's greatest fear—something that had devastated his father when he'd been forced to drop out of college and marry his girlfriend.

He rarely saw Lawrence Robert Moore, who'd been in and out of his life for the first ten years of his life. It ended when he'd returned home after being diagnosed with tuberculosis, a disease he'd contracted from a woman he'd been seeing off and on. Robert resented his mother taking him back, but she claimed she was fulfilling her marriage vows to love him whether in sickness or in health. Five months later, his father was committed to a TB sanitorium where he'd succumbed to the debilitating disease.

After going through his personal effects, Ivy Moore found a duffel bag filled with one-, five-, and ten-dollar bills. Ivy rarely spoke of her husband except to tell Robert that his father had given her enough money to pay for the college of his choice. She refused to tell him how much she had inherited or where the money had come from.

He glanced at the watch on his wrist. "It's time I get you back, because Dennis mentioned that he wanted to be on the road before noon."

"Are you coming to Virginia with us?" Claudia asked.

"No. Not this time. I must study for an exam," Robert said as he escorted Claudia out of the restaurant and onto the sidewalk. "I'll give you my telephone number and then you can let me know when you're going to be available."

He and Claudia retraced their steps and when they stopped under a tree in front of the row house, he met her eyes. "May I kiss you?" The second hand on his wristwatch made a full revolution before she nodded. Cradling her face between his hands, Robert lowered his head and brushed his mouth over hers, inhaling her moist breath and the perfume on her neck. "Thank you," he whispered against her parted lips.

Claudia lowered her eyes and sighed. "You're welcome."

Robert unlocked the door to the small three-bedroom house he shared with his cousin and another student. He found his cousins and roommate in the kitchen, where Dennis and Yvonne were preparing breakfast.

Yvonne smiled. "Have you two eaten?"

"Yes," Robert and Claudia chorused in unison.

Dennis placed strips of crispy bacon on a brown paper bag to drain. "As soon as we're finished eating, I'm going to drive Claudia and Yvonne back to Virginia."

"Don't worry about cleaning up," Robert said. "Ernest and I will take care of everything." Ernest Anderson, swallowing a mouthful of eggs, nodded in agreement.

Robert sat at the round Formica-topped table in the eat-in kitchen. He knew he should've gotten up after he and Ernest cleaned up the remains of breakfast, to go into his bedroom and study for an exam on legal ethics, but he couldn't stop thinking about Claudia Patterson.

He was still attempting to understand what about her was so unique that he wanted to marry her. Robert knew at nineteen he shouldn't have been thinking about marriage, because his mother was still responsible for him, and there was no way he was mature enough to take care of a wife. Even after graduating from law school, he wanted to secure employment before assuming the responsibility of having a family of his own.

He blew out a breath as he pushed to his feet. He was wasting time ruminating about Claudia Patterson when he had to go over his notes for the upcoming exam. His footfalls were heavy as he walked out of the kitchen and into his bedroom, which looked as if it had been hit by a windstorm. He, Dennis, and Ernest had worked out an alternating weekly schedule for cleaning the house while alerting one another in advance whenever they wanted to invite either family or friends over. Robert decided to put his room in order before settling down to study.

Later that day, Claudia sat on her bed, an unopened book on her lap, as she stared into space. She knew she had to read several chapters before tomorrow, yet she couldn't stop thinking about Robert Moore.

"How long is it going to take before you open that book?" Yvonne asked. "You've been sitting there staring into space for the past ten minutes."

She blinked as if coming out of a trance. "I've been thinking."

"What about, Claudia?"

"If I was too brazen when I told Robert that I wanted him to become my boyfriend."

Slipping off her bed, Yvonne sank down to Claudia's. Her dark eyes were filled with amusement. "What did he say?"

Claudia stared down at the book cover. "Let's just say he didn't reject my suggestion."

Reaching over, Yvonne put her arms around Claudia's neck, hugging her tightly. "No, you were not too brazen." She dropped her arms. "You're a grown woman, Claudia, and you shouldn't have a problem speaking your mind."

She met Yvonne's eyes. "You think?"

Her roommate smiled. "I know. There are times when you give off the impression that you're a coy Southern belle where men feel it's their duty to protect you, then there are times when you appear very mature and in control of everything. And from what you've told me about your aunts, you are more like them than you realize."

Claudia closed her eyes, smiling. "That's because I truly want to be like them. The exception is having affairs."

Yvonne's eyebrows rose slightly. "Would you consider having an affair with *one* man?"

Claudia replayed Yvonne's query several times in her head, and then said, "Yes. But only if I believed I loved that man, and he loved me enough to make me his wife."

"So, you believe in premarital sex?"

A hint of a smile played at the corners of Claudia's mouth. "The only thing I'm going to say is I have to think about it."

"Keep thinking, roomie, because something tells me you and my cousin are going to end up together."

"Did he say something to you about me?" she asked, her heart beating a double-time rhythm.

"He thanked me for inviting you to come to D.C. so that he could meet you."

"That goes double for me. I don't know what it is about Robert, but I find it so easy to talk to him about anything. I told him things I've never told my aunts or even my mother, because I didn't want them to judge me. I know they want to protect me, but I need to experience some things without their inference. And if I make a mistake, I must own it and hopefully not repeat it."

Yvonne nodded. "I know you probably don't want to accept it, but I think you spending time in Europe was the beginning of your real education. You saw things and met people who influenced your thinking even though you probably weren't aware of it."

Claudia realized Yvonne was right. Noelle was sleeping with a man of a different race with whom she'd fallen in love, and still she didn't feel pressured to marry him. Then, there were her aunts. Modern women who had assumed complete control of their lives.

"You're right, Yvonne."

Yvonne flashed a smug grin. "I know I am."

Although Claudia and Robert didn't get to see each other in person over the next two weeks, they had kept up a steady stream of letter writing. Most of his were short, while Claudia mailed off pages of what she thought of as aimless details about her coursework and occasionally her classmates. Letter writing had become a source of unburdening her thoughts when she wrote to Robert, her grandmother, parents, and aunts. Most of the missives were filled with lighthearted anecdotes, successfully masking her feelings of homesickness and a disconnect from everything that was familiar. Other than her roommate, Claudia hadn't formed any close relationships with any of the other students.

Her spirits were buoyed when she received a letter covered with strange stamps and a return address from an African country. Tearing open the envelope, Claudia read and reread what Noelle had written. She'd married Adjovi in a civil ceremony in Paris and had a traditional African wedding in Benin. She was now pregnant with their first child.

She laughed hysterically until Yvonne gave her a look which Claudia interpreted as Yvonne thinking she had lost her mind. She finally translated the letter, which had been written in French, to her roommate, and much to her surprise Yvonne didn't have the same response because she'd felt a White woman had beguiled an African prince when he should've married someone from his own race and ethnic group. Even when Claudia tried to convince Yvonne that she couldn't tell the heart who to love, her roommate refused to relent.

She didn't know why, but Claudia felt something change between her and Yvonne. She didn't want to think of her roommate as a racist, yet she was beginning to sound like so many of the bigoted White Southerners who'd passed laws known as the Black Codes following the Civil War to keep Blacks from exercising their rights, and that included interracial marriage. Maybe she viewed interracial relationships differently from Yvonne because of Virginia Bailey's relationship with Jacques Lesperance, while Claudia knew in her heart of hearts that she, like her mother, wanted to marry a Black man.

Yvonne gathered her books and jacket. "I'm going to the library to study."

"Okay." Claudia watched her roommate leave, and a

minute later she heard a knock on the door and wondered if Yvonne had forgotten to take her key. She crossed the room and opened the door. "What are you doing here?" she asked, her voice barely a whisper.

His grin faded. "What happened to 'I'm glad to see you, Robert'?"

Claudia opened the door wider, allowing him to come in. Of course, she was glad to see him. She just didn't expect him to show up unannounced. And it was the first time she'd seen him wearing glasses.

Robert took a step, and then leaned in and kissed her cheek. "I wanted to surprise you."

Feeling his warmth, inhaling the scent of aftershave on his jaw prompted her to put her arms around his neck as she kissed his smooth jaw. "And you did. Come sit down."

Robert took a quick glance around the dorm room Claudia shared with his cousin. Colorful scatter rugs, potted plants, and family photographs had turned the space into an inviting one. And he hadn't lied to Claudia when he'd said he wanted to surprise her. They'd exchanged several letters; however, the contents were not those of a boy or girl who liked each other but of pen pals writing about the passing events in their lives.

He met her eyes, unable to believe she was more stunning than he had remembered. Her hair was a mass of curls framing her face and falling around her shoulders, the image reminding him of photographs of movie starlets in seductive poses as they preened for the camera. Robert continued to tell himself that it was her natural beauty that had attracted him to Claudia Patterson, yet he knew that wasn't the only thing.

Even at eighteen she projected the maturity of a much older woman, and he liked that she wasn't reticent when it came to speaking her mind. And the passion in her voice when she'd discussed the injustices plaguing their race had ignited a similar fire within him.

And that's when Robert informed his mother that he'd planned to attend a Black college in the South to become a civil rights lawyer. Ivy's eyes had filled with tears. They weren't tears of joy but fear. He'd reassured her that he would follow the White man's laws and rules in the South until he joined other civil rights lawyers to begin the undertaking of dismantling the pit viper masquerading as segregation.

"I'd rather we not talk here."

Claudia nodded. "I just have to get a jacket."

"I'll wait for you outside."

Claudia slipped her sock-covered feet into a pair of tennis shoes and put on a wool jacket. She was still adjusting to the change of seasons. She found Robert in front of the building waiting for her. He took her hand, lacing their fingers together.

"Where do you want to go?" she asked him.

"I'm parked in the visitors area."

"You drove?"

"Yes. I have Dennis's car."

"Did he come with you?"

"No. He's staying in for the next few days to study for midterms."

Claudia gave Robert a sidelong glance. "What about you? Did you study?"

"Yes. That's the reason I didn't come sooner. What about you? Are you keeping up with your classes?"

"Yes. I have back-to-back classes on Mondays and Wednesdays, which leaves the rest of the week free for me to study. Yvonne likes going to the library, while I prefer staying in our room." Robert opened the passenger-side door and Claudia got in, sharing a smile with him when he came around to sit beside her. "Where are we going?"

"I thought we would just drive around and then stop to get something to eat."

Claudia detected a hint of laughter in his voice. "What have you planned?"

Robert turned the key in the ignition, starting the engine. "Why is it I can't fool you?"

"That's because your face is an open book. Once you become a lawyer, you're going to have to practice hiding your emotions."

"What is my face saying now?"

"That you want to go somewhere so that we can be completely alone."

"And do what?" he asked, as he drove slowly out of the parking lot.

"I don't know, Robert. You tell me."

He glanced up at the rearview mirror, then accelerated until he turned off onto one of several roads leading out of the campus. "You're half right, Claudia. I am going to take you to a place where we can have complete privacy. But whatever we do will have to be your decision."

Shifting on her seat, Claudia stared at his profile. "What did you do, Robert?"

"I have a distant relative on my maternal grandfather's side of the family who owns a rooming house near Newport News, and he told me I can come and stay over whenever I want."

Claudia had overheard students saying they were driving to Newport News because of several Black-owned seafood restaurants. "That's close. How long are you staying?"

"That depends on you, Claudia. It's Thursday, and I don't have to be back in D.C. until Sunday."

"Are you asking me to stay with you?"

He nodded. "I am. But nothing's going to happen that you don't want to happen. I've never forced myself on a woman and I don't intend to begin now. And especially with you."

"Why me, Robert?"

"You're special, Claudia Patterson. More special to me than you could ever imagine."

"Define special, Robert."

"Special enough for me to consider possibly marrying you in the future. You probably think I'm talking out the side of my neck, but I'm serious. I know you must graduate college and me law school before that can happen. I'm willing to wait for you, and I'd like to know if you're willing to wait for me?"

Claudia felt as if she was drowning in a maelstrom of emotions, making it difficult for her to think realistically. She wasn't in love with Robert, yet she knew there was something about him that would make it easy for her to fall in love with him.

Reaching over, she placed her left hand over his right on the steering wheel. "Yes, Robert. I'm willing to wait for you if you're willing to wait for me."

Robert reversed their hands and kissed the back of hers. "I give you my word that I am."

Chapter 15

A successful marriage requires falling in love many times, always with the same person.
—Mignon McLaughlin in *The Atlantic*

Robert had kept his promise when he'd told Claudia that nothing was going to happen if she didn't want it to. He borrowed Dennis's car whenever his cousin wasn't using it to come see her; however, there were days when he could only stay overnight before driving back to Washington, D.C., the following morning. Claudia would stay with him in the tiny room with views of the James River, snuggling on the twin bed and talking for hours. They would occasionally engage in heavy petting but nothing beyond that because she still hadn't felt comfortable going all the way; yet she knew after two years of their intermittent meetings the day of reckoning could not be postponed forever.

She returned to Mississippi for family holidays and school recesses, and not once had she mentioned that she was seeing a man, and whenever Claudia saw her mother staring at her, she wondered if Sarah had suspected she was dating someone. One evening when they sat together on the porch at Mavis's house, days before Claudia was scheduled to return to college to begin her last semester as a junior, Sarah broached the subject when she said, "I find it odd that you never talk about dating someone."

Resting her head against the back of the rocker, Claudia closed her eyes. "I'm not dating in the traditional sense because he's going to school in Washington, D.C., and we only get to see each other maybe once or twice a month."

"He's at Howard." Sarah's query was a statement.

"He's planning on a career in law."

Sarah leaned forward, her hands tightening on the arms of the rocking chair. "Are you in love with him?"

"Yes, Mama. I love him very much. So much so that I plan to marry him once we both graduate."

"When do you plan on introducing me to the young man who has captured my daughter's heart?"

"I don't know, Mama. He's from New York, and whenever there's a break in classes he goes back home." A lull in the conversation followed Claudia's statement and she knew instinctually what her mother was thinking. "We don't plan to live up North, because Robert wants to become a civil rights lawyer."

A soft sob escaped Sarah's parted lips before she covered her mouth with her hand. "I thought I was going to lose you again."

Pushing off her chair, Claudia sat on the arm of Sarah's rocker. "Mama, you will never lose me. Don't I always come back home?"

Sarah pressed her face against Claudia's shoulder. "I know I sound like a foolish old woman, but every time you leave to go back to college, I keep thinking it will be for the last time."

"Stop it, Mama. Firstly, you're not old and I'm not going anywhere. Once I marry Robert, we're coming back to Mississippi to live."

"Is that what you two decided?"

"Yes. He wants to get a position with the Southern Christian Leadership Conference rather than the NAACP."

Sarah smiled. "I can't believe my baby is going to be a lawyer's wife."

"Let's not count our chickens before they hatch, Mama."

There came another pause before Sarah said, "Are you having sex with your young man, and if you are, are you being careful?"

"No, I'm not having sex."

"Don't you want to?"

She was glad she was having a conversation about sex with her mother because it meant Sarah no longer viewed her as a girl but a woman.

"Yes. Perhaps if I saw Robert more often, I wouldn't be so reluctant."

"Take your time, Claudia, because once you take that step there will be no turning back. The first time I slept with your father I knew he was the man I wanted to spend the rest of my life with."

Easing back, she tried making out Sarah's expression in the light coming through the parlor windows. "You slept with Daddy before you were married?"

A smile softened Sarah's mouth. "Yes. We had talked about getting married during my last year in high school, even though my mother had planned for me to go to college like Mavis and Virginia. But the night I came home and told her that I had given your father my virginity she said I had to marry him."

Throwing back her head, Claudia laughed until tears rolled down her cheeks. "You traded your virginity for a husband, so you wouldn't have to go to college."

Sarah also laughed. "And I'd do it again because I didn't want to lose your father. I never regretted it because there is not a day that goes by that I don't fall in love with your father all over again." Suddenly, she sobered. "You have more options than I did at your age, Claudia. More girls are going to college, and as professional women they don't have to rely solely on a man for financial support. I know you admire my sisters because they come and go as they please without answering to anyone but themselves. But they also gave up having children, and I don't know if that's what you want."

"I want children, Mama. There's no way I would cheat you out of grandchildren."

Sarah smiled. "I like the sound of that. Are you coming back to Freedom with us, or do you still want to stay in Biloxi?"

"I'm going to stay here."

"Well, we're going back tonight, and if you change your mind, then just call me at the shop and I'll come by and pick you up."

Claudia pressed a kiss on Sarah's gray-streaked dark auburn hair. Her mother had begun graying at thirty, and now at thirty-eight the gray strands were quite noticeable. "I have another few days before I have to head back to Hampton, so I'm going to relax here until it's time for me to leave."

"Will I see you before you go back?" Sarah asked.

"I doubt it. I have my return bus ticket, so I'll take a taxi to the station."

Claudia had spent Christmas and New Year's with her family, while Yvonne, Dennis, and Robert drove back to New York City together, and she was looking forward to reuniting with them. Before leaving for the winter break, Yvonne had shocked everyone when she announced her engagement to her boyfriend, Stephen Jones, who was now a first-year medical student at Meharry.

She rarely saw Robert, who was spending all his free time in the law library. Even after two years, Claudia still thought of Robert as an enigma. There were occasions when he would talk nonstop, then other times when he would withdraw, and he would abruptly tell her that he was going back to D.C. She had not asked him about his father again and suspected he hadn't had a good relationship with him.

Although she loved Robert enough to marry him, his inability to talk about his father could possibly become a deal-breaker for Claudia. She did not want to share her future with a man who didn't trust her to disclose things in his past. Her aunt Mavis told her that love was an important component in a marriage, but trust was the glue that held it together. It was the reason Mavis hadn't married, because she hadn't found the man whom she could love as well as trust.

Robert sat across the kitchen table from his mother. Sharing meals with her conjured up happy memories when as a child he couldn't wait for school holidays and the summer recess to spend all day with her. As a teacher, Ivy Moore was off at the same time as school children, and this was the time when she'd planned wonderful outings together.

Reaching into the pocket of her apron, she placed a small package covered in Christmas wrapping paper on the table. "I know we exchanged gifts, but this is a little something extra from me because not only are you an A-student, but you've exceeded my expectations by getting into law school."

Robert met his mother's dark eyes before setting his coffee cup on the saucer. "You never told me I had to make A's, Mom. You used to tell me over and over to do well in school and keep my room clean. And you know you didn't have to give me anything else," Robert said as he removed the paper from the small square box.

"I know that," Ivy said smugly. "But I believe you're going to need this."

He wasn't certain what she was referring to until he lifted the top on the box to reveal a set of car keys. Robert knew his mother didn't earn much as a schoolteacher, and assumed she'd purchased the car from the money her husband had left her. She had been the beneficiary of Lawrence Moore's insurance policy and his pension. He'd worked as a maintenance worker for New York City Parks, before being promoted to supervisor. He'd been the first Black to hold that position.

"It's not new, but the mechanic who sold it to me said it's in good condition, and now you can stop asking Dennis to use his car whenever you want to go see your girlfriend."

Robert's head popped up. "He told you about that?"

"No. My niece did. Yvonne said you hardly get to see her roommate because you don't have a car."

He smothered a curse. He had no idea his cousin was telling his business. Robert placed the keys in the box and pushed it across the table. "I don't need a car now. You can return it and get your money back."

Ivy went still, nothing moved. Not even her eyes. "Why don't you want it, Robert?"

"Because you've done enough for me, Mom. You've covered the entire cost of my college education. You give me gifts of new clothes for Christmas and my birthdays and—"

"Stop it, Robert!" Ivy shouted, interrupting him. "I'm only doing for you what any mother would do to help their child succeed in life. You don't have any brothers or sisters, so that means you're going to have to go it alone in this life when I'm no longer here. And I'll thank you not to monitor my finances."

"Your finances or your late husband's?" he asked in a deceptively soft tone.

"I don't want to talk about that," she said through clenched teeth.

"If you don't want to talk about *that*, then I can't accept the car." Robert had waited years for his mother to be open about the money she'd used to finance his college education. He knew he should've been grateful for her generosity, but something continued to nag at him that the money was tainted. That it was the result of something illegal.

"What if I can't talk about it, Robert?"

"Then I can't accept it, Mom. I want to become a lawyer, and if in the future I decide I want to become a judge, there will be a background check on my past and if anything comes up negative then I might lose my license."

Ivy closed her eyes and slowly shook her head. "I promised your father I would never tell anyone where the money had come from, and that included you."

"If you tell me, Mom, then what is said here stays here."

"He found it."

"Where?"

"It was in Harlem. Your father said he saw this man carrying a suitcase duck into an alley as police cars came down the block. And when the cops went looking for the man, he left the suitcase and took off running. Robert waited until the block was clear and he picked up the suitcase and went inside the building and up to the roof. He crossed the roofs of several tenement buildings until he reached the corner one and then took a taxi across town to his apartment."

"What was in the suitcase?" Robert asked, unaware that his heart was pounding so hard he was certain his mother could hear it through his chest.

"The suitcase was filled with cash and betting slips."

Robert blinked. "Are you talking about numbers?"

Ivy nodded. He had grown up overhearing Black people talk about playing illegal numbers that were controlled by Italian gangsters. They could bet as little as a nickel on a number and get enough money to buy groceries for their family or new shoes for their children. The mobsters had held a tight grip on the number rackets until they allowed Black men to operate in Black neighborhoods as number runners.

Robert recalled reading about the criminals who had controlled illegal gambling, but it had been racketeer Madame Stephanie St. Clair, along with her enforcer Ellsworth "Bumpy" Johnson who had become celebrities in Harlem. She'd refused to pay protection to Dutch Schultz; and when threatened, she'd tipped off the police, who raided his house and arrested more than a dozen of his employees, while seizing approximately twelve million dollars in cash. As the Queen of the Policy Rackets in the 1930s, St. Clair became incredibly wealthy, and as a philanthropist she'd donated money to community programs that promoted racial progress.

"Your father said he burned the slips, and after putting the cash in a duffel bag he cut up the suitcase and threw the pieces in the Hudson and East Rivers. He kept the bag in a storage locker at the Port Authority Bus Terminal. A month later he went to the hospital because he wasn't feeling well. That's when he was diagnosed with tuberculosis. The doctors wanted him to quarantine, but he told them he had to see his wife and son first and promised he would return the next day.

"He went to the bus terminal, retrieved the bag, and came to see me. Your father made me promise to use the money for your education, and if I didn't agree then he would burn it. When I told him to keep it for you, he said he couldn't. That's when he admitted he was sick, and the doctors had given him less than a year to live. They were right, because five months later he was gone."

"You didn't feel guilty taking the money?" Robert asked his mother.

"At first, I did, but then I thought about all the times when I struggled to budget so I could put away a few dollars from each paycheck for your future. Even though I went to a city college, I'd always wanted to attend a Black college in the South because of Black teachers, homecoming, and football games. That's what I wanted for you, Robert, and the money your father gave me made that possible."

He smiled. "They are truly highlights of attending a Black college."

"I did tell him if it had been drug money, I would've burned it myself. Drugs are going through Black neighborhoods like Sherman's March to the Sea, destroying lives. It's become a malignant cancer targeting our people. Kids I taught when they were in second and third grade are now drug addicts, stealing and assaulting folks so they can get money to buy that poison. I just can't understand why some-one would want to stick a needle in their arm to feel good." Ivy pushed the box with the key across the table again. "Tell me about this girl who has you borrowing a car to see her."

Robert picked up the keys. He didn't know why it had taken his mother so many years to reveal where she had gotten the money. "Thank you for your gift." He watched his mother's expression soften when he revealed his innermost feelings about a woman he wanted to share his future with.

"Have you told her that you love her?"

"No."

"Why not, Robert?"

"There's no need to say it because she's already agreed to marry me."

Ivy leaned over the table. "Every woman wants a man to tell her that he loves her."

"She knows that I love her because we talk about getting married once we graduate."

"A woman needs to hear you say it, son."

"Is it really that important?"

"Yes, Robert Lawrence Moore. It is very important. Now, tell me, when am I going to meet my future daughter-in-law?"

"I don't know, Mom. She's really into her books, so I doubt she will come up here with me once the spring semester is over. She's very close to her family and she spends all her free time with them."

"I suppose I'll have to wait until just before the wedding to meet her." Pushing back her chair, Ivy stood up. "I want to give you something your father gave to me when we were dating, and I'd like you to give it to your girlfriend."

He didn't have long to wait when she returned and handed him another box, this one with a delicate gold bracelet. "Lawrence gave me that bracelet once I agreed to us going steady. I don't know if you kids still use that term."

Robert smiled. "We do, Mom." A beat passed. "You and Dad were separated more than you were together. Why didn't you divorce him?"

"I would have if I hadn't known why he was in and out of our lives. His mother poisoned him against me. She blamed me for deliberately getting pregnant and because Lawrence had to drop out of college to marry me. I'd told your father that after I graduated and got a teaching position, I would support him so he could get his degree."

"Did he agree?"

"Initially he did, but his witch of a mother talked him out of it when she said no real man should allow a woman to take care of him. Every time he'd come back to us, she would call and pretend she needed him for something. And that something would stretch into months and, at times, years." Ivy paused, staring at the tablecloth.

"Lawrence would tell me over and over that he loved us, but he wasn't strong enough to break the hold his mother had on him. You were two when I overheard her telling one of her neighbors that she hated me for taking her son away from her, and when I confronted her, she called me names I would never repeat to another human being."

"Is she still alive?"

Ivy shook her head. "I wouldn't know. After I moved out of the old neighborhood, I left everyone and everything behind me."

"I had no idea Dad's mother was so hateful."

"Hateful wouldn't begin to describe her. She was an evil woman, and I hope she repents before she dies."

"Mom, do you mind if I ask you a personal question?"

"I don't mind because I know what it is. And the answer is no. I am not involved with anyone."

"Why not? You're still a young woman."

"I don't have the patience to put up with the BS some men put women through."

"You can say bullshit, Mom."

Robert always enjoyed reuniting with his mother, but this time it was different because she'd answered questions that had nagged at him for years. He was in love with Claudia, wanted to marry her, and knowing what he now knew about his father he was certain not to repeat Lawrence Moore's mistakes.

"I find myself cussing too much whenever I'm upset, so I this year I made a resolution to stop."

The only resolution Robert made for himself was to pass his courses. It wasn't incumbent on him to graduate at the top of his class, as when he had been an undergrad. He wanted to earn a law degree, then put all his energies into passing the bar. It was a new decade, and with the upcoming election for a new president, Robert felt the country was poised for dramatic change.

Chapter 16

Love talked about can be easily turned aside, but
love demonstrated is irresistible.
—W. Stanley Mooneyham, *Come Walk the World*

Claudia hadn't been back in Hampton for more than four
hours when she heard a knock on the door. She'd returned two days before the start of the spring semester because she'd wanted to visit the bookstore and purchase the
books she needed for several of her courses.

"Yes," she called out.

"Open the door, Claudia."

A smile flitted across her features as she forced herself not
to run to the door, fling it open, and jump into Robert's arms.
She didn't know why she'd missed him so much, because it
hadn't been the first time they'd been apart. Claudia knew
her feelings had changed after talking to her mother about
him. Not only had she fallen in love with him, but she also
loved him enough to want to spend the rest of their lives together.

She opened the door and met Robert's eyes behind the
lenses of his glasses. "Happy New Year," she whispered.

"Happy New Year to you, too," he said, smiling.

Claudia opened the door wider. "Would you like to come in?"

"Just for a little while."

There was something in Robert's demeanor that gave her pause. Although he looked the same, she knew instinctively he wasn't.

Had he come to break up with her? Had he found someone else? The silent questions bombarded Claudia until she experienced a tightening band across her chest. "Please sit down."

Robert clasped his hands behind his back. "I'd rather not. I came to ask if you have time to go to Newport News with me for a few hours."

Claudia was certain he heard her exhalation breath of relief. "Yes."

The last time they'd gone to Newport News was days before Thanksgiving because they had established the ritual of meeting off-campus. Some of her classmates had noticed her and Robert coming and leaving together and had asked if he was her boyfriend. And her answer was always yes.

She picked up her coat off the back of the desk chair, smiling when Robert came over to hold it so she could slip her arms into the sleeves. Removing a knitted cap from the pocket, she put it on, and then wrapped a scarf around her neck before reaching for the small purse on the desk. They left the building and walked to the area where faculty, staff, and students parked their cars. Claudia stopped when she saw Robert insert a key into the door of a dark blue Chevrolet.

"Did Dennis get a new car?"

Robert opened the passenger-side door. "Nope. This one is mine."

She slid onto the seat, then waited for him to come around to sit behind the wheel. "You bought this?"

Robert started the engine. "No. It's a gift from my mother. She said I shouldn't have to wait to borrow my cousin's car every time I want to see my girlfriend."

"You told your mother about me."

"Of course. Did you think you would remain a secret, Claudia?"

"I don't know. I thought maybe you would change your mind about us being together once we graduate."

"That's not going to happen, because I love you."

She closed her eyes and exhaled an audible breath. Claudia had lost track of the number of times she'd wanted him to say that four-letter word, while she'd promised herself not to tell him what lay in her heart until she knew what she felt would be reciprocated.

"You love me?"

Robert stared through the windshield as he concentrated on driving. He'd taken his mother's advice to tell Claudia that he loved her, and she had reacted as if he'd told her to jump into a frozen lake.

"Yes, I love you, Claudia Mavis Patterson. Do you think I would've asked you to become my wife once we graduate if I didn't love you?"

"Robert?" she whispered.

"What is it?"

"Do you know how long I've waited for you to tell me that you love me?"

He smiled. "How long?"

"Two years, Robert Lawrence Moore. Two long years of wondering if you liked me for me, or if I was just someone to pass the time with whenever you were bored."

Taking his right hand off the wheel, Robert placed it on Claudia's left thigh under a pair of dark-gray woolen slacks. "I'm never bored, Claudia, and especially not with you."

She laughed, the low, sensual sound filling the interior of the car. "That's nice to know. And since we're into true confessions, I admit that I fell in love with you at first sight. I suppose that's why I was brazen enough to mention you becoming my boyfriend. Also, I never would have even considered marrying you if I didn't love you."

Robert smiled. "You may be a lot of things, but you're hardly brazen. You're confident, outspoken, a tad presumptuous and at times quite opinionated, but I'd never put you in the brazen category."

"Have you ever slept with a woman?"

He gave her a quick glance. "What!"

"You heard me, Robert. Have you ever slept with a woman?"

"What the hell kind of question is that?"

"A question I'd like you to answer."

"What does that have to do with us?" He was hardpressed not to raise his voice, because he didn't know what had possessed Claudia to ask him something so pointless.

"It has everything to do with us. There are times when we don't see each other for weeks, and that's when I believe it's because you're sleeping with another woman."

Robert counted slowly to ten because he knew if he said what had just popped into his head it would destroy whatever relationship he had with Claudia. "To answer your question: Yes, I've slept with women. And to clear up your suspicions about me sleeping with someone whenever I'm not seeing you, then that answer is no. I hardly have time to take a leisurely shit because I'm studying my ass off. Right now, I'm managing about four or maybe five hours of sleep each night because law school is kicking my ass.

"I love you, Claudia, and I want to show you without words how much I love you, but whenever we lie in bed together something in my brain stops me because you're still a virgin, and because of that I don't want to take advantage of you. And I also don't want history to repeat itself. My father got my mother pregnant when they were in college together, and he was forced to drop out and marry her, because of the pressure my grandparents put on him. My mother graduated, while he never went back, and that had become a source of contention and resentment during their marriage.

"If I saw my father more than five times a year the first ten years of my life, then that was a lot. And if it hadn't been for photographs, I wouldn't have remembered what he looked like. The first time I saw a picture of him I thought I was looking at a mirror image."

He gave Claudia an abridged version what his mother had revealed, leaving out how Ivy had saved enough money to underwrite the cost of his education. He told her Ivy was the recipient of her late husband's city pension and life insurance, and that she had used the additional income to move from their Harlem walk-up into an apartment in a Hamilton Heights rowhouse several blocks from Riverside Park and the Hudson River.

Claudia felt as if she'd been chastised not by her grandmother or parents, but by the man with whom she'd fallen in love. Now she understood his reluctance to make love to her. "I would have allowed you to make love to me if you'd trusted me enough to tell me about your father. If we're going to be together, Robert, then there can't be any secrets between us."

"I didn't tell you because I was ashamed of the man who'd refused to accept his responsibility as a husband. Most kids I went to school with had fathers, while I didn't know when I would see mine, or at times if he was dead or alive. And I envied my cousins whenever they celebrated Father's Day with my uncle."

"I can't tell you how to feel, Robert, because we're two different people who come from different places, but I want you to know that I will never pass judgment on you about your past. Your father isn't the first man who has neglected his family for whatever the reason and he won't be the last.

But I do believe in my heart that when I have your children that you will be a phenomenal father."

"And you an incredible mother."

Claudia shared a smile with Robert. "I love you," she whispered.

His smile grew wider. "How much?" he teased.

"I'll have to show you," she countered.

"Really?"

"Yes, really."

"I'm going to have to make a stop at a drugstore before we get to Newport News, to pick up rubbers."

Claudia felt as if it were the first time when she'd come to the rooming house with Robert, watching as he put the key into the lock in the door at the side of the two-story clapboard structure. She followed him up the staircase to a room at the far end of the carpeted hallway. He unlocked the door to what she had come to think of as their boudoir, and she let out a shriek when Robert scooped her up in his arms and carried her inside. He elbowed the door shut and walked over to set her on the bed. There was enough light coming through the lacy curtains on the windows for Claudia to make out his face as he leaned over and brushed his mouth over her parted lips.

"I love you so much," he crooned, as he lowered his body, pressing hers down on the mattress.

Wrapping her arms around his neck, she placed tiny kisses on his jaw. "I love you, too."

It took less than two minutes for them to undress each other, and Claudia felt her breath catch in her throat when she stared at the naked man standing less than a foot away. Her eyes slipped down his chest to his belly and finally to his penis. It was her first time seeing a man without his clothes and she was blatantly aware of the differences in their bodies. She had gotten so used to seeing Robert wear glasses that he appeared like a different person without them.

"You can say no if you don't want to do this."

Claudia shook her head. She knew it was too late to back out now, and if they didn't make love now, then they would have to wait because she was expecting her menses in a few days. "I can't say no, Robert."

He took a step and pulled her close, her breasts flattening against his chest. "You are so beautiful," he whispered in her ear.

"That's because you make me feel beautiful."

Robert nuzzled her ear with his nose as he inhaled the perfume mingling with Claudia's body's natural scent. He didn't think he would ever get tired of smelling or touching her silken skin. Claudia could not fathom how much he'd wanted her from the first time their eyes met. She had confessed to falling in love with him at first sight, and he'd wanted to make love to her at first sight.

Good things come to those who wait had become his mantra. And Claudia Patterson was one of those good things he hadn't realized he'd been waiting for. He placed tender kisses on her moist, parted lips, under her ear, and down the column of her scented neck until he dipped his head and kissed a firm, rounded breast. Robert felt the hair stand up on the back of his neck when she let out a keening when he bit gently on her nipple.

The sound was so primordial that he got so hard he feared ejaculating before he was inside her. Easing her back until she lay half-on, half-off the bed, he picked up the rubber and slipped it on.

Claudia closed her eyes. She'd been around enough girls who'd talked about once they'd given up their virginity to expect some pain the first time, and there were some who admitted they'd never experienced any pain.

She didn't want to think about pain but the pleasure her mother had spoken of whenever she'd had sexual intercourse with her husband; and Noelle, who had talked about making love with her prince.

Claudia let all her senses take over when Robert parted her legs with his knee and pressed his body to hers, while supporting most of his weight on his forearms. He brushed his mouth over hers and at the same time his fingertips explored her inner thighs. Claudia arched off the bed when his thumb massaged her clitoris, and she bit her lip to smother the moans that made her feel as if she were coming out of her skin.

Her hips moved as if they had a life of their own and she wanted to ask him why he was torturing her. Without warning, he removed his hand, and then she felt his erection pushing into her vagina. Claudia tasted blood where she'd bitten her lip, as pain she had never experienced before tore through her when Robert pulled back and then thrust into her body.

Cradling her face between his hands, Robert placed tender kisses over her eyelids. "I'm sorry, baby. I didn't mean to hurt you."

Claudia opened tear-filled eyes and smiled up at him. "I know that."

"Do you want me to stop?"

"No," she whispered. "We have to finish what we started."

She forgot about the initial pain when Robert began moving inside her as wave after wave of pleasure washed over her, leaving her feeling as if she were standing on a precipice unable to stop herself from falling. But she did fall into an abyss where orgasms buffeted her over and over until she struggled to breathe. And when she did it was to moan at the same time Robert's groans overlapped hers, as his thrusts became stronger and faster until he collapsed, burying his face against the column of her neck.

"I love you; I love you; I love you," he whispered over and over.

Claudia wrapped her arms around his moist back. "And I love you, too."

In that moment she recalled her mother's advice verbatim as if she were standing in the room with them. *Take your time, Claudia, because once you take that step there will be no turning back. The first time I slept with your father I knew he was the man I wanted to spend the rest of my life with.*

She moaned again, this time when Robert pulled out of her body. He left the bed and walked to the bathroom. Claudia knew she had to get up and wash herself, but she loathed moving. Now, if she and Robert were married . . . Her thoughts trailed off because she knew they would have to wait another two years before that would become a reality. Then they could remain in bed together after making love rather than get up to go their separate ways until their next encounter.

Sitting up, she swung her legs over the side of the bed, grimacing. Walking slowly, Claudia made her way to the bathroom to find Robert in the makeshift shower. Pulling back the plastic curtain, she smiled at him. "Do you mind if I come in?"

He flashed a wide smile. "Please."

For Claudia it had become a time of firsts: making love with a man and sharing a shower with him. She hadn't felt embarrassed for him to see her completely nude because they had engaged in enough heavy petting for her to familiarize herself with his body and he with hers.

She luxuriated in the feel of Robert's hands on her body when he washed away the evidence of their lovemaking and all too soon the water cooled, and they quickly rinsed off the soap and turned off the water.

*   *   *

During the drive back to Hampton, Claudia could not take her eyes off the delicate gold bracelet on her left wrist. Robert revealed his father had given his mother the bracelet to seal their becoming a couple, and that Ivy Moore wanted him to give it to her as a pre-engagement gift.

"I want to buy you an engagement ring, so you have to let me know what you like," Robert said, as he maneuvered into an empty space in the Hampton parking lot designated for visitors.

Claudia gave him an incredulous stare. "I don't need an engagement ring now, Robert. We still have another two years before we graduate."

He blinked slowly behind the lenses of his round, black wire-rimmed glasses. "Two years will be here quicker than you can imagine. Does it feel like two years that we've been together?"

"No, but I don't want you to spend your money on a ring when you still must buy law books. I have the bracelet, and that's enough for now."

Resting his right arm over the back of her seat, he gave her a long, penetrating stare. "Are you certain that's what you want?"

A smile softened Claudia's mouth. "Very certain. I was yours two years ago, I'm yours now, and I'll be yours two years from now."

Robert angled his head and brushed a kiss over her parted lips. "I like the sound of that."

Resting a hand alongside his jaw with an emerging stubble, Claudia kissed his mouth. "Thank you for everything." She kissed him again. "Love you and get back safely."

"Love you, too."

Claudia got out of the car and walked to the building where she shared a room with Yvonne Chapman. They had gotten along so well during their freshman year that they'd decided to become roommates until they graduated.

Yvonne and Stephen were planning to marry after she graduated Hampton and then she would join him at Meharry when she enrolled in their School of Dentistry. Claudia had teased Yvonne that they would still get to see each other because Nashville and Biloxi were approximately five hundred miles apart. And when she and Robert were married, they would become family and former roomies.

Chapter 17

There may be times when we are powerless to
prevent injustice, but there must never be a time
when we fail to protest.
—Elie Wiesel

Claudia crossed out another date on the wall calendar;
there were three days left before the week ended, on
Sunday—Mother's Day. It would herald two momentous
events in her life. She would become Claudia Patterson, college graduate, and later that evening Mrs. Robert Moore.

Robert had given her a diamond engagement ring on February 14, 1962, for Valentine's Day. He admitted that he'd
called her father to ask his permission to marry his daughter
and he'd hoped to meet her parents when they came to
Hampton, Virginia, for Claudia's graduation.

The weekend before, Claudia met Ivy Moore for the first
time when they witnessed Robert accept his Juris Doctor
from Howard University. She'd been introduced to Yvonne's
parents when they'd come to Washington, D.C., to see Dennis, who had also received his law degree. The elder Chapmans returned to New York after the ceremony with a
promise to come back a week later for their daughter's Hampton graduation.

Meanwhile, Yvonne had shocked everyone when she eloped with Stephen Jones during spring break. He had driven up from Nashville and they were married in Virginia because the state did not have a wait time to secure a marriage license. Yvonne told Claudia that once she moved to Tennessee she and Stephen wanted to live together as husband and wife.

Claudia and Robert had also talked about getting married, debating ad nauseam whether they wanted to live off their meager savings or wait until one of them secured employment. And when Claudia told her mother about their quandary, Sarah admitted she, Earl, Mavis, Virginia, and Earline had all agreed to give them money as a wedding gift. Sarah had also hinted it would be enough for a down payment on a small house in Freedom.

The notion of returning to Freedom to live filled Claudia with a sense of apprehension, and she wondered if after ten years she would still be regarded as a pariah, or if a decade was long enough for those who'd remembered her association with Denny Clark to forgive or forget. And when she'd asked Robert what he'd thought about living in Freedom once they were married, he hadn't hesitated when he said he was looking forward to putting down roots in an all-Black town.

Claudia had packed up most of her clothes, books, and personal items, and had shipped them back to Mississippi. Her cap and gown hung in the closet along with an off-white, raw-silk suit she planned to wear for her wedding. Her aunt Mavis had reserved rooms for their wedding guests at a Hampton bed-and-breakfast owned and operated by a couple she'd met when they were students at Tuskegee Institute. Virgie had sent a cable indicating she was flying back to the States in time to witness her niece's graduation and wedding. Claudia sat at the desk and picked up a ballpoint pen. She'd planned to write Noelle one last time before leaving college, because she knew once she married, she probably wouldn't have much leisure time.

May 10, 1962
Dear Noelle,
I know it has been nearly a year since I last wrote you, and this will be the last letter I will be able to write for a while. I will graduate college in three days and later that evening I will marry the love of my life. Imagine becoming a college graduate and a wife on the same day, and that means Robert has no excuse to forget our wedding anniversary.

Robert and I have decided to wait a couple years before we start a family, because we both want to begin our careers. Speaking of babies—congratulations on the birth of your third son. I've framed the photograph you sent me of your handsome husband and beautiful children, and when anyone asks about them, I tell them I'm an auntie to African royalty.

Race relations in the United States have not improved. Young people put their lives on the line whenever they use nonviolent resistance and civil disobedience. Four students from North Carolina A&T College sat at a "Whites Only" F.W. Woolworth lunch counter in Greensboro. They refused to leave once they were denied service. They were arrested, but the incident was the catalyst for a movement to

desegregate lunch counters all over the
South. The boycott lasted five months,
three weeks, and three days and had affected all of Greensboro businesses. Money
is power and when you take away the
money you also diminish the power.

It isn't only Black high school and college students, but White ones too who have
joined the sit-ins once they receive nonviolence training. Peaceful protesters are
constantly attacked by White mobs, and
during marches the police turn fire hoses
on them. The force of the water is so powerful that it strips the clothes off bodies.
Many are also set upon by police dogs and
then clubbed before they are arrested and
jailed. It is 1962—a hundred years since
the Civil War in this country—yet not
much has changed. Black folks are still
fighting for the rights granted them at
birth.

I keep telling myself to stop reading
newspapers or watching television, but it
is as if I'm hypnotized by what I read and
see and I'm helpless to look away. Last
year activists known as Freedom Riders
traveled on interstate buses into the segregated South to integrate bus terminals,
including restrooms and water fountains.
One bus was firebombed, and the passen-
gers had to flee for their lives. And
another group was beaten so severely by
Ku Klux Klan members that reporters
wrote it looked like a bulldog had gotten
ahold of them.

Public outrage and support for the

Freedom Riders led President John F. Kennedy's administration to issue a new desegregation order. I couldn't understand why there was a need to issue a new desegregation order when bus segregation was ruled unconstitutional in 1956.

The Civil Rights Act of 1957 and 1960 are federal laws, yet Black people are still having to fight and die for their rights. Robert attempts to interpret the laws for me, but I refuse to see his logic. We have the right to vote, yet Black people still can't vote in certain states.

I know this letter is filled with a lot of doom and gloom, but now that I'm finished with college, I can focus my energies on eradicating the cancer in this country that is segregation. I don't plan to march or sit in, but I do want to get involved in voter registration. You've talked about Frenchwomen having the vote but no political power. It is the same here in the States with disenfranchised Black men and women.

I'm going to end this rather lengthy letter and send blessings for you and your family. I will write again once I'm settled.

Much love,
Your sister,
Claudia

Claudia waited for the ink to dry before she folded the page and slipped it into an envelope with the required postage.

She heard three taps, followed by another two on the door, and got up to open it. Claudia and Yvonne had designed the signal because they'd wanted to alert the other to open the door without asking who was knocking.

"You finally got it," she said to her roommate, pointing to the box Yvonne cradled to her chest.

Yvonne grunted at the same time she shook her head. "You can't believe what I had to go through with those assholes at the bursar's office when they told me I couldn't get my cap and gown because I still owed student fees. I told them I wasn't leaving until they went over my account with me standing there. They didn't know I had all of my canceled checks with me. The jackasses had credited someone else's account instead of mine."

Claudia's jaw dropped. "Does this mean the other student isn't going to walk because they owe fees?"

"I don't know, Claudia, but there's no way I wasn't going to walk, after my parents sacrificed to put two kids through college at the same time. Oh, hell no! I was about to pitch a fit the likes of which they've never seen if they didn't give me what I'd worked and paid for."

"Well, I'm glad you resolved that because you studied your behind off to get the grades you needed to be accepted at Meharry."

Yvonne sat on her bed. "When I told Stephen what I was going through he told me to stay calm because he didn't want to come to Virginia and bail his wife out of jail."

Claudia crossed the room and sat next to Yvonne. "You like being married, don't you?"

"What I like is being Stephen's wife. I won't feel married until we live together."

"Have you decided where you want to live after you graduate medical school?'

"We've discussed several places, and so far, we like New York. The South has its share of Black dentists and doctors, so we would like to set up a practice in a Black New York City neighborhood."

"Stephen, who grew up down here, is going to live in New York, while it is the reverse for Robert once we move to Mississippi."

"And don't forget my brother, Claudia. Dennis is moving to Atlanta once he marries his fiancée."

"So, Wendy is finally going to get her man."

Yvonne blew out her breath at the same time she shook her head. "That woman is obsessed with my brother. Personally, I think she's a little crazy, but I would never tell Dennis that, because he loves her."

"Have they set a date?"

"Not yet. But whenever they do I know it will become a spectacle like a Hollywood or even a royal wedding."

"Damn," Claudia said under her breath.

"Wendy gets all of that bougie shit from her mother, who also graduated from Spelman and is an AKA and a member of Jack and Jill."

"That is definitely bougie overkill."

"Well, some folks need all of that to feel worthy," Yvonne said. "I'm not saying it's wrong to pledge a sorority or become a member of clubs that will enhance your social status, but not to the point where it controls your very existence. Wendy was told she had to marry either a Howard man or a Morehouse brother, so she latched onto Dennis like a leech and the rest is history."

"Has she said anything about his wanting to work for the NAACP?"

Yvonne sighed. "She'd rather he'd join her uncle's law firm, but Dennis is adamant about joining the organization, so that's one battle I doubt she will win."

"Robert is focusing on working for organizations like the Student Nonviolent Coordinating Committee, the Southern Christian Leadership Conference, or the Congress of Racial Equality."

Yvonne rested a hand over Claudia's. "I wasn't supposed

to say anything, but my aunt told me she'd rather Robert join the NAACP like Dennis, because she believes it's safer than becoming involved in the grassroots organizations."

Claudia gave her roommate a direct stare. "These organizations need lawyers, too, Yvonne. When protesters are arrested and jailed, they're entitled to legal representation."

"I know that, Claudia, but it's my aunt who's concerned about her only child. I've tried to tell her that Robert will be okay, but she claims she had a dream where she was standing at his graveside."

Claudia felt an icy chill sweep over her body, and she closed her eyes for several seconds. "Please don't say that."

Yvonne let go of her hand and hugged her. "I'm sorry, Claudia. I knew I shouldn't have said anything."

"You're right. You shouldn't have. Let's hope his mother's dream is wrong. That it was just a nightmare." Claudia forced a smile she didn't feel at that moment. "You need to get your gown out of the box and hang it up to let the wrinkles fall out."

Yvonne nodded. "You're right. We only have another three days before all of this is behind us. Sunday is going to be extraordinary because not only will you get your diploma but also a husband."

"It will become a day I know I'll remember for the rest of my life."

Chapter 18

The goal of marriage is not to think alike, but to think together.
—Robert C. Dodds

Claudia met Robert's eyes. "Robert, with this ring, I thee wed. As we are husband and wife today. I promise to be honest and loyal to you. I promise to love, honor, and to cherish you, and to express that love over and over. You are the love of my life and always will be. This I promise for as long as we both shall live."

The justice of the peace nodded. "Robert, you may kiss your wife. Claudia, you may kiss your husband." She felt heat in her face as Robert lowered his head and brushed a kiss over her parted lips. Her eyelids fluttered when he pressed his mouth to her ear.

"I love you more than life," he whispered.

The officiant extended both hands. "Ladies and gentlemen, I present to you Mr. and Mrs. Robert Lawrence Moore."

Applause followed his announcement and Claudia looped her arm over her husband's suit jacket as they turned to face their family members. Yvonne had stood in as her maid of honor and Dennis as Robert's best man. She and Robert had opted for a civil ceremony on the same day as Hampton's graduation because they knew all their family members would be together for the event.

With the ceremony over, an elderly man in a dark suit directed everyone out of the parlor and into the formal dining room where waitstaff stood ready to serve a buffet dinner. "Your aunt really outdid herself when she arranged for us to have the wedding and reception here," Robert whispered in Claudia's ear.

"Aunt Mavis went to Tuskegee with the owners, and she somehow convinced them not to book any of the rooms this weekend."

His eyebrows lifted slightly. "That takes incredible negotiation skills to convince an owner of an establishment like this to turn away business."

"Now that you're a part of the family, you will discover that all of the women in my family are incredibly extraordinary."

A long rectangular table had been set up for the guests, with place cards indicating where the bride and groom, and best man and maid of honor were to be seated. Claudia and Robert sat together at one end of the table, facing Dennis and Yvonne. Claudia shared a smile with her mother, who'd rested her head on Earl's shoulder. Meanwhile Mavis and Ivy were speaking softly to each other, while Earline kept up a steady stream of chatter with Virgie. Yvonne's parents were staring at each other like lovestruck teenagers. The Pattersons, Baileys, Chapmans, and Moores were now an extended family.

"I think I drank too much champagne," Claudia said, moving closer to Robert in the large bed.

Robert wrapped an arm around her shoulders. "You drank too much, and I ate too much."

She laughed softly. "Some wedding night. My husband is

too full to move, and I am a wee bit drunk and on my period."

Robert kissed her hair. "Don't stress over it, baby. Remember, we had our wedding night a couple of years ago."

As a girl she'd fantasized about wearing a long, white, flowing wedding gown and veil, with bridesmaids in colorful dresses processing into the church before her while her fiancé stood with his best man waiting for her father to escort her to his side. And that's what it had been: A fantasy, because she was now a married woman who'd worn a white suit, shoes, and a hat with a veil that covered her forehead. And there were no bridesmaids or groomsmen in the wedding party. There was only her college roommate and her fiancé's cousin.

"Your family really gave us a lot of money as wedding gifts," Robert said after a pregnant pause.

"Yes, they were very generous."

"They were more than generous, Claudia. What your aunt Virginia gave us alone is enough to put down on a house."

"My aunt Virgie is what I could consider a woman of means. She lives in a beautiful house with household help, and she tutors the children of wealthy Parisians in English. Plus, she also has a very wealthy boyfriend who adores her."

"Are you saying she's a kept woman?"

Claudia heard a hint of derision in his voice. "No! She's not a kept woman. I just told you she's a teacher and she—"

"I know you say she tutors, Claudia," he said, cutting her off. "But does tutoring pay so well for her to live in a beautiful house with servants?"

"What are you trying to say, Robert? Are you intimating that my aunt is a courtesan? Or should I say a whore?" She threw off his arm and turned her back.

"Please, baby. I'm not saying your aunt is a whore. I'm just trying to understand why she would give you so much money."

"It's because I'm her niece, Robert. Her *only* niece. And

because neither she nor Aunt Mavis have children, they can afford to be generous with me. Or should I say with *us*," she added.

Robert kissed his wife's bare shoulder. When he and Claudia returned to their room to prepare to go to bed, they'd decided to open the envelopes rather than wait until the next day. His mother, aunt, and uncle had given them checks, but it was Claudia's family who collectively had given them enough money to purchase a modest house. "I don't want to sound ungrateful, sweetheart. I never would've married you if I knew I couldn't support you financially."

Robert did not tell her that his mother had given him the remainder of the money her husband had left her. She'd deposited small amounts into a savings account over the years so she wouldn't alert the tax people that she was saving more than she earned, but most of the cash had been wrapped in oilcloth and packed in empty sanitary napkins boxes.

The money his mother had given him was enough to support them for at least a year, if they didn't squander it, until he could secure employment. The cost of living in Mississippi was much lower than New York, and Robert was confident that he would be able to get a position with a community organization or an entry-level position with a law firm.

Claudia turned to face him. "I know that, Robert. My parents gave me money every time I went home, and most times, I didn't spend any of it. So, you should be proud that your wife isn't a spendthrift. We've decided to live with my parents until we move into a place of our own, and because of the generosity of your family and mine that shouldn't take long. We can use a portion of the money to buy furniture for the kitchen, parlor, living and dining rooms. Then we only must buy furniture for our bedroom, until it comes time to set up a nursery."

"What about a guest bedroom? What if Yvonne or Dennis want to come with their spouses to spend time with us?"

"I didn't think about that." Claudia pulled her lip between

her teeth. "We should wait to see what size house we want before creating a budget."

Robert kissed her forehead. "You're the financial expert in the family, so I'll leave all the budgeting up to you."

Claudia shifted until her breasts were pressed against his chest. "Thank you, my love."

He swallowed a groan when he felt the crush of his wife's breasts through the lacy bodice of the nightgown held up with narrow straps. Claudia was on her period, and he was on fire. It had been nearly two months since they'd last slept together. Both had been too caught up with completing assignments and taking finals to meet each other.

And living with his in-laws was not conducive for them, as newlyweds, to have the privacy needed to become accustomed to each other—in and out of bed. However, their living arrangements would be temporary, because as soon as they returned from their honeymoon, purchasing a home was at the top of Robert's priority list.

It took two days for Claudia to get used to the dizzying fast pace of a city that never went to sleep. The subways ran twenty-four hours, bars stayed open until two in the morning, and in some neighborhoods, diners served customers around the clock. The New York City public school system was in session until the end of June and each morning Ivy got up and left the apartment at eight to take the subway downtown.

Once Ivy left the apartment it had become hers and Robert's time together. They made love, then shared a shower before sitting down to eat breakfast. If Claudia was in awe of the towering skyscrapers and the number of people crowding the sidewalks, or the recklessness of taxis weaving in and out of traffic, she was fascinated by the foods from different countries that had become so much of a staple for New Yorkers. She and Robert rode the subway to Brooklyn, and when they stepped out of the train at the Stillwell Avenue station, she was immediately assailed with the smell of the ocean mingling with popcorn and hotdogs.

She got to sample a Nathan's hotdog with mustard and sauerkraut, and as soon as she finished it, she immediately ordered a second one. Robert introduced her to pizza, bagels with cream cheese, pastrami on rye with mustard, and sodas with unfamiliar names. Claudia felt as if she'd traveled to another country when she walked along the narrow streets in Chinatown and Little Italy. It had been her first time eating Chinese food and she loved it. They managed to find a table in a tiny Italian restaurant that reminded her of the hole-in-the-wall where she'd eaten with Robert during her first trip to D.C.

When she'd asked the waiter in Italian about a dish listed on the menu, he'd stared at her for several seconds, then asked, "*Sei italiana?*"

"*No, ma parlo italiano.*"

The waiter flashed a wide smile. "You speak it very well," he said in the vernacular she'd come to recognize as quintessential New York City.

Claudia lowered her eyes. "Thank you. Unfortunately, I don't get much opportunity to speak it."

The waiter glanced at the ring on Robert's left hand. "If your husband doesn't mind, you can speak with me when you order what you want."

She glanced at Robert, who nodded. "What do you recommend?" she asked in Italian.

"The chicken piccata, linguine with white clam sauce, and our shrimp scampi are customer favorites."

Claudia nodded, then turned her attention to her husband. "Do you want chicken or fish?"

"It doesn't matter. Why don't you order both, then we can share."

"We'll have the chicken piccata and the shrimp scampi."

"With spaghetti or linguine?"

She glanced at the menu again. "We'll have the linguine with garlic and oil."

The waiter smiled. *"Grazie."*

"Prego."

"I had no idea you spoke Italian like that," Robert said, once the waiter left the table to place their order.

Claudia met his eyes. "My French is a lot better. When I write to my friend Noelle it is always in French."

"How about our children, Claudia?"

"What about them?"

"Will you teach them to speak a language other than English?"

"Yes. When they grow up, they may decide to live abroad or get a position with a company that has offices in other countries, and having knowledge of more than one language is an asset."

"There are companies here in New York that are willing to offer more pay for someone with the ability to speak another language."

"Thanks, but no thanks. I like what I've seen of New York, but I don't believe I could live here."

"Why not?" Robert questioned.

"It's too fast for this country girl." Her excuse was only half true. "The buses and subways are too crowded, and I'd never attempt to drive here. I've watched folks step out in front of cars that are still moving and seemingly dare the driver to hit them."

"It's call jaywalking, Claudia. People cross or walk out in the street without any regard for approaching traffic. It's something New Yorkers are famous for. You learn to jaywalk when you're a kid. Even dogs know to stand on the yellow line until the traffic clears before they run across."

"You're kidding?" she asked, laughing. "Dogs, Robert?"

"Yes, dogs, Claudia. Live here long enough and you'll see everything."

"As I said before. Thanks, but no thanks. New York is an exciting place to visit, and that's it for me. When are we going uptown to Harlem?"

"Tomorrow. I'll see if I can get some tickets so we can see a show at the Apollo Theater."

Their orders arrived and Claudia smothered a moan of satisfaction when she bit into the chicken, chewed, and swallowed it before she ate a plump shrimp that was seasoned to perfection. Even the linguine with garlic and oil tantalized her palate.

"I think I'm going to buy an Italian cookbook and try a few recipes."

Robert dabbed the corners of his mouth. "Have you tried cooking French dishes?"

"No," she said, shaking her head.

"Do you like them?"

Claudia scrunched up her nose. "What I like are their pâtisseries."

"Say what?"

"Pastry shops, Robert. The French are masters when it comes to baking."

Smiling, Robert concentrated on winding linguine around the tines on his fork. "So, my wife doesn't believe she's sweet enough, so she feels the need to eat pâtisserie."

"Your wife is very sweet, but it's just that she's addicted to macarons."

"I suppose we'll have to find a pâtisserie and buy some macarons."

"No, we won't. I've done nothing but eat since we've been here and if I continue eating like this, I won't be able to fit into any of my clothes once I begin working."

Robert folded his napkin and placed it next to his plate. He'd suggested honeymooning in New York City because it would give him the opportunity to introduce Claudia to the city he loved, and it would give him more time to spend with his mother.

"What if you don't go to work, Claudia."

Her shock was evident as soon as he'd issued that statement, when she gave him an incredulous stare. "You're kidding me, aren't you?"

Taking off his glasses, he took a handkerchief out of the pocket of his slacks and cleaned the lenses. "No, I'm not. What after we buy the house you stay home to get used to relaxing."

"Relaxing, Robert? Do you think I've spent the last four years of my life busting my brain to sit back and relax? Have you forgotten that I am a modern, educated woman who would like a career? I'm only twenty-two, so if you were to ask the same question at forty or even fifty-two, then maybe I would consider it."

He replaced his glasses on the bridge of his nose. "It was only a suggestion."

"A suggestion that is totally ridiculous." She took a deep breath. "I promise to relax once we have children."

"Are you going to go back to work after you become a mother?"

"It all depends."

"On what, Claudia?"

"On what my job is. I would like to stay home until they are old enough to go to school. Then I would look for something part-time." She slumped back in her chair. "Where is all this coming from, Robert? We talked about what we wanted for our future, so why have you changed your mind now?"

"It's my mother."

She blinked slowly. "What does your mother have to do with us?"

"My mother has had to be the breadwinner ever since she became a wife and mother. She would get up extra early in the morning to get me dressed to drop me off at my grandmother's before she went to her school. Then she would come home exhausted after dealing with a classroom full of kids and picking me up. She'd cook dinner, put aside time with me before putting me to bed, then she was busy marking papers, or writing lesson plans. Monday through Friday she never had a break. It was only the summers when we had what she called our adventures. She called it her time to relax. July and August. Sixty straight days, Claudia. That's how many days Ivy Moore had to relax out of three hundred sixty-five. And I'm not talking about the Christmas and Easter breaks."

Claudia sat up straight and reached across the table to place her hand on his. "I am not your mother, Robert. And you are not your father. And I doubt whether I would've been as strong as your mother, given the hand she was dealt. Ivy Moore is an incredible woman, and when I grow up, I want to be like her. She's intelligent, courageous, beautiful, and a superwoman. She's the embodiment of what generations of Black women have had to do since we were kidnapped from Africa and enslaved here. She kept her family together when her husband and children were sold off, and it continues to this day. Your grandmother stepped up to take care of you when your mother had to work, and I'm certain my mother would do the same if the need arose with our children."

Robert chided himself for bringing up the topic. It wasn't that he didn't want Claudia to have a career. He wanted her to take a break and enjoy being a wife. And he knew he had to stop comparing his childhood with hers.

He reversed their hands and gave her fingers a gentle squeeze. "I'm sorry if I upset you, because that wasn't my intent. I just want you to know that when it comes to our marriage you will always have the option of a career or being a housewife."

"Thank you, sweetheart."

Robert felt as if he'd won a victory—albeit a small one. But still a victory.

Chapter 19

A man who stands for nothing will fall for anything.

—Malcolm X

Claudia fell in love with Harlem. She'd felt the pulsing energy of 100 Twenty-Fifth Street from Eighth to Lenox Avenue, lined with small shops, a department store, five-and-dimes, restaurants, and coffee shops. Speakers outside the Record Shack blared the latest hits, and she was amused to see pedestrians stop, cut a step, then walk on as if no one was watching. Robert had tried to purchase tickets to a show at the Apollo, but they were sold out the day they had wanted to attend.

Robert had taken her on a walking tour of Striver's Row on 139th Street; Lenox Avenue between 122nd and 123rd Streets with a preserved row of late-nineteenth-century homes. The exquisite brownstones were a startling contrast to the ever-present towering brick public housing dotting the Manhattan landscape.

A crowd had gathered around a man standing on a platform and there was something about his voice that drew her to him. "Robert, let's go and see what he's talking about."

"That's Malcolm X."

"I've read about him, but I want to see him in person."

Claudia managed to get close enough to get a glimpse of a slender, light-complected man with cropped reddish hair, and intense gray-green eyes that she felt when trained on someone could look into their soul. She was mesmerized—no, hypnotized—when he began saying what some civil rights leaders were reluctant to say. He said Black people didn't land on Plymouth Rock; Plymouth Rock landed on us. Claudia felt as if he were speaking directly to her when he said, *A man who stands for nothing will fall for anything*. She nodded and whispered *amen* when he stated if Black people weren't ready to die for it, then they should put freedom out of their vocabulary.

Claudia felt Robert tugging on her arm, and she slapped his hand away. "Stop it!"

"It's time we leave," he said in her ear. "He's riling up the crowd, and more cops are heading this way."

She had been so transfixed with what the former Malcolm Little was saying that she hadn't noticed the growing police presence. "Okay."

They walked back to where they could take the subway uptown, in silence. "You don't agree with him, do you?" she said once they were back in their bedroom at his mother's apartment.

Robert emptied his pockets and set his wallet, handkerchief, and keys on the bedroom dresser. "Who are you talking about?"

"Malcolm X."

"He's a troublemaker, Claudia."

She sat on the bench at the foot of the bed. "Why? Because he speaks the truth?"

"He's not a Christian and he's also racist and militant."

Claudia threw up her hands. "Do you hear yourself, Robert Moore? Are all members of the NAACP Christians? No," she said, answering her own question. "I'm certain there are a few Muslims along with Christians and Jews that are Freedom Riders. Not everyone wears their religious affiliation on their sleeve when it comes to fighting for equality. Malcolm X is a Black man who was born in a state where the KKK threatened his father. They claimed he was spreading trouble because he was a local leader in an association that advocated self-reliance and Black pride in their children."

"How do you know all of this?"

"I read, Robert. While you had your face in law books, I had mine in history books." She patted the cushion on the bench. "Come and sit with me." Claudia waited for him to sit next to her and reached for his hand, lacing their fingers together. "Even though you're young, you think like the old folks who say they'll wait for the law to change. Well, the laws do change, but at what cost? Black people are still being beaten and lynched while guilty parties go free. What are the odds of a White man in the South going to jail for killing a Black man?"

"It's probably zero to none."

"Probably? It's zero, Counselor. Our lives don't mean spit to them. What's their expression: *Mule die, buy another. Nigger die, hire another.* They don't even have to pay us in advance to get us to work for them. Aren't we worth more than a mule, Robert?"

"Of course, we are."

"Unfortunately, they don't see it that way. To them we're not essential, except when it comes to cleaning their homes, cooking their food, and taking care of their babies. I don't advocate violence, but if someone comes along and he or she is not afraid of fighting fire with fire, then I'm all for it. And once we get back to Mississippi, I plan to get involved in registering our people to vote. Rather than bullets, we're going to use the ballot box to get rid of the racists."

Robert closed his eyes, not understanding where all this rhetoric was coming from. "Why are you talking like a militant?"

Shifting slightly, she turned to look directly at him. "I'm an activist, or better yet a freedom fighter, not a militant. I don't want to take up arms to effect change. I want to use the White man's laws and rules to beat him at his own game. You plan to challenge laws in the courtroom, while I plan to empower disenfranchised people who have been denied the right to vote."

"Do you know how dangerous that is, Claudia?"

"Not as dangerous as a Black teenage boy being accused of whistling at a White woman."

"What the fuck!" As soon as the curse slipped out, Robert wished that he could retract it as Claudia looked at him as if he were a stranger. "I'm sorry. I shouldn't have said that."

"But you did say it. And I hope it wasn't directed at me because if it was, then I will leave you so fast you'll forget what I ever looked like."

Robert wrapped his arms around her body. "Baby, I love you too much to disrespect you like that. Will you please forgive me?"

"Yes, I forgive you. But no matter how angry we get with each other, I don't want you to curse at me, and I promise not to curse at you."

He smiled. "Are you giving me permission to let loose whenever I get fired up?"

Claudia brushed a light kiss over his mouth. "I've never seen you get fired up. The fact that you're so calm and easygoing is the reason I fell in love with you."

"Really?"

"Yes, really. Do you want me to show you how much I love you?"

Robert didn't believe he would ever get used to making love with Claudia. They'd become so attuned to each other that there wasn't a need for foreplay. As soon as they were naked and after he'd put on a rubber to prevent an unplanned pregnancy, she opened her legs to him and that's when he lost himself inside her warm, moist body.

Six weeks after Claudia and Robert moved into the house belonging to her parents, they were moving into their own home. They'd found a three-bedroom foreclosure that needed minor repairs, and when negotiating with the bank Claudia had convinced the mortgage official to lower the selling price to offset the cost of repairing the roof and plumbing. She'd waited until closing to ask about a position with the bank that had been advertised in the local paper, and when she asked the bank manager to be considered for the position he appeared noticeably flustered and told her the position had been filled. She'd given him a *I know you are lying* look, thanked him, and walked out.

"Lying piece of White shit," she said under her breath as Robert opened the passenger-side door.

Robert came around and sat behind the wheel. "Don't worry about him, baby. You don't want to work in a place where you would be treated like the trash they are. You're better than them."

Claudia stared straight ahead. Robert had secured a position as an attorney for the Student Nonviolent Coordinating Committee, better known as SNCC, while she was still sending out résumés. Robert was right. She didn't want to work at a place with a chip on her shoulder and say something that would endanger her life or those of her family members, and more than anything she did not want a repeat of what had happened ten years ago.

Moving back to Freedom didn't cause the angst Claudia had anticipated. Many of the boys and girls she had gone to school with had married someone in another town or had moved away. She'd caught a glimpse of Janice with stairstep children trailing behind her, but didn't say anything to her. It was obvious Butch Washington didn't know when to stop making babies.

"How long do you think it will take to put a new roof on the house?" Robert asked her.

"It shouldn't take more than a couple of days."

"If it's only a couple of days, then I'll ask my supervisor for some time off."

"You don't have to do that, Robert. My father can come and check on the roofer. He recommended the man because he has done work for him in the past. Besides, you just started working and it wouldn't look good for you to ask for days off."

"Your father is a good man, Claudia."

She smiled. "He really likes you."

"That goes double for me. Your family is wonderful."

Claudia rested her left hand on his arm, and the sunlight coming through the windshield fired the diamond on her engagement ring. "Remember, they are also your family."

"I suppose that's something you'll never let me forget."

Leaning to her left, she pressed a kiss on his ear. "Never ever."

It was mid-August when all the repairs on the house were completed. Claudia felt ready to take up residence in her new home with her husband. She had used a portion of her savings to purchase furniture for the parlor, living and dining rooms, and her grandmother gave them a kitchen set as a housewarming gift. Earline, who'd begun complaining about her arthritic joints, had begun sleeping in the parlor because she'd found walking up and down the staircase difficult. Earl and Sarah had tried to convince her to sell her house and move in with them, but Earline was adamant about sharing the roof with another woman—especially if that woman was her daughter-in-law.

Claudia was unaware that her life would change the day she used her mother's car to drive to Biloxi to do some banking. She always had a few résumés in her handbag, and when she walked into the building and came face-to-face with the manager, she greeted him with a smile.

"Good afternoon, Mr. Gaskin."

"Good afternoon, Miss . . . Mrs. Moore. I keep forgetting that you're now a married woman."

Within days of returning from their honeymoon she and Robert had opened a joint account at the Black-owned bank. "I still have to get used to folks calling me Mrs. Moore."

"How is your husband doing? He is a lawyer?"

Claudia nodded. "Yes, he is."

"And how are you doing?"

"I'm well, but I'm still looking for a job."

"What type of job?"

"Something in business."

"Do you have a résumé?"

Claudia's breath caught in her lungs and then she let it out slowly. "Yes, I do. I happen to have one with me." She opened her handbag and handed him one of the envelopes.

"Please go do your banking while I look this over."

She was too shocked to do anything more than nod. Claudia deposited Robert's paycheck into their savings account and thanked the teller when she handed her back the book after recording the transaction. Mr. Gaskin met her and asked her to sit at his desk.

"I'm really impressed with your résumé, Mrs. Moore. I could use someone like you for our loan department. The young man who is currently in the position will be leaving to attend graduate school at the end of the week, so if you don't mind working for a bank, I'd love to hire you. I will need a couple of letters of recommendation and your college transcript. I hope that won't pose a problem for you."

"Not at all," Claudia said quickly. She paused and took a

breath to slow down her runaway pulse. "I happen to have copies of my transcript and letters of recommendation at home."

"When can you bring them?"

"Tomorrow morning."

"Good. Then I'll look for you tomorrow. After I make a few calls can I get back to you at the number on your résumé?"

"The address and number belong to my parents. My husband and I just moved into our own home, so I'll give you my telephone number. And that reminds me that I must change the contact information on our accounts."

"You can do that at another time. Meanwhile just concentrate on getting me what I need to hire you. I'd like you to begin before Alan leaves so he can show what he's been working on."

Claudia extended her lace-gloved right hand. "Thank you, Mr. Gaskin."

He took it, smiling. "No, thank you, Mrs. Moore, for coming in when you did."

Claudia left the bank feeling as if she were walking on air. She got into the car and drummed her hands on the steering wheel. "I've got a job!" she whispered.

It was their first Christmas as a married couple, and Claudia and Robert had decided to open their home to family members for a festive dinner. Claudia had invited her parents, grandmother, and Aunt Mavis. When Robert's mother declined their invitation because Ivy, her sister and brother-in-law, along with a small group of teachers, were going to Bermuda for a week, he'd called Yvonne, who'd enthusiastically accepted the offer because she and Stephen needed a change of scene and a respite from nonstop studying.

Yvonne and her husband arrived a day before Christmas Eve and Claudia hadn't realized how much she'd missed her former roommate until she saw her again. They'd reverted to adolescent girls talking at the same time, and occasionally screaming at the top of their lungs as if they'd seen their favorite teen idol. Robert and Stephen were less effusive in their reunion when they'd sat in the living room watching television or in the parlor discussing cars, football, and politics.

Yvonne sat on a stool in the kitchen, watching Claudia make deviled eggs. "You really seem to have the hang of it."

Claudia gave her a sidelong glance. "Hang of what?"

"Combining marriage and work. Your home is beautiful, and whenever I ask you about working at the bank you say it is your dream job."

"That's because it is, Yvonne. As a loan officer I'm able to help folks get the money they need to improve their lives. Many of our customers were turned away from the White banks, so that's why they come to us."

Throwing back her head, Yvonne laughed loudly. "You missed your calling, Claudia. You could make a lot of money as a hustler."

"My life as a hustler would be the shortest in history—two seconds."

Yvonne pushed her glasses up the bridge of her nose. "Don't sell yourself short, roomie. I don't know what it is, but there's something about you that men can't resist. I'm not certain whether it is your face or how you speak, but I've watched men stare at you as if they were spellbound."

"I don't think I sound any different from other women born in Mississippi."

"You don't hear it, but I do."

Claudia continued filling egg halves with mashed egg yolks she had combined with mayonnaise, yellow mustard, garlic powder, sweet pickle relish, and salt and pepper. "I knew you spoke differently from me when I first met you, but when I went to New York and heard people speak, it was as if you were in my ear."

"I come from Manhattan, and we speak differently from folks in Brooklyn. There were times when I had a problem understanding them. It took me a while to understand that *earl burner* wasn't a name but *oil burner*. And now that I'm living in the South, I realize slides are not what you find in a park playground, but slippers, and shades are sunglasses and not window shades."

"Do you and Stephen still plan to live in New York after you graduate?" Claudia asked Yvonne.

"Yes. We've talked about doing our residency at Harlem Hospital."

"Isn't Stephen's father a doctor at that hospital?"

"He was until a couple of weeks ago. He's now assistant chief of pediatrics at Bellevue Hospital."

Claudia smiled. "That's wonderful news. I'm willing to bet that if he were a doctor in Mississippi, a White hospital wouldn't let him come in through the front door. I don't know if I told you, but next year I'm going to sign up with a local civil rights organization to get involved in voter registration. I'd been thinking about it for a while, but when I heard Malcolm X speak when I was in Harlem, it was as if his words ignited a fire within me. When he said, *Anytime you beg another man to set you free, you will never be free. Freedom is something that you have to do for yourself.*"

"Does Robert know your intentions?" Yvonne asked.

"Yes. He doesn't like it, but there's nothing he can do to stop me. He's accused me of being a militant, and if being or becoming a militant is what it takes to effect change in the Deep South's most segregated state, then so be it. How many more Emmett Till funerals will we have to go to before we cut off the head of the snake that is segregation?

"Spending the first twelve years of my life here in Freedom did not prepare me for moving to Biloxi, where I had to step off the sidewalk to let a White person pass, or address them with *Yes, sir* and *Yes, ma'am*. And I hated when White men called grown-ass Black men *boy* or refused to call them by their surnames."

"You know you can't change how a person thinks, Claudia."

"I know that. You can't change a racist's mind, but you can change his behavior when he breaks the law. Suffrage is a privilege, and thousands of Black folks have suffered beatings, threats, and death while registering to vote. We will never eliminate segregation until we vote the racist bastards out of office."

"Well damn, roomie," Yvonne drawled. "You are a militant."

"Does that bother you?"

"Hell no! Stephen and I just joined SNCC."

"So, Mrs. Jones, you decided to join the cause."

"There's no way history is going to pass me by without becoming a part of it. And I believe we need someone like Malcolm X because not everyone is a pacifist. You took enough history courses to understand what I'm talking about, Claudia." She paused. "Don't you find it odd that after rooming together for four years we never talked about race relations in this country?"

Claudia turned to give her husband's cousin a direct stare. "I didn't bring up the topic, because of your reaction to my friend marrying an African prince. You seemed so angry that a White girl had married African royalty when you felt he should've married a woman from his own race or tribe."

"That's because I was angry, Claudia. I dated a Black boy throughout high school, and when it came time for our prom, he took a White girl. Unbeknownst to me they were seeing one another and had planned to attend the same college. That's when I asked myself, what did she have that made him prefer her to me, other than she was White?"

"What conclusion did you come to?"

"Actually nothing. I was smarter, a lot prettier, and better born and raised. I suppose it had to be her pussy."

Claudia clapped a hand over her mouth and laughed until tears rolled down her face. She was still laughing when Robert walked into the kitchen with Stephen.

"What's up?" Robert asked.

"Nothing," Yvonne and Claudia said at the same time.

Chapter 20

The future is the past returning through another gate.

—Arnold H. Glasow

Claudia waited until the beginning of 1963 to begin campaigning to register as many Black people as possible before the upcoming local elections, concentrating on the towns of Freedom, Madison, and Hackersville. She'd set up a bulletin board scheduling dates and times when she planned to knock on as many doors as possible of those not listed as registered voters. There were several citizens who were registered but hadn't voted in previous elections.

Whenever Claudia knocked on a door or approached someone sitting on their front porch and introduced herself as a volunteer seeking to register voters, she was confronted with a myriad of reactions. Some threatened to have her arrested for trespassing; others said they weren't interested, and a few told her to come back later once they discussed it with family members.

She was more successful with college students who were twenty-one and willing to register and to vote. It had taken nearly five months and she had registered seventeen new potential voters from the three towns. She hadn't set a goal but hoped, even if she registered twenty-five, that represented a minor victory.

Claudia turned off the lights on the first floor, leaving a lamp on in the parlor, and made her way up the staircase to her bedroom. Robert was in the room she hoped would eventually become a nursery. He'd found a secondhand desk and chairs and several bookcases and had splurged to purchase a new IBM Selectric. Typing on an electric typewriter rather than a manual one for her was as different as night was from day. A side table with a loose leg that had been stabilized with a block of wood held several law books.

Robert had spent all his free time studying for the bar exam, and Claudia rarely disturbed him once he'd retreated to the home office after dinner. Working as a legal assistant for SNCC had changed her husband. His youthful exuberance had been replaced with seriousness and a weariness incongruent with a man in his early twenties, and Claudia attributed that to representing demonstrators who were beaten before being jailed. He'd spoken about one young man who'd lost an eye when a police officer had repeatedly jabbed his nightstick into his face once he'd fallen to the ground.

His concern was that not enough money was being raised to bail demonstrators out of jail, while Rev. King had collected nearly seventy-five thousand dollars in bail money for anticipated arrests in Birmingham, Alabama. Black leaders condemned Birmingham as the "worst big city in the USA." There had been so many bombings in the city that it had earned the nickname of "Bombingham."

Claudia walked quietly into the room. "Can I bring you a cup of coffee?"

Robert's head popped up. "No thanks, babe." He pointed to the straight-back chair next to the rickety table. "Sit down and talk to me for a few minutes. I could use a break right about now."

Rather than sit, Claudia stood behind Robert and massaged his shoulders. "Your muscles are tight as a drum. You need to take a break every fifteen to twenty minutes, sweetheart. Just get up and walk around the room."

He groaned under her ministrations. "That feels so good. You have magic fingers."

Leaning down, she pressed a kiss on his cropped hair. "I'm your fairy godmother and I am here to grant your . . ." Her words trailed off when she glanced at a corner of the desk and spotted what looked like the butt of a handgun in the briefcase she'd given him as a gift for Christmas. "Why are you carrying a gun?"

Reaching across the desk, Robert shoved the gun further inside the briefcase. "I need it to feel safe."

Her fingers gripped his shoulders. "Safe from what, Robert?"

"I should've said to protect myself. We've been getting death threats at the office. The other day someone called to say a bomb was going to go off in five minutes. We called the sheriff, then got everyone out of the building. He came and stood about a couple of hundred feet away, and after an hour when nothing happened, he claimed the caller was *just trying to scare a bunch of niggras.* I was so angry that I had to talk myself into not punching him in his bloated face."

This was another side of her husband that Claudia did not recognize. Where was the soft-spoken, peaceful man she'd fallen in love with and married? He'd accused her of being militant, but his carrying a gun had turned him into someone not willing to turn the other cheek. Did he now agree with Malcolm X when one of his followers overheard Malcolm saying: *Be peaceful, but courteous, obey the law, respect everyone; but if someone puts his hand on you, send him to the cemetery.*

"I don't like you carrying a gun, Robert."

"I'm sorry, Claudia, but it's not about what you like but what I need to do. I carry it whenever I leave this house."

She wanted to tell him that she needed her husband alive. They'd recently celebrated their first wedding anniversary and she loved being his wife. Wrapping her arms around Robert's shoulders, Claudia lowered her head and buried her face against the column of his neck. "Promise me you're going to be careful. I can't imagine my life if something happened to you."

Robert kissed her hands. "Nothing's going to happen to me, babe. I didn't marry you to make you a widow."

"I know we talked about waiting three years before we start trying for a baby, but I've changed my mind. I don't want to wait that long."

Unwrapping her arms, Robert eased Claudia back so he could stand. He cradled her face between his palms, his eyes making love to her face. If possible, she had grown even more beautiful.

"Why have you changed your mind?"

Claudia lowered her eyes. "I don't know what it is, but I keep dreaming about babies."

He smiled. "You want a baby because you've been dreaming about them?"

She met his eyes. "Yes."

"When do you want to begin trying?"

"December."

"Why December?"

"That's when I'll stop taking the pill. It will also be after the election. Maybe if we're lucky we can elect a candidate who isn't a segregationist."

"You're a lot more optimistic than I am, Claudia. Even a moderate segregationist is still a segregationist."

"As long as we don't get someone like Birmingham's Bull Connor, who had his police attack school children with police dogs, we could stand a chance of negotiating with hopefully a peaceful outcome."

"Or we could end up with a governor like George Wallace, babe, who promised his supporters *Segregation now! Segregation tomorrow! Segregation forever!*

She shook her head. "These racists are fighting so hard because they know their days are numbered each time a law is passed to dismantle discrimination."

Robert knew she was right. The Supreme Court had recently upheld in *Edwards v. South Carolina* the right to public demonstrations, thereby allowing Black Americans and others to continue their public protests for civil rights.

He forced a smile he didn't quite feel. "It may be slow in coming, but I know there is going to come a time when there will be a meaningful civil rights law for the entire country. We are going to continue to fight, and the racists are going to continue to fight us, but in the end, we are going to win even though elected officials have no shame. Just yesterday, George Wallace tried to stop the integration of the University of Alabama."

Claudia could not believe Wallace's audacity when he'd blocked the door to the college as he was confronted by the United States Deputy Attorney General Nicholas Katzenbach and asked if he'd intended to act on his defiance of the court. Later that day, the National Guard, backed by federal marshals, asked the governor to step aside. He finally left the campus, and the Black students were accompanied by the marshals and lawyers to their dormitories. The single act broke the color barrier at the University of Alabama. President John F. Kennedy had sent in the military along with his deputy attorney general to make it a reality. In a televised address later that evening, he'd made an impassioned plea for the end of discrimination in the nation.

"Kennedy was forced to make that speech because this spring over one hundred cities have been rocked by chaotic protest, some in the North but mainly in the South. People are tired of waiting, Robert. We've been waiting for hundreds of years to be treated as equals in a nation that refuses to allow us our inalienable rights."

"The Kennedy administration knows that militant demonstrations are a bad look for this country, and I wonder how they are going to react with the upcoming March on Washington."

Claudia gave him a puzzled look. "What march?"

"A. Philip Randolph and Bayard Rustin are the chief planners of the March on Washington for Jobs and Freedom, which is scheduled for August twenty-eighth. It was something they'd talked about last year. The word is Kennedy is opposed to the march because he feels it would negatively impact the drive for the passage of civil rights legislation."

Throwing up her hands, Claudia frowned. "I'm sick and tired of hearing about waiting for civil rights legislation, Robert, while our people are still murdered by White bigots. There are Klan rallies not only in the South, but also in northern cities. We have segregation in schools, housing, and employment. And still, we wait for civil rights legislation."

Robert pressed a kiss to her forehead. "I'm just as frustrated as you. The law works slowly, but once laws are enacted we can never go back. And I'm agreeing with some of what Malcolm X says about being nonviolent. Every time I see our people beaten, fire hosed, or are set upon by police dogs, or blown apart by bombs, I pray, Claudia. Pray that I can remain a pacifist. I know that violence begets violence, and I don't want to be filled with so much hatred that I become like them."

"You have a right to be angry, Robert, just like any other Black person in this country. If you were to ask a White person why they hate Blacks, they wouldn't be able to give you a plausible answer except that they don't like the color of our skin. And what if by divine intervention we wake up one morning and all Black people were white, what excuse would they have to hate us?"

"It's just plain ignorance. And if the power struggle for the races were reversed, we would never deny them the rights they've denied us."

"You are preaching to the choir, my love," Claudia crooned. "I'm going to let you get back to whatever you were doing while I take a leisurely bath and then go to bed."

Robert brushed a kiss over her mouth. "I promise I won't be much longer."

Claudia went into the bathroom and filled the tub with water as she brushed her teeth, then cleansed her face of makeup. She stepped into the tepid water, rested her head on a bath pillow, and then closed her eyes. She was still attempting to come to grips with the fact that her husband was carrying a gun, and she wondered if he was being completely truthful with her. She was aware that folks involved in the civil rights movement had received threats, but she wondered if he had been the object of one. She finished bathing and went through the ritual of applying a rich cream to her face and body. After slipping on a nightgown, she got into bed, leaving the lamp on Robert's side turned to the lowest setting. She had no idea how long she'd been asleep when Robert got into bed with her. She was suddenly jolted awake when she heard the telephone ringing. Claudia stirred, then came fully awake when she heard Robert shouting. Rolling over, she looked at the clock on his bedside table. It was four in the morning. She turned on her lamp and mumbled a silent prayer that whoever had called, it wasn't to give them bad news. Claudia didn't have to wait long for an answer.

"I just got word that Medgar Evers was shot in the driveway outside his home. His wound was so severe that he died within the hour."

Claudia's heart was beating so fast she feared fainting. Evers, a father, husband, distinguished World War II veteran and civil rights leader, had served as the leader of the NAACP's first field office in Jackson, Mississippi. Tears filled her eyes and overflowed.

Robert got into bed with her, and she buried her face

against his chest as he rubbed her back to console her. "Now they are assassinating our leaders," she sobbed.

"They found the rifle that had been recently fired, and hopefully they'll be able to find who fired it."

Pulling back, Claudia glared at her husband. "Even if they identify the shooter, we know that doesn't mean a damn thing. The sheriff will arrest the bastard, he'll be tried by an all-White jury and found not guilty. It's like reliving the trial of Emmett Till all over again, Robert. We'll never get justice when there are all-White juries on cases. That's why we must get more Black folks registered so they can be eligible to serve as jurors."

"How many have you registered?"

"Not enough. Some folks refuse to open their doors when I tell them I'd like to register them to vote in the upcoming election, and those who do let me in say they're too frightened to show up at the polling place because they fear reprisals."

"Reprisals from who?"

"The Klan, Robert. I'm certain you've heard of them," she said facetiously.

"Of course I have. Have you heard of them intimidating our people around here?"

With wide eyes, Claudia stared at him as if he'd taken leave of his senses. "Intimidating? Is that a nice way of saying threatening? When you wake up in the middle of the night to find a burning cross on your property, you know it's not a Halloween bonfire."

"You didn't answer my question, Claudia. Are you aware of Klan activity around here?"

She shook her head. "Not yet, but something tells me that it's inevitable. The more folks talk about being registered and the closer it gets to election day, it's going to bring out those cowardly hood-wearing snakes who will try and keep Black people from going to the polls."

"I want you to be careful, Claudia."

"How careful can any Black person be when they are gunned down in front of their homes?"

Robert smothered an expletive. "I don't want to argue with you, Claudia."

"Then don't!" she retorted. "You have the responsibility of providing legal counsel for civil rights workers while I've volunteered to register voters. Both of us are warriors in this war, and we must stay the course."

Robert was reluctant to tell Claudia that despite working for an organization advocating nonviolence, he had switched his alliance from Dr. Martin Luther King's philosophy of civil disobedience to accept Malcolm X's right to self-defense. Whenever he visited his clients in crowded jails and witnessed the result of them being beaten and maimed and would carry both physical and emotional scars all their lives, he'd experienced a rage that bordered on insanity. That's when he'd wanted to plant bombs and blow up places where Whites lived and/or gathered. The rage lingered, and it was only during his drive home that he was able to let it go. Unlocking the door and walking into the house he shared with Claudia was akin to coming out of the dark and into the light.

"Go back to sleep, babe. Even though it's early I must make a few phone calls."

She snuggled against his body. "I doubt if I can go back to sleep, but I'll try."

The news of the murder of Medgar Evers spread across news wires like a lighted fuse attached to a stick of dynamite. It was if the eyes of the nation and the world were focused on Mississippi. How was it possible that a distinguished World War II veteran hadn't lost his life fighting overseas to end fascism and totalitarianism, yet had lost it organizing protests and voter registration in his own country?

These thoughts plagued Claudia all day as she drove to

Hackersville to register voters. She'd left the bank, went directly home to prepare dinner, then told Robert she was going out to see if she could register one or maybe even two voters. She'd smiled when he cautioned her to be careful. She maneuvered into the driveway to an elderly couple's rental. Claudia knocked lightly on the door of the one-story house that was sorely in need of a new coat of paint. The door opened and she introduced herself to an elderly woman with two long snow-white plaits falling over her narrow chest, and announced why she'd come to see her and her husband.

"Do you mind if I come in, Mrs. Turner?"

"Sure, sweetie. Come and sit a spell. I'll go and get my husband."

She glanced around the parlor filled with mismatched chairs and sofas. A dimly lit bulb hung from the ceiling. She'd checked the census and discovered the couple were in their mid-eighties and voting records indicated they had never registered or voted.

Mrs. Turner came back with her husband. Claudia smiled when she saw them holding hands. Her smile grew wider when Bernard Turner held his wife's elbow, assisting her to sit before folding his body down beside her. Mr. Turner had lost all his hair, while his barely lined nut-brown face belied his eight decades of living.

"I'm forgetting my manners," Lucille said. "Can I get you something to drink?"

Claudia shook her head. "No, thank you, ma'am. But thanks for asking. I don't plan to take up a lot of your time, but I'd like to know if you plan to vote in the upcoming election."

Bernard shared a look with his wife. "I'm not certain about that, because we don't want no trouble. The man that owns this house came around a couple of weeks ago warning us that if we vote, then he was going to put us out. My Lucille and I are too old to pick up and move someplace else."

"I understand your reluctance, Mr. Turner, but if we don't register enough Black voters, when they find the man who shot Medgar Evers, there is no doubt he will go free because an all-White jury will not convict a White man charged with killing a Black one."

Lucille Turner squinted as she looked at the window. "I think something's on fire, Bernard. Best you get up and see."

"I'll check it out," Claudia volunteered when Mr. Turner slowly pushed off the sofa. She went to the door and opened it, her heart stopping when she saw the burning cross on the patch of grass doubling as a lawn. She held on to the door when she saw a half dozen men on horseback with hoods covering their faces. Her heart started up again, and she couldn't believe that she recognized the unhooded man astride a black horse less than ten feet away from her.

There was just enough daylight left to see the eyes she would remember all the days of her life. As a boy he had predicted he would make history. That he'd wanted his name to go down in history books like those she had read to him when she was a twelve-year-old girl. Claudia had read enough about the White supremacist group to recognize the symbol on the robe of the man staring at her. He was a grand dragon—the highest-ranking Klansman in Mississippi. She couldn't fathom how he, only in his mid-twenties, had earned that rank.

"Denny Clark." His name was barely a whisper, but her voice carried where the other men had exchanged glances.

Denny nodded. "Claudia Patterson." He raised his right hand. "Let's go, men." There was hesitation and seemingly confusion among the others. "I said let's get the hell outta here and leave these folk alone." He reached for the sawed-off shotgun tucked into his waistband. "If anyone disobeys me, I'll blow his fuckin' brains out right here. Now git!"

It wasn't until they rode off and the fire from the cross sputtered out that Claudia's knees nearly gave out as she sagged against the door for support. Seeing Denny again was as if her past had returned to the future. And Claudia knew the only thing that had saved the Turners from potential harm and/or intimidation was her presence.

She closed the door and sat down again, her eyes meeting the Turners'. "I don't think they will bother you again."

"Why would you say that?" Bernard asked. "Because this isn't the first time they've come around saying if we vote then they are going to kill us."

"They are not going to kill you, Mr. Turner, because I'm not going to register you." She stood up. "Hopefully we'll meet again under less hostile circumstances."

Claudia returned to her car and rested her forehead on the steering wheel. She'd witnessed firsthand the threatening and intimidating tactics used by racists to suppress the vote. But she never could have imagined the boy whose life she'd saved was now a Klan leader.

Claudia managed to start up her car and head home. Seeing the Klansmen up close was enough for her to curtail her voter registration for a few days. However, she had no plan to give up volunteering. She did not know why, but she'd written down many of Malcolm X's quotes, and the one that resonated with her was: *It'll be the ballot, or it'll be the bullet. It'll be liberty or it'll be death. And if you're not ready to pay that price don't use the word freedom in your vocabulary.* She had chosen the ballot and not the bullet, because she did not want her son or daughter to be treated as a second-class citizen.

Chapter 21

Be bold in what you want to stand for and careful what you fall for.
— Ruth Boorstin in *The Wall Street Journal*

"You're back early."

Claudia walked into the living room, flopped down on the sofa, and stared at the flickering images on the television screen. "That's because I encountered some interference."

Robert moved from his favorite chair to the sofa, his arm going around Claudia's shoulders. "What happened?"

Her voice was a monotone when she told him everything from meeting the Turners to seeing Denny Clark again—this time as a Klansman; and her promise to the elderly couple that she would not put their lives in jeopardy by registering them to vote.

Robert glared at her. "Are you telling me nothing happened to them because this motherfucker from your past decided not to harm them because he's still obsessed with you?"

Claudia couldn't pull her eyes away from the throbbing vein in Robert's forehead. "That's not what I'm saying, Robert."

"Then what the hell are you trying to say?"

"I don't know why he did what he did, Robert. I'm just glad I was there at the time they burned a cross in front of their house."

"Word must have gotten back to those jackals that there was voter registration activity around here, because this is the first occurrence I've heard about a cross-burning. Tonight will be the last time you will go out and register folks."

Claudia panicked. She wasn't going to stop signing up people to vote because of a staged stunt from the Klan. "No, it's not! If you think I'm going to let a bunch of hood-wearing cretins stop me from doing what I signed up for, then you really don't know me, Robert Moore."

Taking off his glasses, he ran a hand over his face. "I forbid you to leave this house other than to go to work or visit your parents."

Claudia was hard-pressed not to spew curses she knew would no doubt put the future of their marriage at risk. "Do you know who you are talking to?"

"Yes, you, Claudia."

"No, you don't, Robert. You can ask me to consider not doing something, but not forbid. I'm not your child or your chattel."

Robert's shoulders slumped as he put back on his glasses. "I really didn't mean it that way," he apologized.

"I know we're still newlyweds, Robert, and it's going to take time for us to get to know everything about each other. Firstly, you will not make demands and expect me to follow them without questioning you. And secondly, if there is something bothering you then I want you to trust me enough to tell me what it is. We're a team, Robert. Partners in life that will have each other's backs in the good and not-so-good times. What I will do is take a week off, but then I'm going back out there again.

"There's no way I intend to let Medgar Evers's death be in vain without continuing the fight for voter registration. It's the same with Fannie Lou Hamer. They've beaten and jailed her yet she refuses to give up fighting for voting and women's rights." Claudia paused to take a deep breath. "And I've gone too far to give up now."

Moving closer on the sofa, Robert took her hand, lacing their fingers together. "I know I overreacted, but I love you too much to lose you—"

"You're not going to lose me, Robert," she said, interrupting him. "I promise to take some time off, then I'm going back out there again."

"Are you finished with your soliloquy, babe?" Robert whispered.

Claudia smiled. "I am for now," she said, as she brushed a light kiss over his mouth, then deepened it when his lips parted as their tongues dueled for dominance. She moaned softly when he eased her back onto the sofa and lay between her legs; she felt his erection through the fabric of her pedal pushers. Passion had replaced her former annoyance once she realized how long it had been since she and Robert had last made love.

Robert rained tender kisses on Claudia's throat. He missed spending time together and making love to her. They were married, living under the same roof, sharing the same bed, yet they were living separate lives.

He moved his hips against her groin. "Will you forgive me for being a horse's ass?"

Claudia moaned again. "I'll have to think about it."

"How long will that be?"

"Just a few seconds. But first I must think about it. Okay. You're forgiven."

Robert moved off her body and pulled her up with him. "Let's go to bed."

She stared up at him. "Don't you have to study?"

"Dammit, woman! Don't you know that making love to my wife takes precedence over studying?"

Robert knew he had been remiss as a husband, partner, and a lover. He'd promised himself that Claudia would come first in his life, yet he had neglected her. He knew if she'd complained he would've attempted to adjust his schedule to spend more time with her. However, she appeared content to go to work, come home to cook and clean, and volunteer to register voters, so he hadn't bothered to ask if she was happy.

Twenty minutes later, he kissed the bridge of her nose before pulling out of her warm body. "You have no idea how much I love you."

"I think I do."

"No, you don't, babe. I love you enough to give up my life for you."

Claudia placed her finger over his mouth. "Please don't talk about death and dying. There's enough of that in the news to make me regret turning on the television or reading the newspaper."

Robert pantomimed zipping his lips. "Done. I want you to know that I've signed on to attend the March on Washington in August." He felt Claudia go stiff. "It's planned as a peace march, babe."

"All marches begin peaceful, Robert, before the police decide it isn't."

"This one is going to be different. There's going to be over five hundred cameramen, technicians, and news correspondents from all the major television networks covering the event, so the entire world will be watching. A. Philip Randolph has planned for the involvement of major civil rights organizations, and the more progressive wing of labor unions and other liberal organizations. I've heard rumors that there will also be a number Hollywood celebrities in attendance."

"How many have they predicted will attend?"

"We don't know currently, but I've heard that bus companies are gearing up to bring folks into Washington from all over the country."

"I doubt if I'll be able to take off to attend," Claudia said, "but I'm definitely going to watch it on the evening news."

Robert smiled. "There are going to be a lot of speakers and speeches."

"It sounds as if it's going to become quite an historic event."

"I'm almost certain it will be," Robert said, hoping he sounded confident enough to convince Claudia of what had been predicted to become a monumental event. Some of the organizers were concerned that only a few thousand people would participate in the march, but Robert was optimistic there would be a lot more.

He and the others in the Hattiesburg SNCC office received weekly reports about the potential participants who had pledged to attend the march. There were updated bulletins about meetings with President Kennedy, who'd tried to persuade the civil rights leaders to call off the gathering with the argument that violence was likely to occur, and he didn't want the country's capital to become a focus of civil unrest. When Randolph and Ruskin refused to cancel the event, Kennedy reluctantly endorsed it when told the themes were unity and racial harmony.

People were informed of the peaceful August demonstration through local churches and civil rights groups, and those traveling from across the country were planning to take what were called freedom buses and freedom trains to Washington, D.C. It would be the first time Robert would become a participant in a public demonstration, and although he doubted whether they would be attacked by police dogs and water hoses, he had drawn up a will leaving everything to his wife.

Reaching for his underwear, he stepped into them. Leaning over, he kissed Claudia's shoulder. "I'm going downstairs to lock up and turn off the lights."

"Are you coming back?" Claudia asked.

"Yes." Not only was he coming back, but he'd planned to spend the rest of the night in bed with his wife. He could always study another day.

Denny slouched lower in the chair on the screened-in porch as the blades of a ceiling fan worked overtime to dispel the lingering daytime heat and humidity. It had been a while since he'd felt so uneasy, and he knew it had to do with coming face-to-face with Claudia Patterson after so many years. It hadn't taken him long to discover she wasn't Claudia Patterson, but Moore, and that she had married a civil rights attorney.

Seeing her again had been like a punch to his gut and for several seconds he'd believed he'd conjured her up. It had taken years before he was able to forget the pretty young Black girl who had saved his life. And although he'd married his employer's housekeeper, whenever he had sex with his wife he'd fantasize that Alice Scott Clark was Claudia Patterson. He was sleeping with his wife and also with a fair-complected woman he suspected was passing for White, who lived in Pass Christian. When he'd questioned her about her race, she'd denied having Black blood, but did admit her grandmother had been half-Natchez.

He detected movement behind him and glanced over his shoulder to find Alice holding a glass of sweet tea. During the eight years he and Alice had been married, she'd miscarried four times, and the doctor had cautioned her about getting pregnant again. However, she had ignored his warning and was now pregnant for the fifth time. Luck was on her side because she had just begun her eighth month of confinement, half on bedrest, which had forced Denny to hire a woman to cook and clean the house.

"Do you mind if I join you?" Alice asked as she handed Denny the chilled glass.

"Is that what you want?"

Alice's dark green eyes filled with tears. "Yes, it is."

"If that's what you want, then sit down."

She sat and rested her bare feet on a low stool. Denny stared at the woman he'd married because he'd gotten her pregnant the first time they'd slept together. He'd been sixteen, she nineteen and a virgin, but at sixteen he hadn't been ready to marry or become a father. And if he'd known she hadn't been able to carry a baby to term, he would not have married her. However, it had been at the insistence of his employer that he do the right thing and marry Alice. Having children out of wedlock went against the Christian principles for someone seeking to advance in the Ku Klux Klan.

Denny took a sip of the tea, finding it much too sweet. "You need to get out and make friends with other women."

"How can I meet other women when I'm forced to spend most of my days in bed, so I won't lose my baby?"

Setting the glass on a side table, Denny stood up and went inside the house. Everything about his wife grated on his nerves—from her whining voice to her constant nagging. She was never happy no matter what he did or gave her. It was never enough. Now he knew why men stepped out on their wives with other women, and he'd never experienced an ounce of guilt whenever he drove down to Pass Christian to sleep with his mistress.

However, it wasn't Alice or his mistress who had invaded his thoughts. It was Claudia Moore, and he knew he had to see her again and warn her of the dangers she faced if she continued to register Blacks to vote.

"Mrs. Moore, there's a Mr. Denny Clark here to see you."

Claudia's head popped up and she looked at the bank guard as if he were a stranger. She did not want to believe Denny had come to her place of business to see her. And she knew it would garner talk that a White man had come into a Black-owned bank to talk to the loan officer.

"Where is he?" she asked, successfully schooling her expression not to reveal the anxiety eddying through her. She feared losing her composure.

"He said he'll wait outside for you."

Claudia glanced at her watch. It was minutes before she was scheduled for her lunch break. "Tell him I'll be out in a few minutes." The guard nodded and turned on his heel to deliver her message.

She opened the bottom drawer in her desk and took out her handbag. She alternated days bringing her lunch and eating in the bank's employee lunchroom or at a nearby coffee shop, and today was her day to eat out. Walking out of the bank without meeting anyone's eyes, she found Denny lounging against the side of the building.

"This is my lunch hour, so whatever you want to say to me, do it now."

"Don't worry about lunch. I bought something for you to eat. I'd like you to come with me to my vehicle so I can take you somewhere we can talk without folks gawking at us."

Claudia stared up at the man who bore no resemblance to the gangly, skinny teenage boy who'd begged her to help him and would've died if she hadn't asked her grandmother to take care of his wounds. He was several inches above six foot and his body had filled out. His hair was lighter than she remembered. It was more gold than brown. He wore a gold band on his left hand that indicated he'd married.

She hesitated and then saw people staring at them. "Okay. But I must be back by one thirty."

Denny reached out to take her arm, then pulled back quickly. "What I need to say to you won't take that long."

Claudia followed him to a parking lot and waited until he opened the passenger door to a pickup before she got in. She'd noticed there was a small picnic basket on the rear seat before she stared out the windshield. What was she doing in the truck of an avowed racist who could possibly murder her and then bury her body where no one would ever find her?

"Don't worry, I'm not going to hurt you," Denny said.

She nodded. He'd read her mind and she managed to relax as he drove out of the lot. He slowed and came to a stop at a park that had been integrated after several demonstrations by Black residents.

"I'm not worried," she half lied. "I'm just curious why what you want to tell me couldn't be said inside the bank."

"I don't feel comfortable being in a Black bank."

"Why not, Denny? Do you think we would treat you any less politely than we would our regular customers?"

"I don't know."

"The answer is no. Money isn't black or white, but green, so it doesn't matter the color of our customers' skin."

"You still have a fresh mouth."

A hint of a smile parted Claudia's lips. "It's called confidence, Denny. And you appeared to have more than enough of that when you and your brethren burned a cross on the lawn of a couple who wouldn't hurt anyone. Does it make you feel like a big man when you threaten folks who can't fight back?"

A muscle twitched in Denny's jaw when he clenched his teeth. "I didn't ask you to come with me so we can argue about things you know nothing about."

"Oh really," she drawled facetiously. "You think I don't know that you're a high-ranking member of the Klan? And that patch on your robe says you're the grand dragon of Mississippi. By the way, how did you obtain that rank so young?"

"That's something I will not discuss with you."

"Oh, but I do remember you telling me that I will read about you in newspapers or in history books. It's apparent your predication came true."

Denny struggled not to lose his temper because Claudia was making it hard for him to remain calm enough to explain to her that she had nothing to fear from the Klan. He maneuvered into an area of the park set aside for vehicles. He shut off the engine, got out of the pickup, and came around to assist Claudia, but she ignored his outstretched hand. Nothing had changed. Even after so many years, she didn't want him to touch her.

Her attitude toward him hadn't changed and it did bother Denny because of their last encounter at her school. If he hadn't approached her the way he had, possibly they could've become friends. It had taken him a while to accept that he'd been wrong. But seeing her again after so many years, he'd realized in an instant his feelings for her hadn't changed.

She had matured into a beautiful woman. His gaze came to rest on her large expressive eyes and full, sexy mouth. But it was her voice with a slightly husky timbre that he'd never tired of listening to. She hadn't cut her hair and had pulled it off her face and into a loose twist on the nape of her long, slender neck. He loathed staring below her neck because he knew if he did, it would trigger an involuntary erection.

Reaching for the basket on the rear seat, he led the way over to picnic tables and benches set up under trees, shading the area from the blistering sunlight. Taking a handkerchief from the pocket of his slacks, he spread it over a bench and waited for Claudia to sit on it before he sat down. He'd opted sitting next to Claudia rather than face her because he didn't want Claudia to see how much he still lusted for her.

Opening the basket, he removed two sandwiches wrapped in waxed paper. "You can choose chicken salad or roast beef."

"I'd like the chicken salad."

Denny smiled. "I'm glad you said that." He reached into the basket again and took out bottles of cola, bags of chips, and individually wrapped pickle slices. He opened the pop and set one bottle in front of Claudia along with the chips. "We can talk while we eat."

Claudia took a bite of her sandwich, chewing it as she waited for Denny to begin talking. Several minutes passed in silence. She swallowed a mouthful of the most delicious chicken salad she had ever tasted, then took a sip of pop, before she gave him a sidelong glance.

"Why are you doing this?" she asked.

"Doing what?"

"Going around threatening folks about laws they're entitled to?"

"Whose laws are we talking about, Claudia? There are laws for White people and laws for nig . . . Black folks."

She noticed he'd corrected himself before saying the offensive word. "That's where you're wrong, Denny. In case you're not aware, federal laws supersede state laws. Jim Crow is going to become a thing of the past, and you know it."

"That's where you're wrong. White people will never accept Blacks as their equal."

"We don't want to be equal to Whites. We just want what we're entitled to under the law."

"You keep talking about the law. Is that because you're married to a lawyer?"

"No. It's because it's reality. What you and your kind must learn is that Black people want freedom; freedom to shop, to eat, attend schools, and to travel wherever they want. We want our children to be able to choose what they want from this life without fearing someone who doesn't like the color of their skin will decide they can't have what they're entitled to."

"But that's not the way it is."

Claudia stared at Denny. His blue eyes reminded her of shards of chipped ice. They were cold and filled with loathing. "You can ride around wearing hoods and burning crosses, believing that you are frightening people, but those days when Black folks were too scared to retaliate are coming to an end."

Denny wiped his mouth with a napkin, and then shifted

on the bench so he was facing her. "Do you think we're scared, Claudia?" he asked in a deceptively quiet voice.

"No, I don't. But neither are we," she countered, giving him a long, penetrating stare. "We are not afraid of dying, Denny, if we're willing to fight for something worthy of giving up our lives for. Men who think like you are becoming relics—objects from the past. And you are still young enough to become part of the future. There will come a day when your children will go to school with my children and the differences in their color will not be an issue. Our men don't want to marry your women. But it's White men like you, Denny, who can't stay away from Black women."

She knew she had hit a nerve with him when he lowered his eyes. She added, "We could've remained friends but that's not what you wanted. I realized that at twelve, when you tried to kiss me. You didn't want to wait to see if I liked you enough to let you kiss me."

"Would you have allowed me, Claudia?"

He was asking her a question she'd asked herself many times after she'd moved in with her aunt. "I don't know. I liked you, Denny, but not the way you wanted me to like you. But that could've changed with time."

Denny angled his head. "We could've become more than friends if we lived someplace other than Mississippi."

"It's not just Mississippi," she countered. "It's everything that's going on down here. You claim you like me, yet you hate Black people. That just doesn't add up."

"It's something I can't explain, Claudia. I liked you years ago, and I still like you. And that's the reason I told my men that you're under my protection."

Claudia blinked slowly as she replayed his words in her head. "What do you mean by *your protection*?"

"My men know who you are, where you live, and where you work. And if any of them were to do anything to you, they will have to answer to me."

"Answer how?"

A beat passed. "I will kill them. You saved my life, so I'm returning the favor and I've sworn to save yours. But I want you to promise me one thing."

Claudia felt her heart beating against her ribs. She did not want to believe the grand dragon of the Mississippi's KKK had issued a decree that she was under his protection. "What?"

"Stop with the voter registration."

"And if I don't?" she asked, unable to disguise the tremor in her voice.

"Then our deal is off."

"Deal, Denny! I didn't make a deal with you."

"But I'm making one with you. Promise me you'll stop."

Claudia didn't want to believe she had to make a deal with a devil to save her life. She knew if she rejected it, then not only would her life be in jeopardy but also Robert's. "Okay," she said after a noticeable pause. "I'll stop."

Tiny lines fanned out around Denny's eyes when he smiled. "Good. After you finish your lunch, I'll drive you back to the bank."

She felt like a traitor, throwing her lot in with the KKK to save her life. The chicken salad had soured on her palate and the fizzy pop tasted flat. "I'm finished," she said, rewrapping the half-eaten sandwich.

"Are you sure?" Denny questioned. "You hardly ate anything."

"I said I'm finished."

"Suit yourself," he said under his breath, as he gathered the remains of her lunch and stored it in the basket.

The return drive was completed in silence, and when Claudia got out of the truck she walked to the bank without a backward glance. She entered the bank and noticed some of her coworkers staring at her. She made her way to her office, closed the door, and struggled not to cry.

Chapter 22

We do not remember days; we remember moments.

—Cesare Pavese, *The Burning Brand*

Claudia knew she hadn't imagined her coworkers' furtive glances whenever she sought to meet their eyes, when she was summoned to meet with Mr. Gaskin a half hour before she was scheduled to leave for the day. She knocked lightly on his door and walked in.

"You wanted to see me?"

He nodded and pointed to a chair in front of his desk. "Please sit down, Mrs. Moore." He waited for her to sit, then said, "I got a call from one of the members on the bank's board of directors who has a concern about your outside activities."

Claudia folded her hands in her lap. "You mean *outside* as to what I do when I'm not working here?"

"Yes."

"What are you implying, Mr. Gaskin? That my position with this bank extends beyond quitting time?"

"No."

"If no, Mr. Gaskin, then what is the problem?"

"The problem is, as an employee of this bank, the board is

concerned that your involvement in voter registration may make this company a target for a potential bombing incident."

Claudia did not want to believe what she was hearing. A Black man was telling her not to register Black people to vote because he feared retaliation from the KKK. "Is the future of my employment contingent on what I do with my private life on my personal time?"

"I'm afraid it is. I want you to go home and think about it. You can give me your answer tomorrow."

She drove home, struggling not to scream when all she wanted to do was to throw things to rid herself of the rage and frustration holding her captive. Her husband wanted her to curtail her volunteering to register voters, and she had promised him she would take some time off before starting up again; while her boss had issued a veiled threat that if she didn't stop, then she would lose her job. And then there was Denny, who'd issued his own ultimatum. He had promised to protect her from Klan retaliation if she stopped registering Black voters.

Claudia arrived home and exchanged her dress for a pair of shorts and a sleeveless blouse and then busied herself putting up a load of wash before preparing dinner.

Robert walked in as she was setting the dining room table. He'd unbuttoned the top button on his shirt and his tie hung loosely under the collar.

She angled her head for his kiss. "You look exhausted. Do you want to relax before we sit down to eat?"

"No. I'll relax after dinner. I'm going to wash up and change into something cooler."

Claudia made up a pitcher of lemonade as she waited for Robert to return. She'd decided to tell him about the meeting she'd had with Mr. Gaskin, but the one with Denny would remain her secret. Her husband failed to understand that she had been responsible for saving the life of an injured White boy and the single act had turned her life upside down when she'd been exiled from her home to escape the shame she had brought on her family.

Claudia had grown up believing Black people had to stick together to fight against Jim Crow, and for the second time in her life her people had betrayed her. It had begun with the principal and the school board member attempting to deny her the right to attend school, and now it was Mr. Gaskin and a member of the bank's board of directors who had threatened her job because they'd wanted her to stop offering disenfranchised people the power that was only possible with their right to vote.

"They can all go to hell," she whispered under her breath.

"What are you mumbling about?" Robert asked as he walked into the kitchen. He'd exchanged his suit for shorts and a white T-shirt.

"My boss at the bank."

"What about him?"

"Sit down and I'll tell you the whole asinine story."

Claudia revealed every detail about the meeting she'd had with her boss, watching as a myriad of emotions flittered over Robert's features.

"What do you propose to do, Claudia? Continue volunteering and lose your job?"

"I'm going to do what you've been wanting me to do and that is to stop volunteering."

His jet-black eyebrows lifted slightly. "Is that what *you* really want?"

"If you want to know the truth it's not what I want, but what I must do. Not only do I like my job, but we need the money."

"I told you before, we have enough money to live on for more than a year without having to adjust our current lifestyle."

Claudia watched her husband remove his glasses and set them on the table beside his plate. "What I don't want is for us to have to dip into our savings, Robert. Between the two of us we make enough to pay the house note, buy groceries, and occasionally new clothes, and deposit money into our savings account. I'd like to continue working until I have a baby, then I'd like to take off at least a year to bond with the baby before going back to work."

"So you're *really* going to stop volunteering?"

"That's exactly what I'm saying—not because I'm a coward, but because I don't want to be responsible for the bank becoming a target for a Klan bombing."

Robert smiled, the expression making him appear boyish without the spectacles. "If I'd suspected you were cowardly, I never would've married you. You are one of the bravest women I've ever met, and I can't promise anything, but I'm going to try to convince those who come into the SNCC office and aren't registered, to sign up to vote."

Claudia placed a hand over her mouth to stop from squealing like a young kid. "Really?"

"Yes, babe, really. Being in the office won't attract as much attention as being out in the field."

"Thank you, my love."

"There's no need to thank me, Claudia. We're a team and that means we must support each other."

Pushing back her chair, Claudia walked around the table and sat on Robert's lap and looped her arms around his neck. "I love you," she whispered in his ear.

"Love you more."

A sense of peace swept over Claudia, and at that moment she knew all was right in their world.

The cocoon that had wrapped Claudia in a contentment of boundless joy was shattered two days before the Fourth of July when her mother called her at the bank to report that Earline had died in her sleep. Claudia was so distraught it took her more than a half hour to compose herself enough to drive home without wrecking the car.

The coroner's office had removed the body by the time

she'd arrived at her grandmother's house, and she found her father sitting on the porch with his face in his hands. He'd lost his father, brother, and now his mother.

She'd taken one look at her father's face and realized she had to be strong, not only for him but for herself. "It's okay, Daddy. Grandma was complaining that she was tired, so now she can rest."

Earl nodded as if he were in a trance. "I tried to get her to see a doctor, but she made up so many excuses that I stopped asking."

"You know Grandma could be as stubborn as a mule when she refused to do something."

The screen door opened, and Sarah walked out onto the porch. Her eyes were red, which indicated she had been crying. Claudia hugged Sarah, kissing her cheek. "Mama, you're going to have to take care of Daddy," she whispered in her ear. "He's not taking this well."

Sarah nodded. "I know."

She steered Sarah away from where her father sat, so he couldn't overhear their conversation. "I called Robert before I left the bank and he's on his way. I told my boss that I'm taking the week off, so I'm going to be here for you and Daddy."

Sarah exhaled a sigh. "That's good to know. I just called Mavis to let her know about Earline. She said she's on her way."

"You need to take Daddy home. I'll wait here until Robert gets here, then we'll be over."

"We have to clean out the house—"

"Stop it, Mama," Claudia admonished softly, cutting Sarah off. "I will take care of everything. I know Grandma talked to Daddy about what she wanted when she passed, so he knows the details when it comes to her funeral."

Sarah's hazel eyes filled again. "She must have known that she was going to die because she kept talking about her late husband waiting for her. And you're right about her leaving explicit instructions about her funeral. She said she didn't want a wake, funeral service, or a repast, just a graveside service.

Claudia forced a smile. "That's Grandma. She had to control everything."

"You're a lot like your grandmother, Claudia. I've come to realize that, the older you get. You've inherited Mavis and Virginia's independent spirit and Earline's stubbornness. That's quite a combination for today's modern woman."

"You don't think of yourself as a modern woman, Mama?"

"Not quite. I'm more of a throwback to my mother's generation when the goal of a lot of women was to be married. Young women nowadays seem to focus on establishing careers before they look for a husband. While there are some who choose to remain single."

"Like my aunts."

"Yes. Like my sisters."

"Do you envy them, Mama?"

"No, because I have you."

Claudia hugged and kissed her mother again. "After we bury Grandma why don't you and Daddy close your shops and take some time off for yourselves. When was the last time you took a vacation?" she asked Sarah.

"I don't know. Even though Earl and I close the shops Sunday through Tuesday, we still don't go anywhere."

"Well, it's time you start planning to close for more than three days and go someplace where you can enjoy a real vacation."

"That's something to think about."

"Don't think about it, Mama. Just convince him to do it."

"I'll talk to him after we bury his mother. Now, he's too distraught to consider going anywhere."

Claudia wanted to remind Sarah other shopkeepers in Freedom had elected to close their businesses because of a death in the family, to go fishing or take extended vacations. The barber and beauty shops would be there whenever they got back.

*   *   *

Two days after the graveside service, Claudia and her mother concentrated on packing up Earline's house. Sarah had suggested she and Robert move into the house because it was larger than the one they'd purchased, but Claudia rejected the offer because it was filled with too many memories of what she'd shared with her grandmother. They were still in the house when they found Earline's legal papers in a metal box she'd stored on a shelf in a spare bedroom closet. Robert handed Sarah an envelope with a copy of her mother-in-law's last will and testament.

Sarah read the single page of type, then handed it to Claudia. "You need to read this."

She read and reread what had been written, unable to believe her grandmother had left her the house, and all its contents; the box also contained a bank passbook with a joint account in both their names. Claudia met her mother's eyes. "I recall Grandma asking me to go to the bank with her and sign on her account because she claimed there might come a time when she wouldn't be able to get to the bank and she'd want me to be able to withdraw money for her."

"Here's the deed to the house, and the title is in your name," Robert said to Claudia. "It looks as if your grandmother made it easy for you to settle her estate. And judging from the dates on these documents she'd made these decisions years ago."

Claudia's eyelids fluttered wildly. She recalled her grandmother hinting that she wanted to make certain her grandbaby girl was well taken care of when she passed.

"I'm going to ask Pastor Davis if he knows of any families who can use the furniture before I put the house on the market." She asked her mother if she wanted anything in the house and Sarah had declined the offer.

The incessant ringing of the telephone jolted Robert awake. He glanced at the clock on the bedside table; it was 3:10 in the morning and he whispered a silent prayer that whoever was calling wasn't the bearer of bad news.

He slipped out of bed and walked into the hallway and picked up the receiver. "Moore residence."

"Robert! He's gone!"

His fingers tightened around the receiver as he sank down to the floor. It was Sarah and she didn't have to tell him who *he* was. "Sarah, please stop screaming and talk to me." His mother-in-law was hysterical. Claudia had just buried her grandmother three weeks ago, and now he knew he had to break the news to her that her father had just passed away.

"I need Claudia. I need my baby with me," Sarah sobbed.

"Okay, Sarah. We're on our way."

"Who are you talking to?"

Robert glanced and met Claudia's eyes. Pushing to his feet, he replaced the receiver on the cradle. "Your mother. Your father's dead." The words were barely off his lips when Claudia collapsed as if she were a rag doll.

Chapter 23

I appeal to all of you to get into this great revolution that is sweeping this nation. Get in and stay in the streets of every city, every village and hamlet of this nation until true freedom comes, until the revolution of 1776 is complete.
—John Lewis at the 1963 March on Washington

1 September 1963
My Dearest Sister,
    I am grieved to hear that you lost your father and your grandmother so close together.
    Please write and let me know how you are doing.
    Much love,
    Noelle

Claudia sat in the kitchen at her mother's house staring at the note card propped up against a covered sugar dish. She had spent weeks attempting to reply to Noelle to let her know how she was doing. And if she were completely honest, not only with herself but with others, then she would say not well.

Claudia had screamed at Robert when he'd suggested his mother-in-law see a psychiatrist because he felt she was suffering from more than grief and feared she might harm herself. She'd tried to convince Robert that her mother hadn't recovered from losing her mother-in-law when weeks later she'd discovered her husband sitting on the sofa staring with lifeless eyes at the television.

Reaching for a fountain pen, Claudia unscrewed the top, closed her eyes, and gathered her thoughts. She positioned the gold nib of the pen at the top of the page and wrote the date:

20 November 1963
Dear Noelle,
Please forgive me for taking so long to reply to your letter and thank you for asking about how I'm doing. I am better than I was several months ago. Losing my grandmother was inevitable given her age and health, but my father's death has devastated my mother. My father was her first and only love, and she is emotionally shattered. I spend more time at her house than I do at my own. I'd taken a week off from my job when my grandmother passed away and had requested and was approved a leave of absence for a month without pay for my father's passing. Then I asked for an extension for another month, and when it was declined, I decided to resign my position as the bank's loan officer.

Aunt Virgie flew over last month to stay with us for a couple of weeks, and Mama appeared so happy to see her sister, while Aunt Mavis comes up from Biloxi on weekends to be with her. Once Mama's back to normal I'm going to suggest to Aunt Mavis that she take Sarah with her to Europe whenever she goes to visit Virgie. There's nothing that's keeping her from traveling because I negotiated the sale of the barber and beauty shops to an interested party looking to go into business in Freedom. I am currently responsible for her finances until she decides she wants to assume control of them again.

I'm not certain if you've either read about or seen footage of the March on Washington. It was televised live, and I because I didn't have to work, I was fortunate enough to view the history-making event. It was estimated that 200,000 to 300,000 Black and White demonstrators gathered in front of the Lincoln Memorial to hear Dr. Martin Luther King Jr. deliver what is now his famous "I Have a Dream" speech. Robert did attend and he said the solidarity among the demonstrators was palpable. Those who'd predicted violence and rioting during the event were profoundly silenced.

Robert has allied himself with a fellow Howard University alum, Stokely Carmichael, who'd been one of the original SNCC freedom riders in 1961 and is now a major voting rights activist here in Mississippi and Alabama. Carmichael is

very radical and refers to himself as a
Black separatist. There are times when
Robert espouses so much extremist rhetoric
that I don't know who my husband is
anymore. And the cry for a Black Power
Movement has garnered the attention of
J. Edgar Hoover, who is the director of the
Federal Bureau of Investigation—the most
feared and powerful law enforcement
agency in the United States. What I fear is
that Hoover has labeled most high-profile
civil rights leaders as subversives or
Communists.

I have cautioned Robert about becoming too militant, but he says he's disillu-
sioned because he feels the Kennedy
administration isn't fully committed to
seeing the passage of the Civil Rights Act
through. That the President doesn't feel as
if he will have the votes in Congress
because of Southern opposition.

It's time I end this rather lengthy letter
and when I write you again, I hope I'll
have better news from this side of the
Atlantic. Please kiss your babies for me
and maybe one of these days I will come
to Benin to meet your wonderful family.

With much love,
Your sister.
Claudia

Claudia detected movement behind her and glanced over
her shoulder to find her mother peering at what she'd written. For the past three days she hadn't had to wake Sarah to
get her ready to brush her teeth, take a bath, or dress.

"Are you ready to eat breakfast?"

Sarah sat at the table and laced her fingers together. "Not right now. I'm just going to put up a pot of coffee. Would you like a cup?"

Claudia smiled. "Yes, please." Sarah offering to make coffee was another indication that she was slowly returning to her former self.

Sarah pointed to the letter. "Is it hard for you to write in a different language?"

Claudia glanced down at what she'd written in French. "No." She tapped her forehead. "If I think in the language, then it's easy for me to speak and write it."

Sarah smiled. "Mavis has taught you well. Speaking of Mavis, I'm planning to stay with her for a while."

"What do you mean, a while?" Claudia asked.

"She's invited me to stay with her for a couple of months. There are too many things here that remind me of Earl. And I can also feel his spirit."

"Does his spirit disturb you, Mama?"

"Sometimes. He keeps telling me that things will be all right and that I shouldn't be so sad."

"He's right, Mama, because you still have wonderful memories of all the good times you shared together. You're luckier than a lot of couples because not only did you get to live with your husband, but y'all also went to work together every day. Daddy died of a heart attack and that's something none of us could've prevented."

Sarah lowered her eyes. "He made me promise not to say anything to you, but he'd had a couple of heart attacks when you were in college."

"But you should've said something, Mama. You could have given me a hint that he wasn't well."

"There were times when I tried, but I kept thinking about what Earl would say if you knew."

Reaching across the table, Claudia placed her hands over Sarah's. "I never would've let on that you'd told me."

Sarah's mouth twisted into a cynical smile. "I know you never would've betrayed me."

She extricated her hands from Claudia's. "I need coffee."

"Don't get up, Mama. I'll make the coffee."

"No, you stay put. You've done enough for me, and it's time you go home and take care of your husband. You've neglected him for far too long."

"Robert's okay. What I don't want to do is leave you alone."

"I'm not going to be alone, Claudia. Mavis is coming up from Biloxi this afternoon to pick me up and take me back with her. She told me I could live with her for as long as I want."

"Is that what you want, Mama? To live with your sister?"

"Of course, it's what I want. I know I've been a burden—"

"Don't, Mama," Claudia said, cutting Sarah off. "Don't ever say that you're burden. You needed me and I'm glad that I could be here for you."

"But you lost your job because of me."

"I didn't lose it. I quit. And when the time is right, I'll get another one."

"I know you really loved working at that bank."

"Liked, not loved," she said truthfully.

Claudia realized she would've been more committed, more loyal to the Black-owned banking institution if Mr. Gaskin hadn't issued an ultimatum: her job or her cause. She'd chosen her job because that decision had been taken out of her hands earlier that day when Denny Clark had made the same request: stop registering Black voters.

"How long do you think it will take for you to find another job?" Sarah asked.

"I really don't know, Mama. I think I'm going to look for something closer to Freedom."

"Does it have to be in banking?"

Claudia felt an emotion she hadn't experienced since her

father's funeral: peace. Her mother was on the road to becoming her former self. She was more animated than Claudia had seen her in weeks.

"No, it doesn't have to be in banking. By the way, I'll hang out here with you until Aunt Mavis comes."

"I'm going to have to pack some clothes."

Claudia stood up. "We'll do that after we eat breakfast. And don't worry about the house because I'll come by every other day to check on everything. I'll empty the refrigerator and turn it off and wash any remaining laundry."

Sarah also rose to stand. "I don't know how long I'm going to live here. I'm seriously thinking about selling this house because it's too big for one person."

Walking across the kitchen, Claudia removed the top on a coffee can. "If you do sell it, then you can move in with me and Robert."

"I can't do that, Claudia."

"Why not, Mama?"

"Because I wouldn't feel comfortable. Please don't get me wrong, sweetie. I like your husband, but not enough to live under the same roof with him."

Claudia's hands stilled filling the basket in the coffeepot with grounds. "Why would you say that? Robert adores you."

"Not enough to want his mother-in-law to live with him."

"I hope history is not going to repeat itself with you and Robert, like you were with Grandma."

"What are you talking about?"

"I shouldn't have to spell it out for you, Mama. You and Grandma never agreed on anything—especially when it came to me. There was always a push and pull, with me in the middle."

"That's because your grandmother was selfish and controlling. From the moment you were born it was all about her grandbaby girl. I know she loved you, Claudia, but I shouldn't have had to compete with my mother-in-law for my child's attention."

"What does that have to do with Robert?"

"Your husband is a lot like your grandmother. He doesn't want to share you—not even with your mother. And he resents you spending nights with me when you should be with him."

Claudia experienced twin emotions of relief and concern. She was relieved that Sarah had dealt with her grief and appeared willing to live her life without her husband, but Claudia was concerned because she didn't know Robert as well as she'd believed she did.

Once Aunt Mavis arrived to take Sarah to Biloxi, she would go back to her own home to sleep in her own bed beside her husband.

Chapter 24

I don't think of all the misery but of the beauty that still remains.
—Anne Frank, *The Diary of a Young Girl*

Claudia set down the iron and stared at the television when a special bulletin flashed across the screen, interrupting a daytime soap opera she'd begun watching since she'd resigned her position at the bank. The image of Walter Cronkite appeared, and she froze when the news correspondent announced that President Kennedy had been shot during a trip to Dallas and was transported by the Secret Service to a nearby hospital.

Turning off the iron, she sat on the living room sofa, her hands sandwiched between her knees. Claudia recalled Medgar Evers's assassination five months earlier. The Klan had murdered Evers, and she prayed it wasn't a Black person who'd retaliated and shot JFK, because the result would be open warfare on every Black man, woman, or child in the country.

An hour later her trance was shattered with the announcement that the president had succumbed to his wounds and Vice President Lyndon Baines Johnson was to be sworn in as the thirty-sixth US President.

The telephone rang, and she reached over to answer it before it rang a second time. "Moore residence."

"Babe, turn on the television."

"I have it on, Robert. Have they caught who killed the president?"

"I don't know. But once I hear something I'll call you."

"Do you think it was a Black person?"

"Hell no! We don't do shit like that, Claudia. I'll bet the police will catch whoever shot the president and he'll be convicted of murder, while that bastard who assassinated Medgar will go scot-free despite the airtight evidence against him."

Byron de la Beckwith had been arrested two weeks after shooting Medgar Evers, once the sheriff verified fingerprints found on the discarded murder weapon matched those in FBI files based on Beckwith's military history.

"What type of president do you think Johnson will be?" she asked Robert.

"Only time will tell. But the country must get past a period of mourning, then we'll see how much influence Johnson has with Congress to push through Kennedy's legislative agenda. With all that's going on I'll probably be here late, so I won't be eating dinner with you."

"Okay."

Claudia ended the call and refocused her attention to the television. She'd been back in her home for two days, yet she and Robert hadn't recaptured the intimacy they'd shared before her father passed away. Robert Moore had changed, and Claudia suspected it was because he'd been wholly indoctrinated by an ideology that no longer included nonviolence. The mention of Black Power had become a part of his lexicon when he stated some in the civil rights movement were tired of waiting for the government to parcel out freedom like crumbs from bread that wasn't fit for human consumption.

The telephone rang again, and she answered it with her pat greeting identifying their residence, but there was no response on the other end of the connection. She could hear someone breathing and after several seconds she hung up. It rang again, and when she answered, the caller hung up before she could. *Maybe they called the wrong number. Or maybe it was someone who wanted to talk, not to her, but to Robert.*

It had been nearly four months following the Kennedy assassination and still Claudia found herself unable to turn off the television during the nightly news. It was as if the networks wanted to keep the incident fresh in the minds of all Americans.

She'd been watching television the day before President Kennedy's scheduled state funeral and a man who was later identified as Jack Ruby shot and killed Lee Harvey Oswald as cameras were rolling. Conspiracy theories were rampant when Oswald—a former marine who had lived in the Soviet Union for almost three years and had married a Russian woman—had been charged as Kennedy's assassin. Journalists had become bloodhounds sniffing out theories that Oswald had been hired by the CIA to kill Kennedy, while they confirmed that Jack Ruby had ties to the New Orleans Mafia.

Newspapers increased their circulation with headlines that hinted that Cuban revolutionary leader Fidel Castro had sanctioned Kennedy's assassination in retaliation for the standoff of the October 1962 Cuban Missile Crisis, when an American spy plane secretly photographed a missile site being built by the Soviet Union on the island ninety miles off the coast of the United States. Kennedy had ordered a blockade of the island and by the end of the year all the missiles had left Cuba.

Claudia drove from Freedom to Biloxi several days a week to share lunch with Sarah, who appeared to have completely recovered from the shock of losing her husband. Claudia had decided to drive to Biloxi earlier than usual because she wanted to stop at the bank where she'd been employed to complete several transactions. She arrived minutes after they opened the doors for business and came face-to-face with her former boss. Claudia gave Henry Gaskin a saccharine smile.

"Good morning, Mr. Gaskin."

He nodded. "Good morning, Mrs. Moore."

"I just came to close out my savings and checking accounts and to get something out of my safe deposit box."

The bank manager seemed to recover from her unexpected visit. "Before you do that, I'd like to speak to you. In my office."

Claudia could not imagine what he wanted to talk to her about, but she was curious enough to say, "Okay." She ignored the curious stares of the other employees as she followed him to his office.

"Please sit down, Mrs. Moore."

She sat, recalling another time when she'd occupied the same chair and was told to stop registering Black voters or lose her job. Henry Gaskin clasped and unclasped his hands. "Believe it or not, I'd planned to call you because I wanted to talk to you about something."

"What do you want to talk about?"

"I'd like for you to consider working here again."

Claudia successfully concealed a Cheshire cat grin as she averted her eyes. It was apparent the bank manager not only missed her but that he also *needed* her.

"Do you currently have a loan officer?"

"I do, but he's new, so he's still learning."

"Isn't that what most people do—learn on the job? It was the same with me when I began working here."

"The difference is it'd only taken you weeks and not months to adjust to the position."

"Are you saying that if you rehire me, then this person will be fired?"

"Yes," Mr. Gaskin said after a swollen pause.

Claudia shook her head. "I'm sorry, Mr. Gaskin, but I will not become a party to someone losing their position because you believe I'm better qualified. What I will do, if I decide to work for this bank again, is train the person, but as your assistant manager."

The bank manager swallowed several times as his expression mirrored shock. "I don't have an assistant manager," he whispered.

"You will when you hire me. And having a Black woman in a managerial position will elevate this bank's image that you're willing to see us as workplace equals. You hired me, Mr. Gaskin, because I have a business degree, and that means I can only be an asset, and not a liability."

"I'm aware of that, but can you wait for me to make a call to the president of the board of directors to get his approval?"

"I have nothing but time, so please make your call."

Mr. Gaskin picked up the telephone receiver. "Can you give me an idea of what you want for a starting salary?" He nodded when Claudia gave him a figure that was ten percent more than she'd earned as the loan officer.

Henry Gaskin ended his call, smiling. "Well, Mrs. Moore, I'm happy to welcome you once again as an employee, and in the position of assistant manager. When do you think you'll be able to begin?"

"Monday." It was Friday and she needed the weekend to prepare to reenter the workforce after not working for seven months.

He nodded, smiling. "Then Monday it is." Reaching across the desk, he extended his hand. "Thank you, Mrs. Moore."

Claudia took the proffered hand. "You're welcome, Mr. Gaskin."

She left his office and walked out of the bank. Now that she would be working there again there was no need to close out her accounts.

Robert stared at Claudia. "Do you really want to go back and work at a place that refused to give you a leave without pay because you were dealing with a family crisis?"

"Yes, Robert. I've been out of work for seven months and I feel like a robot. Now that my mother's living in Biloxi with my aunt, I get up every morning and rack my brain about what I'm going to do for the day."

"You would have something to do if you were a mother."

"I decided that isn't going to happen now."

Robert struggled not to raise his voice. There were times when he lost patience with her as he attempted to explain that he could no longer turn the other cheek when he saw maimed and beaten Black women and children huddled together in overcrowded jail cells, waiting to be charged and hopefully subsequently released on bail.

The phone rang, and Robert pushed back his chair and walked out of the kitchen and into the living room to answer the call. "Moore residence."

"You're dead, nigga."

"Go to hell, motherfucker!"

Robert hung up. He hadn't told Claudia about the threatening calls he'd received at the SNCC office because he knew it would upset her. She'd mentioned someone calling the house but hanging up without saying anything. It was obvious whenever they hadn't reached him at the SNCC office they would call his home. Each time, the same male voice warned him to stop registering Black voters.

"Who are you yelling at?"

He turned to see Claudia staring at him. He hadn't heard her enter the living room. "Some clown deciding they were funny," he lied.

"Was it necessary for you to curse at them?"

"Yes, it was. Because he called me a nigger."

She smiled. "Good for you."

Robert forced a smile. His wife had no idea how dangerous his political activities had become. Not only had he registered Blacks who came to the office, but he'd managed to get signatures of those who'd been jailed, under the guise that he was taking down information he needed to pass along to their family members. Most times the guards were too busy to take an interest in a Black lawyer talking to their prisoners.

He'd told Claudia that he did not marry her for her to become a widow, but he knew that could possibly become a reality with the increasing threats on his life. However, he had taken steps to secure her financial future if anything were to happen to him.

"When do you plan to go back to work?" Robert asked, as if the telephone call hadn't interrupted their conversation.

"Monday."

He forgot about the threatening telephone call when Claudia revealed how she'd negotiated with the manager of the bank to become his assistant. "You are an incredible woman, Mrs. Claudia Patterson-Moore," he said, smiling.

Claudia inclined her head. "Thank you, Mr. Robert Lawrence Moore."

"I think we should celebrate your new position."

Resting her elbow on the table, Claudia cupped her chin on the heel of her hand. "When?"

"What do you think about going away for a weekend to combine your promotion with our second wedding anniversary?"

"I love it," Claudia said, her lids lowering over her eyes and hiding her innermost thoughts from him. "Where do you want to go?"

"I don't know. I'll let you choose the place."

"I'm not going to have any earned vacation time, so we'll have to leave Friday night and return by Sunday."

Robert angled his head. "I'm certain you'll come up with something."

Claudia could not have predicted it would be the last time she would share dinner with her husband, when she got a call the following night from the local sheriff that Robert had been killed when his car had flipped over and rolled down into an embankment.

She existed in what she thought of an alternative universe when she'd called Ivy Moore to tell her Robert was dead, then Yvonne to let her know she had lost her cousin. Her aunt Mavis had called a doctor, who had given Claudia something to keep her calm once she broke down, as she'd become hysterical and she couldn't stop crying.

Yvonne and her husband made all the funeral arrangements, and the church Claudia had attended as a child overflowed with members of various civil rights organizations and demonstrators who'd come to know the soft-spoken, bespectacled attorney advocating for them. Even Henry Gaskin had driven up from Biloxi to attend the funeral and to reassure Claudia to take as much time as she needed to mourn her late husband.

She'd received sympathy cards and telegrams from Dr. Martin Luther King Jr., Myrlie Evers, John Lewis, Ella Baker, Stokely Carmichael, and Fannie Lou Hamer. Local newspapers had carried the story that Robert had been speeding along an unlit, rain-slicked road and had lost control of his vehicle. A motorist going in the opposite direction reported the accident to the local sheriff, who had found her name and phone number on Robert's emergency contact card.

Claudia did not believe it was an accident because she'd never known Robert to speed, especially at night, because he'd admitted to having poor night vision. Her suspicions were confirmed when a worker at his SNCC office revealed that Robert had received several threats against his life. Threats that Robert had failed to tell her about.

Claudia delayed returning to work for two weeks, because she knew the longer she remained at home the more difficult it would be to leave. Ivy had returned to New York, seeming to have aged ten years, and Claudia thanked her for sharing her son with her and promised they would stay in contact.

She woke one morning, ten days after she'd buried Robert

in the Patterson family plot, with a single purpose. And when she sat behind the wheel of her car she knew exactly where she was going and who she wanted to see. It took less than twenty minutes to locate the building with a WHITE MEN ONLY sign on the front door.

Claudia knocked on the door, and when it opened, she knew she'd shocked the man on the other side. Not only wasn't she white, but she was also a woman. "Tell Denny Clark that Claudia Moore is here to see him."

"Can't you read the sign? This place is for White men only."

"I can read, and I'm willing to bet a lot better than you. Now you tell Denny Clark to come out or I'm going to start yelling and won't stop until he does."

He slammed the door in her face and Claudia tapped her foot as she waited for it to open again. She knew it was risky coming to a place where Klan members were known to congregate in Hackersville, but she was past caring.

Claudia had discovered the building's address when she found a map on Robert's desk with the towns and cities with KKK chapters. Denny had come from Madison, which did not have a chapter, but nearby Hackersville did. She'd come to Hackersville on a hunch and had hit the jackpot.

The door opened again, and Denny stared at her with near-colorless blue eyes. "What the hell are you doing here?"

She stood up straighter. "Didn't your man tell you that I want to talk to you?"

"About what!" he said between clenched teeth.

Claudia refused to back down. "My husband. Or should I say my late husband."

Denny grabbed her arm and steered her around to the side of the building. "This will be the first and the last time I'll allow you to come here and talk to me."

"I don't need another time if you answer my question," she retorted.

"What's that?"

"Did you have anything to do with my husband's so-called accident?"

His expression softened. "You think I had something to do with your husband's death?"

"Yes."

Denny shook his head as he met her eyes. "You're wrong, Claudia. When I told you that you were under my protection, that protection also extended to your family. You, your mother, father, grandmother, and your aunt *and* your husband had nothing to fear from my men."

"I don't believe you."

"You don't have to believe me. I know you must think of me as nothing more than a piece of racist shit, and I'll admit that I am a racist, but whenever I give my word, I never go back on it. So, I suggest you look elsewhere if you believe someone ran your husband's car off the road."

Claudia placed a trembling hand over her mouth. If it wasn't the Klan chasing Robert, then who? "Can you find out for me who did?" she asked between her fingers.

Denny reached over and removed her hand from her mouth. "No. You can ask me anything, but not that."

Her eyes filled with tears, and she willed them not to fall. "Why not?"

"Because I will not become a traitor to what I believe in."

"What you believe in is evil, Denny. You're filled with so much hate and loathing that I feel sorry for you."

"You feel sorry for me? That's a load of bullshit."

Claudia knew he was trying to goad her, to get her angry enough to lose her temper. "The days are numbered for you and your kind, Denny. And I hope when that day comes you'll have the courage to put a gun to your head and blow your brains out. If not, then I wish you luck because Mississippi, as you know it, will never be the same." She turned on her heels and walked back to where she'd parked her car.

Claudia drove to Freedom and to the house she'd shared

with Robert. Now she knew how her mother felt when she said she couldn't stay in her house because she'd felt Earl's spirit. It had become the same for her. Not only had she loved Robert Moore, but she was still in love with everything they'd shared during their brief marriage.

Robert had declared he hadn't married her to make her a widow.

But he had.

PART THREE

1968

ASHLEY BOOTH

Chapter 25

Question: What has four eyes and can't see?
Answer: Mississippi
         —children's riddle

Claudia planned to do something she'd believed she would never do—leave Mississippi. It had been her home for twenty-seven years, a place where family roots run deep and a place where she'd buried too many of her loved ones within a short period of time. It hadn't only been the loss of family members but Mississippi's 1964 Freedom Summer. The police, the Ku Klux Klan and the White Citizens' Council had used murder, arson, beatings, increased arrests, and intimidation to prevent Blacks from exercising the right to vote to achieve social equality.

Meanwhile, Claudia felt as if her life had become as predictable as the sun rising in the east and setting in the west. She woke Monday through Friday to go to work, and her weekends were spent with her mother or her aunt. Sarah had sold her house in Freedom after she'd made the decision to live in Biloxi with Mavis, who'd gotten Sarah a position in her school as a cafeteria worker. And once Claudia informed her mother she was moving to New York, she'd offered to take Sarah with her. Sarah refused, stating she would never be able to survive the frigid winters.

Sitting with her mother and aunt in their parlor, Claudia stared at her single piece of luggage near the front door. She'd called a taxi company to pick her up and take her to the Gulfport-Biloxi International Airport for her late-afternoon flight to New York City.

Sarah, who'd recently cut her hair, combed her fingers through the auburn waves. "I can't believe you're moving to New York during one of the coldest months in the year."

"It was either move now or lose my position," Claudia said.

She'd sent out résumés to several New York City banks and when she'd received an offer from one in Harlem, she'd called to arrange an interview. She'd flown up mid-December for her first interview and returned in early January for the second. Both times she'd stayed with Yvonne, who'd graduated dental school two years before and had moved back to New York with her husband, who now was a resident at Harlem Hospital. Yvonne had invited Claudia to live with them until she was able to find an apartment. She'd taken her former college roommate up on her offer because the year before, Ivy Moore had married a fellow teacher and moved to Albany. When Claudia searched for the city on the map, she'd discovered it was approximately a three-hour drive from Manhattan.

"I hope you packed enough winter clothes," Mavis said.

"I did."

She'd ordered sweaters, jackets, and several wool coats and had them shipped to Yvonne's address. And now that minidresses were in vogue, she'd purchased tights and pantyhose in various colors and patterns, while keeping in mind that banking was a conservative institution that fostered a businesslike image for their customers.

Once she'd decided to relocate, Claudia had listed her house with a Realtor and sold the house with all the contents to a young couple who were grateful they didn't have the extra expense of purchasing furniture. She'd shipped all of Robert's personal effects to his mother, donated his clothes to the local church, and his law books to Howard University for needy students. Claudia had boxed up her clothes, textbooks, and family photographs and had stored them in the attic at Mavis's house for safekeeping.

"When do you think you're going to get a vacation so you can come down for a visit?" Sarah asked.

"Probably not until next year, Mama. After I reach my first anniversary, I will be entitled to ten days' vacation."

Sarah grimaced. "That's a long time from now. Maybe once school is out, your aunt and I can come up to New York to see you."

"Don't forget, Sarah, that I'm planning for us to sail to Europe this summer," Mavis told her sister.

Sarah exhaled an audible breath. "I don't know why I keep forgetting that."

"I know you're going to have a wonderful time, Mama," Claudia predicted, recalling the six weeks she'd spent in Paris. "Have you thought about flying to Europe, Aunt Mavis?"

Mavis shook her head. "No. I much prefer sailing because of the onboard services. Sitting out on deck just reading or relaxing is something you can't do sitting for hours in an airplane where you can only get up to use the lavatory."

Claudia nodded. Her aunt was right. "I know if I ever get the opportunity to return to Europe, I'm certain I'll take an ocean liner." The doorbell rang, and Claudia stood and slipped her arms into the sleeves of a wool coat. "That's my driver." She kissed her mother, then her aunt before she picked up her single piece of luggage. "I'll call you when I get to New York to let you know I got there safely." She left the house without a backward glance because she knew it would trigger a rush of tears from her and Sarah.

During the ride to the airport Claudia asked herself if she knew what she was doing. She was moving to a new city to live with a friend until she could secure lodgings of her own. Her need to relocate had been a long time coming. The first time she'd contemplated leaving Mississippi was when she'd celebrated Christmas without Robert. That's when his loss had become so profound that she'd thought about selling their home and moving to Biloxi, where she would be closer to her mother, aunt, and her job.

She'd enjoyed her position as the bank's assistant manager and there had been hints from the board that they were considering promoting her to manager once Henry Gaskin retired. However, they were unaware that she had no intention of becoming bank manager because with each passing year she'd become more and more embittered with Mississippi Democrats who'd excluded Blacks from the political process.

She made it to the airport and boarded her flight, and within minutes of taking off Claudia felt free—freer than she'd felt in years. *What has four eyes and can't see? Mississippi.*

The childhood ditty swirled around in her head like a needle stuck in a groove on a record; it kept playing over and over until Claudia wanted to scream as the plane climbed to cruising altitude. White Mississippians were blind to the truth that what they were attempting to preserve, what they'd fought and died for during the Civil War, was coming to an end. And for Claudia, the irony was that poor White folks were on the front lines fighting for segregation for their wealthier brethren who hid in the shadows to escape prosecution.

Claudia closed her eyes and settled down to sleep before the nonstop flight touched down in New York City. *Give me your tired, your poor, your huddled masses yearning to breathe free.* She knew none of the huddled masses yearning to breathe free would be free until everyone in the country was free.

The plane touched down and within seconds of walking

out of the airport terminal Claudia felt the bite of the frigid
February nighttime temperature attack her exposed skin like
tiny razorblades. Her mother was right. It felt as if she'd
come to the North Pole. Gripping the handles of her carry-on
bag, Claudia waited for Yvonne to drive up. She'd just
packed a carry-on because she didn't want to wait at baggage
claim for her luggage. She ran over to greet Yvonne when she
pulled up curbside and got out of a late-model Buick.

"Welcome back to the Big Apple," Yvonne said with a
wide grin.

Claudia hugged Yvonne. "It's more like a candied apple.
Red, hard, and cold."

Yvonne took her carry-on. "I'm glad you're wearing a hat
and coat because this week the below-freezing temperatures
have been brutal. Get in the car where it's warm while I put
your bag in the trunk."

She opened the passenger-side door, got in, and let out a
sigh when heat enveloped her in a cocoon of soothing warmth.
Claudia knew it was going to take some time for her to get
used to New York's frigid winters.

Yvonne slipped in behind the wheel, checked her mirrors,
and then pulled away from the curb. "How was your flight?"

Claudia met the dark eyes behind a pair of oversized
glasses, and in that instant a chill eddied through her when
she realized how similar Yvonne's and Robert's eyes were.
Not only were they first cousins, but both wore glasses.
Yvonne had recently cut her long hair and wore it in a Sassoon Greek-goddess style, while Claudia had had an inch cut
off the ends of her hair until it was chin-length. She'd set it
on rollers to achieve a smooth, wavy look or left it to dry
naturally with a mass of curls framing her face. Many Black
people were embracing the Afro hairstyle as a symbol of
pride, rebellion, and Black empowerment.

"It was good. I managed to fall asleep as soon as it took
off and didn't wake until we were ready to land. I didn't get

much sleep last night because I couldn't stop thinking about leaving my mother."

Yvonne gave her a sidelong glance before returning her attention to the road. "But isn't your mother living with her sister?"

"Yes. They've been living together for years. It began after my father passed away."

"Good for them. By the way, have you thought about going back to Paris?"

"I have a few times. My Aunt Virgie and I still write each other, and she calls the States several times a year."

"That must have cost her a lot of money."

"Money is something my aunt doesn't have to concern herself with. She's still tutoring the children of well-to-do Parisians to perfect their English and she also has American students as clients who need to improve their French."

"Are you still fluent?"

Claudia nodded. "Yes. Whenever I spend time with Aunt Mavis we speak to each other in French, Italian, and occasionally Spanish. Now that Americans aren't allowed to travel to Cuba, she will alternate and go to Puerto Rico one year and then Mexico the next."

"Your aunt sounds like a real globetrotter."

"She's not married and doesn't have any children, so she travels."

"Do you find it odd that your aunts never married?"

"Not really," Claudia replied. "My aunts are what you would call liberated women who are in control of their own destinies. Both claim they didn't want to be under the yoke of some man telling them what they can and cannot do."

Yvonne accelerated as she moved from a slow lane and into one with flowing traffic. "Not all marriages are like that, Claudia. Take me and Stephen. We're married and both doctors. And when I told him that I wasn't going to drop my maiden name because I wanted folks to be able to differentiate between which Dr. Jones they were referring to, he said he didn't have a problem with that. He's Dr. Jones and I'm Dr. Chapman-Jones."

"Do people call you that?"

"Yes. It's a common practice in England, so some folks think I'm of West Indian descent, because some of them also hyphenate their names."

"How often do you get to see Robert's mother?" Claudia asked after a comfortable silence.

"Not too often since she moved upstate. Have you kept in touch with her?"

"We spoke a couple of times, and maybe I'm wrong, but I think your aunt blames me for Robert losing his life."

Yvonne gasped. "Did she come out and say that?'

"She didn't have to, Yvonne. Ivy had let it slip that if her son hadn't moved to Mississippi, he would still be alive."

"That's bullshit, Claudia. My aunt knew Robert wanted to be a civil rights lawyer and that meant going South and getting involved. And didn't you tell him that he was becoming too militant, and that his actions were attracting attention from the wrong people, while his death could've been what the law concluded: an accident. I loved my cousin, but Robert knew what he'd signed up for, and he was willing to risk his life for his beliefs."

"Speaking of civil rights lawyers, how's Dennis doing?" Yvonne's brother hadn't attended Robert's funeral because his wife was giving birth to their first child.

Yvonne sucked her teeth. "Please don't get me started about the heifer he married who has him on lockdown. Whenever I call to speak to him, she picks up the extension and listens in on our conversation. She finally convinced him to leave the NAACP and join some relative's law firm. He's so henpecked that I don't recognize my brother anymore. And the one time my mother called to speak to him, Wendy told my mother he was tired, and she didn't want to disturb him. Mom went off and cussed her out. That was sometime last summer and that was the last time we heard from either of them."

"How could your brother divorce his family because his wife wants to control his life?"

"I don't know, roomie. I suppose you could say that he's pussy whipped."

Claudia laughed so hard that she struggled to catch her breath. She could always count on Yvonne to make her laugh. To not take life so seriously. She had three days before she was scheduled to begin her job and she was looking forward to starting over in a city with the reputation that it never went to sleep.

Chapter 26

The great courageous act that we must all do, is
to have the courage to step out of our history and
past so that we can live our dreams.
—Oprah Winfrey

During the drive on the bridge leading to Manhattan,
Yvonne told Claudia that Stephen's parents had moved
out of their Harlem brownstone two weeks ago and into a
downtown high-rise apartment building designated for Bellevue Hospital staff.

"The timing was perfect because our lease was due to ex-
pire at the end of this month and we went from living in a
one-bedroom apartment to living in their rowhouse with
more space than we know what to do with. We're living on
the first floor, and if you want you can have the apartment on
the top floor."

"What's on the second floor?" Claudia asked.

"We're going to use that for entertaining sometime in the
future. The third floor is completely furnished and there was
a time when my in-laws rented it out, but after their last tenants moved out, they'd decided not to rent it again. Someone
used to put cigarettes out on the parquet floor rather than
use an ashtray. Stephen's dad thought he was going to have

to replace the floors, but fortunately a carpenter was able to refinish them, so now they look like new."

"I don't smoke, so you don't have to worry that I'll put out butts on the floor or burn down the house."

"I know you'd mentioned finding an apartment, but I'm serious about you living with us for as long as you want, Claudia."

"I appreciate the offer, but I won't feel completely independent until I have my own place. I went from living with my parents, to my aunt's, and then with you at Hampton. And once I graduated it was back with my parents until Robert and I found a house of our own. When I do find an apartment, it will be the first time in my life I won't have to share it with anyone else."

"Now you really sound like your aunts," Yvonne teased.

"Folks used to call Mavis and Virgie uppity because not only were they educated but also independent. They chose the men they wanted to deal with, and they came and went without having to answer to anyone. If that made them uppity, then I want to be just like them when I grow up."

"You're already grown, roomie, and you're more like your aunts than you realize. When you told me what you'd wanted when your boss asked for you to come back to work at the bank, I couldn't stop laughing because I would've given anything to have seen his expression."

Claudia smiled when she recalled the incident. "He was a little shocked."

"Like hell he was," Yvonne countered. "I bet if he could have, he would've cussed you out loud and long for forcing him to do something he didn't want to do. He'd probably never had a woman in his face issuing an ultimatum because he was the HNIC."

"No, you didn't say that!"

"I didn't want to say the N-word, so it's 'Head N In Charge.'"

"Mr. Gaskin did like to throw his authority around every

so often. But after I came back as his assistant, he was a lot calmer because he saw how I'd related to my coworkers."

"How did he react when you told him you were resigning for the second time?" Yvonne asked.

"The only thing I'm going to say is he didn't take it well, because he was visibly upset. I truly felt sorry for the man, but I'd made up my mind that I was leaving Mississippi."

Yvonne exited the bridge and continued along 125th Street, and then made a right onto Lenox Avenue until she reached 130th Street, then another right along a block with beautiful row houses claiming front yards and wooden porches.

Yvonne maneuvered into a space behind a red Mustang but didn't shut off the engine. "New York City isn't the promised land, but it's a whole lot better than any state that claims a flag with the Stars and Bars. Dumbasses still fighting the Civil War don't know when it's time to quit."

Claudia nodded in agreement. "The Black Panther Party for Self-Defense's ideology of Black Power, gun rights, and anti-imperialism is far more militant when compared to Dr. King's philosophy of nonviolence."

"If militant Black people are willing to challenge the United States government, then they damn sure don't fear the Klan."

"How does Stephen feel about the Black Power movement?" Claudia asked Yvonne.

"We try not to talk about it because he claimed I've been radicalized and then I called him Uncle Tom because he wants to appease the White power structure. After that disagreement he wouldn't talk to me for days."

"Politics and religion are sensitive topics friends and families should stay away from if they want to avoid making enemies. I knew Robert was turning into an extremist when he started espousing Marxist and Communist rhetoric, and when I tried talking to him about not setting himself up as a target to be murdered, he completely ignored me." Claudia paused. "Once I moved back home after my mother seemingly had recovered from losing my father, the relationship I'd had with Robert was never the same."

Yvonne shut off the Buick's engine. "Enough talk about racist White devils. It's time I get you settled. Stephen's home and he's probably entertaining company because that cherry-red Mustang belongs to one of his friends." She got out and retrieved Claudia's carry-on.

Claudia waited for Yvonne to open the gate leading to the house and followed her up the steps to the porch. Streetlights illuminated several structures along the block that needed repair, but that did not detract from what made it without question the most beautiful block of rowhouses in Harlem. Stephen and Yvonne had inherited a house that had been built in freestanding pairs.

Yvonne opened the front door and Claudia was stunned by the furnishings in the vestibule, wondering whether they were antiques or reproductions; and even if they were the latter, the tables, chairs, and lamps were exquisite, as was the parquet flooring covered by a rug with black and white geometric shapes.

She followed her friend down a hallway to a first-floor apartment. Yvonne pushed open the door and Claudia entered an expansive living room to find Stephen sitting on a chair holding a glass containing an amber liquid. Her gaze shifted to the man sitting opposite him. Everyone and everything ceased to exist as the man Yvonne had hinted was Stephen's friend stood up and stared directly at her. At first Claudia thought him rude, but then she was flattered because she'd found him so stunningly attractive. He was unequivocally a Black man from his ebony complexion, dark eyes, and jet-black cropped hair. There was something about his face that called to mind the African masks she had seen in art books.

Stephen set the glass on a coffee table, stood up, and extended his arms, smiling. "Welcome home."

Claudia walked into his embrace. "Thank you, Stephen, for opening your home to me."

Wrapping an arm around her waist, Stephen pulled her close. "There's no need to thank anyone because you are family." He dropped his arm. "Claudia, I'd like you to meet a friend of mine. Ash, this Claudia Moore. Claudia, Ashley Booth."

Ashley approached her and offered his hand. "It's a pleasure meeting you."

Claudia took his hand, finding it almost as soft as her own. "Same here." She lowered her eyes before Ashley could see how much she was affected by him. Not only was he gorgeous, but he smelled wonderful. And judging by the cut of his suit she knew it hadn't come off a department store rack. Ashely Booth was the epitome of sartorial splendor from his barbered hair to the shine on his shoes.

Yvonne walked into the living room and laced her fingers through Stephen's. "Ashley, now that you've met Claudia, will you be staying for dinner?"

Claudia stared at Yvonne, then Ashley, wondering if Yvonne had talked to him about her, or if she'd invited him over as a ruse to get them together. Well, if she had, then Claudia wasn't upset, because there was something about the tall, slender man that intrigued her.

Pushing back the French cuff on his shirt, Ashley glanced at his watch. "Sure."

"Are you certain you're not going to stand up one of your honeys?" Stephen teased.

Yvonne extricated her hand from her husband's and landed a soft punch on his upper arm. "Stop, Stephen. You're embarrassing Ashley."

"I doubt that, sweetheart," Stephen crooned before he kissed Yvonne's hair. "It will take more than a little teasing about women to embarrass the Black Prince of Wall Street."

Stephen calling Ashley the Black Prince of Wall Street

piqued Claudia's curiosity. And was the epithet a compliment or a criticism of his character? She stared at Yvonne's husband. He hadn't changed much over the years. He wore his reddish hair longer than what he had in college and medical school, but his light-brown freckled face looked the same. Stephen Jones had grown up in a family of doctors. His grandfather was a family doctor in Washington, D.C., and his father had also become a doctor.

"Stephen, I'm going to take Claudia upstairs so she can change before we have dinner. Meanwhile, can you please set the table in the dining room for four?"

Stephen saluted. "Yes, boss."

"I can't believe climbing two flights of stairs has me winded," Claudia said after stepping off on the third-story landing.

"I'm used to it because Stephen and I lived in a fifth story walk-up. He preferred an apartment on the top floor because he didn't want folks walking over his head when he needed his sleep."

"How long did it take you to get used to it?"

"A long time, Claudia," Yvonne said when she opened the door to the third-story apartment. "I'd find myself pausing at the fourth floor every time to catch my breath." She opened the door wider. "Here you are. I put your stuff in the smaller bedroom, so you can unpack whenever you find time. Stephen's mother ordered new mattresses for both bedrooms after the tenants moved out. There's a supply of towels and facecloths in the bathroom along with a few grooming supplies."

Claudia set the carry-on on the floor next to a dropleaf table. The apartment was spacious, with a quartet of floor-to-ceiling windows in the living room and dining area. The light from gaslight fixtures shimmered on the gleaming parquet flooring. "It's too beautiful," she said, her voice filled with awe. And as beautiful as it was, Claudia knew she would leave it. She hadn't relocated to New York to relive history by sharing a space with her college roommate.

"I put a roasting chicken in the oven before I left, so it should be ready whenever you come down."

"Thank you, Yvonne. I mean for everything."

"Please don't start roomie or I'll start crying and can't stop. Now that I'm pregnant, it must be hormones."

Claudia stared, tongue-tied. "You're what?" she said once she recovered her voice.

Yvonne smiled. "I found out last week that I'm pregnant. I'd forgotten that I didn't get my period in January because we were so busy moving, but then one morning I threw up. At first, I thought it was something I'd eaten that didn't agree with me, but when it happened again, I knew for certain I was pregnant. Stephen and I will become parents in late September or early October."

Claudia hugged Yvonne, but not too tight. "Congratulations, mama!"

"Thank you, and I'd like to ask you if you would become my baby's godmother."

"Of course, Yvonne. I'm honored you asked."

"Thank you, roomie. I'll see you downstairs."

It wasn't often that Stephen Jones called Ashley at his office, but when Ashley had picked up the phone and heard his friend's voice, his first reaction was something had happened to Stephen's father. Fortunately, that wasn't the situation. Stephen was calling to tell him that he and Yvonne were expecting their first child and wanted him to be godfather to their son or daughter. Ashley hadn't hesitated when he'd said yes.

He and Stephen did not grow up together but had become acquainted once Ashley discovered their fathers had attended and graduated medical school together. Ashley's father, Dr. Thaddeus Booth, had invited some of his former medical school buddies and their families to the Booth summer home on Sag Harbor, Long Island, and Stephen, who was a first-year biology student at Hampton Institute, had come with his father and mother. Because Ashley was also a college student, they'd quickly bonded.

Stephen was forthcoming when he'd told Ashley how he'd initially resented his father for leaving him and his mother in D.C. for six years while he'd established himself as a preeminent New York City pediatric surgeon, but once he'd read about how Dr. Stephen Jones had saved the lives of countless Black children, his father had become his hero. Unfortunately, Ashley's father wasn't his hero because Thaddeus had an Achilles' heel: his unfaithful wife.

All thoughts about his parents' bizarre relationship vanished when Claudia Moore walked into the living room in a pair of dark gray slacks, a pale pink cashmere twinset, and black leather loafers. He knew it was rude to stare, but he couldn't pull his gaze away from the cloud of curls framing her beautiful face. She smiled, and Ashley knew she was a woman who made him want to get to know more about her. And the "more" was if she was engaged, married, or single, and if the latter, then he wanted to know if she would be willing to go out with him.

"Hello, again," he said, smiling. He slipped his hands into the pockets of his suit trousers and rocked back on his heels. "So, you and Yvonne are friends."

"Yes."

"How did you meet?"

"We were college roommates. How did you and Stephen meet?"

"Our fathers were in the same graduating class at Howard University College of Medicine."

Claudia moved closer. "Should I assume you didn't follow in your father's footsteps if Stephen referred to you as the Black Prince of Wall Street?"

"You assume correctly. I knew I'd never be able to become a doctor because I wouldn't be able to deal with blood."

"Do you faint at the sight of it?"

Ashley realized she was teasing when he saw her smile. "No. But I can't eat a piece of meat if there's blood on the plate."

"Are you saying your steaks must be well-done?"

"I prefer medium-well. And how do you like your meat cooked?"

"Medium-well."

"You guys are going to have a lot more in common than how you like your meat cooked," Yvonne said, as she entered the room carrying a bottle of wine. "Ashley has agreed to be godfather to our baby." She handed him the wine. "Can you please put the wine on the table?"

Claudia closed her eyes. Ashley taking the wine from Yvonne and walking into the dining room dispelled the soporific spell he'd woven by their just sharing the same space. She had interacted with countless numbers of men throughout her life, but there was something about Ashley Booth that affected her in a way others hadn't. Not even Robert.

He'd removed his suit jacket, rolled back his shirt cuffs, and even in his state of relaxation he still projected a sophistication she hadn't seen in men since returning from Europe.

"Do you want me to help you with anything?" she asked Yvonne.

"No, thanks. As soon as Stephen brings out the chicken we can sit and eat."

Seconds later, Stephen walked into the living room carrying a platter with a large golden-brown roasted chicken. "I don't about y'all, but I'm ready to get my eat on."

Claudia wanted to tell Stephen that she was more than ready to get her eat on. The furnishings in the dining room were as elegant as those throughout the house, and she wondered if Stephen's mother had been responsible for decorating the interior of the historic Victorian home.

Claudia met Ashley's eyes when he pulled out a chair at the table to seat her next to Yvonne. "Thank you."

"You're welcome," he whispered in her ear, before he rounded the table to sit opposite her.

She lowered her eyes, focusing on the designs on the silverware rather than meet the dark eyes that seemed to strip away the invisible façade of confidence Claudia had spent years nurturing.

Stephen uncorked the bottle of rosé and filled four crystal glasses, then passed them around the table. He held his glass aloft. "A toast to Claudia for her new job, and for agreeing to become godmother for Yvonne's and my son or daughter. And the same to Ash as godfather."

Claudia saw a sly smile part Ashley's lips as he angled his head. Now she knew their meeting had been prearranged. She was also aware of Yvonne's insistence that it was time for her to begin dating again; that as a young woman there was more to life than her going to work, returning home, and only interacting with her mother and aunt.

She knew her friend was right, but after burying Robert she had fallen into an emotional rut and didn't know how to get out of it. She'd continued to wear her wedding set, which successfully kept men from coming on to her.

The first time she'd come to New York for her initial interview, she hadn't worn the rings because she did not want to give the impression that she was married when she wasn't. She'd told the bank vice-president the truth. She was a widow and was looking to begin the next phase of her life and make new memories.

Stephen carved the chicken with the skill of a surgeon and passed the platter around the table. Side dishes of collard greens, candied sweet potatoes, and cornbread followed.

Yvonne spread a napkin over her lap. "Thanks to my roomie, I've perfected making cornbread."

Ashley picked up a forkful of greens. "You cook, Claudia?"

"Ashley, please," Yvonne drawled. "Claudia can burn some pots."

Claudia smiled. "Thanks to my grandmother, I can cook."

"Don't be so modest," Stephen said. "The one time Yvonne and I drove from Nashville to Mississippi to spend a few days with Claudia, she made everything from fried chicken to baked ham, mustard and turnip greens, candied sweets, pound cake, green beans with white potatoes and smoked ham hocks, biscuits, and cornbread."

"Stephen, you forgot the deviled eggs, potato and macaroni salads," Yvonne reminded him.

A stunned expression flitted over Ashley's features. "You made all of that?"

"Did you grow up in the South?" Claudia asked him.

"No."

"If you had, then you would know that when folks come to stay a while, good Southern hospitality means to treat them right."

Ashley laughed. "Preparing a banquet is treating them right?"

"Of course. I prepared enough so they could take leftovers back to Tennessee. And there was still enough left for Robert to take for lunch."

Ashley leaned back in his chair. "Robert?"

"Robert was my first cousin who married Claudia," Yvonne explained. "He passed away almost four years ago."

A beat passed before Ashley said, "I'm sorry, Claudia, for your loss."

Claudia bowed her head, while willing the tears filling her eyes not to fall as she chided herself for mentioning the name. She nodded because the lump in her throat wouldn't permit her to speak. Even after so many years she'd discovered she wasn't able to let Robert go, not because she couldn't but because she didn't want to.

Chapter 27

There is great power in letting go, and there is
great freedom in moving on.
                        —Author Unknown

Claudia had almost forgotten how much fun she'd shared
with Yvonne and Stephen when they were in college together. They laughed about incidents she had forgotten about,
while including Ashley in their conversation. She'd gleaned
from tidbits of information imparted from Stephen that Ashley worked on Wall Street, and that meant they both had careers geared to business. Claudia concluded that she liked the
modest, urbane man because he didn't boast about what he
did in New York City's Financial District, despite Stephen referring to him as the Black Prince of Wall Street.

Yvonne put her hand over her mouth to conceal a yawn. "I
don't know about you good folks, but not only am I full as a
tick, but I can't seem to keep my eyes open."

Stephen stood and eased Yvonne up from her chair. "Why
don't you go to bed. I will clean up everything."

"I'll help you," Claudia volunteered.

"Me too," Ashley said, coming to his feet.

Stephen shook his head. "That's okay, Ash. Claudia and I
got this."

"Are you sure?" Ashley asked.

"Of course I'm sure."

"The next dinner is on me. Just call and let me know when you're off and I'll make it happen. And, Claudia, you're also invited. Stephen will give you my numbers and I'd like you to call me so we can get together to plan what we'd like to do as godparents. If you call me at my office and I don't pick up, you can leave a message with my assistant. It's the same with my home number. I have an answering service that will pick up my calls."

Claudia successfully schooled her expression not to let on that Ashley asking her to call him had nothing to do with becoming godparents to Stephen and Yvonne's baby. That was something they could talk about a month or even weeks before the impending birth. "Okay."

Yvonne had gone to bed and Ashley had left, leaving Claudia and Stephen with the task of clearing the table and cleaning up the kitchen.

"You have to know that he likes you," Stephen said as he stored leftovers in Tupperware containers.

Claudia gave him a sidelong glance as she handwashed sterling and crystal. "Who are you talking about?"

"Ashley Booth, Claudia. I've known him a long time, and I've seen him with a lot of women, but tonight he wasn't himself."

"Maybe he was shocked that you'd asked him to be a godfather."

"He'd agreed to become godfather before tonight, so it couldn't be that."

She wiped her wet hands on a dish towel. "Did you and Yvonne invite him here tonight because you knew I was coming up?"

"Yes. I wanted you to meet the person with whom you would be sharing godparent duties. I know Yvonne hadn't asked you, but she was certain you would accept. What I didn't expect was Ash's reaction when he first saw you. He couldn't stop staring."

"Why did you call him the Black Prince of Wall Street?" she asked, deliberately ignoring his remark about Ashley staring at her.

"Because that's what he is, Claudia. Ashley graduated from Baruch College near the top of his class, and when companies were forced to hire Blacks to fill their quotas, Ashley was courted by several major investment companies. The headhunters hired by the companies had a bidding war as to which would offer him the most money and benefits."

"Which did he choose? Merrill Lynch or J.P. Morgan?"

"Neither one. He went with a small firm and within a couple of years their clients were able to double, and some triple their initial investments. It's as if he has a sixth sense when it comes to selecting companies in which to invest."

"That really takes tons of confidence."

"Of which Ash has an overabundance, Claudia. The man knows his stuff and because of that he's very successful."

"Is he still working for that company?"

"In a way he is. It merged with a larger investment company last year and Ash was ready to leave but stayed on once he was promoted with a sizeable salary increase to head their newly formed minority business division."

"Good for him."

"Good for any woman lucky enough to get him to settle down."

Claudia busied herself drying the fragile stemware. "What makes you think he wants to settle down? Some men are okay being a bachelor."

"They are until they meet someone who will make them change their minds."

"Why should a woman force a man to change his mind, Stephen? Either he does or he doesn't. I don't want a man I'd have to coerce into marrying me."

"Are you referring to Robert's mother and father's situation? That he was forced to marry Ivy because she was pregnant?"

"Yes, even though I wasn't consciously thinking about them. It hadn't mattered how much I was in love with Robert, I never would've married him if he didn't love me enough to make me his wife."

"What if you were carrying his child, Claudia?"

"That wouldn't have mattered, because I wouldn't be the first woman to have a child out of wedlock and I wouldn't be the last."

"Not to change the subject, but are you willing to go out with Ash if he calls?"

Claudia gave Stephen a direct stare. "Yes."

"Good. Now why don't you turn in, while I finish up here."

"Are you certain you can handle this, Dr. Jones?"

He winked at her. "Very certain, Mrs. Moore."

Claudia could not have imagined her good fortune when Yvonne had invited her to move into her house on what she'd learned was called Astor Row, because she could walk to work. It had taken her less than ten minutes to walk six blocks—door to door.

She identified herself to the bank guard who opened the door for her, and then quickly closed it, much to the disappointment of several customers shivering on the sidewalk as they waited for the bank to open for business. Claudia removed her wool gloves and put them into the pocket of her coat as the branch manager approached her.

John Brennan was tall and muscular, and despite his intimidating size, he'd quickly put her at ease with his beautifully modulated voice. A voice that was perfect for radio.

"Good morning, Mrs. Moore. It's encouraging to know that I won't have a problem with you coming in late."

"Tardiness is a pet peeve of my mine."

"That's good to know. I'd like you to come into my office

because there's a situation that needs to be resolved before you begin working."

Claudia followed him across the banking floor to an alcove behind the platform, while removing her hat and unbuttoning her coat. When she entered the office, it only took a brief glance to realize the meeting wouldn't be between just her and the branch manager. Another man stood up and came around the desk.

"Mrs. Moore, this is Mr. Hamilton from the corporate office. Please sit down because we need to discuss something with you."

She took a chair, facing the desk, while Mr. Brennan elected to stand. Claudia gave the man who had sat down again behind the desk, a direct stare. "What do you need to discuss with me?" she asked. She'd decided to take the initiative to open the discussion.

"Mrs. Moore, I know you were under the impression that you would be hired as this branch's loan officer. However, there is a problem because we misread the date on his retirement form."

Claudia couldn't help but smile. It was the most asinine excuse she'd ever heard. Did they believe she was that naïve? "How did you misread the date, Mr. Hamilton?"

"We mistook the two for a seven. His retirement date isn't until July eighteenth, not February eighteenth."

She wanted to give them the benefit of the doubt. However, she did have an ace in the hole: a letter confirming her employment. "Are you telling me I have to wait five months before I can become the loan officer at this branch?"

Mr. Hamilton nodded. "Yes, Mrs. Moore. Meanwhile Mr. Brennan and I have worked out a plan where you can work at one of our other branches until July."

"In what position?" she asked.

"We have an open teller position at a branch on Broadway near 106th Street. Of course, you'll have to go through a training period before—"

"I don't need a training period, Mr. Hamilton," she inter-rupted. "If you'd read my résumé, you would have seen that I was an assistant bank manager and that meant I was famil-iar with every position in the bank. I opened and closed the bank and took over when the manager called in sick or went on vacation."

"We are aware of your qualifications, Mrs. Moore," John Brennan said, "and that's why I wanted to hire you, and still want you to work at my branch. That will happen only if you are willing to wait five months."

Claudia felt the branch manager was genuinely sorry about the misread dates, but there was something about the so-called explanation that still nagged at her. Why had they waited for her to begin her first day of employment to reveal their dilemma? They wanted her to wait five months and she would. "Okay," she conceded, "I'll wait." Claudia bit back a smile when both men let out audible sighs of relief. "And I'll work at the other branch until then."

John Brennan sat down for the first time. "You were hired as a loan officer, so your paycheck will reflect that going for-ward. I really thank you for being so understanding."

"Things do happen that are beyond our control," she said, smiling.

John Brennan reached over, picked up an envelope on the desk, and handed it to her. "You'll find the address and the name of the branch manager on Broadway in here. I want you to take the day off and relax before you begin tomorrow. And again, I'm so sorry about the mix-up."

Claudia slipped the envelope in her clutch bag, and then stood, both men also rising to their feet. She walked out of the office, her mind in tumult. She still didn't believe the ex-cuse about misreading a retirement date, but she wasn't going to let them know of her suspicions. And if they didn't want her as the loan officer at the Harlem branch, then why? It couldn't be because she was Black because the branch had Black employees. The only other reason could be her sex.

She walked back to Astor Row, and when she entered the house and opened the front door, she saw Yvonne closing the door to her apartment. "Hey, roomie."

"Good morning, Claudia. I thought you were starting your new job today."

"I was, but that's a long story."

Yvonne's eyes narrowed behind the lenses of her glasses. "What happened?"

"I'll tell you later on tonight when you come home."

Yvonne grabbed Claudia's hand. "Tell me now."

Claudia sat at a table in the Jones's eat-in kitchen and told Yvonne everything. "I don't know why, but something keeps nagging at me that they didn't want a woman in the position."

"Not only a woman, but a Black woman, Claudia." Yvonne stood and picked up the receiver to the phone on the countertop. "I'm going to call Ashley to see what he says."

"You don't have to do that!"

Yvonne rolled her eyes. "Yes, I do. I'm certain he's familiar with this underhanded crap, so you need to hear it from him how you should go forward."

Claudia waited for Yvonne to end the call and return to the table. "Ashley says he's going to come by later tonight and take you out to dinner so you can tell him everything. Meanwhile, I need to get going or I'm going to be late for my first patient. I'm only working until four, so I'll see you before you go out with Ashley. Stephen is scheduled to begin a shift at two this afternoon, so he'll be sleeping at the hospital for the next three days. You can hang out down here if you want."

"Thanks, but I'm going to go to the supermarket and do some more shopping."

Since she'd moved in, Claudia had unpacked all the boxes and gone to a nearby supermarket to buy items to fill the refrigerator in the kitchen in her apartment. She still needed staples to fill the pantry that was built off the kitchen. Claudia had begun to feel comfortable in the furnished apartment after she'd added her personal touches. She'd called the telephone company for them to install a phone, and she was told a technician would come by Tuesday, which was Yvonne's day off.

She left the Jones's apartment, closing the self-locking door, and walked out again into the cold. If she was given a day off, then she'd planned to make the best of it. Aside from shopping for groceries, Claudia knew she had to purchase a television. Although she listened to the radio and read newspapers, television connected her to the world outside, beyond the United States.

Ashley had come to believe that he must be living right. He'd wanted to wait at least a week before calling Stephen or Yvonne about reconnecting with Claudia. He didn't know what it was about Claudia, but she'd intrigued him as no other woman ever had. He had intimately known his fair share of women, enough to know that Claudia Moore was someone special. Not only was she naturally beautiful, but also unabashedly feminine, and he knew intuitively that to become involved with her would not only complement, but also enhance, his image.

He hadn't earned the epithet as the Black Prince of Wall Street because of his business acumen, because that was only a small part of who he had become. It had taken years of hard work to cultivate the persona of a Black man in America who had defied the odds to become successful. Ashley was familiar with well-educated Black men who'd opted to become drug distributors because they were able to make more money in a week selling heroin than they would make in a year as teachers, social workers, or medical professionals.

Ashley's luck continued when he maneuvered into a parking space across from the Jones's residence. He turned the collar up on his topcoat as he crossed the street and rang the bell for her apartment.

"Yes."

He smiled hearing Claudia's voice come through the intercom speaker. "Ashley." Seconds later he climbed the three flights to find the door slightly ajar. "May I come in?"

Claudia suddenly appeared. A black knit minidress emphasized the slimness of her body and displayed her long legs. Rather than wear shoes or go barefoot, she had put on a pair of white socks. The riot of curls that had framed her face when he first saw her was now a cascade of soft waves along her jawline.

She nodded. "Please."

Ashley sniffed the air as he walked into the living room. "Something smells wonderful."

"Did you make reservations at a restaurant?" she asked, closing the door.

"No. Why?"

"Because I decided to make dinner for us."

He stared at her under lowered lids. "What if I had made reservations?"

"Then what I made wouldn't go to waste. I'd just put it away and eat it at another time. I went out twice today and nearly froze my behind off. I wasn't willing to challenge it a third time."

"It's going to take a while before your blood thickens up where you'll be able to tolerate our winters."

"I hope it's soon because my teeth sound like castanets when they begin chattering." She held out her hand. "I'll take your coat."

Shrugging off the coat, he handed it to her. "If I'd known we were going to eat in, then I would've brought a bottle of wine."

"Don't worry about that. I have wine."

"Or flowers."

Holding on to his coat, Claudia turned to smile at him. "I have those, too."

"You are just full of surprises."

"I am until you get to know me," she said.

Ashley longed to tell Claudia that he wanted to get to know her. And very well.

Chapter 28

Whatever you want in life, other people are going
to want it too. Believe in yourself enough to
accept the idea that you have an equal right to it.
—Diane Sawyer

When Yvonne said Claudia could burn some pots,
Ashley knew she had been truthful.

She had prepared a four-course dinner with a vinaigrette
salad of mixed greens topped with shaved Parmesan, black-
eyed pea soup with the meat from smoked neckbones,
broiled baby lamb chops with a rosemary-flavored Madeira
sauce, and bread pudding topped with a bourbon custard
sauce.

Over dinner she'd revealed what had happened at the
bank earlier that morning, and her suspicion that the branch
manager had reneged on giving her the position because she
was a woman.

Ashley stared at Claudia over the rim of his coffee cup.
"He knew you were a woman when he interviewed you, not
once but twice, so it can't be that."

"So, you think everything he said was a lie?"

"It's hard to tell, Claudia, because he's telling you to wait
five months before the position becomes available. Maybe

the current loan officer changed his mind and decided to stay on longer."

"I don't know why, but something keeps nagging at me that it was all a flim-flam. I suppose I'm paranoid because years ago, I applied for a position at a White bank in Biloxi that had advertised for a teller, and when I went in to inquire, I was told the position had been filled. Meanwhile, a week later the ad was still up because they hadn't hired anyone."

"That's because you were dealing with bigots, Claudia."

"Are you saying there are no bigots where you work?"

"I know there are some at my company who resent me, but the difference is they are better actors because they smile in your face while at the same time stab you in the back. I have more respect for a bigoted White man from the South than one up here because I know where he's coming from."

"But why would they resent you because you're an asset to the company?"

Ashley wanted to tell Claudia that she was being naïve. That some of his coworkers would rather wait for another elevator than get into one with him. "Perhaps they I know I was better born and better bred," he said without a hint of modesty. "That it is their color that helped them get to where they are, when it's my color which has limited my people for generations. I refuse to dwell on the White man, Claudia. I do what I must do to make it through the day, and when I leave the office and go home and close the door to my apartment, I become whoever I choose to be."

Claudia rested her elbow on the table and cupped her chin on the heel of her hand. "And what's that?"

Ashley smiled, exhibiting a mouth filled with straight white teeth. "One night I'm a chef whenever I try a new recipe. The next I might go to the theater to watch a film and then come home and critique it."

"Do you go to the movies alone?"

Inky-black eyebrows lifted slightly. "Are you asking if I'm seeing someone?"

"Yes."

"Why?"

"I'm just curious."

"Curious enough to go out with me if I asked?"

A smile tilted the corners of Claudia's mouth. "Maybe."

"Yes or no, Claudia?"

Claudia knew she'd backed herself into a corner, and then reminded herself she was a novice when it came to flirting with men. Robert had been the first and only man she'd been with, and when she compared him to Ashley it was like apples and oranges. "Yes."

He smiled. "Now that wasn't so hard, was it?"

A shiver of annoyance eddied through Claudia. "Please don't to talk to me as if I were a child, Ashley." Suddenly all the air seemed to leave the room when he glared at her.

"I'm sorry if that's how you feel, but I didn't mean it that way."

The seconds ticked as Claudia and Ashley stared at each other. "And I'm sorry if I took your meaning the wrong way."

He nodded. "Apology accepted."

"But you didn't answer my question, Ashley."

"What's that?"

"Are you currently involved with someone?"

"No, I am not involved with anyone. Now, back to your position at the bank. You claim they're paying you a loan officer's salary, so are you willing to wait to see what transpires?"

"Yes, because if I don't, then there's no guarantee that I will find another position with a comparable salary and benefits."

"Do you have to work for a bank?"

"I don't have to, but it's what I'm drawn to even though it is a male-dominated profession."

"There are banks in the Wall Street area that have female

employees. By the way, do you have a résumé I could look at?"

Claudia stared at Ashley, complete surprise freezing her features, and wondered if he was asking to see her résumé to humor her or if he was serious about the possibility of finding a position for her in the Financial District. "Yes. I'll go and get it."

"While you do that, I'll clear the table."

"You don't have to do that, Ashley."

He smiled. "I know, but I want to."

When Claudia had asked him if he was currently involved with someone, he was truthful when he'd told her no. The last woman with whom he'd been involved had decided she couldn't continue to see him because after sleeping together for nearly a year she'd wanted a commitment. Commitment for Ashley meant not cheating on each other, but for her it was marriage, and when he told her he wasn't ready for marriage she'd walked out of his apartment and out of his life.

He thought about Claudia as he stacked dishes and tableware and took them into the kitchen. She appeared to be a woman who knew what she wanted and wasn't afraid to go after it. She'd sought entrée into a world where women had been prohibited for years, yet that hadn't deterred her. Under her seeming fragility was a woman with a backbone of steel, and instinct told him Claudia Moore was going to make those in banking stand up and take notice.

Ashley had cleared the table when Claudia returned and handed him her résumé. He scanned it quickly, smiling. She'd only listed one place of employment, but what she'd indicated was remarkable. She had been hired as a loan officer and had risen to the rank of assistant manager. Now he understood why she was upset about having to start over as a bank teller.

He read and reread what she'd listed as skills. "You are multilingual?"

"Yes."

"You really speak all of these languages?"

"Yes, Ashley. I do."

"Where did you learn them, because you didn't list them under education as a minor."

"I majored in business and minored in history. My aunt taught me. Even though I understand French, Italian, and Spanish, I'm still working on my Spanish. When it gets warmer, I'll go to what you call El Barrio or Spanish Harlem and practice speaking with some of the shopkeepers."

"Are you aware that some banks are setting up branches overseas?"

"No. Why?"

"Because with your knowledge of foreign languages you could remain stateside and get a position in their international department."

"I'm not versed in international banking, so that means I would have to take some courses at a college that offers them."

"That shouldn't be too difficult. You have Baruch College and New York University right here in Manhattan." Claudia's smile was dazzling, reminding Ashley of a sunrise. It lit up her entire face and drew his gaze to her large, luminous eyes.

"That's something I'm going to consider. I know it's too late to register for the spring semester, so I'm going to see about taking a few summer courses. Which college would you recommend?"

"I'm partial to Baruch because it's my alma mater. It's a public college that's under the umbrella of the City University of New York and has free tuition. NYU is private, more expensive, but has excellent business programs."

Ashley mentioning international banking was like offering Claudia a reprieve—that she would have another option than working as a teller and then a loan officer. "Where are these colleges located?"

"Baruch is on the Eastside near Twenty-Third Street and NYU is in Washington Square."

"Thanks, Ashley."

"For what?"

"For giving me something to think about," Claudia said, as she walked over to the sink and filled it with water, then added a liquid detergent.

"Do you mind if I hold on to your résumé?"

"Of course not." Claudia scraped the dishes before placing them in the sink.

"Tell me about your aunt who taught you to speak several languages."

"I have schoolteacher aunts who speak more than one language. My aunt Virgie lives in France as an expatriate and she tutors the children of wealthy Parisians in English, while Aunt Mavis minored in foreign languages in college. I lived with her for six years, and during that time she taught me to speak, read, and write Spanish, Italian, and French."

"Why did you live with your aunt?"

Claudia stared at the soapy water rather than meet Ashley's eyes. "That's a story I'd rather not talk about."

Her response didn't seem to bother Ashley when he asked, "Have you traveled abroad?"

"Yes. I spent six weeks in Paris. It was a high school graduation gift from my aunts."

"Did you enjoy it?"

Claudia washed and rinsed the dishes, then set them on a rack to dry. "It was eye opening, Ashley, for an eighteen-year-old girl who'd been living under apartheid. There were no WHITES ONLY and COLORED ONLY signs, and it was the first time that I felt as if my race wasn't a factor, because I'd become a citizen of the world. I have a friend who was born in Paris but moved to Benin after she married an African prince. At the time she was dating him, the country was referred to as Dahomey or French Dahomey, but officially became Benin in 1960."

"Is she a White girl?"

"Yes. And please don't start in about African royalty marrying a White woman."

Ashley crossed his arms over his chest and rested a hip against the countertop. "What makes you think I was going to say something?"

"Because I saw you scrunch up your nose as if you'd just smelled something bad."

"Maybe my nose was itching."

"Yeah, right. Other than Yvonne, Noelle is the only other woman I trust unconditionally. I feel comfortable telling them things I'm reluctant to tell my mother because they're not judgmental."

"What about a sister?"

"I don't have a sister. I'm an only child. What about you, Ashley? Who do you trust?"

"I would have to say Stephen. I had an older sister who'd just entered high school when she got involved with a piece of shit who was using drugs. She got hooked on heroin and overdosed. Her death nearly destroyed my family. It had become the blame game when my mother accused my father of being overly protective when it came to my sister, and he pointed the finger at Mom because she was the opposite when she let Pamela do whatever she wanted."

Claudia heard the pain in Ashley's voice and resisted the urge to put her arms around him. "I'm so sorry, Ashley. I know it couldn't have been easy for your parents to bury their child."

"I knew it was grief that had them talking about divorce, but after they attended marriage counseling, they decided to stay together."

"Where do they live?" she asked.

"St. Albans. That's a predominately Black middle-class neighborhood in Queens. Dad is a cardiologist at Jamaica Hospital and Mom is an assistant professor at the New School for Social Research."

Now Claudia understood why Ashley said he was better born and bred because he was raised in a family of upwardly mobile Black people. And as professionals, his parents had expected him to follow suit, while his sister had gone in the opposite direction.

"It's good they were able to save their marriage."

"They bought a beachfront house in Sag Harbor and Mom spends the entire summer there, while Dad drives out whenever he's not working weekends. He reconnected with some of his medical school buddies and when he invited them and their families out to Long Island for a Memorial Day weekend reunion, that's when I first met Stephen. Our fathers were not only in the same medical school graduating class, but also fraternity brothers."

"And now you and Stephen are tight."

"We've become very close." Ashley pointed at the sink filled with pots. "I feel bad that you won't let me help you clean up."

Claudia scrubbed a pan with a pad made of steel wool. "I'm territorial when it comes to my kitchen. I really don't like to share it with anyone."

"I'm the complete opposite. I'll take any assistance I can get. But whenever I host a small dinner party I usually have it catered, so it's the caterers who will clean up."

"I haven't reached that stage because that's not going to happen until I move into my own place."

"You don't plan to live here?"

Claudia almost laughed when she saw Ashley's shocked expression. "No. I told Yvonne that I'll live here until she goes on maternity leave at the end of June, even if I find an apartment before she stops working."

"This apartment is perfect for you, Claudia. You'll be able to walk to work once you become a loan officer."

She didn't want to explain to Ashley that living with Yvonne and Stephen wasn't what she needed to become to- tally independent. "A technician will install a phone tomorrow and then you'll be able to call me without having to go through Stephen or Yvonne," she said, deftly changing the topic of her moving out of the Astor Row house.

"That's good news. If you don't have plans for the weekend, I'd like to take you to Sunday brunch before we go to an art gallery in the Village where a friend of mine has a showing of African baskets and masks."

"I'm definitely free this Sunday."

Moving closer, Ashley lowered his head and kissed Claudia's cheek. "Good. Make certain to dress warmly because we'll be taking public transportation. And thank you for dinner. Everything was delicious."

"It was my pleasure. Once I get the phone, I'll call you at home because I don't like calling someone's place of business."

"If I don't pick up, just leave a message with the answering service and I'll get back to you."

"Okay." Claudia waited for Ashley to put on his suit jacket, then topcoat, and walked him to the door. He winked at her before he left and she closed the door, smiling.

When Ashley had asked to see her résumé it was a blessing in disguise because even with her ability to speak multiple languages, she never would've considered international banking, even though she'd taken several business courses geared to banking laws and regulations. Although Claudia hadn't planned on going back to college for several years, she realized it was necessary if she was serious about branching out into another phase of banking.

Chapter 29

Don't count the days, make the days count.
—Muhammad Ali

It took Claudia a week to feel as if she were a true New Yorker when riding the bus or subway, once she realized riders rarely made eye contact with one another. They were more apt to read newspapers, books, magazines, or even feign sleep to divert their attention and mind their own business. And they walked—everywhere.

Claudia also found herself walking across town to Broadway to take the subway from 125th Street to 103rd. She had learned quickly to dress in layers, and when she arrived at the bank, she wore a smock that was the required uniform for all employees. After two days of training, she was permitted to take care of customers without supervision. Claudia was warmly welcomed by the branch manager and his assistants, while her coworkers were friendly and approachable whenever she had a question about a particular account. And when she closed out her drawer at the end of the day she always proved to the penny.

When she climbed the staircase to her apartment Friday night, she realized she could easily survive the next five months working as a teller because she was able to interact with customers in a way that she hadn't been able to do as a loan officer, whom she saw by appointment only.

The portable color television she had ordered was delivered Saturday morning and Stephen came upstairs to take it out of the box and set it on a table in the living room. After adjusting the antenna, he was able to get a clear picture. With a radio, television, and a fully stocked pantry, the apartment had become her sanctuary where she could relax and shut out the sounds of vehicular traffic and the constant wail of police sirens, firetrucks, and ambulances. She'd discovered a laundromat two blocks away with drop-off and pickup service and a dry cleaner with weekly specials.

She'd set aside Saturdays for cleaning the apartment and Sundays to cook enough to last her for several days. Most of her coworkers brought lunch from home and ate it in the employee lunchroom located on the bank's lower level. On the days she didn't bring lunch she'd discovered a small Greek coffee shop, and when she told the waiter that she'd never eaten Greek food he recommended she try the pastitsio and dolma.

Claudia thought of her honeymoon in New York with Robert when he'd introduced her to foods she'd never eaten, and then the floodgates opened when she cried, because even after so many years, she still missed him. She cried for her father, grandmother, and her husband. Images of her past life flooded her mind like frames of film until the ringing of the telephone shattered her reverie. Pushing off the sofa, she walked over to the table to answer it.

"Hello."

"Claudia?"

"Yes."

"Why do you sound so different?"

She marveled that Ashley was able to discern the change in her voice. "I do?"

"Yes, you do. Are you okay?"

"Not really."

"What's the matter?"

"I miss him, Ashley. I miss my husband." Her eyes misted over once again with tears.

"I'm coming over."

"No! You don't have to do that."

"Yes, I do. When I get there, I want you to buzz me in."

"Ashley . . ." Her words trailed off. He'd hung up on her.

Claudia also hung up and headed for the bathroom. There was no way she wanted Ashley to see her with red eyes. She managed to take down some of the swelling in her eyes with a cold compress, but it would take a while for her complexion to return to its natural color. She didn't know where Ashley lived, but it seemed as if she'd just hung up when she heard the intercom. She pressed the button releasing the lock on the outer door and waited for him to come up the staircase.

Ashley felt his heart turn over in pity when he saw Claudia's face. There had been a thread of desperation in her voice when she said she missed her husband, and he feared she would do something to harm herself. He had regarded her as a confident and resilient woman willing to confront challenges and roadblocks in her career, yet it had been her personal life or her attempt to reconcile her past that had become the obstacle for her to overcome in order to move forward.

He shut the door to the apartment and swept her up in his arms. "Everything's going to be okay," he crooned as he pressed a kiss on her hair. "I'll stay as long as you need me."

"I'm okay, Ashley."

He wanted to tell her that she was a liar—a very beautiful liar who had come into his life when he hadn't been looking for a woman to take up the hours when he wasn't monitoring the investments of those who had entrusted him with their money.

He carried Claudia into her bedroom and placed her on the bed, his body following hers down. Reaching over, he switched off the lamp on the bedside table, plunging the room into darkness, then turned to cradle her against his chest.

"Talk to me, Claudia."

There was only the sound of breathing and Ashley silently prayed Claudia would trust him enough to be open with him.

"I'd buried my grandmother, and then three weeks later it was my father. And I was still grieving when less than a year later I lost my husband."

"Where did you meet him?" Ashley asked.

"I met Robert during my first year in college. We didn't get to see each other that often because I was at Hampton and he was in D.C., but we had fallen in love and planned to marry following our graduations. He graduated Howard Law and the following weekend I graduated Hampton and later that day we were married. Both of our families were there for the wedding."

"What happened after you were married?"

"We moved to Mississippi, and we lived with my mother until we were able to buy a house of our own."

Ashley listened intently, not interrupting when Claudia told him about their involvement in the civil rights movement. She had volunteered to register Black people to vote while her husband joined SNCC as legal counsel. He felt tiny shivers of gooseflesh rising on his arms when Claudia talked about being confronted by the Klan and warned to stop her registration campaign and that her boss had also asked her to stop because of an increase in beatings, murders, and bombings in the area.

Her tears flowed again when she said despite the threats against her husband's life, he'd refused to stop registering voters. That he'd died in an automobile accident two months before they were to celebrate their second wedding anniversary.

"Was it really an accident, Claudia?" Ashley asked after a long pause as he waited for her to compose herself again.

"I don't know. But what I do know: Robert couldn't have been speeding because it was after sunset, and he had poor night vision. Someone had to be chasing him if he was going fast enough to lose control and swerve off the road."

"I read that's what happened to Chaney, Goodman, and Schwerner. The Klan chased their car, ran them off the road, and then murdered them."

"It had gotten so bad for Black people in Mississippi that I knew I could no longer live where a Black person's life is worth less than a mule. There's an expression that 'if a mule dies, then you buy another, but if a nigger dies, then you hire another.'"

Ashley buried his face in her hair and inhaled the scent of coconut on the riot of curls. "This country is a time bomb, Claudia, ready to explode. The Black Panthers are challenging the police as they promote social change, while Vietnam War protests are escalating from coast to coast. And like the sit-ins, once again it's mostly college students who are the protesters. Malcolm X spoke out against the United States' involvement in Vietnam before he was assassinated, and last year when Dr. King was invited to speak at Riverside Church, he said it was time to break the silence. He talked about the suffering of the Vietnamese people whose homes were being destroyed and their culture obliterated."

Claudia shifted, putting space between their bodies. "Political assassinations. Vietnam War protests. The civil rights movement. The Black Power movement. Draft card burnings. What's next, Ashley?"

Turning on his back, Ashley folded his arms above his head. "I don't know, Claudia. I don't think anyone knows."

There was silence for a moment, then Claudia said, "I'm sorry, Ashley."

"For what?"

"For the histrionics."

"Don't, Claudia. Don't you dare apologize for being human. You're hurting because you lost someone you loved very much."

"I didn't realize just how much I loved Robert until I lost him."

Ashley remembered all the good times he'd had with Pamela, and when she died, he'd told his thirteen-year-old self she was sleeping, and if he asked her, she would wake up. But she didn't wake up and it had taken him a long time to come to the realization she was gone, and he would never see her again.

"Even though you lose someone, that doesn't mean the loves goes away."

"I know. But what I must do is try and remember the good times we had."

"You're a young woman, Claudia, and you have your whole life ahead of you, and I'm willing to bet that one of these days your name will appear in business magazines."

Claudia couldn't shake off a momentary wave of uneasiness that gnawed at her confidence when she recalled Denny telling her something like what Ashley had just predicted for her. "I had someone say the same thing to me about himself. That I would eventually read about him because he was going to be famous."

"Did he become famous?"

"Yes. But it wasn't for anything good."

"Well, I'm predicting good things for you, Claudia Moore. I made several copies of your résumé and if I meet someone actively looking to hire someone like you, I'll give it to them."

"Thank you, Ashley. You are truly my guardian angel."

"Guardian yes. Angel unequivocally no."

Claudia rested a hand along his jawline. Lying in bed with Ashley felt so natural and comforting. "I beg to differ with you, Ashley Booth."

"We can agree to disagree. Did you eat dinner?"

"No. You?"

"No. Let's go out and get something."

"I'd rather not eat out, Ashley." Claudia didn't want people to see her puffy eyes.

"Then come home with me. No, better yet. Why don't you pack a bag and stay over. That will give us a head start on brunch tomorrow because I won't have to come here to get you."

Claudia sat up and turned on the lamp on her side of the bed. "I can't," she said, watching him staring at her as he slipped off the bed.

"Why not?"

"Because I just can't."

Ashley smiled and rested his hands at his waist. "You don't have to worry about me trying to get you to sleep with me. I happen to have a two-bedroom apartment."

Claudia could not stop the wave of heat suffusing her face. It was apparent he'd read her mind. "You live alone."

"Yes. I live alone. I have a guest bedroom because my parents will occasionally stay over whenever they come into the city for a night on the town and it's too late for them to go back to Queens."

She didn't know why, but Claudia felt as if she'd been ceremoniously chastised. When Ashley had invited her to stay at his apartment her first thought was he'd wanted her to sleep with him. Right then and there, Claudia decided she was a grown-ass woman, and it was time she acted like one.

"Okay. I'll pack an overnight bag."

Ashley's teeth shone white in his dark-skinned face. "What do you want to eat?'

Claudia walked to a closet and retrieved a bag from an overhead shelf. "I don't know."

"Have you ever eaten Chinese food?'

"Yes."

"Is there anything in particular you'd like to eat?"

"No, Ashley. Order whatever you want."

I'm going to drop you off at my apartment before I go to the restaurant."

Claudia opened a drawer in the dresser and took out two sets of underwear. "Where do you live?"

"Across town."

"Across town where, Ashley? Don't forget that I'm still learning how to get around this city."

"I have an apartment on Riverside Drive."

Claudia was familiar with the street that ran north and south with spectacular views of the Hudson River. "Nice."

"I like it."

"What's not to like, Ashley, when you wake up to river views," Claudia said as she selected sweaters, bell-bottom jeans, knee socks, and long-sleeved cotton turtlenecks.

"I must admit that it is therapeutic."

Claudia left the bedroom and entered the bathroom to fill a cosmetic bag with personal items and stored it in the carry-on with her clothes. Ashley was waiting in the entryway when she handed him the bag and opened the closet to get a wool duffel coat with a lambswool lining.

"I hope you didn't leave your place wearing just jeans and a pullover sweater," she said to Ashley as she locked the door.

"I have a jacket in the car."

Claudia followed him down the staircase and out to the street. She couldn't fathom going out without a coat, while Ashley appeared impervious to the frigid weather. He'd parked halfway down the block and when he opened the passenger-side door for her, she sat and waited for him to come around and start the engine.

It didn't take long for the sports car to heat up. "When did you buy this car?" she asked Ashley.

"I bought it a couple of months ago. Why?"

"Because it has a brand-new car smell."

Ashley pulled away from the curb, drove to the corner, and then made a right turn onto Fifth Avenue. "I don't get to drive it as much I'd like because I ride the subway to work during the week."

"If that's the case, then why do you have it?"

"I only take public transportation when it is necessary. If I were to visit my parents, I would have to take the subway to Queens, and then a bus to St. Albans. And I still must walk four blocks once I get off the bus. That's ninety minutes to two hours each way. I don't want to waste that much time when I can drive there in forty minutes."

"You said your parents have a house on Sag Harbor. Is that far from here?"

Ashley stopped at a red light and met her eyes. "Yes. It takes me more than two hours to drive there from Manhattan. I try to go there every other week during the summer months just to relax. And I also schedule my vacation during the summer and stay for two weeks."

It was obvious to Claudia that Ashley Booth had grown up privileged. Both parents were professionals and owned two homes when most Black people were fortunate if they were able to own one. He drove a late model sports car and lived in an apartment building along a scenic thoroughfare offering views of Riverside Park and the Hudson River.

She stared through the windshield at the passing landscape as Ashley headed in a westerly direction and came to a stop in front of a twenty-story building. A doorman came over to open the car door for him. Ashley took her bag off the rear seat and told the man wearing maroon livery he was going to leave the car in front of the building and would return in a few minutes.

The opulence of the lobby in the luxury apartment building was reminiscent of the furnishings in her aunt Virgie's *hôtel particulier*. Ashley escorted her to a bank of elevators, and he punched a button for the fourteenth floor. The car rose smoothly and quietly, and when the door opened it was to a carpeted hallway with framed art on the walls. He un-locked and opened the door to his apartment, and she walked into an expansive space with large picture windows and marble floors covered with colorful rugs.

Claudia followed Ashley across the living room and formal dining room to an alcove with facing bedrooms. He set her bag on the floor next to a table cradling books and magazines. "You'll have your own bathroom, so take your time settling in while I go pick up dinner."

She smiled. "Okay."

Waiting until he'd left, she sat on a padded bench at the foot of a queen-sized bed, wondering how many women he'd invited to his apartment, and how many had shared his bed in the bedroom across from hers. Claudia knew she had to ignore her thoughts about other women because she had no claim on the man under whose roof she would spend the night. She drew the drapes, unpacked, and put away her clothes as she waited for Ashley to return.

Chapter 30

I can be a better me than anyone can.
—Diana Ross

Using chopsticks, Ashley picked up a piece of shrimp egg foo young for Claudia to sample, as he watched intently for her reaction. He repeated the action with orange chicken, and then crispy shredded beef.

"Which one do you like best?" he asked, after she'd swallowed a small portion of white rice.

Claudia picked up a fork and cut off a piece of egg foo young covered with peanut sauce. "All of them, if you don't mind sharing." Ashley had attempted to show her how to eat with chopsticks, but she was unable to manipulate them to pick up enough food to put into her mouth.

"Of course I don't mind. That's why I ordered different dishes."

She picked up a serving spoon and filled her plate from each container and added a small portion of white rice. "I really like Chinese food," Claudia said.

"How often do you eat it?"

"This is only my second time. The first was in China-town."

"Are you talking Mott Street Chinatown?"

Claudia nodded. "Yes. I had roast duck, pork buns, and eggplant with shredded chicken in a spicy sauce. Eggplant isn't a vegetable I grew up eating, but the dish was delicious."

"There's an Italian restaurant on the Eastside that makes scrumptious eggplant Parmesan."

"How often do you eat out?" she asked Ashley.

Ashley lowered his eyes and stared at the food on his plate. "Probably too often. I always order lunch from a nearby coffee shop, and whenever some of the people in the office want to get together after work."

"Where do you go?"

"It differs. Sometimes we go to Greenwich Village or Little Italy. Most times it's any of the restaurants located on Forty-Sixth Street between Eighth and Ninth Avenues, because whatever cuisine you're craving you can find it there." Ashley scooped up pork fried rice with the chopsticks. "What about you, Claudia? How often do you eat out?"

"Not as often as you do. I bring my lunch three times a week and the other two days I try a different restaurant or coffee shop along Broadway. I go home after work and stay in." Claudia saw Ashley's impassive expression change when he gave her a Cheshire cat smile. "What are you grinning about?"

"You need more than just going to work and coming home to stay in."

"Can you define more?"

"Going to a Broadway show, jazz club, or eating in different restaurants."

"Is that where you'd like to take me?"

"Yes." Ashley paused, his smile still in place. "Does that meet with your approval?"

It was Claudia's turn to smile. "Yes, it does."

Their first official date began when Ashley took her to see the Broadway play *Hallelujah, Baby!* She also accompanied him to Minton's Playhouse, Birdland, and Smalls Paradise to listen to jazz, and whenever they visited his favorite restaurants the maître d' addressed him by name.

She'd asked Yvonne for the name of her ob-gyn because it was time for her annual gynecological checkup. The doctor wrote a prescription for an oral contraceptive pill along with a sample two-month supply she could begin taking with the onset of her upcoming cycle. Although she wasn't sexually active, Claudia did not want to be caught unprotected if or when she and Ashley did sleep together. And whenever he kissed her, Ashley unknowingly had rekindled a desire she'd forgotten.

Claudia arrived home and picked her mail off the table in the vestibule and sorted through the envelopes. There was one from Noelle and another from Ivy Moore. She'd written her former mother-in-law to let her know she was now living with Ivy's niece and once she rented her own apartment, she would write to let her know her new address.

She slipped out of her rain boots and left them on the mat outside the door. Claudia had just removed her raincoat when the telephone rang. Walking on sock-covered feet, she rushed over to answer it.

"Hello."

"Hey, sweetheart. I'd like to ask you something, and if you don't want to do it, then it's okay."

"What's up, Ashley?"

"One of the guys on my team is moving to Chicago to marry his fiancée, and I'd like to throw him a little something at my place this Saturday afternoon. It's a going to be a surprise, and I'd like to know if you would mind standing in as my hostess?"

She smiled. "Of course, I don't mind. Are you catering it?"

"Yes."

"Casual or formal?"

Ashley's laugh caressed her ear through the earpiece. "It's going to be casual."

"Don't laugh, Ashley, because as your hostess I have to know what to wear."

"You would look beautiful in a burlap sack."

"Enough with the flattery, lover boy. Do you need help with the menu?"

"Yes. That's why I'm calling."

"Today is Tuesday, so that doesn't give you a lot of time," she said. "Why don't you come over tonight so we can begin planning."

"I'll bring dinner."

"Don't bother, Ashley. I have marinated chicken in the fridge that needs to go in the oven."

"Don't you know it's not safe to leave your door open because anyone could walk in and take advantage of you?" Ashley knew he'd surprised Claudia when she dropped the knife she was using to slice red onions.

"What are you trying to do? Give me a heart attack by sneaking up on me like that?"

Walking into the kitchen, he rested his hand on her chest. She wasn't kidding. Her heart was pumping a double-time rhythm under her blouse. "I'm sorry. The next time I promise to make some noise."

Claudia tilted her head and brushed a kiss over his mouth. "I left the door open because I was expecting you, and not anyone else."

Ashley sniffed her neck. "You smell delicious. What are you wearing?"

"It's called patchouli."

"I don't remember you wearing it before."

"Whenever I come home after work, I take a shower and put it on."

Ashley trailed tiny kisses down the column of her neck. "You smell good enough to eat."

Claudia elbowed him softly in the ribs. "The only eating you're going to do tonight is roast chicken with cornbread stuffing and a mixed citrus salad with red onions and escarole."

"I can't believe you come home every night and cook like this."

"I used to cook on the weekends for the entire week, but now that I have a boyfriend, I've had to modify my timetable."

"Are you saying I'm an interference?"

Claudia rolled her eyes at the same time she sucked her teeth. "You're being ridiculous. If I didn't want to go out with you, I'd tell you. You must know by now that I don't bite my tongue."

"That's only one of the incalculable reasons why I like you."

"I also like you, otherwise you wouldn't be standing here talking to me."

"That makes me a very lucky man."

Claudia wiped her hands on a terry cloth towel and rose on tiptoes to brush her lips against his. "You have no idea how lucky you are."

She wanted to tell Ashley her feelings for him deepened with each encounter, that she'd count down the days when she would see him again. There were times when she'd found herself comparing Ashley to Robert and invariably the latter would come up lacking, while she knew it wasn't fair to compare a nineteen-year-old boy with a thirty-one-year-old man. An erudite man with a monopoly on confidence, who whenever he entered a room seemed to suck the oxygen out of it.

"I left something for you in the living room. It's on the coffee table."

Ashley angled his head. "What is it?"

"You'll have to go and see."

The distinctive ding of the timer told Claudia it was time to take the chicken and the cornbread out of the oven. Reaching for a pair of oven mitts, she opened the door to the oven and removed the chicken and muffins.

Claudia couldn't help but smile when she heard Ashley

whooping in the living room. It was obvious he liked what she'd given him. Ashley had wined, dined, and taken her to events that would not have been possible if she had not met him. She'd removed the chicken from the pan and set it on a platter, then quickly made gravy from the pan drippings, and had poured it into a gravy boat by the time Ashley walked into the kitchen cradling record albums to his chest.

"How did you know I didn't have these?"

Claudia had given him recordings by Charlie Parker, Thelonious Monk, and Dizzy Gillespie. "I must admit that I went through your record collection and made a list of what you owned. I have a customer at the bank who owns a small record shop. When I asked him if he had any jazz records, he said he did. When I walked to his shop I was overwhelmed with his collection of jazz recordings. He even had original recordings of Bessie Smith.

"Where is his shop, because I'd like to go through his stock and see what he has. My father is a jazz enthusiast and maybe I can pick up something for him before we go out to Sag Harbor in a couple of months."

Claudia realized he'd said *we*. Was it his intent to take her to meet his parents? Maybe, she thought, it was just a slip of the tongue. "Either we can go there after I get off from work, or one of these Saturdays."

"It can't be this Saturday, so let's make a date for next Saturday. By the way, how much do I owe you for these?"

She bit her lip to keep from spewing curses. "I'm going to pretend you didn't ask me that, Ashley Booth."

"What are *you* talking about?"

"I can't believe you're asking me how much I paid for those record albums when you take me out every weekend and I never have to open my wallet for anything."

Ashley's expression had become a mask of stone when he glared at her. "That's because I don't believe in taking money from a woman."

"You're not taking money from me, Ashley. I gave you a

gift and I'd hoped you would be gracious enough to accept it as a gift."

Her explanation seemed to satisfy him when he smiled. "Thank you, Claudia. I graciously accept your gift."

She inclined her head. "You're most welcome. Dinner is ready, so do you want the honor of carving the chicken?"

"Yes, ma'am. I'll do it after I wash my hands."

Claudia didn't know why, but Ashley calling her *ma'am* made her feel old, because it was common in the South to address older women as ma'am. However, at twenty-seven and soon to be twenty-eight, she wasn't old.

Ashley took a sip of white sangria and stared at Claudia over the rim of the wineglass. He still could not believe he'd met a woman who embodied everything he'd want in a wife. That is, if he was the marrying kind. Claudia was beautiful, poised, intelligent, ambitious, and independent.

"How many people do you anticipate coming Saturday?" she asked.

"There are eight people on my team, and most are bringing their significant others, so I project we should plan for twenty."

"What about the guest of honor? Will his fiancée be there?"

Ashley's mouth curved into an unconscious smile. "Yes. That's the surprise. David has no idea that his fiancée flew into New York today and checked into a hotel near the airport."

"So, David knows that the party is for him?"

"Yes. I had to tell him, otherwise he never would show up, because he gets upset whenever he's blindsided."

"If you're catering it, do you want buffet-style or sit-down?"

"Definitely buffet. That way folks can select whatever they want to eat."

"What about seating?" Claudia asked.

"The caterers will provide the chairs and tables. I'll have

to move the living room furniture against the walls to provide enough space for the tables. And there's still the dining
room for those who want to sit at that table."

Claudia nodded as she touched a napkin to the corners of
her mouth. "Now the menu. What are you thinking about
serving?"

"That's where I need your help. I figured we'd start with a
cocktail hour before dinner."

"If you want a cocktail hour, then you should serve hors
d'oeuvres like prawns with dipping sauces, tuna or steak
tartare on pumpernickel triangles, or ginger-shrimp toasts for
those without shellfish allergies. Endive with herb cheese and
almond-stuffed dates with bacon should also go over well
with your guests. And if you want meat, then marinated
grilled lamb on skewers with a mint sauce is a nice touch.
Mixed drinks, wine, and iced vodka should cover the cocktails."

"Why iced vodka?" Ashley asked Claudia.

"If you put a bottle of vodka in the freezer the liquid won't
freeze, and the bottle won't crack because of the alcohol content. When you drink it, it goes down smooth and icy."

"How do you know so much about hosting cocktail parties?"

"The summer I spent in France with my aunt she hosted
soirées in her salon every Sunday. That's when I acquired a
taste for olives, caviar, and champagne."

"You mention your aunts a lot, but not your uncles."

"That's because I don't have any uncles. Both my aunts are
single."

Ashley leaned back in his chair. "Are they widowed or divorced?"

"Neither. They decided they didn't want or need husbands."

"What about you, Claudia?"

"What about me?"

"Do you plan to get married again?"

The second hand on his timepiece made a full revolution before she said, "If I'm being honest, then I'd have to say no. It's been almost four years since I buried my husband, and it's still too fresh in my mind to even think about becoming another man's wife."

"Is it because you're still in love with him?"

Claudia gave him a long, penetrating stare. "I will always love him, Ashley."

"Are you saying you can't love another man?"

"That's not what I'm saying. If I happen to fall in love with another man, then that love will be different from what I had with Robert."

"Are you saying there are different degrees of love?" Ashley asked her.

"That's exactly what I'm saying. The love between a husband and a wife is different from the love they have for their children. A husband and his wife do not share blood, while their children do. That's why I believe the bond between siblings is stronger than that of their parents, because a man can divorce his wife, but that's not possible for their children."

"Family dynamics can be messy." He groaned inwardly when he'd spoken his thoughts aloud.

"Every family has mess, Ashley," Claudia countered. "Even mine had its share of eye-rolling, teeth-sucking confrontations that had folks not speaking to each other for days and sometimes weeks. Me and Robert had our share of disagreements and there was a time after we were married that we didn't sleep together, so no one is exempt from chaos."

Ashley had broken the promise he'd made to himself not to mention Claudia's husband because talking about him seemed to put her in a funk. She needed to heal, and she never would be able to do that if he kept dredging up her past.

"What do you suggest for the dinner?" he questioned, deftly changing the topic.

"You should offer meat, chicken, and enough vegetables

for those who are vegetarians. If you're willing to go with a carving station, then it could be prime rib and baked ham with an orange glaze. Chicken choices can be broiled, fried, or baked."

"What about vegetables?"

"Glazed carrots, sauteed spinach with garlic and oil, rice pilaf, string beans, and small roasted potatoes."

"Dessert?"

"I'm partial to macarons."

"Of course, you would be," he teased Claudia, "because it's French."

"Don't knock them, Ashley, because they are masters when it comes to baking."

"I'm not disputing that, but I just happen to like Italian desserts."

"If that's the case, then order tiramisu, cannoli, or *tartufo di pizzo.*"

Claudia continued to surprise him with the extent of her familiarity with foods and languages. "What if I order both French and Italian desserts?"

Claudia smiled. "Nice compromise."

He pushed back his chair and stood. "Do you mind if I use your phone to call the caterer?"

She blinked slowly. "You're going to order now?"

"Yes. Why?"

"You didn't write anything down."

Ashley tapped his forehead. "It's all up here."

Claudia's lips parted in surprise. "You remember everything we just talked about?"

"Yes. Now, may I use your phone?"

"Yes, you may."

Ashley went into the living room and dialed the number to the caterer and told the man what he wanted and when it should be delivered to his apartment. He ended the call and returned to the dining room, leaned over Claudia's chair, and kissed her neck. "It's done."

She smiled up at him over her shoulder. "You are incredible."

"No, baby, you're the incredible one. I'm going to hang around long enough to help you clean up, then I'm leaving."

"You don't have to leave, Ashley."

He went completely still. "What are you trying to say?"

Shifting on her chair, she stared up at him. "I'm not trying to say anything. I am telling you that you can stay if you want."

Ashley felt as if he'd been holding his breath from the first time he saw Claudia walk into the Jones's living room with Yvonne—what now seemed eons ago—and now he could exhale. He knew he'd wanted to sleep with her, but then convinced himself she was different. That he would wait for her to make the first overture.

"I have condoms."

She smiled. "And I'm on the pill."

Chapter 31

In the midst of movement and chaos, keep
stillness inside of you.
　　　　　　　　—Deepak Chopra

Claudia pushed all thoughts of what she'd shared in bed
with Robert to the farthest recesses of her mind when
she raised her arms to allow Ashley to pull her blouse up and
over her head. He'd turned on one of the bedside lamps to its
lowest setting and she'd watched him as he undressed. Everything about him was so different from the only man she'd
slept with. He was taller, more muscular, and even his semi-
erect penis was unmistakably larger.

She closed her eyes as he removed her bra, slacks, and
panties, then cradled her face between his hands.

"Open your eyes, Claudia. Please," Ashley pleaded in a
hushed tone.

Claudia smiled and opened her eyes. She could feel the tension in Ashley's body and a hint of desperation in his voice.
"I want to do this."

"Are you sure?"

"Yes."

They got into bed together. Claudia closed her eyes, this

time losing herself in the weight pressing her down to the mattress, the stubble on Ashley's jaw when he buried his face between her neck and shoulder and she felt his breathing, slow, deep, controlled, and the throbbing hardness against her belly. The fingers of his hand skimmed her abdomen, her inner thigh, and then the opening between her legs.

Claudia moaned as a rush of moisture bathed her core; she was ready to welcome Ashley into her body, her life, and into her future. She smothered another groan as she felt every inch of his penis until he was fully sheathed inside her. She felt the heat of his body course down the length of hers, as her whole being was scorched with a desire she had long forgotten; she gripped Ashley's buttocks, pulling him closer. The rhythm he'd set changed, quickening, and Claudia followed his pace, arching as he thrust into her with longer and deeper strokes.

Ashley buried his face against Claudia's neck, straining valiantly to prolong the ecstasy. But it was not to be. Everything about the woman writhing under him made him forget every other one with whom he'd lain. He had spent weeks fantasizing about making love with her and it hadn't come close to what he was feeling. Claudia Moore was perfect—in and out of bed.

Angling his body slightly, he reached down and rubbed his penis up and down her swollen clitoris and achieved the reaction he sought from Claudia as she screamed his name, then convulsed as the walls of her vagina squeezed his rockhard dick. It was his turn to groan when he ejaculated, the rush of semen leaving him slightly light-headed. He collapsed heavily on Claudia, his chest heaving in exertion.

"Did I hurt you?" he whispered in her ear.

"No."

He kissed her forehead. "I'll be right back. I'm going to throw away the condom."

Ashley returned to the bed and eased Claudia closer until

her buttocks were pressed against his groin. "Are you okay?" He'd asked because he was certain she would experience some discomfort for a few days.

"I'm good, Ashley. Now, please stop talking and go to sleep."

He kissed the nape of her neck. "Yes, boss."

She laughed softly. "I am not your boss."

"You think not."

"I know not, Ashley Thaddeus Booth."

"Damn, woman. Why did you have to go and use my government name?"

"Because I want to sleep, while you're chattering like a mynah bird."

"Do you know that mynah birds are excellent mimics?"

Claudia turned over to face him. "What do I have to do to get you to go to sleep?"

"Make love to me again."

She patted his chest. "That's not happening because I doubt if you would be able to get it up so soon."

Ashley nodded, smiling. "You're right. It's just that I'm so wound up that I can't get to sleep."

Claudia rested her leg over his. "About what?"

"Saturday."

"What about Saturday, Ashley?"

"It will be the first time that the people I work with will come to my home."

"Why does that bother you?" Claudia asked.

"Because I try not to let my work life overlap with my private life."

"Why have you changed your mind?"

"I don't know, Claudia."

Ashley didn't want to tell Claudia that dating her had changed him. That he'd begun to view life differently. She'd grown up under segregation in one of the most racist states in the South and had buried so many loved ones in less than a year, yet it hadn't broken her.

"Are you having second thoughts about inviting them?"

"Even if I did, it's too late to renege now."

Claudia looped an arm over his waist. "I don't view your inviting them to your home as an invasion of your privacy, rather that you're willing to interact with them not as a boss but as a coworker. And that's a lot different from going out with them after work."

"So, you approve of me inviting them?"

"Yes, Ashley, and don't forget I'll be there to help you, so things should go smoothly."

Ashley knew he would never forget Claudia because she'd become his drug of choice. Someone he never wanted to give up.

Claudia had morphed into her aunt Virgie, as she stood in the entryway next to Ashley, greeting his coworkers and welcoming them inside. Casual attire was evident, with the men wearing turtleneck sweaters or Nehru jackets and slacks, while their wives and girlfriends favored mini shifts and tent dresses. The women sported bouffants, beehives, Twiggy cuts, and Sassoon's geometrical and asymmetrical hairstyles. Claudia felt a kinship with the woman with the Afro, because when she didn't set her hair on rollers the result was a riot of soft curls framing her face.

David Kessler was genuinely shocked when he walked in to find his fiancée waiting with his coworkers. He'd lost all the color in his complexion before he recovered enough to kiss her, amid applause and whistling from those who'd come to wish him well. Tall, slender, with bright red hair, David couldn't stop grinning as he clutched the hand of the woman wearing the pear-shaped diamond engagement ring Ashley said David had given her the year before, while Meredith Landau, a recent law school graduate, could not take her bright blue eyes off her fiancé.

Ashley, dressed entirely in black, waited until everyone held a glass of champagne to toast the couple. "David, you must be special for me to invite this motley crew to my home to celebrate the next phase of your life. I'd had my doubts when you asked to be transferred to my department, but thankfully I'm man enough to admit that I was wrong." He raised his glass. "Here's to you, your beautiful fiancée, as you settle in the Windy City."

David waited for the smattering of applause to end. "You all know that I don't like surprises, but I'm willing to accept this one. Ashley, I must say that you're the best boss I've ever had and not because I'm going to drink your booze and eat your food, but because you took a chance on me and for that I'll always be indebted to you. I'm moving to Chicago where I know I'll freeze my ass off, but it's going to be worth it because I'll be with the woman I love."

"This is a celebration, not a wake, so there's no need for you to get sentimental, David," Ashley's assistant shouted.

Claudia was surprised to discover that Ashley's assistant was a Black woman who was responsible for answering his phone, scheduling his meetings, and typing his reports. He'd referred to her as his assistant rather than his secretary because of his dependence on her, as he said she was there to "watch my back." He claimed there were some executives who resented him heading his own unit with a team he'd personally handpicked to staff it—a staff made up of men of different races and ethnic backgrounds.

Lorraine Parker walked over to Claudia and looped her arm through hers, pulling her out of earshot of those who had gathered at the bar. "I really must give it to you. You've succeeded with Ashley where so many other women have failed."

Claudia gave her a questioning look. She'd estimated Lorraine's age to be between mid-thirties to early forties, and she wondered if the woman had something going with Ashley because she appeared quite comfortable touching his arm or resting a hand on his back. "What are you talking about?" she asked, deliberately lowering her voice.

"I've seen your boyfriend with quite a few women when we occasionally run into each other at different venues, but this is the first time he's introduced one to his staff. Whenever we have office parties or even hang out after work, he's always solo."

Claudia wasn't about to tell her personal business to a woman she'd just met. "Ashley and I have friends in common, so when he asked me to help him put this together, as a friend I couldn't turn him down."

Lorraine nodded. "Okay, if you say so."

"I do." Claudia forced a smile. "There's plenty of food, so feel to select whatever you want."

Waiters were circulating with trays of hors d'oeuvres and shot glasses of iced vodka, and Claudia took one and put the glass to her mouth; the vodka chilled her throat before warmth spread throughout her chest.

Lorraine also took a shot glass and downed the alcohol in one swallow, her eyes filling with tears as she blew out her breath. "Well, I'll be damned. That's like swallowing nitroglycerin."

"Do you like it?"

"Girl, please. I could drink about six of these, but two is my limit. My parents are watching my kids at my place, and I can't be late because Mom and Dad have tickets to see James Brown at the Apollo Theater tonight."

"How many children do you have?"

"Three. Two boys and one girl. I left their trifling daddy three years ago and finally divorced the bum last year. He couldn't keep a job if his very life depended on it. What about you, do you have any kids?"

Claudia shook her head. "No."

"Do you want any?"

"Maybe in the future."

"Don't get me wrong. I love my kids, but sometimes they do things that make wonder if all the pain I had giving birth to them was worth it." She took another glass of iced vodka from another waiter and swallowed it. "Ashley is a good man, that's why I make certain to watch his back at work. And you, *Miss Friend*, should watch his back at home."

Claudia couldn't help smiling as Lorraine made her way over to where David stood with Meredith. She knew the woman didn't believe she and Ashley were friends. Well, it didn't matter because she doubted whether she would ever see his coworkers again.

The cocktail hour ended and mouthwatering aromas from chafing dishes filled the apartment amid groans that everyone had stuffed themselves on hors d'oeuvres and hadn't left room for the buffet dinner.

Claudia had just claimed a chair at the dining room table to eat dinner when Ashley sat down next to her. "The caterer said to tell you that you should be a party planner because what you selected for the cocktail hour challenged his culinary acumen. He claims it has been a while since anyone has requested steak or tuna tartare for their dinner parties."

"I only suggested what I like to eat, and it's apparent your guests really liked them, too."

Ashley pointed to her plate with a piece of thinly sliced ham, spinach, two small roasted potatoes. "Is that all you're going to eat?"

"This is all I can eat right now because I filled up on prawns, lamb skewers, tuna tartare, stuffed dates, and ginger shrimp toasts. And I also had a couple of iced vodkas."

Ashley pulled at a curl on her nape. "I have to confess to drinking a little bit more than a couple."

"Where did you find this caterer, because the food and the waitstaff are excellent?"

"The company's top brass has a contract with him. He caters all our office functions and banquets whenever elite clients come in from all around the country."

"Is your company paying for this elegant little soirée?" Claudia asked.

"Nope. This one is on me. And it's worth every penny because it's not often we all get to hang out together with our spouses and girlfriends."

She leaned to her right until their shoulders touched. "Is that what you're telling everyone? That I'm your girlfriend?"

Ashley turned to give her a direct stare, and as their eyes met Claudia felt desire sweep through her when she saw raw passion in the dark orbs. "Would you prefer that I tell everyone we are lovers?"

"Please, no," she said quickly. She wasn't ready to advertise that she was sleeping with the Black Prince of Wall Street.

A hint of a smile parted his lips. "Then, girlfriend it is. And to save you from having to explain our relationship I will emphasize the word *friend*."

Claudia wanted to tell him it was probably too late for that based on what Lorraine had told her about Ashley not introducing his other dates to his coworkers.

"Are you sure you don't want something else to eat?"

"No, thank you. I'm good."

She was good, and she could no longer deny that her feelings for Ashley intensified with each encounter.

And she prayed she wasn't falling in love with him.

Chapter 32

A genuine leader is not a searcher for consensus but a molder of consensus.
—Martin Luther King Jr.

Claudia sat stunned and unable to move when she heard the shocking news that Martin Luther King Jr. had been assassinated in Memphis, Tennessee. She wanted to scream, cry, throw things, yet couldn't. She'd become numb when it came to death. She had left the South, but the South had come to revisit her in the North, because nothing had changed. The telephone rang and she reached over to answer the call.

"Hello."

"Are you watching television?"

"Yes, Ashley."

"I can't believe it."

"Why not? If folks can kill the president, who is protected by the Secret Service, then why not a Black man who the head of the FBI claimed was the most dangerous threat to the country. Martin was allowed to live if he was still talking about civil rights, but when he began speaking out against the Vietnam War that's when he had to be silenced. It was the same with Malcolm X. Once Brother Malcolm met with Martin and encouraged Black nationalists to get involved in voter registration campaigns and other community organizing, he ended up with a target on his back."

"But Malcolm was killed by Black men."

"Don't be so naïve, Ashley. Black men who were directed by the government to kill him."

"And you don't believe it was because he'd severed ties with the Nation of Islam?"

"No. It was because Malcolm spoke directly to people who saw that Black folks were still being brutalized during peaceful protests. Several years ago he sent a telegram to the head of the American Nazi Party because there were threats of increased lynching around Selma, Alabama, stating and I quote: *'This is to warn you that I am no longer held in check from fighting white supremacists by Elijah Muhammad's separatist Black Muslim movement, and that if your present racist agitation against our people there in Alabama causes physical harm to Reverend King or any other Black Americans who are only attempting to enjoy their rights as free human beings, that you and your KKK friends will be met with maximum physical retaliation from those of us who are not handcuffed by the disarming philosophy of nonviolence, and who believe in asserting our right of self-defense—by any means necessary.'*"

"You memorized that?"

"I've memorized a lot of Malcolm's speeches because he was willing to say what a lot of people were too afraid to say."

"Violence will only bring more violence."

"Are you saying Black people shouldn't defend themselves?"

"No, Claudia. I'm saying that rioting doesn't prove anything."

"Somebody should've said that to the White people who burned down Greenwood, Oklahoma, also known as the Tulsa Race Massacre."

"Black folks rioting and tearing up their neighborhoods doesn't prove anything."

"But White folks beating us, turning water hoses on children, and bombing churches and schools, is that okay?"

"Of course not."

"Then, don't talk to me about riots, Ashley. The cameras focus on Black folks venting their anger, while they hardly cover police and state troopers beating the hell out of our people. History books don't even want to acknowledge the atrocities Black people suffered and still endure. You were raised up here, where there is racism, albeit subtle, while I had a front row seat to it." She paused as her eyes filled with tears. "How many more, Ashley? How many more Black leaders will we lose before we're recognized as full citizens in this country?"

"Baby, you're getting upset. Why don't you come and stay with me."

"No. I need to be alone."

"That's what you don't need."

"Please, don't ever tell me what I need."

"I don't want to argue with you, Claudia."

"Then don't! I'm going to hang up now."

"Claudia—"

She hung up, cutting off whatever he'd intended to say. Claudia didn't want to tell Ashley that he was as far removed from the fight for civil rights as his high-rise apartment was above the city streets. Ashley was the Black Prince of Wall Street and that made him a part of the establishment.

The telephone rang again, and she hoped it wasn't Ashley calling her back. "Hello."

"Claudia, did you hear?"

"Yes, Mama. I did."

"Who's next? Reverend Abernathy? Jesse Jackson? They are killing our leaders."

"I don't know."

"Are you safe up there, because you know folks are going to tear up."

"I'm safe, Mama. How are you doing down there?"

"We're good. I'm certain the Klan will be celebrating now that they've killed Dr. King."

"Hopefully they'll catch whoever did it, and if he's tried under federal law, he will probably spend the rest of his worthless life in jail."

"I hope you're right. Mavis has been talking about going to Puerto Rico for Christmas. How would you like to come with us?"

"I must check and see how many vacation days I have coming to me. Once I find out I'll call and let you know."

"You need to let me know as soon as you can because flights fill up quickly."

"How long do you plan to stay?"

"We're planning to leave Christmas Eve and return New Year's Eve."

Claudia knew spending a week in the Caribbean would be restorative not only for her mind but also her body. "Let Aunt Mavis know that I'm coming. Do you know which airport you're leaving from?"

"Yes. We're flying into Miami and then take a connection flight to San Juan."

"I'll make my own reservation to fly into Miami. Then I'll connect with you once I'm there."

"Are you certain you'll have enough vacation days?"

"It doesn't matter. I'll take the days without pay."

"Let me know how much you'll lose, and I'll reimburse you."

"You don't have to do that, Mama."

"But I want to, Claudia. I know things are expensive in New York, so I don't mind paying for your vacation. Think of it as an early Christmas present."

"You need to save your money, Mama."

"For what? If I can't spoil my only child, then it's of no use to me."

Claudia knew it was pointless to argue with Sarah about money. "Okay. You can pay for my ticket."

"Now, that wasn't so bad. Back to those bastards killing Dr. King. Mavis and I were just talking about Martin the other day. The world awards him a Nobel Peace Prize at the same time he's listed as an enemy of the state. This country is going to hell in a handbasket."

Claudia listened as Sarah ranted about the injustices and how Blacks could not give up the fight for civil rights. "They did the wrong thing killing Dr. King, Claudia, because now the militants are going to take up the cause. Even folks down here are talking about Black Power."

Although she was no longer on the front lines in the movement, Claudia continued to read Black newspapers and magazines for information ignored by the White press. "I want you to be careful, Mama, because you're beginning to sound like a militant."

"I wasn't militant when we lived in Freedom because we didn't have to deal with White folks, but it's different here in Biloxi. Even though there are no WHITES ONLY and COLORED ONLY signs, that still doesn't change anything."

"You can change the laws, Mama, but you can't change someone's heart when they are willing to die for what they believe in. There's going to be a temporary pause now that we no longer have Dr. King, but I predict it will never go back to the way it was."

Claudia had no idea how prophetic her words were, when riots broke out across the country. At least 110 cities were affected during the four-day period of violent civil unrest. Chicago, Baltimore, and even Washington, D.C., were not spared from rioting, protests, and looting. More than six thousand were arrested, at least a thousand were injured, and thirteen people lost their lives.

Ashley had waited three days before calling her again. She told him she would call him once she ended her period of mourning Dr. King's death. He hadn't asked her when that would be, and they ended the call wishing each other the best. Claudia had resolved never to discuss politics with Ashley again; he was aware of the civil rights movement, but she suspected he hadn't been willing to jeopardize his career by openly demonstrating.

She liked Ashley Booth because he was so easy to like. And it was obvious all his subordinates liked and respected him, which made her see him in an entirely different light. He was friendly and outgoing, yet she'd noticed his staff continued to relate to him as their boss. It hadn't mattered that he'd invited them into his home; there was still a line of demarcation they weren't willing to cross.

Ashley sat across from Yvonne in her living room, baring his soul. He'd called her earlier that morning to ask if she would be home because he needed to talk to her. It was the second weekend he hadn't seen or heard from Claudia, and he feared she was still in a blue funk because Dr. King's death had dredged up memories of her late husband. He also feared losing her—something he wasn't ready to accept.

Yvonne laced her fingers together and rested them on her belly under a flowing floral top. "You're seeing the woman, yet you haven't taken the time to know who she is, Ashley."

"That's because she refuses to open up to me."

"That's where you're wrong. What you see is what you're going to get. Claudia isn't really that complicated. She's loyal, passionate about what she believes in, and she's the type that if you're starving, she will give you her last piece of bread. We shared a dorm for four years and during that time we talked about everything, but we always respected each other's opinion."

Ashley looped one leg over the opposite knee. "Are you saying you never argued?"

"That's not what I'm saying. We had discussions, not arguments."

"There is something I don't understand, Yvonne."

"What is it?"

"If she wasn't willing to follow the rules of the segregationists, why didn't she get involved in the civil rights movement while in college?"

"It was all about timing. We were sophomores when the Greensboro Four sat at an F.W. Woolworth's Whites Only lunch counter in North Carolina and were refused service. It had become the catalyst to subsequent sit-in movements all over the country, and it helped with the formation of SNCC—the Student Nonviolent Coordinating Committee. After I graduated and moved to Nashville to attend Meharry, Stephen and I joined SNCC, while my cousin Robert, God bless the dead, was legal counsel for an office in Mississippi, and Claudia had volunteered to register Black voters.

"While you were living and going to school up here, Claudia had lived through the killings of Emmett Till, Medgar Evers, and Chaney, Goodman, and Schwerner, all who'd been murdered in Mississippi, so I suggest you check your inflated ego at the door and try to understand where she's coming from. And I shouldn't have to warn you that she's not like the women you've been with who believe you're the cat's meow."

Ashley lowered his eyes. "Why did you have to say that?"

"Because you know it's true, Black Prince of Wall Street."

"Please don't call me that."

"Why, Ashley? There was a time whenever someone called you that you'd preen like a peacock."

"It's getting old."

"So are you, Ashley Booth. When are you going to stop chasing skirts and settle down? Just the other day Stephen and I were talking about you. That you need a wife and children."

Ashley forced a smile rather than tell Yvonne he wasn't ready for marriage and children. "Maybe one of these days," he said instead.

"When is that, Ashley? When you're so old that you'll be shooting blanks?"

"Why are you talking about my sperm count? You should know men can father children well into their seventies."

Yvonne pushed her glasses up to the bridge of her nose. "Seventy-year-old men are grandfathers or even great-grandfathers, so spare me the bullshit, Ashley. I . . ." Her words trailed off when she heard three knocks following two. "That's Claudia."

Ashley sat up straight and planted both feet on the floor. "Did you tell her I was coming here?"

Yvonne blew out her cheeks. "What did I tell you about your overblown ego. No, Ashley, Claudia did not know you were coming here today."

He rose to stand as Yvonne stood up to answer the door.

Claudia was grinning like a Cheshire cat when Yvonne opened the door. "I got the apartment."

Yvonne hugged her. "Congratulations! I know I sound selfish, but I've gotten used to eating dinner with you a couple of times a week whenever Stephen is scheduled to work a double shift."

"I'm not moving that far away."

"Ashley's here," Yvonne whispered.

"Did he come to complain about me?"

"No, roomie. But he knows you're here, so it's time you guys work out whatever you need to do to get back together. Meanwhile, I'm going into the kitchen to get a snack. This baby never stops eating."

Claudia walked into the living room. She stared at Ashley and saw the frown set into his handsome features. It was obvious he wasn't happy to see her but that was no longer important. She'd just signed a six-month lease, with an option to renew for another six, to sublet a furnished studio apartment facing Central Park.

"Hello, Ashley."

He inclined his head. "Claudia. How have you been?"

She paused, then said, "I'm good. You?"

A slight smile parted his lips. "Better."

Claudia also smiled. "That's good to hear."

"Do you think we can go somewhere and talk?" he asked.

"Sure. We can go upstairs." Claudia knew he wanted to talk about why she hadn't called him. She climbed the three flights, Ashley following, and she unlocked the door to the apartment. "Please sit down, Ashley." He sat on the sofa while she took a matching loveseat several feet away. "I found an apartment and I'll be moving at the end of the month."

"Where?"

"It's on Central Park West between 103rd and 104th Streets."

"Nice neighborhood."

She smiled. "Nice views of the park."

"Are you going to need help moving?"

Claudia ignored his flat tone. "No."

Ashley leaned forward and rested his hands on the knees of his jeans. "What's up with us?"

"Nothing, Ashley. I've spent the past two weeks looking for an apartment."

"You could've called and told me that."

Claudia looked at him, not wanting to believe what she was hearing. Did he believe she was obligated to check in with him? "Why, Ashley?"

"Because I would've liked to have known what was going on with you."

"If that's the case, then why didn't you call me?" A swollen silence followed her question. "Since you've declined to answer, I think we should move on."

"Move on to where, Claudia?"

"That's up to you, Ashley. I'm not angry with you, so I don't know why you have an attitude."

"I don't have an attitude. I thought we were a couple and—"

"I'm under the impression that we are still a couple. What

we're not is joined at the hip. You have your life and I'm trying to get mine together. There's going to come a time when we can't spend every weekend together."

Ashley angled his head. "Like these past two weekends."

Smiling, Claudia nodded. "Yes."

Ashley also smiled. "Perhaps we need to start over."

"Okay. What are you proposing?"

"I'm invited to a fundraiser next Sunday afternoon for a local politician. Are you available to come with me?"

"Yes."

"And then there's the Memorial Day celebration at my folks' house on Sag Harbor. Are you up to going with me?"

"Of course. Long Island has a special place in history during the Revolutionary War and Prohibition."

"I keep forgetting you minored in history. And you're right about Long Island. Many of the towns are named for the Indian tribes that had made the island home." He pushed to his feet. "I'm going to head out now. I'll call you next week to let you know about the fundraiser."

Claudia also stood and walked Ashley to the door. "Get home safe."

"I will," Ashley said, and then dipped his head to brush a kiss over her mouth.

She waited for him to disappear down the staircase to close and lock the door. Claudia realized their relationship had hit a slight bump, yet not enough to wreck it completely. She hadn't lied to Ashley when she told him about apartment-hunting. She'd gone to a real estate company with a listing of available apartments in Manhattan and the Bronx. She knew nothing about the Bronx, so Claudia told the agent to concentrate on Manhattan.

She was shown one in Harlem along a block with several abandoned burned-out buildings. She managed to hold her tongue and when they'd returned to the office, she'd expressed to the agent he'd insulted her when he'd referred her to a drug-infested neighborhood because she was Black.

Claudia told him she wanted to rent a place where he'd want his family to live. He did apologize and then asked if she was willing to sublet, and once he explained the guidelines, and when she saw the furnished studio apartment, she was ready to write a check on the spot.

The second-floor apartment facing the park was move-in ready. The only thing she'd planned to purchase was a new mattress for the convertible sofa bed. There was a laundry room on each floor, which eliminated her sending her clothes out. She could walk to work until July, then she would take the bus that ran along Central Park West once she transferred to the Harlem branch.

Claudia had missed seeing Ashley for the past two weeks, but securing an apartment had taken priority. Now that she had a move-in date, she could relax and begin dating again.

Chapter 33

If you're offered a seat on a rocket ship, don't ask what seat! Just get on.
                                           —Sheryl Sandberg

When Ashley called Claudia to tell her the fundraiser was to be held in a hotel ballroom, she decided it was the perfect excuse to go shopping for a new dress. Yvonne had mentioned the B department stores: B. Altman, Bloomingdale's, Henri Bendel, and Bergdorf Goodman. She had also recommended she visit Saks Fifth Avenue and Lord & Taylor.

Claudia had walked into Bloomingdale's and within five minutes walked out because it was too crowded. It was another two hours of going in and out of various stores before she finally found what she wanted. It was a black sleeveless silk dress ending mid-calf. Four-inch black patent leather slingbacks and a small black evening clutch bag covered with bugle beads completed her outfit.

She had washed and set her hair on large rollers and then sat under the dryer she'd purchased after moving to New York. As the daughter of a beautician, she'd learned to do her own hair. The only thing she couldn't do was cut it. Cuts she left to the professionals. Claudia took extra care applying makeup. Black eyeliner, pastel eye shadow, light blush, and several coats of black mascara and opaque coral lip gloss completed her beauty regimen. She opened a drawer in the dresser and took out the case with Giancarlo's gift. It was the first time in ten years she would wear the pearl earrings and necklace.

Claudia put the earrings in her pierced lobes and secured the screw backs. She put on the necklace and fastened the catch. She glanced at the clock and gathered a black shawl and evening bag, opening it again to make certain she had tissues, a small compact with loose powder, and lip gloss.

Ashley checked his watch for what seemed like the umpteenth time when the door to the row house opened, and Claudia walked out at exactly two o'clock. He stared at her, unable to move for several seconds because he couldn't believe she could improve on perfection. He couldn't tear his gaze away from the soft waves falling to her shoulders, and as she came closer, he smiled at the same time as a feeling of pride washed over him. Yvonne had accused him of having an inflated ego and he wanted to tell her hell yeah, he did, because with Claudia on his arm there was no doubt he would be the envy of every man at the fundraiser.

Reaching for her free hand, he pressed a kiss to her inner wrist. "Thank you."

Claudia looked at him through a fringe of thick black lashes. The dramatic eye makeup highlighted the gold in her clear brown eyes. "What are you thanking me for?"

"For looking so incredibly beautiful." She lowered her eyes, the demure gesture he'd found so alluring "The driver should be here any minute."

Claudia's eyebrows lifted questioningly. "You're not driving?"

"No. I arranged for a driver to take us downtown because it's almost impossible to park near the hotel."

"How did you get here?"

"I took a taxi."

He glanced down the street to see a black Mercedes-Benz sedan coming closer. Moving over to the curb, he put up his arm to signal the driver. The chauffer stopped, got out, and opened the rear door. Ashley waited for Claudia to get in, then removed his suit jacket, slipped in beside her, and folded the jacket neatly and placed it over his lap.

With wide eyes, he stared at the earring in her left ear. A large pearl was suspended from a cluster of stones he knew in a single glance were diamonds. There also were diamonds on the clasp holding the single strand of perfectly matched pearls in place around her perfumed neck. Ashley wondered if the jewelry was a gift, and if it was, from whom. And he pondered if her husband had given her the necklace and earrings.

"How familiar are you with the candidate running for office?" she questioned.

"I met him through his uncle, who was one of my college professors."

"Is this his first election?" Claudia asked.

"Yes. He's challenging the incumbent representative from an Upper Westside district."

"Do you think he has a chance of winning his seat?"

"We'll see. First, he must win the primary in June, and if he does then his name will appear on the November ballot. This will be his last fundraiser before the primary. He held his first one last summer in Sag Harbor, and then another just before Christmas."

"I've heard of candidates having fundraising dinners and charging a thousand dollars a plate for so little food that it wouldn't fill up a bird."

"Kenny's fundraiser is a cocktail party. Lots of booze and finger food."

"Dammit!"

"What's the matter?"

"I deliberately didn't eat because I thought there was going to be real food at the fundraiser, not finger food."

"They usually offer deviled eggs, skewered meatballs in different sauces, stuffed mushrooms, cucumber cups with creamy salmon, and bacon wrapped chicken livers."

"That sounds better."

Ashley rested an arm over her shoulders. "If you don't get enough to eat, we can always slip out and find a restaurant."

Claudia rested her head on his shoulder. "That's okay, Ashley. I promise not to faint on you."

Turning his head, he kissed her hair. "Don't worry about fainting because I will catch you before you fall."

Claudia looped her arm over Ashley's when he led her toward a ballroom at the Waldorf Astoria hotel. She chanced a surreptitious glance at the other women heading inside the ballroom with their escorts and she was glad she'd elected to wear what she did. The bodice of the dress was molded to her breasts and waist while the flowing skirt flared around her hips and legs.

She smiled at Ashley when he rested a hand at the small of her back. He was breathtakingly handsome in a slim-cut navy blue suit, white shirt, and blue and white striped silk tie. He always wore his hair cropped because he claimed if he let it grow any longer the strands would stick up like little spikes.

Claudia noticed that some of the attendees were wearing Robert F. Kennedy campaign buttons. The former US Attorney General and currently the US Senator from New York had declared he was running for president and had actively campaigned in Oregon, Nebraska, California, and Washington, D.C. His challengers for the office were Senator Eugene McCarthy and Vice President Hubert Humphrey.

"Come with me, sweetheart, I want to introduce you to the candidate."

Claudia followed Ashley as he wended his way through

the crowd in the opulent ballroom to where a young Black man was speaking as onlookers appeared to be holding on to his every word.

"I'm glad you showed up again to support my nephew."

She watched the approach of a tall, heavy-set man with a soft voice that belied his impressive bulk. He enveloped Ashley in a bear hug, then released him to give Claudia a friendly smile.

"Who is this lovely woman you brought with you, Booth?"

"Professor Bayless, I'd like to introduce Claudia Moore. Claudia, Professor James Bayless."

Claudia extended her hand. "It's nice meeting you."

James Bayless cradled her hand in his much larger one. "The pleasure is all mine. Booth, can you please go and bring me and your date something to drink, while I get to know her better."

Claudia wondered if the man was flirting with her or he was just being friendly. She didn't have long to find out when he asked, "Just what is it you do?"

"I work for a bank." It took her less than two minutes to give him a recap of her employment history, ending with the mishap where she was working as a teller rather than a loan officer.

"Do you like banking, Claudia?"

"Yes," she replied truthfully.

"Where do you see yourself in, let's say, five years?"

"I'd like to get into international banking because I speak several foreign languages."

James Bayless appeared stunned. "Say that again?"

"I can read, speak, and write French, Spanish, and Italian."

"Are you ready to change jobs now?"

Claudia was shocked and thoroughly confused. "I don't understand."

"What is there to understand, Miss Moore? You want to get into international banking and I'm here to help you out. Do you have a résumé?"

"Yes, but I plan to update it and include the loan officer position in July."

"Forget about updating it." Reaching into the breast pocket of his jacket, he removed a small case and handed her his business card. "I want you to drop your résumé off at my house as soon as possible. If I'm not there, then just leave it with my wife. Meanwhile I'm going to call someone who I know would be willing to interview you for a position at his bank."

Claudia couldn't believe what had just transpired as she stared at the card. "I live about five blocks away from you."

James smiled. "That's even better. Drop it off tomorrow evening. Meanwhile I'm going to call my friend and let him know it's time for him to return a favor. There's an Italian proverb that says, *One hand washes the other while both hands wash the face.*"

"*Una mano lava l'altra mentre entrambe le mani lavano il viso.* I just said the same thing in Italian."

Putting his hands together in a prayerful gesture, James gave her a direct stare. "I believe you're going to go places, young lady."

"Do you really believe I can get the position?" Claudia wanted to kick herself for sounding inept. The man was offering her the opportunity of a lifetime; meanwhile she was questioning him about his ability to make things happen for her.

"If you live in this city long enough, you'll learn it's not what you know, but *who* you know. And I happen to know the right people to get young Black professionals into positions where they can thrive."

"Like Ashley."

He nodded. "Yes, like Ashley Booth. I recognized his genius the first day he walked into my classroom. And when I told him this, he didn't question me, Claudia. He owned it. Just like you should own your gifts and never let anyone define who you are."

Claudia smiled, knowing she had been thoroughly chastised. "Yes, sir."

James peered over her head. "Now, where is Booth with our drinks? I should've known he wouldn't be able to go two feet without some woman trying to get his attention."

Turning, Claudia saw Ashley with a glass in each hand, while a buxom brunette held on to his arm as if he were her lifeline. "I think it's time I go and rescue my man."

"That's what I'm talking about," James said under his breath.

Ashley flashed a wide grin when he saw Claudia and his former professor coming in his direction. He'd attempted to extricate himself from the clingy woman, but she wasn't having it.

"Thank you, darling, for getting my drink," Claudia crooned as she eased the glass from his hand and brushed a light kiss over his mouth.

Ashley wanted to applaud Claudia for her award-worthy performance. The endearment must have gotten through to the other woman when she snorted delicately and walked away. "Thank you, sweetheart." He nodded to James. "Sorry about the delay."

James touched his glass to Ashley's. "You looked as if you needed rescuing."

"She's like an octopus."

"Caroline just happens to be an incurable flirt. But she does know when to back off."

Ashley stared at Claudia taking furtive sips of champagne. "I wanted to introduce you to Kenny, but I'll wait until he's finished greeting his supporters."

James glanced over at his nephew. "I was telling your girlfriend that I'm going to see if I can get her a position with a bank with overseas connections."

Ashley looked at his former business ethics professor as if he'd suddenly grown a third eye when he heard *overseas*.

Was he talking about Claudia leaving the States to work abroad? "Would she work here or in another country?"

"Don't panic, Booth. She would be stateside."

An emotion Ashley could only interpret as relief swept over him. He was certain Claudia wouldn't accept an overseas assignment even if it were presented to her, because she wouldn't want to leave her mother.

"I'm not panicking," Ashley lied smoothly. "I'm certain Claudia will excel in whatever position she holds."

Although he hadn't panicked, he was scared of losing Claudia. Not seeing her for two weeks was enough to send him into an emotional tailspin where he'd found it difficult to concentrate on his work. He'd come home and watch endless hours of television while logging less than five hours of sleep each night.

He moved closer to Claudia and put an arm around her waist. "Would you like something to eat?"

"Please."

Claudia exited the taxi and walked into Rao's for her scheduled interview. The restaurant, an East Harlem institution, was based on the quality and authenticity of their pasta sauces. She was surprised when the bank executive suggested conducting an interview at the restaurant because not only was it close to her home, but he'd admitted that Rao's was his favorite Italian restaurant.

She still felt as if she'd entered an alternative universe after attending the fundraiser with Ashley. The event was a rousing success. The attendees were friendly, the finger foods scrumptious, and the quality of the champagne excellent. Ashley had introduced her to the candidate, and she concluded he had the good looks, intelligence, and charisma to earn thousands of votes.

However, it had been her conversation with James Bayless that was seared into her brain. He'd promised to get her a position with a bank with an international division. And if her interview was successful and she was hired, then the next step was to hand in her resignation even before assuming the position as a loan officer.

She gave the maître d' her name and a waiter escorted her to a table where a man with salt-and-pepper hair rose to stand at her approach. A network of attractive lines fanned out around his large blue-gray eyes when he smiled.

"We finally meet," he said in fluent Italian.

Claudia nodded to the waiter as he pulled out a chair for her to sit. "Yes, it is. And thank you for suggesting we have dinner while you interview me," she replied in the same language, watching as his sweeping black eyebrows lifted slightly.

William McNeil smiled. "Your Italian is flawless."

"Thank you. And so is yours," she said, continuing to speak Italian. His warm smile was enough for Claudia to curb some of her anxiety about the unorthodox interview.

"I must thank my Italian mother for teaching her children the language, while my Irish father was completely clueless whenever we talked to him in our mother's tongue."

"He never picked up any of the words or phrases?"

"No. If you don't mind, I'd like to order something to eat before we begin talking about how you've come to speak Italian."

"I don't mind at all. And because I don't get to speak Italian very often, would you mind if we conduct the interview in Italian?"

The banker smiled again. "I was hoping you would say that."

When Claudia walked through the restaurant's red doors, she'd discovered why Rao's had earned a reputation as one of the finest Italian restaurants in New York City. Spaghetti and the saucy meatballs made with veal, beef, and pork in a marinara sauce were the best she'd ever eaten. William had ordered a bottle of red wine to go along with his spaghetti and chicken Parmesan. He'd drunk three glasses of wine to her one.

Over dinner, she revealed how she'd learned to speak different languages and was fortunate enough to perfect her French when she'd spent six weeks in Paris. Claudia was also forthcoming about growing up in Mississippi and why she'd decided to relocate to New York. She'd disclosed the barriers she'd encountered as not only a woman but a Black woman.

William leaned back in his chair. "I must admit when James Bayless called to tell me about you before a messenger delivered your résumé, I was hesitant to hire a woman. I am not a chauvinist, but I didn't want to hire a woman and have her deal with backlash from some of the men who'd openly said they would never work with a woman."

"If you did hire me, and I came to you complaining that someone was ridiculing me, what recourse would I have?"

"If there are any malcontents, then they wouldn't have to deal with their supervisors, but directly with me. I run a tight ship, Claudia, and I expect everyone to follow the rules."

"You're the director of the international department, so how many of your people speak more than one language?"

"My department is not quite a year old, so I'm still not fully staffed. I've hired someone who speaks French, and another person is fluent in Spanish. What I need is someone who can speak, write, and understand Italian. Right now, I'm the only one who speaks Italian and whenever I communicate with our Italian-based branch it takes time away from my other responsibilities."

"How do you adjust to the difference in time zones?" She was aware that Italy was six hours ahead of New York.

"Your work schedule will reflect the difference. For example, if it's eight o'clock in the morning here then it would be two in the afternoon in Rome. And we usually conduct business before or after their siesta. An Italian *riposo* or siesta can last about ninety minutes. It can begin anywhere between noon and one thirty and run until two thirty to four. If you've scheduled an overseas call, then you will inform your supervisor that you won't be working nine to five."

"That means I'll have flexible hours?"

"Yes. Will that pose a problem for you?"

"Not at all."

William extended his hand. "I was hoping you would say that. Welcome aboard, Claudia. You're hired."

Claudia placed a hand over her mouth as she struggled not to burst into tears of joy. James Bayless had made it happen for her. He'd been instrumental in her securing a position where she could use her experience and skills.

"Thank you."

"No, thank you, Claudia," William countered. "You're exactly what I need because you can fill in for the Spanish- and French-speaking team members when they aren't available. Of course, your starting salary will reflect your impeccable qualifications. You will have to undergo a three-month training period before you will be assigned clients, and there may come a time when you may have to fly to Rome to meet my Italian counterpart."

"When do you expect me to start?"

"August first. That's when Europe goes on holiday and it's the best time for you to go through a training course."

Claudia knew she had to inform the bank that she would not accept the loan officer's position. She also planned to hand in her resignation at the end of June and spend the month of July with Yvonne before beginning the next phase of her life.

"The personnel department will mail you the documents we need to put you on the payroll. You should receive a letter of acceptance outlining your starting date, salary, and benefits before the end of the month."

"I know I keep saying it, but thank you, Mr. McNeil."

He signaled for the check, and after paying the bill, he escorted Claudia to the sidewalk. "My driver is waiting for me, and I'll drop you off at home."

Cupping her elbow, he escorted her across the street to a limousine. He tapped on the driver's-side window to get the chauffeur's attention. The man came alert and got out to open the rear door. Claudia slumped against the supple leather seat and closed her eyes. And she did something she hadn't done in a while. She whispered a prayer of thanks that she could cross off another entry on her wish list.

Chapter 34

Giving up doesn't always mean you are weak.
Sometimes it means that you are strong enough to
let go.
                    —Author Unknown

Claudia sat in the racy sports car, watching the landscape
whiz by as Ashley accelerated off the Triborough Bridge.
It was late May and spring had made a brief appearance before it was supplanted by summer. One day she wore a lightweight jacket, and the next she was sleeveless. She wasn't
certain how to dress for the fluctuating temperatures and always left the apartment with a sweater.

She had moved into her studio apartment and woke every
morning to chirping birds and the verdant lushness of Central Park. She'd begun walking—everywhere. Living on the
Westside made it easier for her to walk to and from work and
visit the American Museum of Natural History. She'd become a New Yorker in every sense of the word when she
stopped to buy hotdogs from sidewalk vendors, requesting
they smother them with mustard and onions. Since she and
Ashley had reunited after the fundraiser, they'd spent every
weekend together—Friday and Saturday nights in his apartment, and Sunday night at hers.

If Claudia had imagined herself falling in love with Ashley, now she knew for certain she was. Her feelings for him were different from what she'd experienced with her husband. Robert was an unabashed romantic who wasn't reticent when demonstrating his love for her—in and out of bed. She'd waited over and over to hear Ashley express his love for her when in the throes of ejaculating, but it hadn't happened, and that was when Claudia wondered if he did love her, or had she just become a receptacle for his lust or someone who had served to enhance his image whenever they were out in public.

When she'd called Ashley to let him know she had gotten the job, he'd taken her out to a restaurant and given her a Louis Vuitton wallet as a congratulatory gift. Claudia had long admired the iconic luxury brand when she saw her aunt Virgie's handbags and steamer trunk, and had thanked him in the most intimate way possible.

It was as if events in her life were moving faster than she could have imagined; so were the antiwar protests. The demonstrations weren't just germane to the United States, but violent rallies had also spread across Europe. There were protest marches in London; Frankfurt, Germany; and Rome, Italy, and there was an increase in draft-card burnings in the States, along with violent clashes with police.

The month before, an antiwar rally in San Francisco drew more than fifteen thousand attendees. In attendance was Muhammad Ali, who'd changed his name from Cassius Clay when he'd become a Muslim, members of the Black Panther Party, the Iranian Students Association, Black Muslims, and the Socialist Workers Party.

Claudia had been anticipating spending several days in Sag Harbor just to get away from watching the upheaval gripping the country. She'd left Mississippi, where a Black's life was valued lower than that of a mule, only to be made aware there was no place in the country where Black people could demonstrate for equality and not be labeled as radicals, Communists, or militants.

"Are you okay?" Ashley asked after they'd been on the road for more than an hour.

She turned to him and smiled. "Yes."

After Dr. King's assassination, Claudia had promised herself that discussing politics with Ashley was taboo. Not only had she been an eyewitness to Klan activity but even talking about them made her furious.

"You're very quiet."

"I'm just taking in the sights."

"Once I get off the expressway, I'm going to stop to get gas before we get to my parents' house, just in case they want me to run a few errands."

"How many people are they expecting?"

"I don't know. They always open the house the last weekend in May and don't close it up until after the Labor Day weekend."

"Is the house large enough to accommodate a lot of people?" Claudia asked, because although Ashley admitted his parents knew he was bringing a woman, she wondered if they realized she was sleeping with their son.

"Are you asking because you want to know if we'll be sharing a bedroom?"

"Yes."

"We'll be staying in the guesthouse."

"Is that where you stay when you invite other women to come with you?"

Ashley gave her a quick glance. "Jealous?"

Claudia rolled her eyes. "You wish. Your past is your past, Ashley, and I couldn't care less about what you did or did not do with other women."

"What about you?"

"What about me, Ashley?"

"Are you content with what we have? Or do you want more?"

"I don't know what you mean by more."

"Marriage and kids."

Claudia wondered if Ashley was testing her to see what she would say. "No, Ashley. I don't want or need more. What we have now works for me. But that may change once I begin my new job because I won't have a structured work schedule. I hope that answers your question."

"It does."

"Are you disappointed?"

"No. Because I want whatever it is you want."

Ashley did not want to tell Claudia that even if she changed her mind he could never marry her. That what he'd witnessed seeing his parents nearly tear each other apart after his sister's death had traumatized him. Even after they'd gone to marriage counseling, he still couldn't forget the yelling and threats that were seared into his brain and had triggered nightmares where he would wake up shaking uncontrollably. His parents may have reconciled, but Ashley still had unresolved issues with them.

Ashley left the expressway and took the road leading directly into Sag Harbor. Claudia had slept over Friday night because he'd wanted to get up early and be on the road before seven, since he wanted to avoid the truck traffic on the Long Island Expressway.

He maneuvered into a service station and had the attendant fill up the gas tank. Twenty minutes later he pulled into the driveway and parked behind his father's sedan. The front door opened, and his mother stood on the porch waiting for him. He knew she was curious about the woman he was bringing to her home, because in the past he had always come alone. That had been his time to distance himself from work and the women he'd been seeing at the time. Ashley had called it his "me time" when he did whatever he wanted without having to think of anyone but himself.

Ashley got out and came around the car to open the door

for Claudia. Holding her hand, he led her up the porch, watching Valerie Booth's expression change from impassive to amused. "Mom, I'd like you to meet Claudia Moore. Claudia, my mother, Valerie Booth."

Valerie extended her hand. "It's indeed a pleasure to meet you. And I hope this won't be the last time my son decides to bring you with him when he comes to visit."

Claudia smiled at the tall, dark-complected woman with lightly graying straight black hair she had styled in a ponytail. She was casually dressed in a pair of loose-fitting cotton pants and a short-sleeved camp shirt. Claudia realized Ashley was the more masculine version of his mother's delicate beauty.

"So do I, Mrs. Booth," she said.

"Please call me Valerie."

Claudia smiled. "Then Valerie it is."

The screened door opened, and a short, stocky, slightly balding man joined them on the porch. The first thing Claudia noticed were his eyes, laughing eyes. There was something about him that put her instantly at ease.

"Dad, this is Claudia. Claudia, my father, Thaddeus Booth."

Thaddeus took a step and embraced Claudia. "Welcome. I hope this won't be the last time you'll spend time with me and Valerie."

Claudia wanted to know what was going on that the Booths were so intent on having her come back with Ashley. She nodded because she didn't know what to say. "I left something in the car for the house. Ashley, could you please get it for me?"

"You didn't have to bring anything," Valerie said.

"I was raised in the South, and we were taught never to go to someone's house empty-handed."

"Come inside, Claudia. I know you must be exhausted after sitting in a car for so many hours. Thaddeus and I waited to eat breakfast because we knew you were coming out early. Our other guests aren't expected until later this morning. Come, child, I'll show you where you can wash up. After breakfast you can relax in the guesthouse."

Valerie was talking a mile a minute and Claudia wondered if she was nervous meeting her son's girlfriend or if it was something she always did. She followed her into the house and exhaled an audible sigh when she saw a collection of antique glasses lining a shelf in the expansive farmhouse kitchen. When Ashley revealed that the Sag Harbor summer home had been renovated but still had retained its early nineteenth-century character, she'd found an antique shop with an inventory of Depression glassware and bought a blue fruit bowl as a house gift.

Valerie opened a door off the kitchen. "You can wash up here."

Claudia was looking forward to relaxing before the Booths' other guests arrived. She did what she had to do in the bathroom and when she walked into the kitchen, she saw Valerie setting the table. "I can do that."

Valerie waved her hand in a dismissive gesture. "No. You're a guest, so just sit and let me do this."

"Are you certain you don't need my help?"

"No, she doesn't," Thaddeus said as he walked into the kitchen wearing a bibbed apron. "Valerie and I have agreed that I cook whenever we come here, and she cooks when we're in the city."

Ashley entered the kitchen with a shopping bag containing Claudia's gift. He handed it to his mother. "I don't know what it is, because Claudia refused to tell me."

Valerie removed the box from the bag and took off the black velvet ribbon and black-and-white wrapping paper. Claudia knew from the smile spreading across her features that she had selected an appropriate house gift.

"How did you know I collect Depression glass?" she asked Claudia.

"I didn't know. Lucky guess."

"You better not let this one go, son," Thaddeus said, as he gave Ashley a direct stare. Claudia, how do you like your eggs?"

"Over easy, please."

Ashley took his and Claudia's bags to the guesthouse, kissed her and said he would be back because he needed to discuss something with his father. Breakfast had been easy-going with Claudia charming both his parents.

She smiled. "I'm going to take a shower and change into something cooler."

He found Thaddeus at the rear of the house hosing down picnic tables and benches. "How many are you expecting?" he asked his father.

"Valerie said six have confirmed."

"Are any her lovers?" Thaddeus glared at Ashley, but he ignored it. "Dad, how long are you going to put up with your wife disrespecting you when she flaunts her lovers?"

"Mind your business, Ashley. What goes on between me and your mother doesn't affect you."

"It does affect me, Dad. Do you know why I don't want to get married? It's because I don't want to end up like you," he said. "Loving a woman so much that I'm willing to look the other way when she decides to fuck another man."

"That's enough, Ashley! If you can't respect my home, then you can get the hell out! I don't tell you who to fuck, because I know you're no choirboy when it comes to sleeping with women. And I wonder if that nice girl knows that you'll never marry."

"Claudia doesn't want to get married, so she's not a topic for discussion."

"Then why is she with you?"

"Because we enjoy each other's company?"

"One of these days she's going to get tired of your company and move on. And when she does then you'll realize what you've lost. Your problem is you're so busy looking at me and your mother when you should take stock of yourself, Ashley. If you don't want to get married, then say that and don't use someone else's marriage or relationship as an excuse because you're too selfish to share your success with a woman. Could it be you're afraid she just might take some shine away from the Black Prince of Wall Street? That she might get more attention than you?"

"That's not true!"

"Yes, it is, son. I know you better than you know yourself. You're in love with Claudia, but she will never know that unless you tell her. And if there comes a time when she's ready to marry and you don't ask her to become your wife, then you're going to lose her."

"Claudia's not going anywhere."

Thaddeus ran a hand over his face. "I hope you're right for your sake. And if she does leave you, I promise not to say I told you so."

Ashley did not want to think about losing Claudia, but he didn't want to end up like his father, ignoring his wife's affairs because he wasn't able to satisfy her sexually. The trauma of losing his daughter had affected Thaddeus psychologically and physically, resulting in his inability to achieve an erection.

"Do you want me to get the grills out of the shed and set them up?"

"That would be nice."

"You could say thank you, Dad."

"And you could stop being a pain in the ass."

Ashley walked across the grass to the shed, reliving the conversation he'd just had with his father. Thaddeus was wrong. He planned to have Claudia in his life for a long time.

When Claudia walked into the investment bank several blocks from Wall Street to begin her first day of work, she was escorted into William McNeil's office. She'd spent the past two months mentally preparing herself for this day.

"Please sit down, Claudia. I must ask you something before my secretary shows you your office."

There was something in his voice that gave Claudia pause. Was he going to tell her he didn't need her, after she'd quit her last job? "Okay. What is it?"

"Is there anything in your life that would prevent you from relocating?"

Her eyelids fluttered. "Relocate where?"

"Rome. Our Italian associate is leaving, and I'd like you to replace him."

"You want me to live in Rome?"

"Yes. You'll be provided housing, a travel allowance, and a salary increase that will permit you to live quite comfortably."

"How soon do you need my answer?"

He lowered his eyes. "Actually now."

Claudia found herself in a quandary. There were times when she'd seriously considered moving to France to live with her aunt after she'd buried Robert, but hadn't wanted to leave her mother. She thought about Sarah Patterson and Ashley Booth. Could she leave them and start a new life in a foreign country? William McNeil had hired her based on her résumé and a dinner interview, and now he was offering her an overseas assignment she knew would change her life—forever. Claudia was certain Aunt Mavis would tell her to accept it because it was what she'd prepared her for when she'd tutored her in French, Spanish, and Italian.

"Yes," she said, before she could change her mind. "I'll accept the assignment."

"Thank you, Claudia. You just saved my job."

She blinked slowly. "What?"

"I told you we are a new start-up and not fully staffed. I had a meeting with several board members last night who are planning to dissolve this department because they claim it isn't viable. And when I asked if my people would be folded into the other departments, I was told they wouldn't. I said if they go, then I'm going with them."

"What did they say to that?"

"They want me to put my person in place in the Rome office."

"Why?"

"Because I will be able to supervise you, and we'll pay your salary. If you don't have a valid passport, we can fast-track that for you."

"I have a valid one."

"Good."

"How much time do I have to get my affairs together before I have to leave?"

"A week. I know you're renting an apartment. We will pick up whatever is left on your lease. And if you have a vehicle, we can arrange to have it shipped overseas if you don't want to leave it here."

Claudia did not want to believe what they were willing to do for her to accept the position. "I don't own a car."

William nodded. "Good. We'll set you up with a furnished apartment that's within walking distance to the bank. I'll also arrange to have someone stock the refrigerator a few days before you arrive. Once we finalize your flight arrangements, you'll be picked up at the airport and driven to your apartment. And if you want to ship any personal items in advance, just pack them up and they will be at your apartment before you arrive."

"It looks as if you've thought of everything."

"I didn't get more than two hours of sleep last night wondering if you were going to accept what I'm offering."

"From what you've just told me, if I didn't, then I would be out of a job. And there's no way I can go back to my former employer asking for them to take me back."

"I'm sorry about that, but you could say I was also bush-whacked. Donna will show you your office for now. You'll find some manuals that will give you an overview of the bank and our operating systems. I'll take you out to lunch, where I'll outline your duties and responsibilities. This will be your first and last day in this office because you need to be ready to leave before August tenth. You have my private number, so call me if you encounter a problem. We have a messenger service that will bring you your travel documents." He paused. "And thank you again. I'll make certain you won't regret the sacrifice you've made to save this department."

Claudia followed William's secretary down a carpeted hallway to an office that reminded her of a sitting room. It was small and inviting. "If you have to make an outside call, you must dial nine first."

"Thank you."

She stood, rooted to the spot and unable to move as she thought about how her life was going to change, and the impact on those she would leave behind. Her mother, Aunt Mavis, Yvonne, and Ashley. She wouldn't be in the States when Yvonne had her baby, and that was something she really was looking forward to. And she didn't want to think about Ashley. She hadn't returned to Sag Harbor with him because she'd promised Yvonne they would spend the month of July shopping for baby clothes and decorating the nursery. Ashley had put in for vacation the last two weeks in August and he'd planned to spend that time at his parents' summer home.

Claudia made a mental list to call her mother later that night, but she wanted to tell Yvonne and Ashley about her future in person.

PART FOUR

1968

GIANCARLO FORTENZA

Chapter 35

Unless you try to do something beyond what you
have already mastered, you will never grow.
—Ralph Waldo Emerson

"I had no idea you were going to put out a spread like
this when you told me to come for dinner," Claudia
said to Yvonne.

Her best friend had hosted an impromptu bon voyage
party and Claudia knew it would be the last time she, Yvonne,
and Ashley would all be together until the following summer.
She wouldn't be eligible to go on holiday until she completed
one year of employment.

Yvonne, now very noticeably pregnant, smiled. "You know
I couldn't send my roomie off to a country where if she was
craving soul food, she wouldn't be able to get it."

Claudia clasped her hands together as she stared at the
buffet table lined with dishes Yvonne had ordered from a
restaurant known for serving some of the best Southern cuisine in Harlem. "Whenever I find myself feening for soul
food I will buy the ingredients and make it myself."

"So, are you really ready to leave behind all of this crazi-
ness going on in this country, to lie on some beach in the Italian Riviera?"

Claudia picked up a glass filled with sparkling water. "Yeah, right. I'm moving to Rome to work and not to wear a tiny bikini and frolic in the Mediterranean with the rich and famous."

"But you will be dealing with the rich and famous," Ashley said, as he crossed the dining room to stand next to her.

Claudia gave him a direct stare. "Then, we'll have something in common. You make investments to make people richer, while I'll be responsible for convincing wealthy Italians to invest in American companies."

"True."

"At least we can agree on that," she countered.

What she and Ashley hadn't been able to agree upon was her decision to accept an overseas assignment. He'd claimed she had blindsided him and he felt as if she should've discussed it with him first. Claudia was quick to remind him that she did not need his permission to make changes in her life and to decide what was best for her career.

"When are you coming back?"

Claudia decided to ignore his chilly tone. "Coming back on holiday or coming back to stay?"

"To stay."

"That's not happening, Ashley. I'll come back to visit during holidays, but beginning tomorrow I will call Italy home."

"So, you are going to be like your aunt who lives in France. You're leaving and never coming back."

"The reason my aunt Virgie decided to become an expatriate is because she didn't like this country's political system, and I'm leaving because I've been offered an opportunity I would never be able to get here. You of all people should know that, Ashley. Other than your assistant, where are the Black women in your department?" She held up a hand. "No. Please don't answer that because we both know it's *nada*. And I doubt if you would ever hire one, because you're now a member of the old boys' club. I've lived long enough to know that men, regardless of their color or race, will stick together to keep a woman, regardless of her race, in a subordinate position. But this could've worked out differently if you'd asked me to stay."

"Ask you to stay when you've already committed to accept the position?"

"Yes. I could've negotiated with my supervisor to work in Rome for a year, with an option of staying or returning to the States." She hadn't told Ashley that her accepting the position was contingent on the future employment of four other employees in the international unit.

"Now you tell me."

"Cut the bullshit," she whispered. "If I really meant that much to you, we wouldn't be having this conversation."

Ashley recoiled as if she'd slapped him across the face when she uttered the expletive, because it was on a very rare occasion that she used profanity.

All Claudia wanted from Ashley was to hear that he loved her, and that would've been enough for her to tell William McNeil, *thank you but no thanks* because she couldn't leave the man with whom she had fallen in love. But it was as if the four-letter word was so abhorrent to Ashley that he couldn't allow it in his psyche.

"I'm extending an open invitation for you to come and visit whenever you want. My mother and aunt have canceled their trip to Puerto Rico this Christmas to celebrate the holiday in Rome with me. All you have to do is call and let me know when you're coming, and I'll show you the best of the Eternal City." Claudia paused. "You have a year, Ashley. If you don't contact me about visiting, then this will be the last time you will see me. I refuse to put my life on hold waiting for someone who isn't willing to make me a part of theirs."

"What is it you want, Claudia? You want marriage?"

"No, Ashley. I'm not asking you to marry me because I'm not looking for another husband. I just want someone to love me as much as I love them. One year, Ashley, and not one day more." She was leaving the States on August eighth, and if

Ashley didn't contact her before the same date the following year, then she knew whatever they'd had would be relegated to their past.

"You're a hard woman, Claudia Moore."

Claudia made a fist in a Black Power salute. "No, Ashley. What I am is a fierce Black sister willing to cross an ocean to get what she has been denied in the country of her birth."

Ashley realized Claudia had challenged him when she'd given him one year to decide whether they would stay together. But how the hell could he have a relationship with her thousands of miles away? It just wasn't possible. "It's not going to work," he said softly. "I can't keep up the pretense that we're a couple if I can't see you. And flying to Europe to spend a week or two together will only mess with my head when I come back. You know I care about you and only want the best for your future, so I'm going to say goodbye and good luck."

Turning on his heel he walked out of Yvonne and Stephen's home, praying he hadn't made a mistake rejecting Claudia's offer for them to continue their relationship even if it was long distance. He knew her decision to move to Italy was twofold. It was an opportunity of a lifetime to advance her career, and he knew she was growing more despondent each time another prominent leader was murdered.

It took Claudia two days to settle into her apartment that was conveniently located close to many shops, cafés, and office buildings that she could get to on foot. And it had taken that long for her to recover from jet lag. Her flight from New York had been delayed for more than three hours and when it finally took off and she'd settled down to sleep, bright sunlight came through the shades indicating they had crossed several time zones and her body's circadian rhythm hadn't adjusted to the six-hour time difference.

A driver had met her at the airport and driven her to the apartment that was on the top floor of a two-story building overlooking a charming courtyard. The two bedrooms were clean and spacious, the larger claiming a balcony where she could drink her morning coffee and end the day with a glass of wine or cup of cappuccino. Boxes she'd packed with her clothes and personal items that were shipped days before her departure lined a wall in the living room.

William McNeil had made certain her relocating to Rome was expedited smoothly. The refrigerator was stocked with perishables, and the cupboards in the kitchen filled with various items she would need to put together a meal. The only thing missing was meat, and that was something she would select from a butcher.

The telephone rang and she walked across the living/dining area to answer it. "*Ciao.*"

"*Buongiorno*, Claudia."

"Good morning, William," she replied, speaking English. "What are you doing up so early?" It was five o'clock in New York.

"I just got up and I wanted to check to see how you're feeling."

"I'm better. I slept for at least ten hours yesterday, so now I'm ready to begin working. And I want to thank you for extending my start date by a week."

"There's no need to thank me, Claudia, because you're the goose that lays golden eggs. I knew you would be jet-lagged, so I told the bank president that you would need a couple of days to recover. How's the apartment?"

"It's perfect and so is the location. I'm glad I'm starting now because most of the tourists have left."

"That's why I wanted you to start in August, because many of the businesses close for the month and you should be able to become more familiar with the city without having to navigate crowds of tourists."

"I'm planning to go out later this afternoon to buy some meat and groceries. Then later tonight I'm going to find a café and drink coffee under the stars."

William laughed. "Don't forget to sample gelato."

Claudia had heard once you have gelato, you'd never want to eat ice cream again. "Thanks for reminding me. I will add it to my shopping list."

"I suggest you try it at a *gelateria* to see the different flavors. You'll be given samples in a little cup that you can eat with a flat spade-shaped plastic spoon."

"It sounds as if you're more than familiar with *gelaterie*."

"I spent a month in Italy last year and I ate gelato every day in every city I visited. My favorite is a blood-orange gelato I had in Bologna."

"That sounds delicious."

"Trust me, it is, Claudia. I'm going to ring off now because I have a breakfast meeting with the corporate/commercial banking division. I'll call you again once you complete orientation."

She'd been told that her orientation would last from three weeks to a month, where she would be required to delve into the complexities of international banking, letters of credit, changes in currency values, tax shelters, and to recognize tax evasion and money laundering.

Claudia ended the call, promising William she would call him if she encountered a problem, which she prayed she wouldn't until she completed her orientation. She decided to leave the apartment before it got too hot and when many of the businesses closed in the afternoon for *riposo*.

Dressed in a loose-fitting shift dress and ballet-type flats, she set out to tour the neighborhood with several mom-and-pop shops offering delicate pastries, handmade jewelry, decorative masks, a hair salon, a shop selling baby and children's clothes, and a photographer. She discovered a butcher at the end of another cobblestone street and ordered a whole chicken, rib lamb and pork chops, and ground pork, beef, and veal for meatloaf and meatballs.

The butcher complimented her on her Italian when she told him she was an *americana* who had recently moved to

Italy. He welcomed her in rapid Italian, which she struggled to understand until she finally had to tell him to speak more slowly. He'd introduced himself as Angelo and he told her if she wanted to learn to cook authentic Italian food, then he was willing to share some of the recipes that had been passed down through generations of women in his family. He said whenever she came in again, he would have a few for her.

Claudia felt as if she'd made a friend, and he in turn a loyal customer. Purchasing fresh meat from a butcher was very different from selecting packaged meat from a super-market's freezer case. She found an outdoor market and pur-chased fresh fruit, vegetables, and herbs. She had to purchase two large canvas bags to carry her purchases back to the apartment. The rays of the blistering summer sun were re-lentless, and Claudia felt as if the heat had penetrated her scalp. It was a blatant reminder that she couldn't go out at midday without a hat.

She returned home and put away her purchases, and then sat down and flipped through an Italian cookbook she'd bought at an airport bookstore before boarding her flight. She found a tuna and white bean salad recipe using tuna packed in olive oil, white cannellini beans, minced garlic, chopped shallots, lemon juice, capers, white vinegar, and salt and pepper. She had all the ingredients on hand and decided to make enough for lunch and dinner.

Claudia sat at the kitchen table, her fountain pen poised over a sheet of pale blue stationery. The sun had set, taking with it the intense daytime heat. She'd changed her mind about going out and drinking coffee because she feared the caffeine would keep her up.

13 August 1968
My Dearest Sister Noelle,
I'm now living in Rome. I was offered a
position to work for an Italian-based

bank and I knew it was something I could not refuse. Fortunately, everything was set up for me before I arrived. I have a wonderful apartment within walking distance of the bank, and I don't have to go far to shop for whatever I need.

Now that I'm living in Rome, I will get to see Aunt Virgie more often. I called her as soon as I arrived to let her know that I'm going to take the train from Rome to Paris to spend a weekend with her.

My mother and Aunt Mavis plan to come to Rome to celebrate Christmas, and I'm going to try to convince Virgie to come, too. I don't know what it is, but I haven't been here a week, yet I feel as if I'm home. Did you feel that way when you moved to Benin? I'm not experiencing the angst that I felt when living in the States. But then again 1968 isn't a good year for the United States and it will probably go down as one of the worst in our history.

Writing to you in French is my way of staying fluent. So far, I haven't had the opportunity to speak it a lot. It is only when I talk to Aunt Mavis that we will converse in French. Perhaps one of these days I'll find someone who speaks Spanish, then I'll be able to practice with them like I did with Giancarlo Fortenza when I wanted to improve my Italian.

I occasionally think of him whenever I wear his gift. I'm beginning to think of the pearls as a good luck charm because the last time I wore them I met someone

*who was instrumental in my getting a po-
sition here. I keep thinking that I will run
into him one of these days because his
company is based in Rome. And I also
wonder if he will remember me after ten
years. I will always remember him
because he treated me like a woman and
not a girl. And it wasn't anything sexual.
It's just that I felt so grown-up with him.
     I know you're busy with your family but
try and write me back at my new address
whenever you get the chance.
     Love you much.
     Your sister,
     Claudia*

Claudia waited for the ink to dry, then folded the page and slipped it into an envelope. It had been ten years since she last saw Noelle, yet there were times when it seemed so much longer. Perhaps it was because her friend's life revolved around her husband and children, while for Claudia it had always been herself and her career.

She smiled as she affixed postage stamps to the envelope and realized she was the second coming of the Bailey sisters—Virgie and Mavis. They'd chosen career over marriage, while her marriage had been short-lived. Now as a young widow she was able to make decisions about her life without discussing it with a partner.

Claudia often thought about Ashley and if they had married, would she have been content being Mrs. Ashley Booth. And now that they were separated by an ocean, her answer would be no. Ashley's ego would not have permitted her to outshine him. After all, he was the prince, and she would always have been his subject.

But there were so many things she did like and love about

him, yet what she'd felt for him wasn't the all-consuming love she'd had for Robert. He was her husband *and* her partner who was willing to sacrifice his life for his beliefs. Tears filled Claudia's eyes and she managed to blink them back before they fell. Claudia had cried so much in her life that she had come to believe that she had no more tears to shed.

Chapter 36

I've learned that people will forget what you said, people will forget what you did, but people will never forget how you made them feel.
  —Maya Angelou

Claudia felt as if her brain was going to explode as she tried to remember all she'd covered in orientation. The complexities of international banking were just that—complex. She'd had a different instructor for each of the subjects, which had forced her to conform to four different personalities. Her orientation was pushed back when a trainer, an expert in tax shelters, fell and shattered his leg and hip and was estimated to be out of work for several months.

She accepted the news as a temporary setback and took the extra time to go over the manuals and notes she'd taken during the other three sessions. Claudia discovered she was transfixed with tax evasion and money laundering—two crimes that had become the focus of the FBI and Internal Revenue Service when investigating organized crime. She was anxious to uncover if any of the bank's customers were investing in businesses overseas to cover up criminal activities in Italy.

Not only had Claudia settled comfortably into her new apartment, but also in her new city. She had quickly embraced *riposo* when the bank closed for ninety minutes, and she was able to go home and eat at her leisure. It had also become a time when she would prepare the ingredients for dinner. Angelo the butcher, as promised, had given her recipes for sole piccata, traditional Italian meatballs, and lemon pasta with shrimp. She'd followed the recipes to the letter and the result was lip-smacking deliciousness.

It was mid-September and she'd received a letter from Yvonne with a photograph of her wearing a tent dress. Her roomie said she was counting down the days when she would give birth and get to see her feet again. She said Stephen was more anxious than she was to find out the sex of the baby, while she didn't care whether it was a boy or girl so long as it was healthy. Yvonne said she still wanted Claudia to be her child's godmother, even in absentia. She also admitted she cried when opening the box with all the knitted and crocheted garments and promised they would become heirloom pieces that would be passed down to the next generation of Joneses.

There was no mention of Ashley in Yvonne's letter and Claudia wondered if he had moved on and had begun seeing another woman. And if he had it would not make a difference to Claudia because she wished him the best with whomever he'd chosen to become involved with. Ashley Booth was her past and she was never one to look back and wonder *what if*.

Claudia had no idea her past would revisit her when she left her apartment one Saturday morning in late September and saw Giancarlo Pasquale Fortenza talking with another man near the Spanish Steps. She'd recognized him immediately because of his height and thick, wavy blond hair. It had been ten years, but it appeared he hadn't changed. And if there were changes, they were the threads of silver in his golden hair.

Then, without warning he turned and looked at her. He appeared as stunned as she until a smile lifted the corners of his firm mouth. It was apparent that he'd recognized her, and Claudia, still unable to move, met the large, dark green eyes under sweeping light brown eyebrows as he approached her.

Giancarlo thought the woman he'd finally recognized as Claudia Patterson was an apparition—someone he'd often thought about over the years since they'd parted. Then she'd been a young girl on the threshold of womanhood, while this flesh and blood Claudia was undeniably a woman. She was tall and slender, yet there was a lushness about her body that hadn't been there at eighteen.

Smiling, he dipped his head and kissed her on both cheeks. "What are you doing in Rome?" he asked in English.

"I live here now," Claudia replied, speaking Italian. "I'm working for a local bank with ties to one in America."

Giancarlo did not want to believe that Claudia was more beautiful than he'd remembered. And he surely did not want to believe that she was now living in Rome. He'd gone to Paris on holiday and when he'd stopped by to see Claudia's aunt, Virgie hadn't mentioned that her niece was now living in Europe. After she'd warned him about keeping her niece out all night, he knew mentioning Claudia would become a source of contention between them.

"Where are you going?" he asked.

"I thought I'd do some sightseeing this morning."

"Would you like some company?"

Claudia glanced over at the man standing a short distance away. "What about your friend? Is he going to come with us?"

Giancarlo was so enthralled with seeing Claudia again that he'd forgotten he'd arranged to meet a business associate at the Spanish Steps. "No." Reaching into the breast pocket of his suit jacket, he took out a pen and a case with his business cards. Opening the case, he handed Claudia a card and the pen. "Please write down your phone number and address because I would like to see you again so we can reminiscence about our time in Paris." He hoped he wasn't being presumptuous about her agreeing to see him, because he noticed she wasn't wearing any rings, which he hoped indicated that she was still single.

Claudia jotted down the information on the back of the card. "I work five days a week, so I'm only available on weekends."

"What about this weekend? Are you free tonight for dinner?" He couldn't pull his gaze away from her light brown eyes. What he hadn't forgotten were her eyes and sexy contralto voice.

"Yes, I'm free tonight."

He smiled. "Good. I'll pick you up at eight."

"I'll be downstairs waiting for you."

He nodded. "I'll see you later tonight."

He stared at Claudia as she disappeared, then returned to talk to his friend. "Sorry about that. She was someone I haven't seen in years."

Luca Contorni laughed loudly. "With her face and body, it's a wonder you even remembered I was standing here."

Giancarlo deliberately ignored Luca's comment about Claudia's appearance.

"I must give it to you, Giancarlo."

"What about, Luca?"

"You didn't waste any time asking her to dinner."

Suddenly Giancarlo was annoyed with the man. He'd set up a meeting for them to talk business, not about his personal life. "Let's go so we can talk about the cost of the new components for the latest model of the Veneto Spider."

He had assumed control of the automobile design company three years ago when his father died suddenly from a massive heart attack, and he'd begun restructuring the company, keeping only essential personnel while offering those willing to take early retirement an increase in pension benefits and a generous severance package. Giancarlo was interested in bringing Luca onboard because of his reputation as a

financial efficiency expert with an innate knowledge to identify excess and maximize profits.

They found a small café with a table in the rear where they
could discuss business. Giancarlo had suggested meeting outside the Rome-based company office because despite Luca's
reputation, he still hadn't decided to hire him. Over coffee
and slices of melon-wrapped prosciutto Luca outlined his
proposal to make Fortenza Motors a brand as popular as
Ferrari, Fiat, and Lamborghini, which was officially established in 1963.

Fortenza Motors not only designed cars, but built the en-
gines, and some of their models were as recognizable as Germany's Porsche and Audi, and the United Kingdom's Aston
Martin.

Giancarlo had been working closely with the engineers on
developing a sports car with an engine that could be used for
car races. His focus was a single-seat, fast car that would
compete in Formula 1 races. That would be possible only if
the company's profits could offset the cost of designing the
vehicle.

"I'm going to look at your numbers and compare them to
what my accountants have, and I'll contact you again with
my decision," Giancarlo told Luca.

"That sounds good. And thanks for taking the time to
meet with me, Giancarlo."

"It was my pleasure. Giancarlo took care of the check and
walked to where he'd parked his car.

He drove back to his apartment and tossed the car keys
on the table in the entryway. The aroma of freshly brewing coffee wafted to his nostrils as he entered the kitchen.
His mother sat at a table reading a newspaper. Although his
apartment was large enough that Myriam could have her
own suite of rooms, she claimed she preferred visiting her
son and not living with him.

"Anything good in the paper?"

Myriam Fortenza glanced over her reading glasses at her

son and shook her head. "Is there ever anything good in the newspapers? It's the same with television. They like reporting bad news."

Giancarlo leaned over and kissed his mother's silver hair. "Good news doesn't sell newspapers, Mama."

Myriam had recently celebrated her sixtieth birthday yet could pass for a woman almost ten years younger except that her son was forty. His mother complained constantly that she refused to die until she saw him married and she a grandmother.

"How was your meeting?"

Giancarlo sat opposite his mother. She'd been inconsolable when her husband died, and it was only when he'd taken her on a cruise of the Greek Isles that she returned to the upbeat, vibrant woman he knew and loved unconditionally. Myriam was sixteen when she'd fallen inexorably in love with twenty-two-year-old Pasquale Fortenza, and after renouncing her religion and encountering the wrath of her family, she married him.

"It was interesting."

"Interesting how, Giancarlo?"

"I like what Luca was saying but I'm going to go over his numbers with our accountant before I make a decision."

Myriam removed her glasses and stared at Giancarlo with the green eyes he had inherited from her. "Take your time. You don't need to rush into anything until you're sure this is what you want to do."

"There's no rush. It's a long-term plan of mine. It's going to take at least three to five years to develop the engine."

"Good. Now what about your long-term plan to marry and make me a grandmother? All my friends constantly ask me when you are going to give me grandchildren."

Giancarlo frowned. "They're not friends, Mama, if they continually ask you that."

"What are they?"

"Hyenas looking to grind bones. You need new friends."

"I'm too old to make new friends, Giancarlo."

"You're never too old to get rid of people and things that upset you." He glanced over at the coffeemaker. "The coffee's finished brewing. Do you want me to pour you a cup?"

Myriam smiled. "Yes, please. And thank you. You need to buy a machine that can make espresso."

"If I buy one, will you move in here with me?"

"You can't bribe me, Giancarlo. I told you I'll come and visit but I will not move in with you. The only woman who should live with you is your wife, and not your mother."

"You're as bad as your so-called friends, Mama. You won't stop badgering about me getting married."

"I did not give up everything that made me who I am to have a child who's too selfish to share his life with a woman. I know you sleep with women, Giancarlo, even though you try to be discreet. But do you ever consider how they feel when you get up and leave them after using their bodies for your selfish pleasure, and they continue to sleep with you because they're hoping that one day you'll ask them to marry you?"

"Mama."

"What?"

"This discussion is over."

Pushing back her chair, Myriam stood up. "And my visit is over," she said as she walked out of the kitchen.

Giancarlo knew it was useless to try and convince her not to leave because she was as stubborn as a mule. He realized she was worried if he didn't father children then the family dynasty would end with him.

For him, becoming a father wasn't as important as finding a woman to become his wife.

Myriam reappeared carrying her handbag. "I'm ready to go home now."

Giancarlo went to retrieve the keys to his car and drove his mother back to her house several miles outside the city. He loved his mother and wanted her happy but realized that after losing her husband he was all she had.

After dropping her off, Giancarlo returned to his apartment and stared at the card where Claudia had written her address and telephone number. He thought about taking her to his favorite restaurant in the city, then quickly changed his mind. He would take her to a small, intimate dining establishment across the Tiber River. He found the number and made a reservation for two at eight thirty. Not only was he looking forward to reuniting with Claudia, but he was also anxious to know what had been going on in her life over the past ten years.

Chapter 37

Life is not measured by the number of breaths we take, but by the moments that take our breath away.

—Maya Angelou

Giancarlo drove up to Claudia's apartment building ten minutes before eight and found her waiting downstairs for him. He quickly exited the car and saw her smile at his approach. It was as if ten years could have been ten seconds since he'd come to her aunt's house to pick her up so they could spend time together tutoring each other in English and Italian.

Even though he spoke English, he hadn't been as fluent as Claudia, and asking her to tutor him in the language had been a ruse to get to see her again and again. Giancarlo had been more than aware of the twelve-year difference in their ages, and at no time had he thought of seducing her. At thirty, deflowering virgins hadn't been in his sexual repertoire.

He couldn't pull his eyes away from the body-hugging black, off-the-shoulder, long-sleeved dress ending at her knees, and sent up a silent prayer that he would be able to make it through dinner without blurting out how she had affected him in a way no other woman had before or since meeting her. When he'd first noticed her at Jean D'Arcy's wedding, Giancarlo knew there was something special about Claudia. So special that when he discovered she was Virgie's niece he realized luck was with him, because not only was he acquainted with Jacques Lesperance but also his mistress, Virginia Bailey. Virgie had invited him into her home on Sunday afternoons along with a small group of her friends to discuss politics, music, art, and occasionally, just occasionally, to sit and listen to jazz while eating canapés and drinking wine.

Giancarlo leaned in to kiss Claudia's cheek; the soft curls floating around her face tickled his nose as he inhaled the subtle scent of her perfume. He recognized the notes of bergamot, jasmine, and vanilla. Not only was it sensual and romantic, but the fragrance was different from the one she'd worn at eighteen.

"Thank you," he whispered in her ear.

"For what, Giancarlo?"

"For looking so incredibly stunning." Claudia lowered her eyes, unaware that Giancarlo was affected by the modest gesture. How, he mused, could she look so sexy and innocent at the same time? The young, pretty girl had matured into a beautiful woman.

"Thank you, Giancarlo," Claudia said, smiling.

Tucking her hand into the bend of his elbow over his white shirt, he led her to the car. He seated her, and then came around to sit behind the wheel.

"I remember this car," Claudia said, as Giancarlo started up the low-slung sports car.

Giancarlo gave her quick glance. "This was the prototype for a limited edition model my family's company produced the first year it was introduced to the public."

"How many cars did you make?" Claudia had to talk, to say anything so she wouldn't concentrate on the man sitting close enough for her to feel his body's heat. Everything she'd forgotten about Giancarlo Fortenza flooded her mind like frames of a film. He still wore the same cologne that would allow her to pick him out in a dark room filled with other men. And when she saw him near the Spanish Steps and he'd turned to meet her eyes, she was cognizant of how her body reacted to his intense stare.

"Thirty-five."

"Why only thirty-five?"

"My father decided not to mass-produce them, so they were made to order."

Claudia stared at the feathering of blond hair on the back of his right hand as he expertly shifted gears. "It drives nice."

"All of the cars Fortenza Motors make are top quality and are built to last years. Unlike American companies, we don't put out new models every year, and rarely do the designs change from year to year."

"Are you involved in designing and engineering?"

"Yes. I graduated university with a degree in engineering, so you can say I have a fair knowledge of how a car engine works. Do you drive?"

Claudia smiled. "Yes."

"Automatic or standard?"

"Standard. Why?"

"Just asking."

"There has to be a reason why you're just asking, Giancarlo."

"Maybe I'll let you drive back."

"That can't happen because I don't know my way around the city to drive at night. And I don't have an Italian driver's license."

"Do you have an American license?"

"Yes."

"That means you know how to drive. Don't worry, I'll act as your navigator."

"Maybe another time."

"Will there be another time, Claudia?"

"There will if you ask me out again," she said without hesitating.

"It will be like old times when we were in Paris."

"Speaking of Paris."

"What about it, Claudia?"

"Your note said you had to go back to Italy because of business. Was it serious?"

Claudia was asking Giancarlo a question he did not want to answer because he wasn't certain whether it would cause bad feelings between her and Virgie. But then if he wanted to see Claudia again after tonight, he knew he owed it to her to be truthful.

"*You* were the business, Claudia."

"What are you talking about?"

"Your aunt was angry because I'd kept you out so late and she figured I'd somehow compromised you." Silence filled the interior of the vehicle.

"She thought you had slept with me?" Claudia asked, her voice a breathless whisper.

"Yes. I told her that I'd taken you to dinner and then a jazz club, but she was furious because she didn't want me to take you to places where I'd taken other women on holiday. Then she told me it was the last time I was to see you. That's when I wrote the note telling you that I had to return home for business."

"When was the last time you saw my aunt?"

"It was three years ago. I was on holiday. I stopped in to see her because it's something I've done for years, and I didn't want her to think that a little misunderstanding would ruin our friendship. I've never brought up your name, and neither has she."

"Didn't she know that you were always a gentleman with me?"

Giancarlo wanted to tell Claudia that even though his actions were gentlemanly his thoughts weren't. And knowing she was a virgin was the only reason he hadn't attempted to seduce her. "She was trying to protect you, Claudia."

"I suppose she meant well. I missed seeing you because I felt so grown-up whenever I went out with you."

"You're grown-up now and I'm a middle-aged man."

"Even though there's still a twelve-year difference in our ages, twenty-eight and forty sounds a lot better than eighteen and thirty."

Giancarlo gave her a sidelong glance. "So, you don't think I'm too old for you?"

"Too old for what? To been seen with you?"

"Yes."

"Of course not." She paused. "I forgot to ask. Are you married?"

Giancarlo laughed, the sound low and throaty. "You wait until now to ask me if I'm married?"

"Why is that so funny?"

"Do you think if I was married, I'd ask you out?"

"I don't know, Giancarlo. Some men have wives and girlfriends on the side."

"I'm not one of those men, *bella*. Once I marry, then my wife will be the only woman in my life."

"Were you ever married?" Claudia asked.

"No."

"Why not?"

"I haven't found the woman I'd want to spend the rest of my life with. What about you, Claudia? Why haven't you married?"

"I was married."

Again, there was deafening silence in the car as Giancarlo wondered what had happened in Claudia's life that had ended her marriage. "What happened?"

"He died."

The two words were filled with so much pain that Giancarlo wanted to pull off the road and take Claudia into his
arms.

"I'm so sorry, Claudia. How long have you been a widow?"

"Four years."

Giancarlo was surprised by this revelation. He thought
maybe she'd decided to leave the States and move to Europe
to distance herself from the memories that she'd shared with
her husband. "You married very young."

"I married my college sweetheart at twenty-two. We were
a couple of months shy of celebrating our second anniversary
when he died in an automobile accident. I mourned him for a
long time, but then I started dating again."

"What happened?"

Giancarlo was anxious to know about the men in Claudia's life because he didn't want complications now that
they'd agreed to see each other again. And he knew this time
it would be different because her aunt wouldn't be able interfere in what he hoped would become an ongoing, mature relationship with her niece.

"It ended once I decided to move here. I was offered an
opportunity I never would've been able to get in the States,
and he wasn't leaving with me, so we parted as friends. But I
did offer him an out."

"What was that?" Giancarlo questioned. He didn't want
to start something with Claudia only to have an ex reconcile
with her.

"I told him he had a year to contact me, to see if we could
make a go of it."

"You're very generous, Claudia."

"Why would you say that?"

"Because a lot of things can happen in a year. He could
meet someone else and as they say, out of sight, out of
mind."

"It's the same with me, Giancarlo. I've been here almost

two months and I don't think I've thought of him more than a couple of times. However, he made it easy for both of us because he rejected my offer."

"Were you in love with him?"

"No. I loved him, but I wasn't in love with him."

"Is there a difference?"

"Yes, there is. You can love someone's voice, or how they treat you, but that doesn't necessarily translate into being in love with someone. Ashley has a lot of good qualities, but then I wasn't aware of the negative ones until I'd made the decision to move here. And I knew if I'd married him, then I wouldn't be able to be myself."

"Had he proposed marriage?"

"No."

"Why not, Claudia?"

"He didn't want to marry, and I wasn't looking for another husband, so that's something on which we did agree."

"Do you want to marry again?"

"I don't know, Giancarlo, because that's something I've asked myself many times over. And to be honest, I'm not looking for a husband because I want to concentrate on my career."

"You don't believe you can balance the two?"

"It all depends on my husband. I'd be his wife, but I'd also expect him to support my decision if I wanted to work outside the home."

"What about children? What if you become pregnant?"

"I'd take a few years off to bond with my child, then when they're ready to attend school, I would like to go back to work part-time."

"You sound like a woman with a plan."

"Don't be facetious, Giancarlo. You're a businessman with a successful company and you know you have projections where you want to see your company five or even ten years from now. It's the same with my life."

"You're right. It's just that I haven't a met woman who's as focused on her career as you."

"That's because you've been seeing the wrong women. Colleges and universities are filled with women who think like me."

Giancarlo knew Claudia was right about him dating some women whose sole objective was getting married and having children. And listening to her talk about a career reminded him she was like her aunts, who lived their lives by their leave. They were educated, professional, independent women who determined their own destinies, not depending on a man to enrich their lives.

"We'll be there in a few minutes," he said, as he slowed along a narrow cobblestone street where the restaurant was built into a stone wall. He found a parking spot, shut off the engine, and reached for his jacket and slipped his arms into the sleeves.

Giancarlo came around to the passenger side and opened the door, his eyes lingering on the length of Claudia's long legs in sheer black stockings and matching patent leather heels. He found her stunning, whether wearing a simple dress and flats, or haute couture. And she'd cut her hair so a wealth of curls framed her face like the mane of a lion. He smiled. *Il leone d'oro* had found his mate.

Claudia was totally charmed with the carriage house turned restaurant. As soon as Giancarlo opened the door the mouthwatering aromas of grilling meat and fish greeted her, reminding her that she hadn't eaten anything since earlier that afternoon. The interior was illuminated by candles and wall sconces.

She moved closer to Giancarlo when he reached for her hand, threading their fingers together, marveling that she felt so comfortable with him. It was as if they'd picked up where they'd left off ten years ago.

A waiter came out of the kitchen carrying a bowl of pasta, and another with a tray of grilled fish. "*Ciao*, Vittorio," Giancarlo said to the one with the pasta.

"*Ciao*, Giancarlo. Please find your table and I'll be right with you," the waiter replied in rapid Italian.

Giancarlo gave her fingers a gentle squeeze. "Are you hungry?" he asked as they wended their way around tables to one with seating for two near a grotto.

"I wasn't, until I smelled the food."

Claudia sat when Giancarlo pulled out a chair for her, then he took the one opposite her. The flames from the flickering candle flattered the lean contours of his face. There was something about the more mature Giancarlo that was more sensual than when she first saw him in the courtyard at the French château, which now seemed like eons ago. Then she'd thought he was the perfect model for Michelangelo's *David*, but now there were a few attractive lines around his large expressive eyes that she found mesmerizing. There was something about him, whenever he looked at her, that stirred feelings that were totally foreign to her. It was if he could read her mind even if she vehemently denied she'd always had feelings for him.

She glanced at the plastic-covered menu. There were listings with which she was totally unfamiliar. "What is *guanciale*?"

"That's pig's cheek. It's like bacon or pancetta but it has a more delicate flavor. You do eat pork, don't you?"

"Yes. Everything except chitlins."

"What are chitlins, Claudia?"

"Pig intestines. I used to eat them as a child, because whatever was placed on my plate I had to eat. But since becoming an adult I won't touch them."

"We call them *budellini a treccia* in Italian. We also eat tripe, or *trippa*, which is the stomach lining of a cow."

Claudia shuddered visibly. "No, thank you. I'll stick with pieces of meat I can easily identify."

"I thought you were the adventurous type."

"I am, except when it comes to food, then I'm a little insular."

Giancarlo rested an elbow on the table. "Well, it looks as if I'm going to have to introduce you to more than spaghetti and meatballs."

She registered his teasing tone. "That's not all I eat."

"We'll see, once you come to my place where I'll cook for you."

With wide eyes, she stared at him. "You cook?"

He chuckled softly. "Yes, Claudia, I cook. Why does that surprise you?"

"I don't know. I just thought maybe you'd have a live-in staff that would cook and clean for you."

"You're only half right. I do have someone who comes in to clean, but I prefer cooking for myself."

"Who taught you?"

"My mother. She taught my father, and when I was old enough to look over the stove, that's when my lessons began."

Claudia smiled. "Are you any good?"

"Come to my house tomorrow and find out."

Claudia knew she had walked into a situation of her own making. "Okay, but only if you let me return the favor and I'll treat you to a traditional Southern Sunday dinner."

Reaching across the table, Giancarlo picked up her hand. Rising slightly and leaning over the table, he pressed a kiss on her inner wrist. "You've got yourself a deal," he said in English.

Claudia felt a shock of nerves racing up her arm and pretended interest in the menu rather than meet Giancarlo's intense stare. His holding her hand, kissing her wrist, was what she thought of as foreplay to seduction. He was subtly seducing her, and she was helpless to resist. She didn't know what it was about the sophisticated, worldly man who had come into her life not once but twice, that made her aware of why she'd been born female. It hadn't been that way with Robert or Ashley.

She ordered grilled sole and linguine with *aglio olio*. She preferred garlic and oil on her pasta to tomato-based sauces, while Giancarlo ordered his *guanciale* with *cacio e pepe*, spaghetti with grated Pecorino Romano cheese and black pepper. Both had declined to drink wine and shared bottles of fizzy water.

Over a leisurely dinner Claudia gave Giancarlo an abbreviated version of her work history, watching his expression change, becoming a mask of stone, when she revealed how she'd had to wait five months to secure the position as a loan officer, but then turned the tables on the bank officers when she resigned before the purported transfer.

"Do you think it was their intent all along not to give you the position?" he asked.

"I'll never know because I got something so much better."

A slow smile crinkled the skin around Giancarlo's eyes when he smiled. "Their loss, our gain." Raising his glass of sparkling water, he touched it to hers. "*Saluto.*"

"*Saluto,*" she echoed, smiling at him over the rim of the glass as she took a swallow.

Dinner was delicious, her dining partner charming, and Claudia felt more relaxed than she had in a very long time.

Giancarlo wasn't ready for the evening to end after spending more than two delightful hours with Claudia. And despite her smiling, he'd glimpsed sadness in her eyes. It was obvious she still missed her husband, and although she'd had a lover since becoming a widow, he suspected no man could ever replace the one she'd loved enough to marry. He wouldn't even begin to try.

Giancarlo concentrated on the road as he drove back to Claudia's apartment. However, when he thought of his own life since his father's passing, work had become all-encompassing;

he arrived at the office at dawn and didn't leave until hours after the scheduled quitting time. It was as if he'd become obsessed with designing and engineering components for the Veneto Spider. Claudia said she was available only on weekends, and he knew if he wanted to spend time with her, then he had to give up going into the office on Saturdays.

He took a quick glance at Claudia's profile. "Do you have any idea what you'd like to eat tomorrow?"

"Nope. Surprise me."

"You're not making it easy for me, Claudia."

"That's because I'm not easy, Giancarlo."

"Thanks for the warning, *signora*."

"You're welcome, *signore*."

Giancarlo found an empty space across the street from Claudia's apartment building and placed a hand on her forearm when she attempted to get out of the car. "Don't move. I'll walk you up."

"That's not necessary, Giancarlo. My building is safe."

He increased his grip on her arm. "As long as there are crazy people, no one and no building is safe. Now please, I'll help you out and walk you to your apartment. And I will leave as soon as you're inside—safe."

Giancarlo felt the stiffness of Claudia's body as he assisted her out of the car and walked her across the street. A full moon and streetlamp illuminated the salmon-colored two-story building with curved terra-cotta roof tiles and a façade covered with tendrils of ivy. Holding her hand, they walked side by side up the winding staircase to the second floor, he releasing her hand when she reached into her handbag to take out a set of keys and unlocked the door.

"Would you like to go inside and check to see whether anyone has broken in?"

"Yes. Please wait here." Giancarlo brushed past her and walked inside.

He discovered Claudia's apartment was neat and inviting. He checked the bedrooms, the half bath in the master bedroom and the full bathroom across the hall from the smaller one. Giancarlo smiled when he studied photographs of her family, then remembered she was waiting for him.

"It's all clear," he said, meeting her eyes.

A slow smile spread across her features, bringing his gaze to linger on her parted lips. Lips he'd kissed once and wanted to kiss again.

"Thank you for a wonderful evening," she said.

He nodded. "The pleasure has been all mine."

"What time is dinner tomorrow?"

"I'll come here at three to pick you up. And please don't wait downstairs for me. That's not a good look." Giancarlo took a step and cradled her face. "Good night, Claudia." He pressed a kiss to her forehead, then turned on his heel, walked out of the apartment, and closed the self-locking door behind him. He got into the car and started the engine and instead of going home, he headed in the opposite direction.

Giancarlo drove around aimlessly as he tried to sort out his feelings for Claudia. It had taken years, and nothing had changed. He still liked her. Too much. And things were different this time because she didn't have a scheduled date to return to the States. She was staying. This time for good.

Chapter 38

It's your place in the world; it's your life. Go on and do all you can with it, and make it the life you want to live.

—Mae Jemison

The bell to her apartment rang at exactly three, and Claudia walked across the living room to press the button on the intercom. "Yes?" she asked, even though she knew who had rung the bell.

"Giancarlo."

Claudia tapped the button, releasing the lock on the door leading into the vestibule. She opened the apartment door, smiling when Giancarlo stepped off the landing. The green shirt he'd paired with black slacks was an exact match for his eyes. "*Buon pomeriggio.*"

"Good afternoon to you, too," Giancarlo replied in English.

Claudia gave him a questioning look. Since reuniting with him their conversations were conducted entirely in Italian, and it sounded strange to hear him speak English. "Do you still want me to tutor you in English?" she asked.

"Yes. I want to learn all the slang."

She laughed. "That's impossible because I don't know all the slang."

"Your downstairs neighbors asked me if I was *corteggio di te*."

"What did you say when they asked if you were courting me?"

Giancarlo's lowered his eyes, smiling. "I told them of course I was."

"And what was their reaction?"

"They seemed quite pleased, especially Signora Sapienza."

When she'd first moved in, the elderly woman had welcomed Claudia with a jar of her homemade marinara sauce and said if she wanted to learn to make it, then she would teach her. Claudia had repaid Signora Sapienza with a pasta machine after she'd heard the woman complaining to her husband that the one she'd used for years had outlived its usefulness, and knew in that instant they'd become fast friends. "Because we've become sympatico."

"You're sympatico because you have a good heart, Claudia."

She scrunched up her nose. "Being sympatico doesn't make me easy, Giancarlo," Claudia teased.

"That's something I'm certain you won't let me forget. Are you ready to leave now?"

"Yes, but I have to get something first."

Claudia returned to her bedroom to get a jacket, her handbag, and a canvas bag with Giancarlo's house gift. She returned to find him looking at the framed photographs on a table with several potted plants.

"You were really a cute kid with a head full of curls."

She rolled her eyes. "I looked like Little Orphan Annie without the red hair."

Giancarlo turned to stare at her. "I happen to like your curly hair."

"It's convenient when I don't want to set it on rollers and sit for an hour under a dryer."

Giancarlo slowly shook his head. "I don't understand women. They complain if they have straight hair because they want curls. Then the ones with curls want straight hair."

She handed Giancarlo the bag. "There's a little something in there for you."

"What is it?"

"You'll see after you unwrap them."

"You didn't have to get me anything, Claudia."

"I know, but I wanted to," she said, as she scooped her keys off the table.

"I'll take whatever is in here this time, but I really don't need for you to buy me anything."

"Don't you know how to be gracious and accept a gift?"

"Yes, but I don't want you to spend your money on me."

Claudia's jaw tightened as she clenched her teeth. "I don't need you to monitor my bank balance, Giancarlo, because I'm definitely not interested in yours."

Giancarlo had learned the art of negotiating when it came to business, but what he was hoping to have with Claudia had nothing to do with business. He knew it was time to retreat, because he did not want to get into a debate with Claudia about accepting things from her.

He bowed as if she were royalty. "Thank you so much for your gift."

"Liar," Claudia retorted, smiling.

"Let's go, *bella*, because this morning I've only had coffee and yogurt and berries."

"Is that what you normally eat for breakfast?" she asked as she locked up the apartment.

"No. I usually have a continental breakfast of coffee, sweet breads, and fruit."

"We Americans love our bacon or ham and eggs, grits,

French or home fries, toast or biscuits and occasionally English muffins, with juice, coffee, or tea."

Giancarlo noticed Claudia had referred to herself as an American. And she was until she made the decision to become an Italian citizen. "If I ate that much in the morning, I'd have to go back to bed to sleep it off."

"I only indulge like that when I'm not working."

"What do you normally eat for breakfast?" he asked.

"I'll have coffee and toast, a bagel, or sometimes a Danish."

"Danish?"

"It's a flaky, buttery pastry usually filled with prunes or cheese."

"I don't believe I've had a Danish. Mascarpone coffee éclairs are my favorite sweet breads."

"Do you make those also?"

Giancarlo held the passenger-side door open for Claudia. "No. Whenever I go to Paris, there's this patisserie that makes them, and I try to get there as soon as they open because they always sell out in a couple of hours."

"Do you ever go anywhere else other than Paris on holiday?" she asked.

"I will occasionally sail down to the Greek islands and every couple of years I'll go to Monaco or Costa del Sol."

"You're quite the European traveler."

"I still haven't spent time in Vienna."

"Why not, Giancarlo?"

"It is on my to-do list."

"Where do you plan to spend your next holiday?" she questioned.

Giancarlo wanted to tell Claudia it would all depend on if they were still seeing each other, and if they were, then the choice would be hers. "I don't know. What about you, Claudia? Are you going back to the States on holiday?"

"No. I have no wish or plan to return there for a while."

Giancarlo knew her decision not to go back to America wasn't based on her breakup with her boyfriend, so it had to be something else that made her sound so bitter about the country of her birth.

"Do you want to talk about it?"

Claudia gave him a quick glance before she looked out the windshield. "I may as well tell you everything."

Giancarlo held the steering wheel in a death grip as he listened intently to Claudia reveal what she'd lived through in the United States. He was no stranger to hate and bigotry because even though he hadn't experienced it directly, it still had destroyed the lives of family members whose blood he carried. "I understand what you had to go through," he said when her voice faded.

"Do you, Giancarlo? How can you understand what I've gone through when you've had a charmed life from the first time you drew breath."

"Don't be so quick to judge, Claudia."

"Are you saying the Golden Lion has been denied eating in certain restaurants, or attending social events?"

"Don't call me that."

Why not, Giancarlo? Isn't that what people call you?"

"People say a lot of shit!" he spat out in English.

"You should curse more often in English because that was flawless."

He glared at her grinning at him. "Like motherfucker?" Much to his chagrin, Claudia doubled over laughing. Her laugh was so infectious. He was still chuckling under his breath when he drove into the driveway leading to his home. He shut off the engine and rested his arm over the back of Claudia's seat. "Are you ready to enter the lion's den?"

"Should I be concerned about being eaten?"

Giancarlo went completely still, wondering if she was joking or if she was referring to something sexual. Because tasting her, his tongue tracing every inch of her body, was something he'd craved since reconnecting with her. He wanted to make love to Claudia in a way that would make her forget every man she'd ever slept with. And then it suddenly hit him that he wanted to be the last man in her life, and she the last woman in his.

"No, *amore mia*, there's no need for you to be concerned."

"Is that what I am?" she whispered. "Your love?"

Giancarlo nodded. "Only if you choose to be. I'm forty, Claudia, and much too old to play games. You must know I had deep feelings for you when we first met in Paris, but I couldn't act on them because of your age and because you were going back to the States to attend university. If circumstances had been different, I would've let you know that I was falling in love with you. And when your aunt told me I couldn't see you again, that's when I realized I loved you. Yes, Claudia, I love you. I've always loved you."

Claudia felt like weeping because Giancarlo was telling her what she'd wanted Ashley to say. That he loved her. She liked Giancarlo but she wasn't in love with him. But then she asked herself, could she? Could she come to love this man as much as he loved her?

"I need time," she whispered.

Giancarlo combed his fingers through her curls. "Take all the time you need. I've waited ten years, so what's a few more years."

"It's not going to take that long for me to make up my mind." Shifting on her seat, Claudia turned to meet his eyes. Resting her right hand on his jaw, she leaned close and brushed a kiss over his mouth. "Thank you."

"For what?"

"For loving me."

"That's because you're so easy to love, Claudia. With you there's no pretense, and that's what I've been looking for in other women. For them to be themselves."

Claudia placed a finger over his mouth. "There will be no

more talk of other women, Giancarlo Fortenza. Starting now it's just you and I."

He smiled. "*Sì, signora.*"

She waited for him to come around and assist her out of the car, as she attempted to process that one of Italy's most eligible bachelors had fallen in love with her as she walked with Giancarlo into his home. However, she realized it was something that had been ten years in the making, and if she had been more worldly at eighteen, she would've recognized what she'd shared with Giancarlo was more than mere friendship.

She'd gotten up every morning knowing she would see him, and it had been the first time that she'd felt like a sophisticate instead of a shy young woman who'd spent the last six years of her life completely isolated from boys her age. She'd entered puberty without knowing how to flirt or accept compliments. It had taken a man twelve years her senior to awaken her dormant femininity—and if he'd wanted, he could've seduced her.

Claudia now realized Virgie had short-circuited her association with Giancarlo at the right time, because the next time he kissed her she would've wanted more. And the *more* was her sleeping with him.

"You're very quiet," Giancarlo said, breaking into her thoughts.

Claudia smiled. "I was just thinking about Aunt Virgie."

"What about her?"

"I was just thanking her for sending you away because I know I wasn't ready for you at that time."

Light brown eyebrows lifted, questioning. "And now?"

"I'm more than ready," Claudia said without a hint of guile.

Giancarlo dipped his head and covered her mouth with his in a kiss that stole the breath from her lungs. "We're going to have fun, Claudia, rediscovering each other." He kissed her again. *"La mia casa è la tua."*

"You may regret telling me your house is my house when I move in here and run your household like a military drill sergeant."

Tiny lines fanned out around his luminous eyes when he smiled. "I can't wait."

Chapter 39

Take a chance! All life is a chance. The person
who goes the farthest is generally the one who is
willing to do and dare.
—Dale Carnegie

Claudia discovered Giancarlo's apartment was a duplex,
that he'd purchased the property after his father's passing because he'd hoped his mother would sell her house and
move into the adjoining apartment.

"I take it your mother is very independent," Claudia said
as she ran a hand over the back of an antique leather dining
room chair.

"Independent and very stubborn," Giancarlo confirmed.
"My mother prefers living in the country to the city because
she claims she sleeps better when it's quiet."

Claudia followed Giancarlo into a renovated kitchen with
vaulted ceilings. She found *tutto in ordine*, everything in
order, in the uncluttered space that was conducive to preparing meals for two or a dozen. A collection of gleaming copper pots lined one wall and herbs in hand-painted pots were
positioned on a ledge to take advantage of sunlight coming
through the casement windows.

"This kitchen is magnificent, Giancarlo."

He set the canvas bag on a stool near a prep table. "It's my favorite room in the apartment."

"How long have you lived here?"

"It will be two years this December. I have a little place in the country, but unlike my mother there are times when I find it too quiet."

"There's something I don't understand, Giancarlo."

"What's that?"

"I assume you're quite wealthy, yet you don't have a driver and you live in what would be considered a middle-class neighborhood in the States." Giancarlo looked directly at her—no, he glared at her—and Claudia wondered if what she'd said had struck a nerve with him.

"My wealth has nothing to do with how I prefer to conduct my life."

She heard the sarcasm in his voice and regretted bringing up the subject. "I'm sorry for being nosy."

Giancarlo didn't want to believe he'd snapped at Claudia for asking him a question he had asked himself over and over since he'd purchased the property. He'd spent more than half his life attempting to distinguish himself from the image that was Signor Pasquale Fortenza.

"No," he said in a quiet voice. "I should be the one apologizing." Giancarlo held out his arms and he wasn't disappointed when Claudia moved into his embrace. He rested his chin on the top of her head. "I live the way I do because I never wanted people to relate to me the way they had with my father."

Easing back, Claudia looked up at him. "How did they relate to him?"

"Whenever he walked into a room everyone stood up as if he were royalty, or a judge in a courtroom, or even a Mafia godfather. I'd watch his face and know that he loved the adoration. He owned a magnificent villa in the country, had drivers and servants at his beck and call, and he ran Fortenza Motors like a despot. The workers would cower in fear whenever he visited the factory, and after a while I told him to stay away because he was disrupting production."

"You and your father didn't get along?"

"We got along because he owned and managed the company. However, there were issues on which we didn't agree. I only challenged him when there was something I truly believed in. One time he threatened to disinherit me after I accused him of going to hell because he was intent on breaking four of the seven deadly sins. The exceptions were sloth, gluttony, and lust. Pasquale adored his wife and didn't cheat on her, and he would never be accused of being lazy, while he monitored every morsel of food he put into his mouth because he didn't want to gain weight."

"What did he take offense to?"

"My calling him vain, greedy, and an attention-seeker. He was rarely seen wearing the same suit more than once in a month, and he was obsessed with making more money than he could spend in a lifetime, even if he pissed it away buying yachts, private islands, and priceless jewelry. He'd stay up nights worrying about how he could design a car that was faster than a Ferrari, and I'd tell him it wasn't about competing with Ferrari but establishing Fortenza Motors as a company that could produce vehicles comparable to Rolls-Royce Motor Cars and Bugatti, but with a vastly lower selling price. I told him to disinherit me if that's what he wanted. That's when I began spending holidays in Paris, where I met your aunt."

"How long did it take for you and your father to reconcile?"

Giancarlo smiled. Claudia was asking him a litany of questions that he felt comfortable answering. "It took a couple of months. Once I returned to Rome, he decided we needed to talk. I was forthcoming when I told him about his dictatorial way of running the company and that I wanted to be the point person when dealing with our employees. He agreed and that continued until he passed away three years ago.

"I transformed the company and offered some in top management additional compensation if they took early retirement. Many did, and the result was a streamlined payroll. Most of those in management were individuals who were my father's friends, so it was nepotism that made them loyal to him."

"So, the engineer is also an astute businessman," Claudia said, smiling.

"I learned from the best, Claudia. I may not use the same tactics as Pasquale Fortenza, but he had an innate sixth-sense when it came to making money." Giancarlo dipped his head and pressed a kiss to the bridge of Claudia's nose. "I did promise to cook for you, so as soon as I wash up, I'll start."

"What are you making?"

"Grilled chicken and pasta with sausage, fennel, and garlic."

"That sounds delicious. Is there anything you want me to do?"

"No. I prepped everything this morning, so it won't take long before we sit down to eat."

"Do you mind if I take a tour of your house?"

"Of course, I don't mind. I told you before that my house is your house."

Going on tiptoes, Claudia kissed him. "*Grazie.*"

Sitting at the table in the dining room and eating succulently broiled chicken and al dente spaghetti with ground sausage, fennel, and minced garlic, Claudia realized Giancarlo was an enigma. He claimed he loved jazz, but she discovered he also liked R and B and soul when he stacked records of Aretha Franklin, the Four Tops, the Temptations, and the Rolling Stones on a turntable. Despite owning and operating a successful car company, he'd avoided the lifestyle of his flamboyant father. His home was modest and furnished in a style for family living rather than a bachelor. Claudia thought of Giancarlo Fortenza as an onion, where she would have to peel off each layer to discover who the man really was.

There was one thing she did know, and that was that he loved her and had been in love with her for years. The pearl earrings and necklace were the only tangible reminder of the man who had made her trip abroad unforgettable. And when she'd attempted to recall the times they'd spent together, Claudia could not remember what she'd said or done to make him fall in love with her.

"You are just full of surprises," she said, after swallowing a mouthful of pasta.

"Why would you say that?"

"Your choice in music. I know you like jazz, but I didn't know you liked soul music."

Giancarlo picked up a water glass. "I like American music. I feel it here." He patted his chest with his free hand.

"I must admit I'm partial to it, too. There's a shop on 125th Street in Harlem, New York, that has an outdoor speaker and they always play the most popular records heard on the radio."

"I'm certain it worked to get people to come in and buy the records."

Claudia nodded. "I must admit I did buy a few."

"Did you bring them with you?"

"No. I only shipped my clothes and personal effects. I wanted to bring my typewriter but decided to leave it behind. My mother said she would bring it when she and Aunt Mavis come for Christmas."

"Your mother is coming to Rome for Christmas?"

"Yes," she said, smiling. "Why does that surprise you?"

Giancarlo set down his glass. "I don't know."

And he didn't know why the knowledge that Claudia's mother was planning to come to Italy disturbed him. If she'd said her aunt Mavis, he knew he would've felt a lot more comfortable seeing her again. Giancarlo had planned to introduce Claudia to his mother once their relationship changed, because he'd promised Claudia he wouldn't put any pressure on her about the possibility of sharing their future.

"They're only going to be here a week. They're planning to fly in Christmas Eve and leave on the last day of December. Have you made plans for Christmas?"

"Not yet. I close the company on Christmas Eve for the week, to give the employees time to spend with their families."

"What did you do last year?"

"I went to Venice."

"I've always wanted to visit Venice. Especially when I saw pictures of the festival during Carnevale."

"If you really want to go, then I'll take you next year. I want to warn you that it can last as long ten days."

"That's a lot of partying."

"It is," Giancarlo confirmed. "Do you want to get dressed up or attend as a tourist?"

"I live here, so don't you dare call me a tourist."

He held up both hands. "Point taken, *bella*."

"You like calling me that, don't you?"

"Does it bother you that I call you beautiful?"

Claudia shrugged her shoulders under a white man-tailored blouse. "I don't know."

"Is it because it was what your husband called you?"

"No! He called me by my name." A flush suffused her face. "Why are you bringing up men from my past?"

"I don't want to compete with a dead man who will always hold a special place in your heart. I don't want you to forget him, but what I want is to make new memories—for both of us."

"I told you I need time, Giancarlo."

"And I'm willing to give you all the time you need."

Claudia lowered her eyes. "What if I can't love you?"

"Can't or won't?" he questioned.

Claudia ran her fingers through her hair, holding curls off her forehead. "I'm so confused, Giancarlo. You must know that I have feelings for you, but I keep thinking there are things that would come between any happiness we could possibly have together."

Giancarlo decided to press his attack. He had to know now whether to walk away from the only woman he'd ever loved or stay and fight for her. "What are they?"

"Race, religion, and culture."

"That's bullshit and you know it."

Her jaw dropped. "What did you say?"

"You heard me. It's bullshit, Claudia. Do you think any of that matters to me?"

"I don't know because I'm not inside your head."

"It's a good thing you're not because then you would know what I'd like to do with you." Giancarlo sobered when he saw Claudia's stunned expression. "But that's not going to happen unless you want it, too. Yes, I'm going to be the same gentleman I was in Paris and not touch you. I'll pretend you're that eighteen-year-old virgin who Virgie told me I could see but was forbidden to touch, and you have no idea how hard it was for me to keep my hands off you."

"But you did touch me, Giancarlo, the night you took me to dinner and then to the jazz club. You kissed me and I kissed you back. And if you hadn't taken me home, I would've asked you to make love to me. Now, close your mouth because you were not the only one who had naughty thoughts that night."

Giancarlo was momentarily speechless in his surprise. "And if I'd taken your virginity, it wouldn't have ended there because I would've married you."

A secret smile flitted over Claudia's lips. "How honorable. Did you believe I would've traded my virginity for a wedding ring, Giancarlo? I slept with my boyfriend before we were married. Unlike some women you may have known, I don't use my body when brokering a deal. And if we do sleep together, it wouldn't necessarily translate into matrimony."

"What would?"

"Love. I would only marry you if I loved you."

"If that's the case, then why did you mention religion, race, and culture?"

"Because I need to know if they matter to you."

"They don't." He touched a napkin to the corners of his mouth. "Now I want to see what you brought me."

"It's not much."

Giancarlo pushed back his chair and stood. "Let me be the judge of that."

Claudia had admitted to Giancarlo that she had feelings for him, but refused to let him know how deep they were. She didn't know why, but he was the only man, other than her father, with whom she'd felt protected. With Robert and Ashley, it was as if she'd met them as equals, but it wasn't the same with Giancarlo. Claudia knew she was creating problems when there were no problems that would prevent her from sharing her life with Giancarlo.

She smiled when Giancarlo returned to the dining room with a tray and the demitasse cups and saucers she'd given him as house gift. When she'd seen the small white porcelain set for six, with a gold trim, she couldn't resist purchasing them.

"How did you know I didn't have any?"

"I didn't." He set the tray on the table and then pulled back Claudia's chair and picked her up. "Thank you."

Claudia's arms circled his neck; she rubbed her nose against his. "You're welcome," she whispered, as she buried her face between his neck and shoulder.

Everything about the man holding her to his heart seeped into her: the strength of his arms holding her effortlessly, and the hauntingly sensual cologne that she never tired of inhaling. She didn't know what it was, but Giancarlo had made it so easy for her to love him. He lowered her to her feet but not before she felt his hardness pressing against her thighs.

Nothing had changed. It could've been ten years ago when Giancarlo kissed her for the first time, and she thought she'd

imagined the bulge in his groin. Then he'd ended the kiss before she knew for certain that he'd had an erection. But now
she knew she'd turned him on, and in return he'd aroused
her, and Claudia knew she had to put even more distance between them.

"I'll help you clean up the kitchen." She wasn't certain
whether Giancarlo had noticed the tremor in her voice that
she hadn't recognized as her own.

"That's okay. There's not much to clean. I'll take you
home now because I know you want to call the States."

Claudia nodded. Since leaving Mississippi and now the
States, she'd made it a practice to call her mother anytime on
Sundays after twelve noon. "Next Sunday is on me."

"I'm looking forward to what you call a traditional Southern Sunday dinner."

"I know you're not used to eating dinner so early, so why
don't you come over at eleven for brunch and I'll make something that will sustain us until we eat later that night." Claudia still hadn't adjusted to eating dinner at eight or even as
late as ten at night.

"Okay."

Giancarlo drove her back home, walked her upstairs, and
as she put the key in the lock, she heard her telephone ringing. "I have to answer that." It was a rare occasion that she
got a call.

Giancarlo kissed her cheek. "Go answer the phone."

Claudia closed the door and hurried to pick up the receiver. "*Ciao.*"

"Claudia?"

"Yes, Stephen. I've gotten into the habit of answering the
phone in Italian."

"Is this a bad time?"

"Of course not."

"I'm calling to let you know that Yvonne had the baby. It's
a boy."

Claudia clapped a hand over her mouth to keep from screaming. "Congratulations, Daddy."

"Thank you. He's a big, healthy boy weighing in at almost nine pounds."

"How's Yvonne?"

"Exhausted. She was in labor for fifteen hours before Robert Claude Jones decided to make his appearance."

Claudia gripped the receiver as she folded her body down to the sofa next to the table. "You named him . . ." Her words trailed off when she registered the significance of the names.

"Yes, Claudia. Yvonne wanted to name our son for her cousin and best friend."

"Please thank her for me." Whenever she'd asked her friend if she had selected names for her son or daughter, she'd said no. "Yvonne has my address, so tell her to send me pictures of the baby whenever she can."

"Will do. I want to tell you before I hang up that I ran into Ashley the other day. He has a new girlfriend. He didn't ask about you, so I didn't mention your name."

"I'm glad you didn't."

Claudia reached over to turn on the table lamp once Stephen ended the call. Her former roommate was now a mother. So much had changed since that memorable day when she'd walked into her dorm room at Hampton Institute to introduce herself to Yvonne Chapman.

So many things had changed. She had changed—and Claudia believed for the best. She'd encountered challenges and had emerged stronger than before. She picked up the receiver again, this time to call her mother.

Chapter 40

Every great dream begins with a dreamer. Always
remember, you have within you the strength, the
patience, and the passion to reach for the stars to
change the world.
—Harriet Tubman

As she walked to work, Claudia thought about the phone
call she'd had with her mother the night before. Sarah
revealed she and Mavis had driven up to Bogalusa to console
a friend whose son had been killed in Vietnam. Her mother
mentioning the war had conjured up images of the many
protests sweeping the States, images that were rarely seen on
Italian television.

Then Sarah asked her if things were going well for her because she could discern something cheerful in Claudia's voice
that was different from the last time they'd spoken. She didn't
want to tell her mother that she'd been reunited with someone from her past and that she really liked him.

After she hung up with Sarah, her phone rang again and
this time it was William McNeil. He told her he wanted her
to go over the accounts of the international clients who'd in-
vested in his bank and send him a report before the end of
October. Claudia wanted to remind him that she hadn't com-

pleted the mandated orientation, but agreed. After he ended the call, she wondered if he'd wanted her to investigate some illegalities that could possibly damage his bank's reputation.

Claudia arrived at the bank, went to her cubicle, and placed her handbag in the desk drawer. She'd gotten used to working at a desk without a door. The cubicle was small, with enough room for a desk and chair, but there was an upside because it had a window where she could look out onto a side street. Picking up the phone, she dialed an extension and told the person on the other end of the line what she needed. Twenty minutes later a young man pushing a cart set the files she'd requested on the chair.

"*Grazie,* Paolo." The shy clerk nodded and quickly left without meeting her eyes.

She picked up the top file and opened it. There was a star next to the name of the company, which indicated whoever owned the account was an elite client. There had been a transfer as recently as the week before. Claudia reached for a legal pad and pencil and began the task of writing down the dates and the amounts of the various transfers.

William had confirmed his department was not quite a year old, and the client had begun transferring funds to the States almost immediately, and Claudia wondered if the man was using the bank to launder money. Unfortunately, she wasn't privy to the internal financial status of the clients, which hampered her efforts to rule out money laundering. Once she went through all the files, she planned to contact William to ask for authorization to examine the other bank accounts and if possible, company financial records. And she wasn't certain whether her request would be approved because she wasn't an employee of the bank, but a liaison between two banking institutions.

Claudia was more than ready for the weekend. She'd spent the past five days looking at numbers that after a while she'd begun dreaming about. She got up early Saturday morning to shop for the items she needed to prepare for Sunday. It took her more than an hour to find a store that stocked grits. When a shopkeeper told her she could substitute polenta for grits because both were made from corn, Claudia thanked him and walked out.

Fortunately, she did find a shop that had an inventory of packaged grains, including grits. She bought grits and cornmeal, and then set off to find a fish market for shrimp. Her last stop was at Angelo's butcher shop, where she bought a chicken and dried sausage that was as close to andouille as she could get. There were variations of the traditional Southern recipe for shrimp and grits made with bacon or andouille, cheese, green onions, minced garlic, and Worcestershire sauce.

She'd discovered an Italian recipe for greens. It called for her to sauté escarole, spinach, and collards together in olive oil, with grated yellow onion, minced garlic, crushed red pepper in chicken broth and topped with freshly grated Parmesan cheese. It varied slightly from Southern collard greens, but Claudia decided to try it. The greens and potato salad would serve as side dishes for fried chicken and cornbread. She'd planned for dinner to be followed with coffee and her grandmother's recipe for pound cake.

Claudia returned home with her purchases and as she climbed the staircase to her apartment, she hadn't realized how much energy she'd spent shopping. She stored the perishables in the refrigerator and after opening a bottle of rosé, she filled a glass, and then sat on the sofa to sip it. She had slipped into a state of total relaxation when the telephone rang. Reaching over she answered it before it rang a third time.

"*Ciao.*"

"*Ciao* to you, too."

She smiled. Claudia hadn't spoken to Giancarlo since Sunday. "How are you?"

"That's what I should be asking you. You sound sleepy."

"That's because I've been drinking wine."

"Are you celebrating something?" he asked.

"No. I'm just trying to unwind. I spent most of the morning and early afternoon shopping for what I need to cook tomorrow."

"Why are you overdoing it?"

"I'm not overdoing it, Giancarlo. I had to go shopping."

"Have you had lunch?"

"No. Why?"

"I'm going to come and take you out to eat."

"But I have to—"

"No buts, *bella*," he interrupted. "Are you dressed?"

"Yes."

"Then I'll be over in fifteen minutes."

"I can't stay out too long because I need to start making certain dishes today."

"I promise not to take up more than three hours of your time."

Claudia sighed softly. "Three hours and no more, Giancarlo." She did not want to stay up half the night boiling potatoes for potato salad, brining chicken, and washing and cutting up greens.

"I promise, my love."

Claudia heard the tone that indicated Giancarlo had hung up. Giancarlo Fortenza made her feel things she'd never felt with any man, and that included her late husband. Whenever he looked at her it was as if he knew what she was thinking. And just his stare aroused passions so foreign that it frightened her.

As she walked into the bedroom to exchange her blouse for a twinset, Claudia thought about Noelle. Her friend had given up her family, country, and culture for a man who was not her race, a man she loved enough to become his wife and the mother of their children, so why shouldn't she?

She opened the door, stared up at Giancarlo, and could

feel the sexual magnetism that made her vulnerable to his subtle seduction. "I'm ready."

Giancarlo swept her up into his arms, kicked the door shut, and carried her into the living room, his mouth covering hers as she held on to his neck as if he were her lifeline. Claudia wasn't certain whether her attraction to Giancarlo was purely physical; however, that no longer mattered because she didn't need time to conclude that she wanted him to make love to her.

He carried her over to the sofa, and sat, bringing her down to straddle his lap.

"You have no idea how much I've missed you," he whispered against her parted lips.

Claudia closed her eyes as she buried her face against his warm throat. "I think I know."

A chuckle rumbled his broad chest. "Do you?"

"Yes, because I missed you, too."

Giancarlo groaned. "Don't move."

Easing back, Claudia met his eyes, which had darkened until they appeared almost black. "Why?"

"Because I don't want to embarrass myself."

She felt his erection under her behind, through the fabric of her slacks, and it had taken Herculean strength not to move her hips. Pressing her mouth against his ear, she said, "I promise not to move until it goes down."

"What if it doesn't go down?"

"I can't help you, *amore mio*, because it's the wrong time of the month for us to even think of doing anything." Her menstrual period had come earlier that morning. Claudia placed tiny kisses on his face. "I'm going to get up and you can take all the time you need to get yourself together so we can go out."

Claudia felt as if she and Giancarlo had stepped back in time. Instead of drinking coffee with croissants in an outdoor

Parisian café, it was antipasti followed by espresso and biscotti in a café on the outskirts of Rome.

She stared across the table at her dining partner as a rising wind ruffled his hair. "Where do you find places to eat where there are hardly any crowds?" When they'd arrived, they were seated immediately and served quickly.

Giancarlo angled his head and smiled. "I have a short list of restaurants where I don't have to make a reservation."

"Do you go home for *riposo* or eat at your office?"

"Most days I go home. We have a kitchen and dining area at the office for the employees who don't want to drive home. What about you, Claudia? Do you go home for *riposo*?"

"Yes. It's very different from when I lived in the States. I only had an hour for lunch, and I alternated bringing my lunch with eating at nearby delis or coffee shops."

A slight frown furrowed his forehead. "Delis?"

She laughed softly. "It's short for delicatessen. It's usually a small restaurant where you can buy sliced meats and cheese."

Giancarlo expression brightened. "That's like a *salumeria*."

"Yes. I couldn't think of the Italian equivalent for deli."

"I meant to ask you if you like working at the bank?"

"Yes."

"You have a degree in business, and that means with your experience you can get a position with a number of companies."

"Are you saying that opportunities for women here are better than in the States? I doubt that, because women here didn't get the right to vote until five years after we did in the States, and then they were limited to only local elections. They weren't granted full suffrage until 1945. And that's only twenty-three years ago."

"You really know a lot about our history."

"I minored in history in college, Giancarlo. And once I knew I was going to live here, I researched as much as I could about your country."

"And knowing what you do didn't deter you from moving here?"

Claudia set down her demitasse cup. "It's the people who inhabit countries who are the ones who commit sins, whether for greed or power. And I believe it is greed that takes precedence."

"It sounds as if you don't have much faith in your fellow man."

"I'm just a little cynical when it comes to my fellow man. How about you, Giancarlo? What do you think of your fellow man?"

"I know they're not perfect, but I try to see the good in them."

"You're a lot more idealistic than I am," Claudia said, as she recalled her last meeting with Denny Clark. It hadn't mattered that a Black girl and her grandmother had saved his life; that hadn't lessened his hatred for Black people.

"You're very young to be so cynical, *bella.*"

"I have a right to be cynical, Giancarlo. I was exiled from my hometown at twelve, denied a position with a White bank because of my color, my life was threatened by a White man belonging to a terrorist group because of my voter registration activity, and I was warned by my Black boss to stop signing up people to vote because he feared his bank would be bombed."

Giancarlo ran a hand over his face as he slumped in his chair. He tried to imagine what it would've been like to live under apartheid; he wanted to feel Claudia's pain, but he couldn't because he'd never personally faced racism or prejudice within his native country.

"You've told me what you went through when living in the States, and it was horrific, but what I don't want is for you to think of me like some of the racist White people you've encountered."

"I don't think of you as a racist, Giancarlo."

"Then why do you shut me out?"

"What are you talking about?"

"I've never had to work this hard to get close to a woman as I have with you."

Claudia's eyes crinkled when she smiled. "Don't you remember me telling you that I'm not easy?"

"Yes, I do recall you saying that."

Her smile faded as her expression grew sober. "How many Black women have you dated?"

Giancarlo was slightly taken aback by the query. "One."

"Only one?"

"Yes. You."

"Why me, Giancarlo?"

"Why not you, Claudia? Do you think you're not worthy to be adored by any man regardless of his race or religion? Not only are you a female, but you're a magnificent woman in every sense of the word. When I look at you, I see bloodlines from Africa, Europe, and maybe even the indigenous people from the Americas, and the result is a breathtaking beauty. And when I'm out with you I notice men—young and old—staring at you because they see what I see and like, and I'm not ashamed to admit it does boost my ego."

"Does your ego really need boosting?" Claudia asked, smiling.

"Why not? I must admit when I saw you for the first time at Jean D'Arcy's wedding, I couldn't take my eyes off you. But then when you opened your mouth and spoke French I felt as if I'd been hit with a jolt of electricity that left me unable to breathe. Once I recovered and began spending time with you, I realized you weren't just a pretty face. You were only eighteen, but you didn't talk or act like a typical teenage girl."

"That's because I'd lived with my aunt who'd taught me to speak, read, and write different languages. My aunt Mavis is what I call a woman of the world, and that's what she wanted me to be when I grew up."

"Are you, Claudia?"

"I suppose you could say I am because I'm currently living in a foreign country."

"Do you consider yourself an Italian?"

"I'm an American living in Italy."

Claudia mentioning she was an American made Giancarlo aware that she could return to the United States anytime she chose. He didn't want to think of losing her again. She wasn't the eighteen-year-old virgin he'd been warned not to touch, but a twenty-eight-year-old educated woman who'd loved and lost and was confident enough to leave all that was familiar to move across the ocean to start over. Giancarlo glanced at his watch. "It's time I get you home."

He signaled for the waiter and left enough lire to pay for the meal and a generous tip. He drove Claudia back to her apartment and walked with her up the staircase, waiting until she unlocked and opened the door to kiss her cheek. "I'll see you tomorrow."

Instead of going home, he drove to his mother's house. He knew Myriam was surprised to see him because he never came without calling her first. The villa where he'd grown up hadn't changed much over the years. However, the only exception was the garden. His mother had commissioned a landscape architect to redesign the garden to include a waterfall and ornamental grasses.

Myriam, sitting under the pergola, knitting, glanced up at him over her glasses. "What did I do to be graced with the sight of my beloved son without his calling first?"

Giancarlo kissed his mother's cheek, then took a cushioned woven chair opposite her. "I just wanted to see my mother."

Myriam placed her knitting in a basket next to the chair. Her green eyes narrowed. "What's bothering you, Giancarlo?"

He knew it was pointless to lie to her. That was something he'd learned as a child. Myriam had told him that whatever he'd done couldn't be so bad that he couldn't tell her the truth. But if he lied, then she found that unforgivable.

"A woman, Mama."

Smiling and resting her head against the back of her chair, she closed her eyes. "Should I assume this woman is very special to you?"

"Very special."

Myriam opened her eyes and gave him a direct stare. "What makes her so different from the others you've played with in the past?"

Giancarlo took offense to her reference that he'd played with women. "I met her ten years ago when she came to Paris on holiday, and now she's living in Rome."

"Living and not on holiday?" Myriam questioned.

Giancarlo nodded.

"What does she do?"

"She works in a bank."

Myriam's lips parted in a smile. "She sounds like a smart woman."

"She is. She graduated from university."

"So, she is smart. What else should I know about this woman who has my son twisted up in knots?"

"She's an American."

"And what else, Giancarlo?"

"She's Black and she's not Catholic."

Myriam removed her glasses and placed them in her lap. "You find her race and religion problematic?"

"No, I don't."

"Then, what's your problem?"

"She was married before."

"Are you telling me she's a divorced woman?"

"No. She's a widow."

"Does she like you?"

Suddenly Giancarlo felt as if he were on a witness stand with a prosecutor bombarding him with rapid-fire questions. "She says she does."

"Then what is the problem, Giancarlo Pasquale Fortenza?"

He knew his mother was annoyed when she called him by his Christian name. "I want to marry her, Mama."

"Have you asked her?"

"No."

"*Scopata!* Why the hell did you come to me with this *merda* when you haven't told the woman you want to marry her?"

Giancarlo froze. He'd never heard his mother say *fuck* before. Even when she'd argued with his father, she'd never uttered the word in his presence. "I haven't asked her because she said she would only marry for love."

"You love her, but she doesn't love you."

"At least not yet."

Myriam grunted softly. "So, it looks as if the Golden Lion can't claim the lioness with whom he wants to mate for life."

"That's not funny, Mama."

"You think not?" she countered angrily. "I've watched you date women for more years than I can count, and whenever I ask about them you claim they're just someone you can pass the time or have fun with. Now that you've found a woman who's not impressed with one of Italy's most eligible bachelors, you fold like a squeeze box and come crying to Mama."

Giancarlo jumped like a jack-in-the-box. "I don't have to take this."

"Yes, you do. Sit down, Giancarlo. I said *sit down*," she ordered between clenched teeth when he hesitated.

He sat as anger roiled over his body from his head to his feet. He hadn't come crying to his mother. Giancarlo wanted advice, not her opinion on his dating life. "Well," he drawled. "What else do you want to say to insult me?"

"If what I say is insulting, then I'm sorry. What you must do, *mio figlio*, is treat this woman differently than you do the others. First, she's an American, she's educated and liberated, which means she doesn't have to depend on a man to support her. I consider her race irrelevant because there are Black Italians. Her religion may pose a slight problem because if she's not Catholic and she doesn't want to convert, then you cannot be married by a priest."

Giancarlo felt his anger dissipating when Myriam called him *my son*. He was her son, the only child she'd claimed in her marriage of almost forty years. "I came to you because you faced the same dilemma with Papa that I'm facing with Claudia. I need you to tell me what I can do to convince her that I want to spend the rest of my life with her."

"Patience, *mio figlio*. No woman likes to be pressured into doing something she's not ready for, because there will be nothing but resentment in your relationship. Give her time to come to love you as much as you say you love her."

"I do love her, Mama."

"You don't have to try and convince me you do, because when you came back from holiday ten years ago, I noticed you'd changed."

"Changed how?"

"You took more interest in the family business, and you stopped your merry-go-round of dating a different woman every couple of months. Pasquale had predicted that once you turned thirty you would act more mature, and you did."

Giancarlo knew having to leave Claudia without telling her he'd fallen in love with her had had a profound effect on him. And every woman he'd dated after her he'd found himself comparing to Claudia.

"That's because I'd fallen in love for the first time in my life."

Myriam smiled. "And ten years later you're still in love with her."

"I love her with èvery breath I take." Giancarlo knew he'd shocked his mother with his impassioned revelation when she stared at him, unblinking.

"I hope that one of these days I will be given the pleasure of meeting this remarkable woman who I will call daughter."

Giancarlo smiled. "So do I, Mama." He rose to his feet, then eased Myriam up to stand. "Thank you for listening to me."

Myriam wrapped her arms around his waist. "That's what Mamas are for." She rested a hand on his chest. "You know what they say about patience."

"Yes. It's a virtue."

"Good." She kissed his cheek. "Now, go home and have a glass of wine and think about what we just talked about."

Giancarlo dropped a kiss on her hair. "I will."

It was hours later when Giancarlo, after drinking several glasses of wine, lay across the sofa in his living room listening to the Four Tops singing "Baby I Need Your Loving" and recalled his conversation with his mother, and knew she was right about him having patience. He hadn't realized he'd been waiting ten years for the girl with whom he'd fallen in love to come back into his life as a woman who had experienced sorrow and continued to be tormented by the turbulence in her homeland.

Italy had gone through centuries of bloody conquests, wars, Fascism, and political and religious scandals, but somehow like in most countries there are winners, losers, and survivors. Claudia had reminded him that she was a descendant of survivors and had been given the task of never doing anything that would make her ancestors weep for all that they'd had to sacrifice for her to live free without the physical shackles of slavery. However, she'd risked her life to fight for equal rights because her people weren't free; they were still shackled by what she'd called Jim Crow.

Giancarlo realized Claudia knew more about the history of his country than he did hers, and if he hoped to share her life and future, then it was time he read about the history of the United States, beginning when it was a British colony.

Chapter 41

Challenges are what make life interesting and
overcoming them is what makes life meaningful.
—Joshua J. Marine

Claudia and Giancarlo bonded over food, music, and history lessons. They'd alternated cooking on Sundays at their respective apartments, while he'd surprised her with the gift of a television because he wanted to watch football, which in the States was called soccer. Then came another gift of a record player, because again he claimed he liked listening to music whenever they cooked together at her place.

Giancarlo had become obsessed with Sunday brunch and pleaded with her to prepare shrimp and grits and mimosas. Claudia had teased him, saying he was turning into a real Southerner. However, it was his request that she tutor him in American history that Claudia found most interesting. He said he wanted to know all the events, beginning with written records of Europeans stepping foot on North America for the first time to the present day. When she told him it would take at least a year to cover all the facts written in books by the victorious, and those not included in books by the vanquished, he claimed he had nothing but time.

She'd called her aunt Mavis, asking her to find the box

with her history textbooks and ship them to her and she would reimburse her aunt once she arrived in Italy for Christmas. Mavis promised to send them, then chastised her for being gauche when mentioning money. She managed to apologize for the faux pas seconds before Mavis hung up on her. The books arrived a week later, and she became the tutor and Giancarlo the tutee when he came to her apartment a couple of nights a week for her lectures.

Claudia felt as if she and Giancarlo had come full circle as their relationship mimicked what they'd had in Paris. They'd shared meals and, instead of his helping her perfect her Italian, she had introduced him to American history. What she still hadn't figured out were her feelings for Giancarlo. He was attentive, generous, affectionate, and even-tempered. He was perfect, yet there was something that would not permit her to open her mouth to tell him that she loved him, because she knew he wanted to marry her.

Giancarlo came to her apartment late one night in December, and when she saw his solemn expression, she thought something had happened to his mother.

"What's the matter, Giancarlo?"

"I'm going to be away for a while."

"Going where? And what is a while?"

"I'm giving everyone paid vacation the last two weeks of the month when I close the office and the factory, because I promised my mother I would take her on a cruise to Egypt and the Holy Land. My father passed away just before Christmas three years ago, so it's always a bad time for her."

Claudia cradled his face. "It's okay, sweetheart. Your mother needs you more than I do." Going on tiptoes, she brushed a light kiss on his mouth. "I'm not going anywhere, Giancarlo. I'll be here when you get back."

"Are you sure you're not going back to the States with your mother and aunt?" he teased.

"Very sure. Don't forget I do have a job."

Giancarlo rested his hands at her waist. "A job and me."

She closed her eyes and smiled. "You and a job, Giancarlo, in that order. You mean more to me than my job." When she opened her eyes, she saw him staring at her under lowered lids and hiding his innermost thoughts from her.

"I know I haven't said it in a long time, but you can't imagine how much you mean to me."

Claudia nodded. "I think I do."

His eyebrows lifted. "You think?"

She smiled. "I know. And when you come back there are few things we need to talk about."

"Do those few things have anything to do with us?"

"Yes, they do. I was just getting ready to go to bed because my boss is going to call me here in the morning before I go to work. He wants to discuss some reports I telexed him."

"Why doesn't he call you at the bank?"

"I don't know. Maybe he discovered something in the reports he doesn't want the bank to know about because all incoming calls are recorded." She didn't want to tell Giancarlo that she'd detected some irregularities with two accounts but hadn't alerted the bank officials because she'd wanted to run her suspicions by William, who had the authority to disclose to the managers what she'd unearthed.

"Well, I'm going to let you get your beauty sleep. I'll call to let you know when we can get together again."

"Good night, Giancarlo."

"Good night, love."

Claudia let the telephone ring twice before picking it up at six o'clock, aware it was midnight in New York. Whenever William called her, it was always after twelve midnight—his time.

"*Ciao*, William."

"Good morning, Claudia. At least it is where you are," he said, speaking English. "I went over your reports, and I think you're right about the discrepancies you flagged. I'm going to reserve a flight to Rome later today and meet with the bank managers in person. I don't want you to mention that I'm coming."

"Why not?"

"Because you never warn your prey when you're ready to spring the trap. They must know that their clients are using our bank to launder dirty money. Meanwhile, our bank has frozen their accounts, so there won't be any outgoing transfers."

"What reason will you give for freezing the accounts?" Claudia asked.

"We'll say there have been some improprieties at our bank and we're currently being audited by the OCC."

Claudia was aware that the Office of the Comptroller of the Currency was an independent branch of the United States Department of the Treasury. "Do you think they'll believe it?"

"It doesn't matter, Claudia, whether they do or don't. What they do know is that our banking institutions are closely regulated by our government and if they want to send us their money then they must abide by our laws and regulations."

"Now if you determine that the money is used for criminal activities, what does my future look like here?"

"Don't worry. I'll get you a position in another bank that we've been actively courting. Remember, we're the ones who pay your salary."

"What about your position, William?"

"I'm good. I was just promoted to VP of International Banking."

Claudia smiled. "Congratulations."

"Thanks. I hope you'll set aside some time when I come for us to spend a few hours together."

"Of course."

"Good. I'm going to ring off now and try to get some sleep before it's time for me to get up again."

"Sleep tight and don't let the bedbugs bite," she teased.

William's laugh came through the earpiece. "And you have a good day."

Claudia hung up, not feeling as confident as she had when she'd answered the call. When she'd gone over the files, several accounts had raised flags about fraudulent activity and she'd passed her findings on to William McNeil for confirmation, but she hadn't thought it would result in the freezing of funds and the possibility of charges being filed against Italian bank officials.

And when he'd mentioned getting her a position with another bank she wondered if it would be in Rome or in another city like Florence or even as far away as Milan. Claudia couldn't imagine not living in Rome or not seeing Giancarlo.

"Here are the checks for your signature."

Giancarlo glanced up from reading an article. He read two newspapers a day, *La Stampa* and *Corriere della Sera* to keep abreast of the country's political climate. He smiled at the bookkeeper as she handed him a stack of envelopes with employee names.

"Thank you, Lucia."

He'd asked the bookkeeper to make up payroll checks for the Fortenza Motors office and factory employees, for an additional two weeks' paid vacation as year-end bonuses. Giancarlo had hired Luca Contorni as an analyst and the man had proven his worth as a financial genius when he was able to streamline some expenditures and maximize profits, and Giancarlo decided to pass along a portion of those profits to his workers. The company traditionally closed for the week between Christmas and New Year, but this year he'd extended an extra week. They wouldn't start up again until the week following the New Year.

Giancarlo had begun taking his mother away during the

holidays because it kept her from reminiscing about the many Christmases and New Years she'd shared with her husband. They were four months shy of celebrating their fortieth wedding anniversary when Pasquale Fortenza had begun complaining of pains in his chest before collapsing. Myriam had called Giancarlo, crying hysterically, and when he told her to call for an ambulance to take him to the hospital and that he would meet her there, she'd said it was too late. His father had died in her arms.

Giancarlo signed the checks and inserted them in their respective envelopes, and then put them in an office safe until he distributed them at the scheduled office Christmas party later that afternoon. He closed the door to his office and sat at his desk staring out at the streets in the EUR. His father had moved the office to the modern district south of Rome fifteen years before, while Giancarlo had preferred working in an older section of the city with Baroque-style buildings erected during the Renaissance. After the party he planned to go home and pack for the cruise. He'd been staying at his mother's house and only returned to his apartment when he needed an additional change of clothes.

Myriam hadn't asked him about Claudia, and he was grateful she hadn't, because he still didn't know where their relationship was heading. And he didn't want to admit to his mother that the woman with whom he'd fallen in love treated him like a friend. Aside from chaste kisses, there was no indication from Claudia that she was interested in their sleeping together. She'd promised they would talk after the New Year, and Giancarlo knew the day of reckoning couldn't be postponed forever.

Claudia felt as if she could finally exhale. She hadn't lost her job. William had come to Rome to meet the bank administrators and they identified a manager who'd systematically diverted funds from several elderly wealthy clients into international accounts; he would then withdraw monies and deposit them into an account belonging to a cousin. William had attempted to keep a straight face when he described the police coming into the bank with a warrant and arresting the man, who was so distraught that he had to be carried out bodily. She and William celebrated at a popular restaurant before he caught a flight back to the States. Claudia had wanted to share the good news with Giancarlo, but he was thousands of miles away in the land of pharaohs and pyramids.

She took one glance around her apartment before she had to leave to meet the driver who would take her to the airport to pick up her aunt and mother. William had approved that she take the week off, even though she wasn't eligible for holiday until the following August. It was his way of rewarding her for uncovering the banking scam.

Claudia couldn't stop smiling when she saw Sarah and Mavis as they cleared customs. Both sported Sassoon haircuts. They were a tangle of arms and kisses until she reminded them a driver was waiting for them. It had taken her moving to another country for them to reunite.

Mavis looked out the side window at the passing landscape. "I can't remember the last time I was here," she said.

"Everything looks so old," Sarah said.

Claudia reached for her mother's hand, threading their fingers together. Like fine wine, forty-five-year-old Sarah was aging beautifully. The gray in her hair appeared more gold than silver, and there were a few new minute lines around her large hazel eyes.

"That's because it is old, Mama. This city was inhabited at least seven hundred years before the birth of Jesus."

"Do you like living here?" Sarah asked.

"I love it."

"Are you saying you don't plan to return home?"

Claudia stared straight ahead. "Right now, Italy is my home."

"I can understand why you're living here, Claudia, because of what's happening in the United States, but you can't keep running. First New York and now Italy. Where next? Africa?"

She squeezed Sarah's hand. "No, Mama. I think I'm going to stay here for a while." Claudia didn't want to tell her mother that she'd fallen in love with an Italian and was seriously considering marrying him if he did propose.

"There are times when I don't blame Claudia and Virgie for living abroad based on what went on in the United States this year," Mavis said. "They killed Dr. King and Bobby Kennedy, and National Guardsmen going on a rampage clubbing and gassing hundreds of antiwar demonstrators at the Democratic National Convention in Chicago was disgraceful when a country turns their military loose on their own people."

Sarah glared at Mavis. "Are you saying you're thinking about leaving, too?"

Mavis patted her younger sister's shoulder. "No, Baby Sis. I wouldn't leave because I know you'd never come with me."

Sarah nodded. "You're right. I'm too old to even think about trying to learn another language unless you'd consider moving to England."

"Mama, you'll learn that many Europeans also speak English."

"That may be true, but I've never had a desire to live anywhere else but in the United States, even though it looks as if it's going to hell in a handbasket."

She noticed both her mother and aunt nodding, and assumed they were exhausted from flying from Mississippi to New York, then boarding another plane for the trip from New York to Italy. Claudia paid the driver, giving him a more than generous tip when he carried the luggage up two flights to her apartment.

"How charming," Mavis crooned as she walked inside.

"It is," Sarah said in agreement.

Claudia experienced a rush of pride that her mother and aunt liked her apartment. Although the space had been furnished with a seating grouping covered in an off-white cotton fabric, she had selected accessories that had added a personal touch. Live plants in glazed pots, family photos, scented candles in hurricane holders, and pen-and-ink prints of the Coliseum, St. Peter's Square, the Grand Canal, and St. Mark's Square in Venice decorated the living room walls.

Sarah concealed a yawn behind her hand. "Sorry about that."

"Don't apologize, Mama. I have two bedrooms, so you'll share one with me, while Aunt Mavis will have the other one. It has twin beds. I want . . ." Claudia's words trailed off when the distinctive buzz of the intercom echoed throughout the apartment.

"Are you expecting someone?" Sarah asked as she slipped out of her coat.

Claudia walked over to the panel on the door. "No." She knew it wasn't Giancarlo because he'd left three days ago for his cruise. "Maybe it's the driver," she said as she tapped the button. She hoped they hadn't left something in his car. "*Si?*"

"Let me in, Claudia."

"Aunt Virgie?" She didn't want to believe her aunt was in Rome without telling her she was coming.

"The door, Claudia," came Virgie's voice through the intercom.

She tapped the bell, releasing the lock on the downstairs inner door, then opened the door to the apartment.

"Did you know she was coming?" Sarah asked.

Claudia shook her head. "No. I spoke to her a couple of

days ago and she never mentioned she was coming to Rome."
Virgie had called Claudia to thank her for her Christmas gift.

Mavis was grinning like a Cheshire cat. "The last time all
the Bailey sisters were together was when she flew in for your
college graduation, Claudia."

My graduation and my wedding. It was a day she would
remember all her life. "It looks as if this Christmas is going to
be very special with a house filled with Bailey women." Despite being a Patterson, and then Moore, Claudia had always
thought of herself as a Bailey.

Virgie's smile matched Mavis's when she walked into the
apartment wearing a tweed Chanel suit while holding a
Louis Vuitton handbag. She was the epitome of elegance with
a fashionably cut hairstyle and gray Tahitian pearls in her
ears and around her neck. Claudia's shock was twofold when
she spied the tall, tanned, silver-haired, impeccably dressed
man standing off to the side holding Virgie's monogrammed
Vuitton suitcase.

"Aunt Virgie, aren't you going to introduce us to your
friend?"

Virgie pointed to where the man could set her suitcase.
"Please excuse my poor manners," she said in French. "This
is Monsieur Henri Maison. I wanted him to meet my family
because he was generous enough to allow me to share his
compartment on the train ride from Paris."

"Are you staying, Monsieur Maison?" Claudia asked in
French.

"I'm sorry, mademoiselle, but I cannot stay. I just wanted
to help Madame Bailey with her luggage." He bowed his
head. "It's a pleasure to see so many beautiful women in one
place, but I must leave because my driver is downstairs waiting for me."

"Merry Christmas, Henri," Virgie drawled, smiling.

Henri dipped his head again as if greeting royalty. "Merry
Christmas to everyone."

Virgie closed the door and kissed Claudia on both cheeks. "I know you weren't expecting me, but I wanted to surprise everyone."

"Surprise," Mavis said, coming over to hug Virgie. "You shocked us. And what did you do or say for Monsieur Henri to invite you to share his compartment?"

"I didn't understand a word he said, but whatever it was it sounded so romantic," Sarah said," as she hugged Virgie.

"Hush, Sarah," Mavis admonished, "I want to hear how our sister, looking as if she just walked off the cover of *Vogue* magazine managed to finagle a first-class compartment with a man who couldn't take his eyes off her."

Virgie kicked off her shoes and wiggled her nylon-covered toes. "When I went to the station to purchase my ticket, I was told all the first-class compartments to Rome were sold out. Henri overheard me arguing with the ticket agent and offered to share his with me. I bought a ticket for standard class and the rest is history."

"What does he do?" Sarah asked.

"He owns a vineyard in the Loire Valley and he's in Rome on holiday and business. You know how much I love wine, so I went on to tell him about my collection of Sauternes."

"So, there's nothing romantic going on between the two of you?" Sarah questioned.

"Of course not. The man has been married to the same woman for more than thirty-five years and has four grand-babies with another on the way. There's no way I would give up Jacques for all the money in the world."

Mavis moved Virgie's suitcase next to hers. "Why aren't you spending the holidays with him?"

"He's in Benin for a couple of months visiting his daughter and grandchildren."

Claudia wanted to ask her aunt why she hadn't gone to Africa with her lover, but decided it was something she would ask her in private. "Aunt Virgie, you'll sleep in the bedroom with Mavis, while Mama and I will share a bed. "I'm going to set the table and then heat up something I prepared earlier because I knew y'all would be hungry."

"Listen to you with the *y'all*," Mavis teased. "You can take the girl out of the country, but you can't take the country out of the girl."

Claudia smiled. "Like y'all ain't country, too."

"Yeah, we are!" the sisters chorused, laughing.

Chapter 42

Two roads diverged in a wood, and I—I took the one less traveled by, and that has made all the difference.

—Robert Frost

Claudia sat on the sofa, her sock-covered feet tucked under her body, and stared at Virgie, who'd exchanged her suit for a pair of capris and a blouse as she lounged in an armchair with her bare feet resting on a low stool. After dinner, Sarah and Mavis had retired for bed, claiming they were exhausted from their daylong traveling.

Virgie closed her eyes, sighing. "It's a wonder Mavis and Sarah stayed awake long enough to eat. A few times I saw both nodding off to sleep," she said, speaking French.

"Mama told me they were up at four to get to the Gulfport-Biloxi Airport to take a seven o'clock flight into New York," Claudia replied in the same language. "And once there they had to wait more than ten hours before their Alitalia flight took off. I'm willing to bet they won't get up until late tomorrow morning."

Virgie adjusted the headband holding her hair off her forehead. "Well, they did eat well before turning in. I must admit that you've become a phenomenal cook, Claudia. The veal meatball appetizers, spaghetti with garlic and oil, and the chicken piccata were delicious."

"I'm still experimenting preparing Italian dishes."

Virgie smiled. "If I had to grade you, then you would get an A. Even after all the years I've lived in France, I still haven't mastered French cuisine."

"That's because you pay someone to cook for you, Aunt Virgie. I live alone, so I cook for myself."

"You can call me a meddling old aunt, but I want to ask you something."

Claudia met her aunt's eyes, wondering what she was thinking that could possibly upset her. "What is it?"

"You're a young woman, Claudia, who has been widowed for more than four years. When are you going to stop mourning and begin dating again?"

Claudia lowered her eyes. She hadn't told her mother or her aunts about her relationship with Ashley. And when it ended, she was glad she hadn't because she didn't want to answer a litany of questions as to why it hadn't worked out.

"I am seeing someone."

Virgie sat up straight. "How long have you been seeing him?"

"Four months."

A slight frown appeared between the gray-green eyes. "Didn't you move here four months ago?"

"Yes. The man is someone I met a long time ago."

Virgie covered her mouth with her hand. "Giancarlo Fortenza," she whispered between her fingers.

"Yes, Auntie. The man you told he could see me but not touch. He didn't touch me ten years ago and he hasn't touched me now, even though we spend a lot of time together."

Virgie lowered her hand. "He told you that I wouldn't allow him to see you anymore?"

"Yes."

"I was just trying to protect you."

"I know that, Auntie, and I'm not angry with you because of that. The night he brought me back so late, you should've talked to me before you banished him, and I would've told you everything. I spent the last two weeks in Paris miserable because I missed my friend."

"I'm so sorry, Claudia. He'd stopped in to see me a few times over the years after that, but he never mentioned your name and neither did I. The last time I saw him was about three years ago."

"His father died three years ago, so now he's running the family business, which probably doesn't allow him a lot of time to leave the country on holiday."

"Is what you have with him serious?"

Claudia pondered the query for a full minute, then said, "It is for Giancarlo. He's in love with me."

"What about you, Claudia? Are you in love with him?"

Virgie's question was one she'd asked herself over and over until she wanted to scream just to release the tumult of confusion that kept her from a restful night's sleep. "Yes, Virgie, I'm in love with him."

"Have you told him?"

"Not yet."

"What are you waiting for? The man's not getting any younger and I must assume he wants children."

"We haven't talked about marriage or children."

"And why not?" Virgie snapped angrily.

"Because we haven't, that's why."

Virgie threw up her hands. "I don't understand you, Claudia Mavis Patterson. You've succeeded where so many women have failed, and that is to get Giancarlo Fortenza to fall in love with you. There was a time when he was touted as one of Europe's most eligible bachelors. The first time he came to Paris he was about twenty-five and all the gossip reporters were writing about this young, golden, gorgeous, wealthy Italian who had women taking off their underwear and throwing them at him."

"How did he react to all the attention?"

"He seemed to take it in stride, because he probably had experienced the same reaction here in Italy. Have you been followed by photographers whenever you go out with him?"

"I haven't noticed any. Whenever I go out with Giancarlo it's usually to out-of-the-way places where people hardly look at us. And if they do it's probably because we're an interracial couple."

"You think it's race when it could be that you and Giancarlo are an incredibly beautiful couple. The few times I saw the two of you together I couldn't believe how perfect you looked." She let out an audible breath. "It's funny how what goes around comes around. I tried to keep you and Giancarlo apart, not knowing you would reconnect years later."

Claudia nodded. "That reminds me of the Robert Frost poem about 'The Road Not Taken.' It was as if we'd taken different roads, only to meet up together again ten years later."

"It's called destiny, Claudia. Life can be cruel, but things happen for a reason. You had to lose Robert to find Giancarlo again. But it doesn't have to be that way with you and Giancarlo. The fact that the man never married after meeting you means you are the love of his life. And not many people get to be that. You claim you love him, but what's different from the love you felt for Robert?"

"I think it's because I feel safe with him. And the only other man who made me feel safe was my father. Whenever I'm with Giancarlo it's as if I don't have to worry about anything, and that has nothing to do with his wealth; I believe it's because he's older and more worldly."

Virgie smiled. "That he is. Take it from me, Claudia, because I've lived long enough and known enough men to predict that if you marry Giancarlo, he will not only make you happy, but he will introduce you to a world that will be beyond your wildest dreams."

Becoming Signora Fortenza excited and frightened Claudia, but then she remembered that Giancarlo had given her time—time to accept what he perceived was the inevitable. They were destined to be together.

"I know you and Aunt Mavis never wanted to marry, but did you ever want children?"

Virgie folded her hands in her lap. "I'd thought about it a few times, but then realized becoming a mother wouldn't allow me to do all the things I wanted to. I know I sound selfish, but it would've been unfair to bring a child into the world then resent it, and that wouldn't have made me a good mother. I'm quite fond of Noelle and I'm glad she's found happiness with her husband and children, but whenever they come to Paris to visit, I never consciously think of her children as my grandchildren, even though her father and I have been together longer than some married couples. Her mother is their children's grandmother."

"You're right about destiny. Events happen for a reason, because I never could've imagined falling in love with a man who's not my race. All my life I've always said I wanted to fall in love and marry a Black man and I did, but circumstances beyond my control took him from me."

"We can't help who we fall in love with, Claudia, because the heart knows what it wants. I remember Pearl Bailey saying after she married her White husband, 'What the world needs is more love and less paperwork.' Marry the man who will love you as much or even more than you love him because tomorrow is not promised to any of us. And please give your mama a grandbaby so she can stop whining about wanting to become a grandmother."

Claudia was taken aback by this revelation. She recalled her mother talking about having grandchildren, but that was before she'd married Robert. "Mama's only forty-five and that's kind of young to be talking about becoming a grandmother."

"Remember, she was a mother at seventeen, so to her forty-five isn't young."

"Here we are talking about me having babies when I'm not even married."

"You could be when you say to that man who loves you that you're ready to become his wife." Virgie lowered her feet and stood up. "I'm going to take my tired behind to bed because at fifty-four I need all the beauty sleep I can get."

"You're still beautiful, Aunt Virgie."

"Yeah, right."

Claudia watched her aunt walk. She hadn't lied to her. Virginia Bailey's delicate, ethereal beauty had not faded with age, and it was the reason why her traveling companion had extended an invitation for her to share his compartment. And no doubt the long-time married grandfather enjoyed every minute of sitting across from her during the long train ride from Paris to Rome.

Her mother and aunts weren't the only tired ones. Claudia had gotten up early to prepare what she wanted to cook for later that day. She adjusted the thermostat, then headed for the bathroom where she took a shower, and then slipped on a nightgown before walking into her bedroom and getting into bed beside her mother. Sarah stirred but didn't wake up.

Claudia walked out of the bank to go home for *riposo* and found Giancarlo waiting for her. Her heart stopped, then started up again when she saw the obvious changes. The desert sun had bleached his hair and darkened his face until their complexions were similar. He'd turned up the collar of his topcoat to keep warm from the chilly winter weather.

She wasn't certain who moved first when she found herself in his arms as his mouth covered hers in a possessive kiss that stole the air from her lungs. Claudia clung to him, not caring who saw her sharing a passionate kiss with the man to whom she'd given her heart.

"When did you get back?" she whispered as he held her hands.

"Two nights ago."

"How was the trip?"

"Good, but it would've been better if you'd come with us."

"I don't think your mother would've appreciated me becoming an interloper."

"That's nonsense, Claudia. It's my mother who wants to meet you."

She felt her heart lurch again. "She does?"

"Of course she does. Why wouldn't she when I told her all about you. I know you're on your way home for *riposo*, but I want to pick you up when you get off and take you to meet my mother."

"Okay," she said with more confidence than she felt at that moment.

Giancarlo dipped his head and kissed her again. "I love you."

He was there, then he was gone, leaving Claudia staring at his broad shoulders under the cashmere topcoat.

"Please don't tell me that I'm imagining things."

Claudia turned to find one of the bank secretaries staring at her. She'd had very little contact with any of the female employees because she held a higher position in the bank.

"What are you talking about?"

"You and Giancarlo Fortenza. It looks as if he prefers American women rather than his own kind."

Claudia did not intend to stand on a sidewalk in Rome with an obviously jealous woman and defend or explain her relationship with Giancarlo. "Enjoy your *riposo*, Sabine."

"You do the same, Claudia."

Claudia walked home, her mind in a tumult. She'd expected Giancarlo to call her once he returned to Italy, not just show up at her job to inform her that his mother wanted to meet her. And what exactly had he told Signora Fortenza about her? Claudia knew she would've missed him for two weeks if not for her family coming to visit. It'd rained for three days but that didn't dampen her mother's and aunt's enthusiasm when they visited Vatican City, the Coliseum, and

Trevi Fountain. They were exhausted from all of the sightseeing when they took a return flight to the States on New Year's Eve, while Virgie delayed returning to Paris for three days because Jacques was still in Benin. She'd enjoyed the extra time with Virgie because it gave her the opportunity to speak French.

She reheated and ate leftovers from the prior day's dinner, and then retreated to the bathroom to shower and change into a black wool suit with a slim skirt and fitted jacket with a shawl collar. She searched her closet for shoes and found a pair of black suede T-strap pumps. A black wool three-quarter coat replaced her ubiquitous lambswool navy pea coat. Claudia then applied a little more makeup than she normally wore to work, and after fluffing up her curly hair, she left the apartment to return to work.

She managed to keep a straight face when she walked back into the bank after it reopened and ignored the curious and knowing glances directed at her. There was no doubt Sabine had been gossiping about seeing her kissing Giancarlo. For the past four months they had kept their relationship out of the spotlight because they rarely ventured outdoors to eat, spending most of their time together at their respective apartments. Well, she thought, the timing couldn't have been better, because she was going to tell Giancarlo that she was ready for the next phase of their relationship.

Giancarlo waited outside the bank for Claudia to emerge. He knew he had shocked her, showing up without warning, but he didn't want to give her the opportunity to reject his invitation and say that she wasn't ready to meet his mother.

Myriam was ready and so was he. And if it were feasible, he would marry her tomorrow, but there were other factors they would have to work through before becoming husband and wife. It was as if he were seeing Claudia for the first time when he saw her smiling at a coworker when she came through the doors. Everything about her screamed understated elegance, from the halo of curly hair framing her incredibly beautiful face to the toes of her shoes. Giancarlo couldn't pull his eyes away from her long legs in sheer black nylons.

He approached her and pressed a kiss to her forehead. "You look beautiful."

Claudia smiled up at him. "Thank you. There's a lot of gossip going around the office after some of the employees saw you kissing me."

Giancarlo held her hand. "Let them talk, love."

"It doesn't bother you?"

"No, Claudia. I don't care what they say about me. But I'm not going to be so benevolent if they talk about you. That is something I will not accept or tolerate."

"You can't stop people from thinking or saying what they want."

"They can think it, but they better not say it where I can hear it. There is one thing you should know about me before we talk about starting a future together. And that is, I will always protect what belongs to me."

"I am not your possession, Giancarlo."

Giancarlo stopped where he'd parked his car. "No, you're not. But if you do become a Fortenza then you will belong to me and I to you."

Chapter 43

Put your future in good hands—your own.
—Author Unknown

Claudia felt the warmth of Myriam Fortenza's smile even before embracing her. "How lovely you are," she whispered in Claudia's ear. "My son has chosen well."

"Thank you so much, Signora Fortenza," she replied in Italian.

Myriam eased back and gave her a direct stare with a pair of green eyes Giancarlo had inherited from his mother. "None of that Signora Fortenza, my child. If I'm going to call you Claudia, then you must call me Myriam."

"Then Myriam it is."

Myriam looped her arm through Claudia's. "Come with me, my dear. We need to talk before we sit down for dinner."

"Your home is beautiful, Myriam."

The older woman nodded. "It has taken a long time for me to get it to where I really can enjoy it. My husband used to complain because I'd move the furniture around so much that he didn't recognize his own home."

Giancarlo had mentioned that his mother preferred living in the country because it was a lot quieter than the city, and Claudia had to agree with Myriam. The two-story converted centuries-old villa reflected the influence of countless Mediterranean cultures with two-foot walls that protected the interiors against heat and cold. Although the house had running water, there was a private well with a carved marble font in the courtyard that was a memento from the past.

"Please sit down, Claudia," Myriam said, pointing to a chair covered in a finely stitched tapestry depicting a hunting scene.

Claudia stared directly at Myriam. She'd spent the afternoon mentally preparing for this encounter and planned to answer every question as truthfully as possible. "I suppose you want to know all about me."

"No, my dear. I know what I need to know about you. I want you to know something about me before you marry my son."

"Did Giancarlo tell you we were going to marry?"

"Perhaps I used the wrong word. I should have said if you're considering marrying my son."

"I am considering marrying Giancarlo."

"But there is something stopping you."

"Yes, there is. He's Catholic and I'm not. I went to church every Sunday as a child, but not as often since becoming an adult. There have been things in my life that have me questioning my faith."

"Do you still believe in God, Claudia?"

"Of course."

"Then that shouldn't be a problem for you to reclaim your faith. I was faced with the same dilemma when I fell in love with my son's father. I was born a Jew, and it was expected that I marry a Jewish man and pass along our religion to our children."

Claudia stared wordlessly at the woman who she suspected had given up her faith to marry a man she loved. "You converted?"

A hint of a smile flittered over Myriam's features. "Yes. I was a sixteen-year-old girl who was smitten with a young man the first time I met him. And the fact that he wore a crucifix and I a Star of David meant nothing to either of us. I would sneak out to meet him, and once my father discovered us together, he forbade me to see him again. My father subsequently arranged a marriage between me and a boy from a wealthy Jewish family. That's when I planned to escape. I knew my family was going to a wedding and I feigned being sick and was left home with my grandmother. Nonna helped me escape and once I made it to Pasquale's house, I begged his mother to take me in."

"Did she?"

"Not initially. She made me stay outside, but when Pasquale came home, he told his parents everything. I lived with them for a year and shared a bedroom with his sister. It was the first time I ate pork. His mother took me to a priest, where I began instruction to convert. Meanwhile, my family sat shiva once they realized what I'd done. Shiva is a Hebrew word meaning *seven*, and that's the seven-day period of mourning by the immediate family of the deceased. My family had ceremoniously buried me, so that meant I was lost to them forever. My only contact was with my grandmother, who'd been in an arranged marriage with a man she hated.

"Converting saved my life when everyone in my immediate family was rounded up and sent to Auschwitz and gassed along with over eight thousand other Jews from Italian-controlled areas in France and Greece. A few ended up in Bergen-Belsen and Buchenwald, but I never knew if they died or left the country once the Allies liberated the camps. Mussolini's notorious racial laws were passed in 1938 when marriage between so-called Aryan Italians and North African Semites, or all other non-Aryan races, was forbidden."

"But you married Giancarlo's father before 1938, when it wasn't illegal for a Jewish person to marry a non-Jew."

"That's true. I'd converted because Pasquale's mother insisted and because my family shunned me, Claudia. I was dead to them."

"Are you saying I should convert to become a Catholic?"

Myriam shook her head. "No. That must be your decision. But if you don't convert, then you can't marry or have your children baptized in the Church."

"How long will that take?" Claudia asked.

"It depends. To be fully initiated into the Catholic Church you must receive three sacraments of Christian initiation that include baptism, confirmation, and Eucharist. If you start now, perhaps you'll be fully initiated in six months." Myriam closed her eyes and seemingly appeared to be praying. When she opened her eyes, they were filled with tears. "The only thing I'm going to ask of you is to marry my son and give me beautiful brown grandchildren before I die."

Claudia lost her composure when she saw Myriam's tears as she placed a trembling hand over her mouth to cut off the sobs in her throat. "Yes," she whispered, as tears streamed down her face. "I will marry Giancarlo."

Myriam smiled through her tears. "I've waited all my life for a daughter, and I never would've imagined she would look like you." She sniffled. "I'll show you where to go so we can fix our faces before the others see us."

Claudia rose to her feet, smiling. "You're right, because if my mascara starts running, I'll definitely look like a raccoon." She followed her future mother-in-law into a powder room and blew her nose, then touched up her eye makeup with a guest towel.

She shared a smile with Myriam in the mirror over the pedestal sink. Claudia admired the woman who'd sacrificed so much for love. She'd been shunned, had forsaken her religion, then lost her family when they were murdered in Nazi death camps, and all Claudia had to do was embrace a religion with different rituals from the one she knew.

She and Myriam returned to the living room where Giancarlo sat, his hands sandwiched between his knees. His head popped up when he saw her, and he slowly rose to his feet.

"Yes," she whispered.

"Really?"

"Yes, really. We are going to be married as soon as I become a Catholic."

"I'm going to leave you two alone so you can have some privacy before dinner is served," Myriam said as she turned and walked out of the living room.

Giancarlo reached into the pocket of his slacks and went down on one knee. "Claudia, will you do me the honor of becoming my wife?"

Her eyes filled with tears for the second time within a matter of minutes when she held out her left hand. "Yes, Giancarlo." She gasped when he slipped a magnificent emerald-cut diamond ring on her finger. She'd seen enough of Virgie's diamond jewelry to know it was more than three carats.

He stood up. "If you don't like it, then you can exchange it for another one."

Claudia cradled his face. "I love it. I love you." She felt his lips touch hers in more of a caress than a kiss.

Giancarlo ran his fingers through her hair. "You just made me the happiest man in the world."

Claudia smiled at Myriam across the table and was rewarded with a bright one that indicated the older woman was more than pleased with the outcome of their prior conversation. Myriam's personal chef had prepared an exquisite dinner beginning with tortellini soup; a salad of Swiss chard, pancetta, and hard-boiled eggs; and an entrée of pork tenderloin with glazed sweet onions and grilled asparagus. Dessert was espresso granita topped with ground cinnamon and sweetened whipped cream, and coffee.

Myriam touched a linen napkin to the corners of her mouth. "You don't have to wait for Giancarlo to bring you to visit me. Just give me a call and I'll come and pick you up so we can begin planning your wedding. Of course, I want your mother to be involved. It's not going to be easy because of the time differences, but I'm certain we'll be able to work out something."

Giancarlo set down his coffee cup. "As soon as Claudia gets an Italian driver's license, I'll get her a car."

"I don't need a sports car," Claudia told him. "I was thinking about a Fiat."

His eyebrows shot up. "You want a Fiat when you could have a car from Fortenza Motors?"

"Giancarlo's right, Claudia. You're going to become a Fortenza and that means we only drive cars produced by the family business."

"I don't want anything that goes too fast."

Giancarlo winked at her. "Don't worry. I'll make certain you'll get one you can handle."

Claudia could hear Virgie's voice telling her, *If you marry Giancarlo, he will not only make you happy, but he will introduce you to a world that will be beyond your wildest dreams.*

Well, it didn't take long for her aunt's words to come to fruition. Her fiancé was going to give her a luxury car, while his mother was already planning her wedding. And she prayed that, as Signora Giancarlo Fortenza, she would be able to maintain a modicum of independence as Claudia.

"Where do you want to live?" Giancarlo asked Claudia as he drove her back to her apartment. "Do you prefer the city or the country?"

She gave him a sidelong glance and smiled. "I have a choice?"

"Of course, you have a choice. I will always give you a choice when it comes to our lives. It's not about you or me, but us, Claudia."

"Does it take long to drive to the house in the country?"

"Forty minutes."

"That's far, Giancarlo. What if we stay in the city during the week and spend our weekends in the country."

"I was hoping you would say that. What are you going to do with your apartment?"

"I'm going to live there until we're married."

"You don't want to live with me now?" Giancarlo questioned.

"No, Giancarlo. I'll stay with you on weekends, but I won't live with you until we are husband and wife."

"Didn't you say that you're a modern woman? That you slept with your boyfriend before you were married?"

"I do think of myself as a modern woman, because I'm willing to engage in premarital sex, but I draw the line when it comes to shacking up with a man."

Giancarlo gave her a quick glance. "Shacking up?"

"It means a man and woman living together without the benefit of marriage."

"Like a man and his mistress?"

"Yes."

"But it's different for us, Claudia, because we're engaged to be married."

"I was engaged to my first husband, but we didn't live together until we were married. And even though I spent more time at my boyfriend's apartment than at my own, at no time had I considered giving up my place to move in with him."

"Do you believe I'm going to treat you any differently than I do now?"

"I hope you won't, but speaking from experience there may be situations that may force you or I to change."

"We've been talking about where to live, when we haven't discussed children."

"What about them?"

"Do you want children?"

She smiled. "Yes, I want children."

"Do you want to wait or start trying right after we're married?"

"I don't want to wait." Claudia had planned to stop taking a contraceptive two weeks before their wedding date.

"Good."

"It sounds as if someone's ready to become a papa."

Giancarlo chuckled. "Only if you have my children."

"I'm going to pack a few of my things for you to take back to your apartment. There's going to be enough gossip about our engagement, and I don't want to add to it when my co-workers see me coming and going with an overnight bag."

"You can't stop people from gossiping, Claudia."

"I know, but I'm not used to being in the spotlight."

"When you become a Fortenza you will be in the spotlight whether you want it or not."

"Doesn't that bother you, Giancarlo? Being in the spot-light."

"No, because I've learned to ignore it."

"What if I can't ignore it?"

Giancarlo stopped at a red light and rested his hand on her thigh. "You will after a while. I think once we move to the country, you'll enjoy the anonymity."

"Do you plan to sell your duplex?"

"No. I prefer living in the city during the workweek and staying in the country on the weekends. Once we have our family the country house will become our primary residence and we'll use the apartment for social events."

"That sounds perfect."

"Now that we're making plans, where do you want to honeymoon?"

"Paris."

"So, you want to go back to where all of this began," Giancarlo teased.

Claudia couldn't help grinning. "Yes."

"Once we set a wedding date, I'll make a reservation at the Hôtel Plaza Athénée."

"I need you to make an appointment with a priest so I can begin studying to convert."

"I'll do that tomorrow. Do you still want to go to Venice for Carnevale?"

"Of course, Giancarlo."

"I want to warn you that Venice is an incredibly romantic city. After you see it, you may change your mind about honeymooning in Paris."

Claudia placed her left hand over his right on the gearshift. "We have a long list of things to do before we marry. And when it comes to the wedding, I don't want some big spectacle, Giancarlo. I want a private ceremony with family and close friends followed with a dinner at your mother's house."

"You can have whatever you want."

Giancarlo telling Claudia she could have whatever she wanted had lessened her stress when she thought about the months ahead. She called her mother to let her know she was engaged to marry and would arrange for her and Mavis to come to Italy before the ceremony to meet Giancarlo's mother. She also called Virgie to tell her that she and Giancarlo were planning to marry and that she wanted her in attendance.

She made a third call to Yvonne, bringing her up to date on the events going on in her life and told her she would've selected her as her matron of honor if she got over her fear of flying to come to Rome. Yvonne claimed her fear of heights was too deep-rooted to overcome, even with hypnosis, and told her to take lots of pictures.

12 February 1969
Dearest Noelle,
I'm engaged to marry Giancarlo Fortenza later this year. We were reunited when I moved to Rome last August, and it was as if we never parted. He claims he fell in love with me when we were in Paris, and I suppose a part of me did love him, not in the romantic sense but because he made me aware of myself as a woman.

I met his mother and she's a remarkable woman who raised a remarkable son, and I can't wait to make her a grandmother. Giancarlo and I talked about starting a family and we agreed to begin trying as soon as we are married. I am converting to Catholicism and began studying with a priest several weeks ago. Fortunately, it is going well, and I expect to be fully initiated into the Church before the end of May, which will allow Giancarlo and I to marry sometime during the summer. Write back whenever you get the time and I promise to send you lots of pictures from our wedding.

Much love.

Your sister,

Claudia

Chapter 44

The best is yet to be.
—Robert Browning

"What do you think of Venice?" Giancarlo asked Claudia as they sat in the water taxi heading for their hotel.

"If Paris is romantic, then Venice is ethereal. I want to come here for our honeymoon," she said in his ear.

When she and Giancarlo arrived in the lagoon city built on small islands in the Adriatic Sea, Claudia felt as if she had entered another universe. She was aware there were no roads, just canals, but seeing it for herself was breathtaking. She moved closer to Giancarlo to share his body's heat. The temperature in Venice was at least ten degrees lower than Rome's.

Giancarlo's arm went around her waist. "So, you changed your mind about Paris."

"Yes."

He pressed a kiss on her hair. "There was a time when I'd thought about buying property here."

Claudia eased back and met his eyes. "Would you have rented it to tourists?"

"No, my love. I would've used it as a holiday retreat. Instead of driving to Paris or London, I would spend holidays right here in Italy."

"You've driven to London from Rome?"

"Not nonstop. I usually stay overnight in Paris before taking the ferry from Calais to Dover, and then I drive from there to London."

"You're quite the world traveler," she teased.

"I was before my father passed away."

"Did you ever consider going to the States?" Claudia asked.

"I did a few times. But there were too many cities and countries in Europe I wanted to see before leaving the Continent."

"Whose idea was it for you to go to Egypt and Jerusalem?"

"It was my mother's. She's been talking about visiting the Holy Land for years, so when I discovered a cruise with those destinations, I booked it."

"Is it really that important to her that we marry in a Catholic church?"

"As a convert, my mother is rather fanatical in her beliefs. She sacrificed everything she'd known up to that time to marry a man who wasn't Jewish. It wouldn't matter to me if we were married by a magistrate, but I know my mother would see it not as an act of defiance but betrayal."

"Do you think she regrets giving up Judaism?"

"No, because she still holds on to some of the traditions. During Passover she won't eat bread, pasta, cereal, or cookies for seven days."

"You grew up going a whole week without eating bread and pasta?"

"No," Giancarlo said, laughing. "There would've been a mutiny in my house if my father had to go without eating bread or pasta for a week."

"Can you go a week without pasta?" Claudia asked.

"Nope. I eat pasta at least three times a week."

"I'll remember that when I prepare our menus for the week."

"I'm thinking about hiring a cook once we're married."

"We don't need a cook, Giancarlo. There's only going to be you and me."

"I'll wait on the cook, but I'm not getting rid of the house-keeper."

Claudia wasn't going to debate Giancarlo about the house-keeper. Her two-bedroom apartment was smaller than his living and dining rooms, and if she had to clean the duplex it would probably take her at least two full days. Each apart-ment contained a bedroom, kitchen, bathroom, and a half bath, while his so-called little country house was anything but.

They arrived at the hotel as the sun was setting, and the streaks of oranges and blues crisscrossing the darkening sky created awe-inspiring images that were picture-postcard perfection, and Claudia became increasingly aware that it would be the first time she and Giancarlo would share a bed. She shrugged off her jacket as Giancarlo tipped the bellhop who'd helped him carry their bags up the staircase. "I'm going to use the bathroom to freshen up before we go out to eat."

The train ride from Rome to Venice took more than three and a half hours, and Claudia had spent most of the time watching the passing landscape while Giancarlo slept. She wanted to shower and change her clothes, but her stomach was making embarrassing noises, which reminded her that she'd hadn't eaten since breakfast.

She walked out of the bathroom five minutes later. "It's all yours."

Giancarlo removed his toiletry case from his luggage and went into the bathroom. He knew Claudia was uneasy about them sleeping together, but he hadn't been able to find a hotel room with two beds because he'd waited too long to make a reservation. Hotels, guesthouses, palazzos, and villas had filled up quickly prior to Carnevale, with tourists coming to

Venice to take in the sights in the floating city, and if fortunate, attend the many costume parties.

Giancarlo brushed his teeth, and then gargled with mouthwash. He knew the next two nights would be a prelude to what he could expect once he and Claudia married. They would not only share a bed but each other's bodies as husband and wife. It had taken Herculean strength not to make love to Claudia since reuniting with her months ago. Each encounter tested his self-control as he waited for a sign or word from her that she wanted him as much as he wanted her.

He emerged from the bathroom to find Claudia unpacking their bags. Giancarlo smiled when he saw the blood-red and raven-black ball gowns she'd purchased for the parties. He'd found a retro vintage jacket with gold rococo eighteenth-century braiding, black trousers, a white shirt with a ruffled front and cuffs, and a black Gothic seventeenth-century trench coat.

"You can finish that later, love. It's time we leave to get something to eat before the restaurants get too crowded. I did hear your stomach making noises while we were on the train."

He smiled seeing a rush of color darken Claudia's face. She'd brushed her hair and secured it in a twist on the nape of her neck. Giancarlo had gotten so used to seeing her unbound curls that he'd almost forgotten that she'd worn her hair in the sleek style when he'd first met her in Paris.

Claudia lowered her eyes. "I was hoping you hadn't heard that."

Dipping his head, Giancarlo kissed her parted lips. "Let's go, my love. I can't have you fainting on me."

Claudia sat across from Giancarlo in a café sipping white wine as they dined on quail on toast with polenta. She didn't know what she enjoyed more, watching throngs of tourists or the many pigeons flying around the Piazza San Marco.

"I don't know what it is, but I've fallen in love with this city, Giancarlo."

"That's because you're a romantic, Claudia."

She set down her glass. "Do you think there's something wrong with being a romantic?"

"No, *bella*. It is one of the reasons why I fell in love with you, because you love with your heart."

Claudia smiled. "Virgie accused me of the same thing," she said quietly. "She said I'm like my mother because I love with my heart and not with my head."

Giancarlo gave her a long, penetrating stare. "We are alike, Claudia. Because I, too, love with my heart. If I didn't, then I would've married years ago."

"And why didn't you?" she asked.

"Because I hadn't found a woman who made my heart beat a little too fast when I looked at her. And I hadn't found the one who wanted me for me, not for my family's name or wealth."

"That's because to me your name and money are neither here nor there, Giancarlo. I would marry you even if you didn't have a lira to your name."

He placed a large hand over his heart. "You wound me, love. Even if I were a pauper, I would be a proud one because I never would've allowed a woman to take care of me."

"What if we both were paupers like the starving artists who lived in freezing garrets and existed on stale bread, moldy cheese, and bad wine, but were happy because they loved each other."

Throwing back his head, Giancarlo laughed, causing diners sitting at nearby tables to glance over at him. "You are truly a romantic."

Resting her elbow on the table, Claudia cupped her chin on the heel of her hand. "A romantic who loves your life."

He sobered quickly. "Claudia, my love and my heart, *please* don't make me beg to make love to you," he said sotto voce.

She lowered her arm, unable to pull her eyes away from the man to whom she'd pledged her future. She'd been aware of the increasing sexual tension between them for months, but this was the first time Giancarlo had verbalized he wanted to make love to her, and it was one of the reason why she'd fallen in love with him because he hadn't treated her as a sex object, someone available for his lust.

"You never have to beg, Giancarlo. Just ask."

The seconds ticked, then he said, "Claudia?"

"Yes, Giancarlo?"

"Will you permit me to make love to you?"

Claudia wanted to laugh because Giancarlo asking to make love to her reminded her of herself as a child, when she would ask her mother or grandmother to buy candy, which they claimed would not only ruin her teeth but also her complexion.

"Yes."

The single word, pregnant with emotion, galvanized Giancarlo into action as he reached into the breast pocket of his jacket, removed a money clip, and left enough lire on the table to cover their meal and a gratuity. He nodded to the waiter, then rounded the table to ease Claudia from her chair.

They held hands as they walked back to the hotel, each lost in their thoughts. Claudia felt as if she'd been counting down the seconds, minutes, days, and months since reuniting with Giancarlo, waiting for him to ask or initiating making love with her. Giancarlo swept Claudia up in his arms, carried her into the bedroom, and placed her on the bed, his body following hers down, and bracing his greater weight on his forearms. "I want you to stop me when I do something you don't like," he whispered in her ear.

Claudia nodded, closed her eyes, and then let her senses take over when she felt rather than saw Giancarlo undress her. She opened her eyes when he left the bed to take off his clothes, and she couldn't pull her eyes away from the perfection of his body. His tailored clothes had concealed a lean, muscled physique verifying that he had the face and body reminiscent of Michelangelo's *David*.

She'd believed she was ready for Giancarlo, but not when he returned to the bed to put his face between her legs as his tongue made her feel things she'd never experienced before at any time and with any man. Claudia grabbed his hair to extricate his mouth but failed when Giancarlo held her wrists to hold her captive as his marauding tongue made her feel as if she were losing touch with reality.

She screamed, then bit down on her lip to smother another one when one orgasm and then another and still another swept over her like waves crashing on a beach. She'd just returned from her flight of freefall when Giancarlo moved up her body and kissed her; she tasted herself on his tongue when he slipped it into to her mouth. She gasped as he penetrated her, and Claudia felt every inch of his engorged flesh against the walls of her vagina as he revived her passion all over again.

Giancarlo slipped his hands under Claudia's buttocks, lifting and positioning her where his erection rubbed against her swollen clitoris, increasing his pleasure and hers at the same time. He had waited ten years to make love to Claudia in the most intimate way possible and the wait had been more than worth it. He loved tasting her, inhaling the subtle scent of her perfume on her silken skin, and her moans that threatened to send his libido into overdrive where he feared ejaculating too soon. And her response to him was as natural and as unrehearsed as her orgasms that squeezed him like a too-tight glove.

The rhythm he'd set changed, quickening as Claudia followed his pace, her body arching as he drove into her, his blood-engorged penis plunging in and out with longer and deeper strokes. Giancarlo buried his face in Claudia's neck, straining valiantly to prolong the ecstasy, but it was not to be when he felt his scrotum tighten and then he released himself inside the body of the woman he loved with every fiber of his being.

He lay on her body and waited for his heartbeat to resume a normal rate. "I love you so much," he said reverently.

"I love you, too," Claudia said softly.

Claudia felt like a fairy-tale princess in voluminous yards of the black satin cape covering a red ball gown. A full-face red mask was festooned with black ribbons and feathers. She smiled up at Giancarlo, resplendent in all-black. He'd revealed that even though the two-week celebration began before the start of Lent, he'd learned from experience to limit his participation to no more than two to three days. And when she'd questioned him about his decision, he'd admitted that he'd done things when he was young and foolish that he regretted and had sworn never to repeat them.

They'd taken a gondola with another opulently costumed and masked couple going to a get-together along the canal. The entire city was decorated like an outdoor party. Many of the pastry shops were filled with *frittelle*—sugar-dusted donuts eaten only during Carnevale.

She'd grown up reading about carnivals in New Orleans, Rio de Janeiro, and Salvador de Bahia in Brazil, but it was Carnevale in Venice that claimed the most extravagant costumes and decorative masks. Giancarlo explained that the significance of masks covering the entire face was not only to hide someone's identity but their social status, so the poor were able to interact with the city's more affluent citizens.

Although she and Giancarlo planned to spend two nights in Venice, Claudia wanted to return for their honeymoon, as tourists, to visit some of the smaller islands and browse the many shops to furnish and decorate their country home. Thinking about sharing a home with Giancarlo conjured up their early morning, seemingly endless lovemaking, where each had refused to yield to the burning passions threatening to ignite both. It finally ended with them experiencing *la petit mort* as they climaxed simultaneously where Giancarlo's unbridled lovemaking had left her shaken, yet she'd craved more.

Giancarlo gave his invitation to the masked man at the door to the Venetian villa, and Claudia felt as if she'd stepped back in time when they were shown into a magnificent ballroom with a frescoed ceiling and a balcony overlooking the rear garden. The ballroom was crowded with costumed and masked revelers eating, drinking, some dancing to music played by a small band.

Claudia, after removing her mask, leaned closer to Giancarlo as they stood on the balcony sipping champagne. "This garden reminds of some I've seen in Paris."

Giancarlo had also removed his mask and pressed his mouth to her ear. "That's because wealthy families, during the Republic of Venezia's golden baroque and rococo periods, commissioned their homes and gardens to be designed as small versions of Versailles. This villa has belonged in the same family since the sixteenth century. They have a six-hundred-acre farm in addition to a vineyard that produces Chardonnay, pinot grigio, and Cabernet, and they also cultivate tobacco, onions, and peaches. My friend's father recently added a greenhouse where he raises more than seventy thousand house plants." He squeezed her free hand. "Vittorio and his family will be invited to our wedding."

"How many people do you intend to invite?"

"Not too many, because you claim you want it small and private."

She nodded. "Yes, but will it be small enough to host the reception in your mother's house?"

"I don't know. Maybe we should have it at a restaurant. We can arrange for the owner to close it for the day to accommodate us. That way my mother won't panic if it becomes too overwhelming for her."

Claudia took another sip of champagne. "You're right. Let's have it at a restaurant."

She knew Giancarlo's guests would vastly outnumber hers, but that didn't bother her, because he'd talked about inviting friends, business associates, and his company's employees, while she had her mother, aunts, and William McNeil and his wife as her guests. William had volunteered to give her away in marriage once he was made aware that she wouldn't have any male relative or friends in attendance.

After several hours she and Giancarlo decided to leave, and instead of taking a gondola back to the hotel, they'd opted to walk. They skirted throngs of merrymakers by taking narrow alleys and bridges back to the Grand Canal. After undressing, washing her face, and brushing her teeth, Claudia got into bed with Giancarlo, and as soon as her head touched the pillow, she fell asleep in his embrace.

Chapter 45

The two most important days in your life are the day you are born and the day you find out why.
—Mark Twain

Mrs. Sarah Patterson
Requests the Pleasure of Your Company
At the Marriage of Mrs. Patterson's Daughter
Claudia Mavis
to
Giancarlo Pasquale
Son of
Signora Myriam Fortenza
Sunday, the Twenty-Ninth of June 1969
6:00 PM
at
Il Nostro Santo Nome Church
Via del Conte
Rome, Italy
Reception Dinner to Follow at
Ruffino's
Via del Conte
Rome, Italy

The wedding invitations were printed in English and Italian, with Mavis acting as the interpreter for Sarah whenever she spoke to Myriam about the wedding plans for their son and daughter. The day had finally arrived. It was the last Sunday in June and in less than five minutes Claudia would exchange vows with Giancarlo.

Claudia shared a smile with William McNeil as he extended his left arm. She placed her gloved right hand over the sleeve of his suit jacket as her left hand gripped the bouquet of pink roses. Once she'd completed her religious instruction to become initiated into the Catholic Church, her mother and Giancarlo's had sent out wedding invitations. She'd worn a suit to her wedding with Robert but had vacillated whether she wanted to wear a white gown to her marriage to Giancarlo. She'd always heard that white was for virgins.

Virgie had solved her dilemma when she traveled from Paris to Rome to take her to a dressmaker known for designing wedding gowns. Claudia had tried on several samples and finally selected a spaghetti-strap gown made entirely of soft French lace in a solid pattern on sheer netting that needed only minor alterations, and the overall result was dramatic and undeniably romantic for the semiformal evening affair.

Earlier that morning a stylist had washed and set her hair on large rollers, and she sat under the dryer for an hour before her hair was brushed off her face in soft waves and styled in a bun wrap for the double-tier veil secured with pearls. She'd decided to wear her good luck jewels—the pearl earrings and necklace Giancarlo had given her.

"Are you ready for your next adventure, Claudia?" William asked.

She nodded. "Yes."

Reaching over, William pulled the veil over her face. "Giancarlo has waited ten years for this, so let's not make the man wait any longer." William had flown in the week before to visit with some of his mother's relatives and when Claudia introduced him to Giancarlo the two men bonded quickly.

"I'm ready."

Claudia placed one foot in front of the other as she focused on Giancarlo's white dinner jacket rather than his face as he waited with the young priest who'd been assigned as the officiate. She'd told William she was ready, but she wasn't as confident as she appeared. This was to become her second marriage and everything about it was so different from when she'd married Robert. They'd been surrounded by both their families, while now it was just her three family members who had come to witness her marriage to a man twelve years her senior. When Sarah expressed concern that she might not see her grandchildren, Claudia told her she would pay for her to come to Italy during summer school breaks and the Christmas recess, because she hadn't changed her mind about returning to the United States.

Claudia handed her bouquet and gloves to her mother, who stood up when she neared her row. Moving closer to Giancarlo, she glanced up at him through the lace veil, smiling when he winked at her. She felt as if she was having an out-of-body experience while listening to the priest intone about the sanctity of marriage. Then she repeated her vows and slipped the gold band on Giancarlo's left hand after he'd placed a matching one on hers. Reality returned when Giancarlo raised her veil to kiss her for the first time as his wife. It was over. They were now husband and wife.

After being showered with flower petals, Claudia and Giancarlo walked the one block to the small restaurant, their wedding guests following while eliciting curious stares from passersby. He gave her hand a gentle squeeze as she stared at her mother and new mother-in-law leading the procession. Sarah didn't speak any Italian but she and Myriam, with her limited English, managed to communicate with each other.

"Do you have any idea how much I love you, Signora Fortenza?"

"I think I do," Claudia said, smiling. "Do you realize there are now two Signora Fortenzas?"

"You can't be Signorina Fortenza, because you're married."

"I suppose Myriam and I will work something out whenever we're together and someone wants to talk to Signora Fortenza. Are you also aware that we had a very unconventional wedding? There were no groomsmen or best man. I didn't have bridesmaids, and my boss stepped in to walk me down the aisle."

"It doesn't change the fact that we're married, Claudia."

Claudia had consulted with Myriam when planning for the reception dinner. They didn't want their guests to wait to sit down to eat an hour after the ceremony, so they'd arranged for the photographer to take pictures of friends and family after the dinner and before the dancing began. Giancarlo had also arranged with the restaurant owner of the intimate dining establishment to hire a small band to provide music during and after dinner.

She was glad Giancarlo had suggested holding the reception at the restaurant because it was large enough to accommodate the sixty attendees, and the atmosphere was warm and relaxed as the factory employees, in their Sunday best, were able to rub elbows with the company's office workers and to personally meet their boss's new wife. Most, if not all, were surprised to discover she spoke fluent Italian.

The restaurant's chef and his staff had outdone themselves when they set up a buffet fit for royalty. They'd set out a roast suckling pig, pheasant, crown rib, a risotto mold, spider crabs with orange slices, goose liver pâté, lamb chops with herbs, egg ravioli, gnocchi with Parmesan cheese, and a variety of grilled fish and meats, pasta, sauces, and salads. Another table groaned with cheese, fruit, and endless desserts including cannoli, tiramisu, zabaglione, and panna cotta, while a bartender was busy pouring wine and mixing cocktails.

Once they'd finished eating, Claudia, Giancarlo, Myriam, Mavis, Sarah, and Virgie posed for photos as a group, as couples, and individually. Claudia had asked for one to be taken of her and William McNeil. She and Giancarlo shared their first dance as a married couple to Herb Alpert's "This Guy's in Love with You." The male singer sung it in Italian, then his female counterpart sung it in English, substituting *girl* for *guy*.

They switched partners for the next song when she danced with William, and Giancarlo with Myriam, then Sarah. William spun her around and around until she begged him to stop. "You know I'm going to miss you."

Claudia gave him a puzzled look. "What are you talking about?"

"When you go on maternity leave."

Now she was totally confused. Claudia knew for certain she wasn't pregnant.

"I'm not pregnant, William," she said in his ear.

"I'm talking about when you do become pregnant, Claudia. I've begun training someone to take your place once you call me to say you're in the family way."

She laughed when he'd referred to pregnancy as the *family way*. "If find myself in the family way, then I'd like to work at least the first three months."

"You can work even longer if your doctor recommends it. You sit at a desk, and you have little or no contact with the bank's customers who come in every day, so I don't have a problem if you want to work until you're ready to deliver. I mentioned training someone because it's going to take a while before they'll be able to take over for you."

Someone tapped her shoulder and she turned to find Luca Contorni extending his hand.

"May I have this dance, Signora Fortenza?"

She placed her hand on his outstretched palm. "Of course."

Giancarlo had introduced her to his financial analyst when he'd come to the apartment late one night to drop off a report he'd been working on. She couldn't warm up to the middle-aged, married man with a lecherous grin. Whenever he looked at her Claudia felt as if he were undressing her with his eyes. Luca held her too close for propriety, but Claudia endured it until one of the engineers cut in.

She noticed her mother and aunts didn't lack dancing partners as some of the single men pulled them out onto the dance floor. Sarah and Mavis planned to stay in Italy for two more days, then accompany Virgie when she returned to Paris. Sarah had been more animated than she'd been in years, and Claudia knew her traveling abroad had given her a new outlook on life.

It was close to ten o'clock when Giancarlo pulled her into a corner near the rear door. "I've settled the restaurant bill, and arranged for drivers to take my mother, your aunts, and your mother home."

"What about our guests?" she whispered.

"They can leave whenever they choose. Meanwhile, you and I are going home to get some sleep because we must be up early to catch the first train to Venice."

Claudia, having removed her veil and given it to Myriam for safekeeping, nodded. "Okay. Let's blow this nightclub," she teased.

Giancarlo ran the back of his hand down her cheek. "What am I going to do with you, *bella*?"

"Love me, Giancarlo. All you have to do is love me."

Wrapping his arm around her waist, Giancarlo pulled her against his body. "And I do. With all my heart."

Claudia held on to Giancarlo's neck as he carried her over the threshold to their apartment. Smiling, she rested her head on his shoulder. The past few months had her feeling like a hamster on a wheel, going around and around and nowhere until today. She'd met with a priest several times a week to prepare to convert; she and Myriam got together on weekends to plan the wedding and menu for the reception dinner; once she got her Italian driver's license Giancarlo had her road test a few cars before she selected one of the rare models Fortenza Motors built with an automatic transmission. She'd packed up all the personal items in her apartment and taken them to the country house she planned to decorate during the summer months, with the express hope that she and Giancarlo would be able to take up permanent residence before the end of the year when her mother and aunts had promised to return to Rome for Christmas.

Giancarlo carried her into the bedroom and set her on her feet. "I'm going . . ." His words trailed off when the telephone rang. "I'd better answer that."

Claudia watched his expression as she removed the pins from her hair and placed them in a small dish on a table in the corner of the bedroom. She knew it couldn't be good news as evidenced by Giancarlo's scowling.

"What's the matter?" she asked when he hung up.

"That was the hotel manager in Venice. He says after three days of nonstop rain the streets are flooded and he's closing the hotel until the water recedes."

Claudia walked over to Giancarlo and wound her arms around his waist. "It's okay, sweetheart. It doesn't matter where we honeymoon. It can be here in this apartment, or on a rooftop hotel in Florence. It doesn't matter to me."

Giancarlo stared down at her under lowered lids. "You really aren't disappointed?"

Rising on tiptoe, she kissed his ear. "Of course not. Who are we to argue with Mother Nature? They are getting too much rain up north, while we're not getting enough."

Giancarlo combed his fingers through her hair. "Do you want to see Florence?"

She smiled. "Yes. I've always wanted to visit the Uffizi Galleries to see Botticelli's *The Birth of Venus* and his *Pri-*

mavera, and of course Leonardo da Vinci's *Mona Lisa*. And maybe we can go see Michelangelo's *David*."

"You seem to know a lot about Italian art."

Claudia rolled her eyes. "I probably know the name of every museum in Paris, Rome, and Barcelona." She dropped her arms and turned around for Giancarlo to undo the tiny, covered buttons on the back of her gown.

Giancarlo pressed a kiss on the nape of her neck. "I love you so very much."

"Well, my beloved husband, I need you to show me how much you love me."

Giancarlo smiled as he cradled her face and dipped his head to kiss her mouth before he placed nibbling kisses along the column of her neck, throat, and then the swell of her breasts. Time seemed to stand still for Claudia when Giancarlo undressed her, then himself before he placed her on the bed as if she were fragile porcelain and made love to her in a way that was different from their other encounters. It was more controlled as he stopped her from climaxing twice until she begged him to release her from the sexual torment threatening to short-circuit her senses.

Giancarlo rolled off her, their bodies still moist from their lovemaking, and threw an arm over his face as he waited for his heart to slow down enough for him to reach over and pull Claudia against his chest. He gloried in the peace and contentment he felt at that moment. The Golden Lion had found his lioness, a lioness he would love and mate with for life.

Chapter 46

The great thing about marriage is that it enables
one to be alone without feeling loneliness.
—Gerald Brenan, *Thoughts in a Dry Season*

Giancarlo had called Claudia to tell her he was working
late, and he would eat something before the meeting.
Although he'd promised not to bring his work home, she'd
overheard him on the phone yelling at whoever was on the
other end of the line that if he didn't step up and do his job,
then he should look for a position where he could come and
go without consequences.

It was the first time she'd heard him raise his voice, and
she'd discovered when she'd shared lunch with Myriam it
was a distant cousin who had been the recipient of his anger.
Her mother-in-law also revealed there had been bad blood
between Giancarlo and his cousin because of his habitual tardiness and absences.

Claudia decided to reheat leftovers and save what she'd intended to prepare for dinner for the following night. She
quickly cleaned up the kitchen and then went into the living
room to pick up the envelope addressed to her that had been
delivered earlier that day, and slid a letter opener under the
flap.

18 August 1969

Dear Sister and Greetings from Benin,

I received your letter and the photographs of your wedding to your prince. I knew when Giancarlo first looked at you what now seems a lifetime ago that you were destined to end up together. And you have succeeded where so many other women have failed because you're now Signora Giancarlo Fortenza. And you must tell me how it is being married to the Golden Lion. You looked incredibly beautiful as a bride, and Giancarlo is still as handsome as ever. I see where you get your beauty from because your mother is stunning. And of course, Virgie and Mavis were the epitome of fashion in their Valentino and Chanel couture. I'm sorry you didn't get to honeymoon in Venice because of the floods, but you can always go back next year for your first anniversary.

Now that you're living in Italy, you should think about coming for a visit. I would come to visit you, but with six children ranging in age from two to nine, it's not easy. I was okay when I had four, but these last two have me on my knees praying every day not to regret bringing them into the world. I love my children, Claudia, but there are times when I just need a break. You'll discover this once you start having babies. Write back soon.

Love and hugs,

Your sister,

Noelle

Claudia reread Noelle's letter and smiled. Even though her friend complained about her rumbustious brood, she knew Noelle was having the time of her life. That was evidenced by her unruffled expression whenever she included photographs of her family with her letters.

Not only did she owe Noelle a letter, but also Yvonne. She and her roomie always seemed to miss each other's telephone calls. And she wasn't home when Yvonne returned her call and left a message with Giancarlo that she was going to write rather than call.

Claudia got up from the sofa and sat at the desk Giancarlo used whenever he brought reports and blueprints home, and picked up the Parker Duofold Centennial Lapis Blue fountain pen Myriam had given Claudia for her birthday. The pen had belonged to Myriam's grandmother, who'd given it to her granddaughter during one of their clandestine meetings. Claudia found a shop that sold vintage writing instruments and had replaced the eighteen-karat gold nib with a new one.

30 August 1969
Dear Sister,
I always look forward to reading your letters, and I promise to write more often. I moved to Italy this month a year ago, so now I think of myself as an Italian. I have an Italian driver's license, but my passport authenticates that I am a citizen of the United States of America. I still have a few years before it expires, so that's when I'll decide whether I want to keep or give up my American citizenship.
My mother-in-law is wonderful, and I always look forward to the times when we can get together. I'm learning to cook many of the more traditional Italian dishes she's taught me, and now I can

make sauce from ripe tomatoes rather than those in a can. Of course, it takes hours to cook, but I make enough to last a week or more when I freeze the leftovers.

The next time you come to Paris, please let me know in advance so I can take the train to come up and see you. Hopefully when we do get together it will be like old times when we used to gossip about Adjovi and Giancarlo. As you can see from my wedding pictures, I'm wearing the pearls he gave me the last time we were together. Every time I put them on good things happen, and if or when I have a daughter, I want to give them to her for the next generation of Fortenza women. Kiss all your babies for me and give Adjovi my best.

Love always. Your sister,
Claudia

Claudia set the page aside and then reached for another sheet of stationery. She paused, then remembered she had to write Yvonne in English.

August 30, 1969
Hi Roomie,
It seems as if we can't connect by phone, so I'm going to bring you up to date on what has been happening in my life over the past few months. Firstly, the weather has been brutally hot. You would think . . .

The telephone rang and Claudia capped the pen. She picked up the receiver before it rang a second time. "*Ciao.*"

"Roomie?"

"Hey, Yvonne. You're going to live a long time because I just sat down to write to you."

"Well, you can stop writing. The last time I called you it was on the weekend and your husband said you were out. So, I decided to take a chance and call you tonight."

"How are you?"

"I called to tell you that I'm pregnant—again."

Claudia's jaw dropped. "Congratulations—again!"

"Girl, please. We did not plan this one. I wanted to wait until Robert was at least two before trying for another baby."

"How's Stephen taking the news?"

"He's as happy as a pig wallowing in slop. He keeps talking about having a dozen kids like Ethel Kennedy, but I won't repeat what I told him about that. I didn't go to college and dental school to become a brood mare for a man."

Claudia had always believed Yvonne and Stephen were the perfect couple, but it was apparent they weren't on the same page when it came to the number of children. Her friends weren't in agreement as to how large a family they wanted, while she and Giancarlo had decided they would have at least two.

"Enough about me, roomie. How's married life?"

"It's good, Yvonne."

"Just good?"

"It's better than good. My greatest fear was that Giancarlo would change and become bossy, but it's as if we are still dating."

"Good for you. Giancarlo sounded very nice on the phone."

Claudia smiled. "That's because he is, Yvonne. I wouldn't have married him if he wasn't."

"Ashley came by last week and when I told him you were married, he was so shocked that he couldn't say anything for a while. That's when I told him he didn't realize what he had until he lost you. And he couldn't have been in love with you because if he was, then he would've married you."

"Ashley couldn't love me, Yvonne, because he is in love with himself." She paused. "Ashley is my past, and I wish him the best."

"You're probably right about him being in love with himself. Enough about your ex. Do you have any plans that include returning to the States?"

"No. My mother and aunts are coming to visit again this Christmas."

"I was hoping to see you around the holidays."

"I'm sorry about that, Yvonne. My mother seems to like traveling as much as my Aunt Mavis, so I know I'll be seeing them whenever school is on recess. And once we move into the house they can stay for as long as they want."

"You bought a house?"

"No. Giancarlo bought it years ago as a country retreat. It's a converted eighteenth-century farmhouse that has been updated with electricity and indoor plumbing."

"How large is it?"

Claudia smiled. "Very large. There are six bedrooms, seven bathrooms, and two kitchens. One is large enough for a chef and his staff to prepare a banquet, and the smaller one is about the size of the kitchen in your home. There's also an outbuilding I'm thinking of turning into a guesthouse."

"It sounds as if you'll be living in a mansion."

"I don't think so, roomie. It's like most farmhouses built hundreds of years ago when people had large families and needed living space for their workers."

"If I didn't have this severe fear of flying, I would come and visit."

"You can always take an ocean liner like I did when I first came to Europe."

"That's something to consider. But any plan of traveling will have to be put off until after I push out this baby."

"When is Jones baby number two due?"

"Mid-March."

"Just in time for spring."

"Hopefully by that time Robert will be walking, talking in full sentences, and not shitting in his diapers."

Claudia laughed. "You're asking a lot from an eighteen-month-old."

"No, I'm not. There's no way I'm going to be able to hold him on my hip while taking care of a newborn."

"I know he's not quite a year old, but is he trying to pull up and walk?"

"Hell no! He's crawling but that's it."

"They say boy babies are slower than girl babies when it comes to walking and toilet training."

"He ain't slow when it comes to eating, Claudia. He cries when I'm not feeding him fast enough."

"That's because he's a big boy, Yvonne."

"That he is. The last time I took him to the doctor for his checkup he weighed twenty-six pounds. Speaking of my son, I hear him crying, because he probably needs changing."

"Go take care of your baby, Yvonne. If I don't talk to you again in a couple of months, I'll write. Love you."

"Love you back, roomie."

Claudia hung up at the same time she heard Giancarlo talking to someone. Not only had he come home earlier than expected, but he'd brought someone with him. She got up and walked out of the living room, stopping when she saw her husband cradling a puppy against his chest. He indicated where he wanted the man to set down a crate and a large shopping bag. He handed the man a bill, thanked him, and then closed the door behind him.

"What do you have there?" she whispered, grinning from ear to ear.

Giancarlo's smile matched hers. "I thought you'd need a little something to keep you company before we move to the country."

"But we're not moving until December." She couldn't pull

her eyes away from the puppy with black curly fur and four white paws.

"I figured you would need time to bond with each other before we move."

Claudia extended her arms. "Please give him to me." Holding the puppy against her breasts, she pressed a light kiss on the top of the dog's head.

"You want him?"

She gave Giancarlo an incredulous stare. "Of course, I want him."

"He has all his shots and he's also potty trained, so you don't have to worry about him soiling the floors."

"Does he have a name?"

"Nico. He's a poodle and black Labrador mix, and he has hair and no fur, so he won't shed all over the place."

Claudia rocked Nico gently when he opened his dark eyes to stare up at her. "I like the name. What does he eat?"

"His former owner fed him whatever she cooked for herself. She had to give him up because she's moving to a facility that won't allow pets."

"Well, now he has a new home. Do you like spaghetti and meatballs, or eggplant Parmesan, Nico?"

"I'm sure he does. Where do you want me to put his crate and bed?"

She continued rocking the dog. "You can put his crate in the pantry. I'm not certain where I want his bed."

Giancarlo picked up the crate and a shopping bag, Claudia following and carrying her new pet. She didn't want to tell Giancarlo even if he hadn't brought the puppy, she wouldn't be lonely long because she suspected she was pregnant. Her menses was late, and she'd wanted to wait another week before saying anything to him. And if she was pregnant, she would celebrate motherhood and her thirtieth birthday in the same month.

They set up the crate in the space between the kitchen and

pantry, and the bed outside the kitchen. Giancarlo opened a package with wee-wee pads and spread them on the floor next to the bed. Claudia set the dog on the floor. He climbed into the bed, tucked his muzzle against his side, and went back to sleep.

She wrapped an arm around Giancarlo's slim waist. "Thank you."

Giancarlo rested his chin on the top of her head. "For what?"

"For thinking about me."

"I always think about you, love. I've had to restructure the company again, because I've given the factory supervisor three months off to take care of a personal problem, so I'll have to spend more time at work. That's the reason why I decided to give you a dog."

Claudia knew he was talking about his cousin, but because Myriam had told her about him in confidence, she pretended ignorance. Giancarlo had offered to take her to his company to show her around, but she'd declined because she didn't want to ingratiate herself in his business.

"Are you going to do double duty running the office and the factory?"

"Not really, but I want to keep a closer eye on the production schedule. Right now, we're under contract to build two new cars before the end of the year."

She was aware that Fortenza Motors cars, like Rolls-Royce vehicles, took at least six months to build because they were handcrafted by engineers and technicians once the design was approved by Giancarlo and several designers.

"How far along are they?"

"Not as far as I'd like, but if I were to offer some of the employees overtime, we should be able to make the deadline."

"Give them the overtime, Giancarlo."

"I think I will."

"Don't think, sweetheart. Just do it."

"If you didn't work for that bank I'd definitely try and entice you to come and work with me."

Claudia patted his back. "That's not going to happen because I don't believe in mixing business with my personal life. Have you ever heard of the expression not shitting where you eat?"

"Yes, I have, and that's something I've always subscribed to."

"Has it worked?"

"Not completely, because I can't control what people do on their own time."

Claudia lowered her arm. "Have you eaten?"

"Yes. I ate something before going to pick up the dog."

"I have to address a letter to Noelle, then I'm going to bed."

"Are you feeling all right?"

"Yes. Why are you asking?"

"Because you've been going to bed earlier than usual."

Claudia knew it was time to let her husband know what she'd suspected since not having a menstrual flow for six weeks. "I think I'm pregnant."

Giancarlo closed his eyes for several seconds. "Are you sure?"

"I think so. I missed my period two weeks ago, but I want to wait another week before making an appointment with a doctor."

"No, Claudia. You're not going to wait another week. I want you to call the doctor and get an appointment as soon as possible. And once you get one, I'm coming with you."

"That's not necessary. Your mother can come with me."

"Please, let's not argue. I'm going with you."

"Okay."

"Why don't you finish what you must do and then go to bed. I'm going to hang out here with Nico to make certain he's comfortable in his new home."

"Thank you again for the puppy."

Cradling the back of her head, Giancarlo kissed her, his tongue tracing the fullness of her lips before they parted. The warmth of his mouth on hers made Claudia return his kiss with reckless abandon and she knew if they didn't stop, they would end up in bed. She managed to end the kiss, her breasts rising and falling as she struggled not to moan as she waited for the pleasurable throbbing between her legs to subside. She returned to the living room and addressed the envelope, then folded the letter, slipped it inside the envelope, and sealed it.

Claudia was glad Giancarlo had suggested she go to bed because she doubted whether she could stay awake long enough to watch television with him. She completed her nightly ablution in record time and after turning on the table lamp on Giancarlo's side of the bed to the lowest setting, she got into bed and quickly fell asleep.

Chapter 47

Kids are always the only future the human race has.
—William Saroyan

The day her pregnancy was confirmed changed Claudia's life. Not only was she going to become a mother, but the doctor had recommended bedrest for the first three months of her confinement because she'd begun spotting. And despite her protests, Giancarlo had hired private duty nurses to take care of her. She'd placed a call to William McNeil to give him an update on her health and he congratulated her and reassured Claudia that she would be proud of her replacement because she'd set the standard to which he would have to measure up.

Myriam had closed her house to temporarily take up residence in the duplex. Claudia was disappointed that the country house wasn't fully furnished for Christmas, but Myriam had volunteered to act as hostess for when her family arrived for the week.

Claudia felt like a prisoner in her own home with Myriam hovering over her like a guard in a penal colony. Nico had become Giancarlo's companion when he fed, bathed, and walked the puppy, who was rapidly losing his puppy looks as he grew taller.

She'd completed her first trimester and was rapidly losing her waistline when her mother and aunts arrived a day before Christmas Eve. She'd begun wearing Giancarlo's shirts over pants with elastic or drawstring waistbands rather than maternity blouses. Claudia didn't know who shed more tears—she or Sarah.

Sarah ran a hand over Claudia's longer hair. "You look absolutely beautiful."

"I can honestly say that she is glowing," Mavis said, smiling.

Claudia watched Giancarlo and Virgie as they stood off to the side talking quietly to each other. She smiled when Giancarlo hugged her aunt. "It looks as if they've finally made up," Mavis whispered in Claudia's ear.

"They don't have a choice, Aunt Mavis. This baby I'm carrying is a Bailey *and* a Fortenza."

"It was nice of your mother-in-law to open her home for us to stay for the week."

"Myriam is a warm and generous person, and I've come to love her dearly."

"And she loves you, too, Claudia. You can tell that by the way she looks at you."

"I know you're probably tired, so why don't y'all change into something more comfortable before you eat."

"You don't have to tell me twice," Mavis said, as she picked up her luggage. "I need you to show me to my room."

Claudia led the way to the bedroom suites with adjoining baths before she returned to where Giancarlo sat talking to Myriam. Nico lay near his feet, his muzzle resting on his front paws. She sat on an armchair and rested her feet on an ottoman.

"How are you feeling?" Giancarlo asked for what now seemed like the umpteenth time.

"I'm good."

"You don't feel tired?"

Myriam rested a hand on her son's arm. "Let her be, Giancarlo. You keep asking her the same thing and the answer is always the same. Claudia knows enough to lie down if she's feeling tired."

"I've slept enough these past few months to last me for years. The doctor says I can resume my normal activities if I don't overdo it."

"And that doesn't mean you going around the city looking to buy doodads for the house."

Claudia laughed. "What do you know about doodads, Giancarlo?"

"Enough, my love. Right, Mama?"

Myriam rolled her green eyes at him. "Your father never had a problem with what I bought for this house."

"Your home is beautiful," Claudia confirmed. And it was. Myriam had decorated the villa with the skill of a professional decorator. "And that's why I need your opinion whenever I go shopping."

Myriam nodded, smiling. "We'll wait until spring before we go shopping together again."

"Mama, please don't encourage her."

"That's enough, Giancarlo," Claudia warned. "I'm not going to become a prisoner again. I followed the doctor's orders and went on bedrest. I want this baby as much as you do, so I'm not going to do anything that will jeopardize my life or that of our son or daughter." She lowered her feet and stood. "Myriam, I'm ready to start cooking whenever you are."

Myriam rested a hand at the small of Claudia's back as she stirred a pot of marinara sauce. "I hope Giancarlo survives this pregnancy without losing his mind. You must know he's more concerned about losing you than the baby," she said in a quiet voice.

"I plan to carry this baby to term and hopefully deliver a healthy son or daughter. Then I plan to wait a couple of years and try for another one. I intend to end the only-child syndrome that has plagued our families, because the bloodline can't end with us. My mother had me, then miscarried over and over until the doctor warned her against becoming pregnant again, so she underwent a hysterectomy."

"I was married for three years before I had Giancarlo, but I didn't know he would become my only child because even though me and Pasquale tried to have more children it never happened."

Claudia smiled as she placed a lid on the pot of sauce. "Do you remember telling me to marry your son and give you beautiful brown grandchildren before you die?"

Myriam blushed. "Yes, I do. I never knew when I asked you that it would become a reality."

"It's because Giancarlo and I were destined to be together, like you and Pasquale."

"You're right, Claudia. Have you selected names for your baby?"

"Not yet. I told Giancarlo to give me two names for boys and two for girls, and I'll do the same and hopefully we can come up with ones on which we can agree."

Being on bedrest hadn't been a total waste for Claudia because it allowed her time to knit and crochet baby items. She'd crocheted two crib blankets, and knitted four sweaters with matching hats, booties, and socks. And when she ran out of yarn, she'd made a list of what she needed from a local handicraft shop and gave it to Giancarlo. He'd complained that he didn't want people to see him in an establishment frequented by women but relented when she threatened to get out of bed and go herself.

Myriam opened the refrigerator and took out packaged and labeled fish from the freezer compartment and placed them on a platter on a shelf in the refrigerator to defrost before she prepared them for Christmas Eve dinner. "Do you think your mother and aunts will be upset if I don't serve meat Christmas Eve?"

It was to become Claudia's first introduction to the Italian tradition of the Feast of the Seven Fishes. "Of course not. We are Southerners and we do eat a lot of seafood. What do you plan to serve?"

"Linguine with white clam sauce, and Seven Fishes Fra Diavolo pasta made with clams, mussels, shrimp, anchovies, calamari, scallops, and halibut."

"That sounds delicious."

"I'm also thinking about serving crab cakes with tartar sauce or one made with clarified butter, garlic, and chives. And we can start off with shrimp cocktail and baked clams. I also have fresh oysters that we can grill in the oven. Giancarlo usually makes a greens and seafood salad with endives, radicchio, and arugula with grilled scallops. I also have several whole red snappers. I'll stuff one with herbs and breadcrumbs and bake it, and fry the other two."

"That's a lot to prepare, Mama. Why don't . . ." Her words trailed off when she saw Myriam become teary. "What's the matter?"

"Do you realize this is the first time you've called me mama?"

Claudia hadn't realized that calling Myriam *mama* had slipped out. "That's because I think of you as my Italian mama. If it bothers you, then I won't call you that."

Myriam hugged Claudia. "And you're my Italian daughter, so you can call me mama all you want."

Claudia smiled as she struggled not to also get emotional. There were times when she'd found herself crying when she least expected, and blamed her vacillating moods on the hormonal changes in her body. And being pregnant triggered a sexual craving that had triggered erotic dreams, but it couldn't be assuaged because she'd been instructed not to have sexual intercourse during her first trimester. It was only a week ago that her doctor had given her the go-ahead to make love with her husband; however, she and Giancarlo, as a precaution, decided to wait an additional two weeks.

Myriam placed two large eggplants on the countertop. "To save time, I've decided to make eggplant rollatini instead of lasagna, because I know your mother and aunts want to eat after their long journey."

"You can grill them, and I'll drain the excess water."

Myriam moved a package of mushrooms from the refrigerator. "Claudia, I need to use these before they go bad."

"Have you used all the sausage?"

"No. I still have a few links left. Why?"

"You can use them to stuff the mushrooms."

"Excellent. Do you want to stuff them?"

"Yes." Claudia loved making appetizers. Stuffed mushrooms and deviled eggs were her favorites.

"Do you think it'll be too much if I make a caprese salad?"

"Why don't you save the caprese salad for tomorrow because it's going to be meatless, while tonight you're going to serve prosciutto and melon, eggplant rollatini, sausage-stuffed mushrooms, Italian wedding soup, and pasta Bolognese."

Myriam pressed her palms together. "That is a lot of food."

"I agree," Claudia said, smiling. "You made almond cake and tiramisu, so that takes care of dessert."

"Speaking of desserts. I haven't made *torta di noci* or hazelnut tarts, or vanilla panna cotta in a while."

"Isn't panna cotta similar to flan?" Claudia asked.

"Yes. I'll write down the recipe to that, too."

Two great-aunts and two future grandmothers. Giancarlo felt a kinship with the four sitting at the table, even before the birth of his child. He raised his glass of pinot noir and smiled at Virgie, who acknowledged him with a nod.

He and Virginia Bailey had declared a truce when she'd come to Italy for his wedding to her niece, but Giancarlo couldn't shake the nagging feeling that she still felt he wasn't good enough for Claudia. But when he'd confronted her earlier that day, Virgie did admit there was a time when she'd felt he was too worldly for her niece, but had changed her mind once he married Claudia. And now that she was pregnant, their families were inexorably linked for future generations.

Giancarlo sought to put Sarah at ease when he told her in English that he would protect her daughter with his life, and he had taken steps to secure her financial future if anything were to happen to him. Sarah thanked him and said Claudia didn't need money, as much as she needed his love and protection.

He was content to listen to the conversations floating around the table in Italian, French, and English, and he wondered if Claudia would continue the tradition of teaching their children different languages. His French was passable, but his English had improved appreciably since living with Claudia. There were days when she spoke English to him and insisted he reply in the same language. He'd noticed she'd stopped drinking wine because she claimed it made her dizzy, and most times opted to drink water and milk.

Claudia draped an arm over Sarah's shoulders. "Mama, why don't you go to bed now?"

Sarah dabbed the corners of her mouth with a napkin. "You're right, because even though the clock says six, my body is on midnight."

"Do you need anything before you turn in?"

"No, baby. I have everything I need. And right about now my bed is calling my name."

Mavis pushed back her chair and stood. "I'm sorry to be a party pooper, but I'm going to join Sarah and go to bed. Y'all can count on me to help you cook tomorrow to celebrate the Feast of the Seven Fishes."

Myriam clasped her hands together. "We could use all the hands we can get."

Mavis smiled. "Thank you again for opening your home."

"There's no need to thank me, Mavis, because you're *la mia famiglia*."

"And know that I speak for my sisters when I say that you're also our family."

Claudia felt her heart turn over with the affirmation that the Baileys were now a part of the Fortenza dynasty because of the child growing in her womb. The blood of Myriam's ancestors and those of her own were now connected for perpetuity.

Virgie folded her napkin and placed it next to her dessert plate. "I'm available for kitchen duty."

"No, no, Virgie," Myriam protested. "You are a guest."

"Guest, my ass," Virgie said in French. "I'm not going to sit on my behind this week and expect you to wait on me hand and foot and not help out," she continued in the same language.

"What did she say, Claudia?" Myriam asked.

"You don't want to know, Mama," she replied in Italian. "Just let her help."

Giancarlo stood up. "While you ladies are arguing about who's family and who's a guest, I'm going to walk Nico and then come back and help clean up."

Claudia assisted Myriam and Virgie as they stored leftovers in containers, experiencing an indescribable joy that all her loved ones would live together under one roof for the next five days. Virgie and Giancarlo were more affectionate than they'd been at her wedding, and she hoped their former enmity was now in the past.

And Claudia was looking forward to her first celebration of the Feast of the Seven Fishes, a tradition she knew she would pass along to her children, because unconsciously she'd become an Italian. She thought in the language, spoke the language fluently, and it was on a very rare occasion that she prepared a Southern dish. The exception was shrimp and grits, the American version of Italy's *gamberetti* and polenta.

However, she planned to teach her children English, while introducing them to the foods she'd grown up eating. Claudia wasn't certain what lay in the future for the United States, but there was still a part of her that loved her country of birth and the events that had shaped her into the woman she'd become.

Giancarlo returned after walking Nico and Claudia told him she was going to bed. She didn't tell him that she was tired, because he would start complaining that she was doing too much. And she'd taken her doctor's advice to do things in moderation and to take naps whenever she felt fatigued.

"I'll see you later," he said, as he brushed a light kiss over her mouth.

The doors to Sarah's and Mavis's bedrooms were closed as she walked down the hall to the bedroom she shared with Giancarlo. Fifteen minutes later, after a brief shower, she pulled a nightgown over her rapidly changing body and got into bed. She knew she was pregnant but hadn't felt pregnant until her stomach started getting bigger. That's when she realized for certain that there was a baby growing inside her. Giancarlo had talked incessantly about wanting a son to carry on the Fortenza name, while Claudia wanted a healthy baby, because to her the sex of the child was inconsequential.

She'd just closed her eyes when she heard the tapping of Nico's toenails on the wood floor as he got into his bed. The six-month-old puppy followed Giancarlo around like he was the pied piper, rarely letting him out of his sight. Her husband had bought several doggie beds and placed one in the corner of their bedroom where Nico spent nights, and she knew if she'd permitted it Giancarlo would've had the dog sleep in the bed with them.

"Good night, Nico," she whispered, and was rewarded with a soft woof.

*   *   *

"I still can't believe you eat this many fish every Christmas Eve," Sarah said to Giancarlo, after she'd swallowed a mouthful of the greens and seafood salad.

He smiled at his mother-in-law. "It's a tradition that is widely celebrated by Italians all over the world. My mother buys her fish at least a week in advance and freezes them, because if she waits any later most of what she wants will be sold out."

Sarah smiled. "It's a tradition I wouldn't mind adopting because I love fish. Back in the South we have fish fries. The men would go fishing and bring back a mess of fish. If we were lucky they would scale and clean the fish before bringing them home. Then we would dredge them in a paper bag with seasoned cornmeal and fry them in hot lard and serve them with potato salad, coleslaw, and cornbread. Then some families would charge other folks for plates, to raise money to pay their bills."

"They sell food to make money?" he asked.

"Yes. Tell him in Italian, Claudia, about how house-rent parties came about."

Sarah had put Claudia on the spot when Giancarlo and Myriam gave her direct stares. "People would get together and cook and then advertise they were selling dinners to those who didn't want to cook or couldn't cook dishes they liked. The women would pool their money and buy fish or chicken along with the ingredients they needed for side dishes. They'd spend all morning and afternoon cooking, then charge folks for each plate. If they charged five dollars, then a mother could get enough food to feed herself and at least a couple of kids."

"They give that much food?" he questioned.

"Yes. And the money they raise they put aside to pay their rents. That's where the term house-rent parties comes from."

"I like that they are so resourceful," Myriam said.

"It's called survival," Claudia countered. "Poor people are forced to devise ways to make it day-to-day on their limited resources."

"Claudia!" Mavis admonished. "That is not acceptable dinner conversation."

"It's true, Aunt Mavis. Why do you think so many Black people left the South during the Great Migration? Not only was it to escape Jim Crow, but for better economic opportunities."

"I beg to differ with you, Mavis," Giancarlo said in Italian. "Racism and poverty should be a topic of dinner discussion because too often people believe if they don't talk about it then it will go away, or it doesn't exist."

Mavis gave him a long, penetrating stare. "It appears as if my niece has turned her husband into a freedom fighter."

Giancarlo smiled. "Your niece has taught me a lot about your country's history, and even though the United States is touted as the leader of the free world, they still have many sins to atone for. No country has clean hands, Mavis, but what we must do is acknowledge the pain and suffering we have caused others and try to right the wrongs."

"Bravo," Myriam said, applauding. "I agree with my son, because my family died in Nazi death camps because of the crime of being Jewish."

Mavis stared at Myriam. "My niece married a Jew."

"Your niece married an Italian who just happens to have Jewish blood. When I fell in love with a Catholic man, I converted and was shunned by my Jewish family and later lost them all to the Holocaust, and converting saved me when the Nazis began rounding up Jews to put them in concentration camps. I'm proud of who I am, and I can say with all sincerity that I don't hate German people, because they were following a madman who told them what they wanted to hear. Hitler was no different from Benito Mussolini, Napoleon

Bonaparte, Julius Caesar, or even Genghis Khan. They were megalomaniacs who wanted to gain the world but, in the end, lost their souls."

It was Mavis's turn to applaud. "Well said, Signora Fortenza."

"So, you don't have a problem with your grand-niece or nephew having Jewish blood?"

A flush swept over Mavis's face as she lowered her eyes. "No. Not at all. I once had an . . ."

"You had what, Aunt Mavis?" Claudia asked when her aunt didn't finish her sentence.

"It's not important," she said under her breath.

Claudia didn't have to be a mind reader to know that her aunt had had a liaison with a Jewish man, while Sarah and Virgie looked totally confused because they didn't understand Italian.

The topic, once more, turned to food and this time the conversation was conducted in English, and Claudia would translate a word that Myriam did not understand. She'd tutored Giancarlo in English more than a decade ago, and now it was Myriam's turn. Claudia planned for her children to speak Italian and English, so it was incumbent that their grandmother have a grasp of both languages.

It was after midnight and Christmas when gifts were exchanged. Claudia had done her Christmas shopping earlier that summer and gifted her mother and aunts with matching eighteen-karat gold bar pins set with rubies, pearls, and sapphires. When she'd seen them in the window of a jewelry shop, the owner told her he'd bought them in an estate sale and if she wanted all three then he would give her a good price. She bought the pins and a pair of oval drop Etruscan-designed earrings in yellow gold for Myriam. She'd been in a quandary about what to buy for Giancarlo but finally decided to give him a monogrammed vintage fountain pen and pencil set. She hadn't known once she'd completed her Christmas shopping that she would be on bedrest for three months.

Virgie gave her a large bottle of her favorite French perfume. Mavis's gift was a colorful Hermès silk scarf, and her mother had given her a crocodile-covered monogrammed journal. When Myriam handed her a small box, Claudia knew instinctually that it contained a piece of jewelry. She opened the box to find an exquisite Asscher-cut emerald ring flanked by white baguette diamonds. Myriam said it had been Pasquale's grandmother's ring that had been passed down through several generations of Fortenza women, and now it belonged to Claudia.

Everyone waited to see what Giancarlo had given her, and there was complete silence when Claudia opened the iconic Tiffany blue box to find a pair of diamond earrings.

There were hugs and kisses from everyone as they retired to their respective bedrooms to sleep after celebrating the first annual Fortenza-Bailey Christmas.

Chapter 48

Hold fast to dreams / For if dreams die / Life is a
broken-winged bird / That cannot fly.
—Langston Hughes, *The Dream Keeper and
Other Poems*

It was a rainy day in early May when Leandro Dominic
Fortenza came into the world red-faced and crying loudly,
much to the surprise of many in the delivery room. Claudia
closed her eyes, wanting to drift off to sleep after going
through more than eighteen hours of labor, but she needed to
see if her son was born with all his fingers and toes.

"You have a healthy seven-pound son, Signora Fortenza,"
the doctor told her after the baby had been cleaned and
weighed.

"Thank you," she sighed.

"We're going to take your son to the nursery and you back
to your room, where your husband is waiting for you."

Claudia felt as if she'd entered the twilight zone when she
was wheeled from the delivery room and into one where Giancarlo had sat for hours waiting for her to give birth. His
hair looked as if he'd combed it with his fingers and there
was a noticeable golden stubble on his jaw. And judging from

his rumpled clothes it was obvious he'd hadn't gone home to change.

Giancarlo waved aside the nurses, then gathered Claudia up in his arms and gently placed her on the bed. "Thank you, Mama, for our son."

She gave him a weak smile. "Congratulations, Papa. Our son has a healthy set of lungs. The doctor didn't have to slap his behind to make him cry because he came out bawling."

"He probably wanted to stay inside you a little longer."

"That's not funny, Giancarlo."

He brushed her hair off her forehead. Claudia had endured a long and hard labor, refusing drugs to ease the pain, to give birth to their son. "Are you in pain?"

"It's nothing compared to the labor pains that were kicking my ass."

Giancarlo kissed her forehead. "You were quite brave to go through natural childbirth for all those hours."

"I didn't want our son to be born with drugs in his system." She closed her eyes. "I need you to call my mother and let her know she's now a grandmother."

"I'm going to go and see the baby, then I'm going home to change. When I'm there I'll call everyone and give them the good news. Do you want me to bring you anything?"

"I don't think so, Giancarlo. Everything I need is in the bag you brought when we came to the hospital."

He kissed her parched lips. "I know you're exhausted, so try and get some sleep. I'll be back later."

"Okay."

Giancarlo left the room in the small, private hospital where Claudia had given birth.

He followed the signs to the nursery and stared through the wall of glass until he found the bassinet with a sign identifying Baby Fortenza. He couldn't discern the color of his son's hair covered by a blue cap, or if he had any hair. It had taken several days before he and Claudia had decided on a name for their son or daughter. It was to be Leandro Dominic for a boy and Daria Joelle for a girl. Leandro meant *li-onlike* and Dominic *of the Lord*, while Daria meant *wealthy* and *queenly*, and Joelle was Hebrew for *the Lord is willing*.

"Welcome to the world, my son," he whispered.

Giancarlo felt like a new man once he came out of the bathroom at the duplex apartment where he and Claudia lived during the week because it was closer to Fortenza Motors than the house in the country. Claudia stated she'd planned to move into the house permanently once their child had his or her six-week checkup. Giancarlo knew it would take him twice as long to drive to the office, but his wife's well-being was worth the sacrifice. He'd noticed the difference in her mood whenever they were in the country. She was more relaxed and appeared totally content with her surroundings and admitted she was born a country girl and would die a country girl.

Giancarlo picked up the phone and called Biloxi, Mississippi, hoping someone was home to answer his call. It rang four times before he recognized Mavis's voice.

"*Ciao*, Mavis. I'm calling to let you know that Claudia had a baby boy today."

"Congratulations, Giancarlo."

There was something in Mavis's voice that sent a chill up his spine. "What's the matter, Mavis?"

"It's Sarah."

He sank down to the bed. "What's the matter?"

"She's not well."

"What the hell do you mean, she's not well?" Giancarlo hadn't realized he was yelling at his wife's aunt.

"She has cancer, Giancarlo, and it doesn't look good. They opened her up, then closed her right away because it has metastasized throughout her body."

"Oh shit, oh shit, oh shit," he said over and over. Giancarlo blew out a breath as he struggled not to break down. "Where is she?"

"She's in hospice where they are managing her pain with drugs. Promise me you won't tell Claudia."

"Doesn't she have a right to know that her mother's dying?"

"Yes, but don't tell her now. She just had a baby and she's emotionally too fragile to deal with this news."

"When are you going to tell her, Mavis?"

"I'll call her once Sarah passes. You have no idea how much grief Claudia has had to go through in her young life. First it was her grandmother, and then her father and husband. And now it's her mother, and that means she's going to need you more than ever."

Giancarlo ran a hand over his face. "I don't know how I'm going to deal with this, Mavis."

"You're going to deal with it by being strong for your wife and baby. She's going to rely on you to get her through this crisis."

"She just went through eighteen hours of hard labor, so she's not going to be strong enough to travel back to the States."

"She doesn't need to come back. Virgie is flying in tomorrow, and together we'll take care of all the arrangements for Sarah's funeral. Once she's buried, I'll call Claudia and give her the news. But before I tell her, I'm going to call you at your office and tell you exactly when I'm going to call you at home, because I want you there with her."

"Okay, Mavis." He didn't want to agree, but it was apparent Mavis was more familiar with how Claudia dealt with grief than he was.

"Take care of my niece and my brand-new nephew, Giancarlo."

He smiled for the first time since making the call. "Don't worry. I will."

Giancarlo hung up, then he did something that he hadn't done in years. He cried. He cried because he knew once Claudia heard the news that she had lost her mother it would devastate her, and Mavis was right because he had to be there for her both physically and emotionally.

Claudia sat in a cushioned rocker, her bare feet on a matching stool, breastfeeding her son. The rocker and stool were a gift from Myriam, who when she saw her grandson for the first time could not stop grinning. Myriam had held him while Claudia, who'd spent the past three days in the hospital, took a shower and then slipped into a pair of loose-fitting cotton slacks and one of Giancarlo's old shirts. She was glad to be home.

Giancarlo, who'd adjusted his schedule to work fewer hours, walked into the bedroom. He ran a finger over the wisps of reddish-blond hair on Leandro's head. "It looks as if he's fallen asleep."

Claudia tilted her head for his kiss. "He's just taking a break before he starts up again."

Giancarlo hunkered down next to the chair. "Did you have lunch?"

She nodded. "Yes. Your mother made pasta with grilled chicken." Claudia had decided to modify her diet to elimi-nate alcohol, caffeine, highly processed foods, and garlic, onions, and spices that would go into her breast milk, and in-creased her intake of protein, poultry, eggs, and dark green vegetables.

"I'm not going back to the office because I want to spend the rest of the day with my wife and son." What Giancarlo could not tell Claudia was that her aunt had called him at his office to inform him that Sarah had passed away earlier that morning. And she would call him at home within the next hour. It had been five days since he'd received the phone call from Mavis telling him about Sarah's condition.

"Are you certain your boss isn't going to write you up for slacking off?" she teased, as Leandro began suckling again.

"No, because I have the best boss in the world."

"Are you sure?"

"Very sure, *bella*."

"How many days do you plan to take off?"

Giancarlo smiled and stood up when he saw the baby's tiny fingers clutch Claudia's breast. The nipple slipped out of his mouth, and Claudia reached for a diaper and put it over her shoulder and held Leandro against her chest until he burped. She then stood up and placed him on his back in the crib.

"I'll probably work part-time for a couple of weeks," he said, watching Claudia as she buttoned her shirt.

"You don't have to take off, Giancarlo, now that your mother is here. And don't forget we have a housekeeper, so I don't have to clean."

The telephone rang and he stood straight and walked to the bedside table to answer it. "*Ciao*."

"Giancarlo. Is Claudia there?"

He turned his back rather than look at Claudia. "Yes, she is. Do you want to talk to her?"

"Yes."

"Hold on." He covered the mouthpiece with his hand. "It's Mavis."

Claudia smiled and took the receiver from him. "*Ciao*."

Giancarlo watched Claudia's expression crumple like an accordion as she opened her mouth to scream but no sounds came out. He reached for the receiver and pried her fingers from the instrument. "I'll call you later." He hung up, and then swept Claudia up in his arms and carried her out of the bedroom and into the living room.

"What's the matter?" Myriam asked as she walked in.

He sat on the sofa. "Mavis called to say Claudia's mother passed away this morning."

The natural color drained from Myriam's face; she crossed herself with a shaky hand as she gripped the arms of a chair before flopping into it. "Oh, that poor child," she whispered.

Giancarlo rocked Claudia as if he were comforting a child. "It's okay, baby. It's okay to cry." He wanted her to cry, scream to let out her grief before it swallowed her whole.

"Why? Why do they all seem to leave me?"

"Not everyone, love. We're here. And you still have Virgie and Mavis."

Claudia pushed against his chest as tears streamed down her face. "I have to call Mavis so she can let me know about the funeral so I can reserve a flight."

"You can't travel, Claudia. You just had a baby, a baby you are breastfeeding. And you can't take him with you because he hasn't had his shots."

Giancarlo realized he must have gotten through to Claudia when she broke down completely, sobbing uncontrollably. If she hadn't been breastfeeding, he would've called the doctor to come and give her a sedative. He held her until she quieted and then fell asleep in his arms. Pushing off the sofa, he carried Claudia into the bedroom, laid her on the bed. He stood there, watching her sleep before going back to the living room to sit.

"We have to take care of her, Giancarlo," Myriam said.

He nodded. "I know."

"Where's the baby?"

"He's sleeping. Claudia just fed him."

"I know you wanted to wait for a couple of months, but I think you should take her out to the country. She always seems so happy there."

"I think you're right, Mama."

"I'm going to stay with her, so don't worry about her being alone."

"And I'm going to take a couple of weeks off. Now that Giacomo has straightened out his personal life, he can sit in for me." His cousin had finally worked through his problems with his long-time girlfriend, and they were now engaged to marry.

"Claudia is going to need me more than she ever has."

"She's going to need the both of us, Mama."

"That's true, but what she needs is her mother, and I'm going to make sure she has one."

"What are you talking about?"

Myriam gave him a direct stare. "I'm going to sell my house and move into the guesthouse on your property." She held up a hand when Giancarlo opened his mouth. "Please let me finish, Giancarlo. Claudia has been hinting ever since she renovated the guesthouse that I come and live there on holiday. Well, I'm going to take her up on her offer and live there permanently. I'll have my privacy, while at the same time I'll get to see my daughter and grandson every day."

"Is that really what you want?"

"It's what I want and what I need to do."

Giancarlo did not want to believe his mother was talking about selling the villa whose interiors had appeared on the glossy pages of an architectural magazine as one of Rome's most beautiful homes. It was where Myriam and her husband had hosted elegant dinner parties and it was where his mother claimed she wanted to live out the rest of her life.

"Are you certain, Mama?"

"Very certain, Giancarlo. The house is much too big for one person, and now that Pasquale's gone, I rarely have company. Yes, I want to sell the house and give Claudia the choice of selecting whatever she wants to finish decorating your home. I'm sixty-two and it's time I adopt a simpler lifestyle, and moving into the guesthouse will be the beginning."

Giancarlo could not believe Claudia had succeeded where he'd failed when he'd asked his mother to move into the duplex with him. He'd begun to worry about her living alone in the large house. "You're going to have to tell Claudia your plans."

"Once she's gotten over the shock of losing her mother, I'll let her know my plans. Meanwhile, you need to pack up a few things for the baby to take with us."

"You're planning to leave now?"

"Yes, Giancarlo. The nursery is already set up, so the baby can have his own room."

"Mama, we can't just spring it on Claudia that we're leaving today."

"Spring what on me?"

Giancarlo's head popped up when he saw Claudia standing at the entrance to the living room. Her eyes were puffy from crying, and there were red splotches on her cheeks. "Mama wants us to go to the country."

"Mama's right. I want to go now."

Claudia was so calm it frightened Giancarlo. It was as if she'd taken a tranquilizer that had put her in a state of total relaxation. "Okay. I'll help you pack the baby's clothes and whatever you need for him, then we'll leave."

She nodded as the beginnings of a smile lifted the corners of her mouth. "Thank you, Giancarlo."

PART FIVE

1980s
THE FORTENZAS

Chapter 49

A problem is a chance for you to do your best.
—Duke Ellington

Claudia watched as Giancarlo buried his face in his hands. He'd seemingly aged overnight with the lines of frustration bracketing his mouth and furrowing his forehead. It was 1986, and the Wall Street stock trading boom was coming to an end. It was the decade of greed and debauchery, and unfortunately family- and privately-owned Fortenza Motors had been swept up in the fall when Luca Contorni was charged with embezzlement and wire fraud. Luca had directed his broker-cousin in the States to purchase and then sell worthless junk bonds. His broker was arrested for securities fraud and Fortenza Motors fined millions of lire. The man her husband had trusted to oversee his company's finances had betrayed him and Giancarlo was talking about declaring bankruptcy.

Giancarlo lowered his hands. "If I'm going to save the company, then I'm going to have to lay off more than half the workers at the factory and cut the office staff."

"Don't do anything until I look over your books, Giancarlo."

He stared at her as if she'd grown a third eye. "No, Claudia. You claimed once you left the bank that you just wanted to be a mother and housewife."

"I am a housewife and mother, but I'm also a Fortenza, Giancarlo. And because I am a Fortenza it is incumbent on me to protect the family business."

He shook his head. "Your children need you."

"Our son is sixteen, soon to be seventeen, and our daughter is fourteen. They are not babies, Giancarlo. Leandro is planning to attend college in the States next year, and Daria is an accelerated high school student. I need you to pack up all the financial and bank statements from the past twenty years and have them shipped here. It's going to take me a while to analyze everything, but I need to find a way for you to keep the company running without closing or laying off your loyal workers. I also need for you to purchase a computer for the house, because it will go faster than with pen, paper, and calculator."

Reaching over, Giancarlo held her hand. "I really don't want to dump all of this on you."

"You're not dumping anything on me, Giancarlo. We're partners. We're family. And once we straighten out this mess, only you and I will sign checks. And once Leandro takes over the company, he will also be authorized to sign checks."

Giancarlo rested his head against the back of the sofa. "Okay, Claudia." He closed his eyes. I can't believe our son is planning to attend college in the States."

Claudia stared at the man with whom she'd spent the past seventeen years. He'd aged like fine wine, with a few new lines around his brilliant emerald-green eyes, while his thick hair was more silver than blond. His physique was still slender because he'd begun a regimen of rising early and walking two miles a day before driving to the office. Living in the country had had a positive effect on her own physical and emotional well-being. It was a place where she was able to heal after losing her mother. It was where she'd begun meditating and being surrounded with just the sounds of nature, which had become a healing balm that kept her sane.

After Virgie and Mavis buried Sarah in the cemetery next to her husband in Freedom, Mississippi, they came to Italy to spend the summer with her, and every summer from that time on. They'd become the doting aunts when they indulged Leandro and Daria with items Claudia had not approved of. Mavis was talking about moving to Paris once she retired, but changed her plans when Leandro informed her he had applied to several historically Black colleges and universities in the States. He claimed he wanted to follow in the footsteps of his mother and aunts by enrolling in a Black college. His first choice was Howard's College of Engineering and Architecture in Washington, D.C., and the second was North Carolina A&T in Greensboro, North Carolina.

Daria had inherited her father's blond hair, green eyes, and her mother's complexion, while Leandro was all Bailey. Whenever he stood next to Virgie, his resemblance to his great-aunt was startling because of his large gray-green eyes, palomino-gold complexion, and wavy brown hair with streaks of copper. Girls liked her son, and he liked them back, but not so much that they'd interfered with his studies.

However, it was Daria whom Claudia compared to a wild mare racing across the prairie because she didn't want to be saddled. And when she complained to Giancarlo that his daughter needed a firm hand, he claimed she was going through a stage as a typical rebellious teenager, and it would take time for her to mature.

"Leandro surprised me, too. I thought he would've selected a university either here or in France." Last year Giancarlo had taken Leandro to Paris and their son had immediately fallen in love with the City of Lights.

"He would have, but he claimed the women were too distracting."

"Giancarlo, please. Once he hits the States and takes one

look at all the beautiful Black sisters, he's going to lose his mind."

"Like his father when he saw a young girl who ensnared him in a web from which there had been no escape. And even after all these years I still don't want to escape."

"Keep talking, sweetheart, and I'm going to take you to the bedroom and have my way with you."

Giancarlo smiled and attractive lines fanned around his luminous eyes. "Oh, you think because I'm approaching sixty that I can't keep up with you?"

Claudia straddled his lap. "There's only one way to find out," she whispered in his ear.

Giancarlo wasted no time unbuttoning her blouse and staring at the swell of breasts rising and falling in the black lace bra. "I think you were planning to seduce me, because I've never seen this bra before."

"You've never seen it because it's new. Do you want to see the matching panties?"

"When did you get so nasty?"

Claudia unzipped her jeans and shimmied them off her hips. "If I'm nasty, then you made me that way." She hadn't planned on making love with Giancarlo, but she would do it if it got him out of his funk. He pushed off the sofa and Claudia wrapped her arms around his neck, and her legs around his waist. Desire darkened Giancarlo's eyes as he took his time undressing Claudia. He quickly shed his clothes and joined her on the bed.

Giancarlo wasn't given time to react when Claudia straddled him again and everything ceased to exist as she eased his erection inside her. He loved having her on top because it prolonged their lovemaking, but not this time. Claudia let out a soft cry when he reversed their positions and his rapacious tongue charted a sensual path from her mouth to her scented throat, shoulders, and breasts, suckling her until she arched off the bed. Continuing his downward exploration, he planned to taste every inch of her.

"Giancarlo!"

He heard the desperation in Claudia's voice when she screamed his name, and he moved up her trembling body and positioned himself between her legs. A sensual groan came deep from within his chest as he pushed into her body. Her hot, tight flesh closed around his erection, and within seconds her heat was transferred to him.

Together, they found a rhythm that quickened, slowed, then increased as shivers of giddy desire and ecstasy became explosive currents that shook them from head to toe as he and Claudia climaxed simultaneously.

Pressing his mouth to her ear, he whispered, "You were incredible."

Claudia chuckled. "You weren't so bad yourself."

Raising his head, he smiled. "Does that mean I can expect seconds?"

"Yes, but only if you're sure you can get it up."

Giancarlo nuzzled her neck, and then changed their position to lie side by side. "Give me a few days and I'll gladly oblige you."

Claudia held his hand. "It wouldn't bother me if you never had another erection."

"Why would you say that?"

"Because I still would love you even if we no longer made love with each other. Friendship is what keeps us together, Giancarlo."

"I thought it was love."

"That, too, but people fall in and out of love. Whenever I talk to Leandro about some girl he's interested in, I try to remind him they should become friends before sleeping together."

Giancarlo stared at Claudia. "You talk to my son about sleeping with girls?"

"He's also my son, Giancarlo, and yes, I talk to him about sleeping with girls, because he needs to hear it from his mother how a woman feels when a man takes advantage of her. When he only wants to use her for sex. And I also tell him there is a difference between fucking and making love."

"Have you had similar discussions with my daughter?"

"Yes, I've talked to *our* daughter about sex."

"But she's only fourteen."

"Fourteen, and physically able to make us grandparents. I'm not going to wait until she finds herself in a situation that will derail her future, so yes, I talk to our children about sex."

"I suppose I should've let you give Leandro the talk about where babies come from."

"If you hadn't wanted to do it, then I certainly would have."

Giancarlo could not imagine his daughter sleeping with a boy. The instant he'd held his newborn daughter his response to her was different from what he'd experienced with Leandro. Having a son had filled him with pride because it perpetuated the Fortenza bloodline, but with Daria it had elicited an overwhelming urge to protect her at all costs because she was his little *principessa*.

When Leandro had come to him with the announcement that he wanted to study abroad, Giancarlo had successfully hidden his disappointment; he'd wanted his son to attend his university. However, after several conversations, he'd finally relented when Leandro claimed he'd always wanted to travel to his mother's country of birth, and enrolling in an American college would afford him the opportunity to connect with his Black-American ancestry.

Giancarlo wanted to remind his son that although the blood of his African ancestors ran in his veins, he was not an American, but an Italian. And despite the social and racial advances in the United States, Claudia had chosen to give up her American citizenship to become an Italian citizen.

Leandro had bonded with his great aunts whenever they came to Italy on holiday and Mavis, now a retired schoolteacher, had extended the invitation for him to live with her if he decided to attend a Mississippi college and/or stay with her during college recess if he enrolled in any American university. His son had expressed from an early age that he wanted to become involved in the family business because he'd become obsessed with cars after a Fortenza model came in second in a Formula 1 race in Monaco. Daria loved science and said she wanted a career in medicine but hadn't decided on which field she wanted to study.

When he'd come home earlier in the afternoon, he hadn't planned to spend it in bed making love with his wife; however, it did assuage some of his anxiety about the future of Fortenza Motors. Giancarlo hadn't meant to unload his business woes on Claudia, because like his father he never discussed business at the dinner table, but her volunteering to provide oversight of the company's finances had come as a complete surprise. He'd agreed not only because he trusted her, but he was aware of her expertise with financial fraud from when she'd uncovered a money laundering scheme at the Rome-based bank where she'd been employed as their international liaison.

"Oh, sweet heaven!" Claudia gasped as she touched her forehead, chest, and then her left and right shoulders. She'd seen Myriam make the gesture so often that she had also adopted it herself.

When Myriam had whispered that she wanted her to come to her home, Claudia could not have imagined why her mother-in-law had sounded so mysterious. Although Myriam had maintained an independent lifestyle after moving into the guesthouse, she'd established a routine of sharing dinner with her son's family.

Claudia closed and then opened her eyes. Her heart was beating so hard she could hear it in her ears. "How? Why?"

Rings, tiaras, bracelets, necklaces, and earrings with precious and semiprecious stones covered a black velvet cloth on Myriam's dining room table. There were even diamond-encrusted combs, belts, hairpins, and buckles. And she didn't have to be an archeological historian to assess the value of the many platinum and solid gold pieces dating back centuries.

Myriam smiled. "To answer your question as to how: Nonna gave me a few pieces every time we had our secret meetings. It began with the rings and bracelets, and then when she became bolder it was a lot more. If she hadn't given them to me the Nazis surely would've stolen them as they had from so many European Jewish families. I'm a descendant from a line of Jewish merchants, bankers, and financiers dating back centuries. There were rumors that their wealth rivaled that of the powerful Medici dynasty.

"And the *why* is, what you see here represents what's left of my family heirlooms and I'm giving them to you because not only are you a Fortenza, but because the blood of my ancestors also runs in your children. I know you haven't tried to hide their Jewishness from them, and because of that I'm giving you everything you see on this table before I'm gone. Some you can sell to offset the fines Fortenza Motors was forced to pay for that piece of shit who almost ruined the company. This way Giancarlo won't have to file for bankruptcy or lay off his employees. And what's left over you can set aside for Leandro and Daria."

"Have you had these pieces appraised?"

Myriam smiled. "Of course."

Claudia was glad she was sitting when Myriam removed a written appraisal from the pocket of her apron and gave it to her. The total amount was more than triple the fine Fortenza Motors was forced to pay for securities fraud, and her mind was working overtime as to what she would do with the proceeds if she sold even half the pieces on the table.

"What are you thinking about, *mia figlia?*"

The first time Myriam had referred to her as *my daughter* was when Claudia had lost her mother. Myriam had consoled her and said although she couldn't replace Sarah, she was now her mother and Claudia her daughter. Her mother-in-law was no longer Myriam, but Mama.

"What do you think if I sell a few pieces and buy one or two abandoned properties, renovate and then sell them for a profit?"

Myriam's smile spoke volumes. "I think it's a wonderful idea. Do you intend to tell Giancarlo of your plan?"

"Yes, only because he trusts me enough to provide oversight of the car company."

"He trusts you, because he doesn't have a choice, Claudia. He'd adopted the same stance as his father, grandfather, and his uncles, that they didn't want their women involved in the company, but that antiquated nonsense has put Fortenza Motors in financial jeopardy because if Giancarlo had involved you, knowing how you'd uncovered the money laundering scheme at that bank, he wouldn't be talking about shutting the doors and putting people out of work."

Claudia picked up a platinum bracelet with alternating blood-red rubies and blue-white diamonds. "I'd like to give this to Daria once she graduates college."

"What about Leandro?"

"I'm certain he will find an engagement ring and a wedding band for his future wife once he sees this collection."

"That's what I was hoping you would say, Claudia. Do you want to pick out what you want to sell and what you want to keep? Because I was told by someone at an auction house that they have a few clients who are interested in adding some antique jewelry to their vast collections."

Claudia met Myriam's green eyes. "Will you help me choose?"

"Of course."

Chapter 50

Be on guard against excess. Zeal that is too ardent burns more than it reheats.
—Alec Pelletier, *Le Festin des Morts*

"Where do you think you're going, young lady?" Claudia asked Daria as she picked up a set of car keys off the table in the entryway.

"Out, Mama. Didn't I tell you that I was invited to Francesca's birthday party?"

Claudia rested her hands at her waist. "No, you didn't tell me."

Daria ran her fingers through a profusion of blond waves framing her small, rounded face. "You must have forgotten."

"There may be a few things I forget, but not my eighteen-year-old daughter telling me that she was invited to a party."

It wasn't the party as much as it was Claudia's apprehension that her daughter had just secured her driver's license and she tended to drive much too fast. And she was scheduled to attend college in two weeks.

"I'm not going to stay too late, Mama. It's going to be the last time I'm going to party with my friends because many of them are going away to college and we won't get together again until later in the year."

"Okay. But if the police stop you for speeding, then your father is going to take back the car."

"I promise not to speed."

There was something about her daughter that reminded Claudia of Noelle's bohemian phase when she opted to wear all black, which was a blatant contrast to her pale hair and café au lait complexion that gave her the appearance of being perpetually tanned. However tonight she had foregone all-black attire to pair a brightly colored silk blouse with a pair of slim jeans and multicolored mules with two-inch heels. Standing five-ten in her bare feet, Daria had constantly complained that she was so much taller than some boys in her classes, but as they matured, she'd become more comfortable with her height after she'd been approached by representatives from modeling agencies that were interested in her. But after researching what models had to go through to stay thin, she claimed she had no intention of starving herself.

Claudia forced a smile. She didn't want to dampen Daria's enthusiasm to have fun before becoming a college student, but it was the nonstop partying that was troubling. Since graduating high school she'd gone out at least three to four times a week. And the one night when she'd come back home just hours before dawn Giancarlo was waiting for her, and it wasn't what he'd said to her but how he'd looked at her that caused Daria to burst into tears and apologize, vowing she would never stay out that late again.

Two weeks. That was all the time left before Daria would stop her late-night carousing and settle into her dorm room at the University of Padua. The city was approximately twenty-five miles west of Venice and Claudia was looking forward to revisiting Venice once she and Giancarlo got Daria settled.

"Later, Mama."

"Later, Daria." She was there, then she was gone when the door closed after her.

The house was eerily quiet, and Claudia knew it would become even more quiet once Daria moved. Leandro had just completed his second year at North Carolina A&T and claimed he'd fallen in love with the South. He'd moved into an off-campus apartment, joined Phi Beta Sigma Fraternity, and was dating a girl who was also an engineering student. When Claudia had questioned him about whether he intended to stay in the States, he said no because of his obligation to eventually take over Fortenza Motors.

The jewelry she'd put up for auction generated a great deal of attention and the result was more money than she and Myriam had originally anticipated. Claudia reinvested in Fortenza Motors, making it fiscally sound, then as planned, she purchased several abandoned palazzos in Venice, renovated them and sold the houses to wealthy Americans, Middle Easterners, and Europeans who wanted to use them as vacation properties. She'd always kept her promise to Giancarlo to carefully monitor every lira that was deposited and disbursed by the company and now at fifty she was chief financial officer for Fortenza Motors.

Giancarlo had gone to bed, but it was still too early for Claudia to turn in, so she decided to watch television. She'd set up a room in the house that had become her retreat. She'd found an antique desk where she continued to write letters using her favored fountain pen while many people were using the Internet to send messages to each other.

She'd bundled her letters from Noelle, who had kept her abreast of the lives of her many children, some who had graduated from university and were lawyers and teachers. Yvonne and Stephen, now the parents of two boys and one girl, had sold their home in East Harlem and bought a large house in Mount Vernon, a city in Westchester County where there was enough property for them to install an inground pool and eventually a tennis court. Their daughter had become a tennis phenom and there were plans for her to compete at Wimbledon, while their older son, Robert, had decided to follow the Jones family tradition of becoming a doctor.

It had been twenty-two years since she had seen Yvonne in person, but she and Noelle were reunited last year at Noelle's father's funeral. As a middle-aged woman dressed in the latest Parisian haute couture, Noelle looked nothing like the bohemian-chic young woman Claudia met during her first visit to Paris. Adjovi had accompanied her, and it was the first time Claudia met the extraordinarily handsome African prince in person. Virgie was so distraught losing Jacques that Mavis told her sister she was moving to Paris to be with her. And, as promised, Mavis Bailey sold her home and moved to Paris and into the *hôtel particulier* with Virgie. Claudia realized that except for Leandro, all who'd claimed Bailey blood had left the States. And once he graduated, he would also leave to return to the country of his birth.

Claudia watched a movie dubbed in Italian and when it ended, she turned off the television and prepared to go to bed. She had just emerged from the bathroom when the telephone rang. Quickening her steps to answer it before it woke Giancarlo, she realized she was too late because he'd already answered the call.

She felt her knees buckle slightly when she saw him go completely still before he hung up and flung off the blankets.

"Daria's in the hospital."

The only thing Claudia heard was *hospital*. She didn't remember getting dressed or Giancarlo driving like a madman until they walked into the same hospital where she'd given birth to both of her children. When the attending doctor said she'd been beaten in an attempted rape, that's when everything went dark, and she collapsed and fainted.

She woke what seemed hours later when it was only seconds, to find Giancarlo pounding his fists against a wall. "Stop it, Giancarlo!" She knew he was blaming himself for their daughter's predicament but that wasn't going to change anything.

She must have gotten through to him because he dropped his hands. His knuckles were bloody. Claudia beckoned a nurse. "Can you please take care of his hands?"

"Yes, Signora Fortenza."

"When can I see my daughter?"

The nurse signaled for another nurse. "She will take you to her room while I treat your husband's hands."

When Claudia entered the room and saw the young police officer, she wondered if he had been the one to bring Daria in. And where were her friends? Had they witnessed the assault? Or were any at the party responsible for her daughter's vicious beating as evidenced by her blackened eyes, cut lip, or the bruises on her throat?

"What do you know about the assault on my daughter?" she asked the police officer.

"We got a call that a young girl had been assaulted at a party, but when we started questioning those in attendance, they all claimed they hadn't seen anything."

"That's bullshit and you know it!" Claudia spat out. "They didn't see anything, yet they knew to call the police."

"Don't worry, Claudia. I have my ways of finding out who did this to our daughter."

Claudia turned to find Giancarlo in the doorway, his hands wrapped in gauze. The police officer suddenly stood up straight.

"Signor Fortenza, the police will follow up with a thorough investigation and whoever did this to your daughter will be brought to justice."

Claudia felt a chill sweep over her body when she saw something in her husband's eyes she had never seen before, and it bode ill for the boy who had attempted to rape his daughter. "Giancarlo, we have to let the police handle this," she whispered.

"They will handle it their way, and I'll handle it my way."

"Signor Fortenza, you can't do anything to complicate a police investigation."

"Fuck you and your investigation! That's my daughter, not yours, lying in that bed, and meanwhile you say you spoke to those at the party, and no one saw anything. You can continue with your investigation while I'll carry on with mine."

A doctor entered the room, frowning. "Signore, you must keep it quiet because you're disturbing other patients."

"I want him out of here," Giancarlo said, pointing at the police officer.

"But this is a police matter," the officer protested.

"If the patient's parents don't want you here, then you must leave."

Claudia waited until the officer left the room, then turned to the doctor. "Are you certain she wasn't raped?"

The doctor nodded. "Very certain. She fought whoever attacked her because there were a lot of skin cells under her fingernails. We collected them as evidence for DNA testing. Once the police identify all who were at the party, and look for scratch marks on any of the males, then they'll have their suspect."

Claudia felt a little more relaxed than she had when she first walked into the room. "Can we stay with her?"

"Yes. You can stay as long as you want."

Giancarlo rested a hand at the small of Claudia's back. "You can take the first shift. I'll be back later."

"Where are you going?"

"I'm going home to take off the gauze and put some bandages on my hands."

"But they can do that here."

"I also want to call Leandro to let him know about his sister."

She knew Giancarlo wasn't telling her the complete truth because he'd refused to meet her eyes. "Okay. Drive carefully, sweetheart. We don't need another Fortenza to lie in a hospital bed."

* * *

Daria was discharged from the hospital two days after she'd been brought in, and four days after her attack Leandro flew in from the States to be with his family. The police finally arrested the boy who had attempted to rape Daria because she'd rejected his advances. He'd walked into the police station and surrendered. He looked as if he'd gone a few rounds with a professional boxer, and when questioned why he'd voluntarily come in, he'd claimed he was safer in prison than out on the street. Claudia heard, but refused to listen to the rumors that her husband had paid someone to snitch, and then had someone else severely beat the boy until he finally agreed to turn himself in.

Her daughter had turned into a different person before Claudia's eyes, and she wondered if the attack would scar her for life. She spent hours in her bedroom, and when Claudia approached Daria with the announcement it was growing close to the time when she would have to leave Rome for college, she said she wasn't going.

Sitting on the side of the bed, Claudia reached for her hand. "What do you want to do, baby?"

"I don't want to stay here."

"Where do you want to go?"

"I want to go to North Carolina with my brother."

Claudia clasped her fingers together in prayerful gesture. "He's leaving in three days."

"And I want to go back with him. I asked him if I could come, and he said yes."

She didn't want to believe her son and daughter had made plans and hadn't said anything to her. Claudia knew she couldn't stop Daria because her daughter didn't need her permission to travel abroad. She had a valid passport and money in her bank account.

"Let me talk to your father."

"Thanks, Mama."

Claudia found Giancarlo sitting on a chair in the courtyard with the dog he'd bought home after they'd had to put

Nico down. She sat in a chair next to him. "Did you know she wants to go to the States with Leandro?"

"He'd mentioned it to me last night and I told him I had to discuss it with you."

"Well, Giancarlo. What you think?"

"I think we should let her go. There's always the chance that she'll run into her so-called friends, who didn't have the guts to tell the police who tried to rape her until they were threatened."

With wide eyes, Claudia stared at him. "You threatened kids?"

"No. I threatened their parents."

"Giancarlo!"

"Fuck it, Claudia! I did what I had to do to get the person responsible for attacking my daughter. And what makes you think he wouldn't try to rape another girl? The boy's a rapist and that's all there is to it. He's lucky I didn't put my hands on him because his parents would be burying their son, not visiting him in prison."

Claudia shook her head as if to rid her mind of what her husband had done to identify their daughter's attacker. "Now, back to Daria."

"What about her, Claudia?"

"Is she going or staying?"

"She's going, but only if you agree."

Claudia didn't want to think of her daughter living so far away, but then it was the same with her and Sarah when she'd agreed to accept an overseas assignment. "Okay, Giancarlo. She can go. And she can live with Leandro, and if she wants to go to college there then she can enroll on a student visa."

"Let's go and give her the good news."

Claudia held Giancarlo's hand as they watched their children walk into the airport terminal. They hadn't believed they would become empty nesters this soon. If Daria had gone to college in Padua they would see her more often, but now that she was going to live in the States, they weren't certain when either of their children would return.

"She is going to be okay." Claudia had said it as much for herself as to reassure Giancarlo that his little girl was going to make it.

"I know. I had a long talk with Leandro, and he says he will take good care of her."

"We did good, Giancarlo. I'm proud of our kids."

"You did good, love. If I'd listened to you about not letting Daria—"

"We're not going to start that again," Claudia said, cutting off what had become his rant about what he should've done but didn't do when it came to Daria's self-destructive behavior. "It may sound insensitive, but maybe she had to go through what she did to save her life, Giancarlo. Who knows, if she'd continued it could've escalated into her taking drugs like those she hung out with. There were times when she came home reeking of marijuana, and when I asked her if she was smoking dope, she swore she wasn't even though some of her friends were not only smoking but also snorting cocaine."

"Leandro told me he's going to make certain she's not going to get in any trouble and he's going to put the word out to the guys on campus that they can look but they better not touch his sister."

"That sounds serious, Giancarlo. Leandro must allow her some freedom, or she will rebel."

"And if she does, then she'll find herself back here where she will become a prisoner. She will go into the office with me every morning and leave with me at night. I will close her bank account and she will even have to ask me for money to buy her feminine products."

"She won't have to ask you for money for her tampons because she could always use mine, sweetheart."

Giancarlo gave her a sidelong glance, then smiled. "You have an answer for everything, don't you?"

"Sometimes. Do you know what I want?"

"You want Papa to make you feel good?"

"No! You're a nasty old man."

"And you love this nasty old man, don't you?"

"With all my heart. I was talking about gelato. It's been a while since I've had some."

"Let's go get your gelato, then go home and run around naked as the day we were born."

Epilogue

Look at everything as though you were seeing it
either for the first or last time. Then your time on
earth will be filled with glory.
 —Betty Smith, *A Tree Grows in Brooklyn*

Claudia closed her eyes and smiled as the Statue of Liberty came into view. She'd spent a week on a ship crossing the Atlantic Ocean. She was coming back to the States for the first time in more than fifty years.

She'd gone through weeks of reflection after she buried Giancarlo and knew if she didn't come now, then she would never again step foot on United States soil again. She was eighty-three years old, and most of her life was behind her. But when she thought of Virgie, who'd recently celebrated her 109th birthday, Claudia realized she still had a lot of living to do. She'd tried to get Virgie to come and live with her after Mavis passed away, but her aunt refused to leave France. Virgie felt about France the same way Claudia felt about Italy. She'd fallen in love with her adopted country, and she'd left explicit instructions for Leandro and Daria to bury her next to Giancarlo and Myriam. Her mother-in-law had passed away at eighty-four from a brief illness and Claudia had known she had to be strong not only for Giancarlo, but also for their children.

Leandro graduated college and married his college sweetheart and they had given Claudia the beautiful brown grandchildren Myriam had spoken of. It had taken her daughter-in-law a while to learn Italian, and after two years she was fluent. When she'd asked Claudia why she had left the States, she was forthcoming about encountering racial injustice when she was growing up in Mississippi, and as a Black woman she'd felt freer in Italy than she had in the country of her birth.

Claudia had grown to love her African American daughter-in-law because she'd witnessed the love between her and Leandro, who adored his American wife, and between them they had given her three grandchildren—all boys.

Daria had chosen to live in North Carolina, where she'd married a fellow medical student. They opened a clinic with the money Giancarlo had set aside for her trust fund to provide medical care for impoverished families. Daria had also given her beautiful brown grandchildren—two sets of twin girls. She'd joked that she wasn't willing to become pregnant again because she feared having another multiple birth.

Claudia had come to New York to reunite with Yvonne before traveling on to Mississippi to visit the graves of her family. Then she planned to spend time in North Carolina with Daria before sailing back to Europe after the Labor Day weekend.

Claudia had been in North Carolina for three weeks and she was constantly asked by her granddaughters when they could come back to Italy to visit with her. Two were in college and the other two were finishing up high school, and she told them they could come for Christmas, and with their parents' permission they could live abroad for a couple of years.

"Why don't you go and sit on the porch, Mama. We can finish up here."

Claudia smiled at Daria. "Okay."

Most nights she sat on the porch after dinner, and it was her time to relax and think about her life. There were times when she could hear her mother's voice telling her she had done well.

Glancing up at the late summer sky, she gasped when she saw a shooting star, and made a wish that the lives of her children and grandchildren would be filled with all the happiness they deserved.

"Mama."

"Yes, Daria."

"There's someone named Ashley on the phone asking for you."

"Tell him I'll be right there."

Claudia pushed to her feet, and then went into the house. She knew when she went back to Italy, she wouldn't be alone.

Discussion Questions
to spark conversation and enhance your reading of
Take the Long Way Home by Rochelle Alers

1. What do you think is the significance of the novel's title, Take The Long Way Home? What is the "home" it refers to? Would you choose a different title, and if so, what would it be?

2. When Claudia finds Denny in the woods, do you think her grandmother Earline was right to take him in? What would you have done?

3. Do you feel any empathy for Denny Clark? Why or why not?

4. When Claudia gets her period for the first time, her mother, father, and grandmother turn it into an occasion to celebrate her "new womanhood." All three generations of Pattersons get dressed up and go to a local restaurant for a big dinner complete with champagne toasts. What did you think about their reaction to this rite of passage? What are some of the milestones your own family celebrates and in what ways?

5. Did you agree with Claudia's parents' decision to send her to live in Biloxi with Aunt Mavis? Would you have made a different decision?

6. At various points in the novel, each of the Patterson / Bailey women—Claudia, her mother, and her aunts Mavis and Virginia—are referred to as "uppity." Do you agree? Why would that be considered an insult?

7. When Claudia visits France in 1958, she and Noelle have a conversation about how French women are fighting for political equality while Black women in America are fighting for equal rights under the law. What is the difference between political equality and

equal rights? What were some examples you noticed of how the status of a Black woman in France was different from the status of a Black woman in America at that time? Were you surprised by how different Noelle's awareness of race was compared to Claudia's?

8. Do you think Claudia's aunt should have warned Giancarlo Fortenza to stop seeing her niece when they first meet in France? How do you think things would have turned out differently for Claudia and Giancarlo if Aunt Virginia hadn't intervened?

9. Claudia ends up learning significant life lessons from the relationships she forms, including those with her close female friends. What do you think is the most important lesson she learned from her relationship with her college roommate, Yvonne? What about Noelle?

10. Were you surprised when Claudia and Robert moved back to Claudia's hometown of Freedom, Mississippi after they got married? Where would you have chosen to live?

11. In what ways do you think Robert's relationship with his father influenced his relationship with Claudia?

12. Robert's work as a civil rights lawyer makes him a target. When Claudia pleads with him to curtail his activities, do you think he places his role as an activist above that of a husband? Why or why not? What do you think he should have done?

13. Why do you think Ashley didn't marry Claudia when he had the chance?

14. Though the main characters are fictional, there are many references throughout this novel to real people and historical figures, such as Thurgood Marshall, Charles Hamilton Houston, Martin Luther King, Jr.,

gender equality activist Dr. Pauli Murray, Bayard Rustin, Emmett Till, Julius and Ethel Rosenberg, Harlem racketeer Madame Stephanie St. Clair, Jackie Robinson, Roy Campanella, and many more. Were you unfamiliar with any of the real people who were mentioned in the novel? If so, which ones and what did you learn about them?

15. Following the loss of those closest to her, what does Claudia's decision to move to New York reveal about her? Have you ever made a major life choice in the wake of a big loss? If so, what led you to that choice, and did you have any regrets?

16. Throughout the novel, Claudia meets four men who impact her life in crucial ways: Denny Clark, Robert Moore, Ashley Booth, and Giancarlo Fortenza. Why do you think she includes Denny on this list even though he's the only one with whom she didn't fall in love?

17. What do you think are the best and worst qualities of each of these men—Denny, Robert, Ashley and Giancarlo?

18. You may have noticed each chapter begins with a quote. Which of these quotes was your favorite and why?

Visit our website at
KensingtonBooks.com
to sign up for our newsletters, read
more from your favorite authors, see
books by series, view reading group
guides, and more!

BOOK ▮▮▮/▮/▮ CLUB

BETWEEN THE CHAPTERS

Become a Part of Our
Between the Chapters Book Club
Community and Join the Conversation

Betweenthechapters.net